Kathleen Herbert go_____
Oxford, where hearin_____
in the Dark Age – she prefers _____
Britain. She learned Welsh in order to trace the _____
Arthurian literature, and although she lives in London
spends most of her free time on foot with a camera in
northern England and southern Scotland, co-relating
early history and literature with the physical evidence.
She is working on a non-fiction book on the relationship
of the history and historical traditions of Dark Age
Cumbria and the development of the Arthurian
legends.

Also by Kathleen Herbert
GHOST IN THE SUNLIGHT
QUEEN OF LIGHTNING
and published by Corgi Books

BRIDE OF THE SPEAR

Kathleen Herbert

CORGI BOOKS

In memory of Edgar George Herbert, R.N.

BRIDE OF THE SPEAR
A CORGI BOOK   0 552 13331 0

Originally published in Great Britain by
The Bodley Head Ltd.

PRINTING HISTORY
The Bodley Head edition published 1988
Corgi edition published 1989

Corgi Books are published by Transworld Publishers Ltd.,
61 – 63 Uxbridge Road, Ealing, London W5 5SA, in
Australia by Transworld Publishers (Australia) Pty. Ltd.,
15 – 23 Helles Avenue, Moorebank, NSW 2170, and in
New Zealand by Transworld Publishers (N.Z.) Ltd.,
Cnr. Moselle and Waipareira Avenues, Henderson,
Auckland.

Reproduced, printed and bound in Great Britain by
Hazell Watson & Viney Limited
Member of BPCC plc
Aylesbury, Bucks.

The North after the Death of Arthur

□ Roman sites
• non-Roman sites
† Monastic sites
— Roads
〜〜〜 Roman walls

ALBA or PICTLAND

Culenros
Alclud
MERIN IUDEU
Din Eidyn
Din Pelidr
LOTHIAN
Mailros
Gefrin
Metcaud
Din Guayroi
Segloes
Calchfynedd
BERNICIA
Brewyn
COED CELIDON
ARGOED LLWYFAIN
Caer Ehedydd
Banna
Caer Voran
Befriana
Onnum
Maia
Caer Luel
Candida
Casa
Guasmoric
Alauna
MERIN
RHEGED
Caer Mollt
Penrhyd
Catraeth
DEIRA
MANAU
ELMET
Caer Efrog
CUMBRIA or RHEGED
THE LONG HILLS
Petuaria

STRATH CLYDE

MÔN
Rhos
Deganwy
GWYNEDD

N

0 10 20 30 40 50 miles

PLACE NAMES

THE WEST

Aballava	Burgh by Sands
Alauna	Maryport
Alclud	Dumbarton
Argoed Llwyfain	Bewcastle Fells
Banna	Birdoswald
Caer Ehedydd	Ward Law Fort
Caer Luel	Carlisle
Caermollt	Caermote
Candida Casa	Whithorn
Guasmoric	Wigton
Idon	River Eden
Llwyfenydd	Lyvennet valley and district
Maia	Bowness on Solway
Manau	Isle of Man
Merin Rheged	Solway Firth
Penrhyd	Penrith
Petriana	Stanwix

THE WALL

Caer Voran	Carvoran Fort
Onnum	Halton Chesters
Tina	River Tyne

THE EAST

Bernicia	Northumberland
Brewyn	High Rochester
Caer Efrog	York
Caer Weir	Durham
Calchfynedd	Kelso
Castle of Maidens	Castle Rock, Edinburgh
Catraeth	Catterick
Culenros	Culros
Deira	East Yorkshire
Din Eidyn	Arthur's Seat, Edinburgh
Din Guayroi	Bamburgh
Din Pelidr	Traprain Law
Gefrin	Yeavering
Glein	River Glen
Mailros	Old Melrose
Metcaud	Lindisfarne
Petuaria	Brough on Humber
Segloes	Eildon Hill Fort

CHARACTERS

WEST OF THE HILLS
Urien, King of Cumbria, murdered *c*. 585. In the Arthurian legend he is the husband of Morgan le Fay.

Owain, his elder son. In the Arthurian legend he is the hero of the romances *The Lady of the Fountain* and *Le Chevalier au Lion*.

Rhun, his younger son.

Llywarch, their cousin.

Riderec, King of Strathclyde, died *c*.612. In Welsh history and tradition he is Rhydderch Hael (the Generous).

Madog, Owain's armour-bearer.

Custennin, a member of Urien's Council.

Guendolena, wife of a councillor.

Heledd, Urien's ward, Owain's mistress.

Heulwen, a hill-farmer's daughter, Owain's lover.

Dinogat, her son by Owain.

Viventius, Bishop of Caer Luel.

Mavorius, the palace doctor.

Iarddur)
Riwallon) members of Owain's warband.
Idris)

Gwion, a farm boy.

Anthun, headman of Guasmoric.

Dunwal, a horse-coper and spy.

CAER VORAN
Garmon, lord of Caer Voran.

Penarwan, his daughter.

Meurig, his elder son.

Padarn, his younger son.

Essyllt, his niece.

Ressona, his mistress.

Pluma, her daughter by Garmon.

Wulfric, head groom, later captain of Penarwan's bodyguard.

EAST OF THE HILLS
Loth, King of Lothian.

Gwalchmai, his son by his second wife. In the Arthurian legend he is Sir Gawain.

Taniu, his daughter by his first wife, later revered as a saint.

Kentigern, her son, died 612. Founder of Glasgow, churches in Cumbria and (traditionally) St Asaph's in Wales. Patron saint of Strathcylde.

Luned, Loth's mistress.

Gorthyn, captain of his warband.
Morien)
Cynon)
Brychan) members of the warband.
Dunawd)
Marchlew)
Talhaearn, the bard.
Selyf, the royal jewelsmith.
Hoel, the royal swineherd.
Collen) his daughters.
Eirlys)
Ancarat, the royal nurse.
Nia, her daughter.
Cadwal, Nia's husband, a hill-farmer.
Leucu, their daughter.
Morcant, King of Eidyn, Loth's cousin.
Lovan, his armour-bearer, son of an exile from Gwynedd.
Nefyn, a lady of the royal kin, Essyllt's sister-in-law.
Ceinwen, a noblewoman.
Elcu, a pedlar.
Arthgal, a fisherman.
Eurnaid, a net-maker.
Dumna, an alewife.
Gwallog, King of Elmet.
Eudeyrn, last British king of Bernicia.

OUTLANDERS

Servanus, an Irish missionary priest, revered in Scotland as St
   Serf.
Monenna, an Irish missionary, foundress of a convent in Edin-
   burgh, revered as a saint.
Agatha, her infirmarian.
Drostecca, Loth's second wife, a Pictish princess.
Lurga, her foster-sister, a priestess of the Mothers.
Brude)
Talorg) warriors of her bodyguard.
Nechtan)
Bran)
Rigan) fisherfolk of Culenros.
Annis)
Isag, a trader.
Ida, a sea-rover from Lindsey, first English king of Bernicia.
Bebban, his latest wife.
Theodric 'Flame-Bearer', his son and war leader.
Ethelric, his son, later conqueror of Deira and founder of united
   Northumbria.

8

CHAPTER
1

It was cold for June. The wind was from the east; by nightfall it had freshened to a gale. It stormed the ramparts of Din Pelidr, the Fort of Spears, forced its way through chinks between timbers of the royal hall, pulled at its hangings, beat the smoke down on the great hearth, made the torches eddy and gutter. The wavering flamelight played across the feasters at the long tables. At one moment a shoulder-brooch blazed out, or the rim of a drinking horn lifted to a mouth, white teeth bared in a roar of laughter, the emerald eyes of a hound lifting its head from a bone as it caught its master's voice.

The taste of smoke got into the queen's throat as she drank. She was with child; for a moment both the smoke and the sweet mead were swamped by rising vomit. She fought it down, for decency and pride, but her body was clammy with sweat. The enamelled bronze circlet on her head and the heavy plates of her belt seemed to be nailed to her flesh. She shifted her hips restlessly for ease.

A flicker of flame touched a nymph on the broad silver platter in front of the king. She was dancing wildly under a vine branch, her robe had slipped from her breasts and streamed past her thighs. The king's silver dinner service, and the red cloak he wore when he went into battle, were the only traces about the court of Lothian that the land had once been Roman. King Loth was proud of his tableware, though totally ignorant of the classical legends displayed on it. The breasts and thighs of the silver nymph, suddenly gleaming out at him made a simpler suggestion.

The queen's restless movement against his flank seemed for a moment to answer his thought. A sidelong glimpse of her thickening figure and sullen face diverted his eyes and his mind. No pleasure there tonight, or any night till the child came out of her. Another son, if the Goddess was kind.

Whenever Loth thought of his coming child, and the hopes and plans that would be crowned by his birth, he always said a quick litany to the Goddess. He said one now in his mind. He called on her by all her holy names and in all her holy places, woodland, sacred springs and the standing stones on the moors—Rigantona, Mighty Queen—Brigit of the Sacred Flame—Epona, Great Mare ... and Mary Virgin, added his mind. He wanted every possible blessing on his line.

His queen, Drostecca, was Pictish; among her people kingship came through the mother. Loth's imagination, stimulated by mead, showed a future where his elder son led the warriors of Lothian while the younger one ruled the Picts beyond Merin Iudeu. Loth had never heard the words 'statecraft' or 'politics'. He would have been unable to grasp the ideas they stood for. He simply pictured the dismay and fury of his cousin Morcant, who ruled from the rock of Eidyn, when Loth's line held all the lands to his north and south. The picture was very pleasing.

Loth leaned back and stretched his long legs with a great sense of well-being, present and to come. He looked beyond his queen, beyond the fawn-gold head of his daughter Taniu, to the little group of bower-women sitting in a cluster apart from the warriors to the left of the royal bench.

Luned happened to glance up at that moment. She was small and plump, with dark curly hair and brown eyes. Her upper lip was short and lifted slightly over pearly little teeth, so she seemed always ready to laugh or kiss. She was laughing now at some joke among the women; her eyes laughed into Loth's. He smiled back, slightly raising his goblet before he drank. He saw she understood; his night would pass to his satisfaction. Now he could settle back happily to listen to his bard. Talhaearn had come forward to the hearth, tuned his harp and now began an ode of praise to the king's courage and victories:

> 'Bull of battle, host-protector,
> Pillar of armies, eagle of prey . . .'

Princess Taniu had edged her stool a little back from the royal bench. Partly shielded by Drostecca's bulk, she sat quietly as usual, her clear grey eyes taking in the scene. She had noticed the wordless question and answer that had passed between her father and Luned. She was almost sure Drostecca had seen it too. She was perfectly aware that her father's eyes had passed over herself as if she were invisible. She was used to this and accepted it without resentment. Not only had she, the king's first child, failed to be the boy that his kingdom needed but her delicate mother had been so injured by a long and difficult labour that she had never been able to bear another child. Worse; instead of dying soon, as would have been proper since her life was of no further use, the unhappy lady had lingered on for seven years. She couldn't give the king a son to make up for the unwanted girl-brat, and she stopped him from taking a healthier and more satisfactory wife.

Not that Loth had been bound to his first queen by any personal tenderness or respect for the marriage oath. His men bragged that he had a bastard in every village in Lothian. He would gladly have cast off his queen or put a pillow over her face, but her brother was King of Strathclyde and would have attacked him at once to avenge the insult. Strathclyde was a powerful kingdom and could bring a great war-host against him. Loth would have found a war hazardous and costly, even if he had not been sure that his cousin Morcant would take him in the back at the earliest safe opportunity.

So Queen Languoreth had been left to drag out her life to its natural term, uncared for by anyone except the old nurse who had come with her from Alclud when she married.

Taniu's life had been loveless from the start, so she hardly knew what was missing. Loth's family pride ensured that she was richly dressed and treated with outward respect by his household. She had always been a quiet child, giving no trouble, attracting no notice even now that she was a woman, turned fourteen. Unobserved herself, her watchful grey eyes considered the world around her, not always respectfully.

The feast had reached the hard-drinking stage. Faces were red and sweaty. Heads were thrust forward to exchange jokes or boasts; heads were flung back to laugh. As the heads moved, torchlight and firelight shifted over

11

them, turning them to bronze or gold or making them monstrous with shadows.

Taniu was passing her time by deciding which animals they brought to mind. Gorthyn, captain of the warband, with his bristly hair and beard, was a boar. Cold savage Brychan, long-nosed and thin-lipped, was a wolf. Dunawd of the sly narrow eyes and reddish hair could only be a fox. As for Morien—handsome Morien, who could have any girl in the court if he beckoned her—with his fleshy cheeks sticky with sweat, Morien was a plump young pig at the trough! She pressed her lips together to stop her laughter breaking out.

Morien caught the princess staring at him, her lips curved in a smile. His full wet mouth fell into an encouraging grin. Taniu looked away at once and drew back even more into Drostecca's shadow. She was suddenly ashamed of her game and very weary of the feast. It was too soon for Drostecca to move but Taniu felt she could not bear another moment in the hall. Covered by the approving roars and stamping that broke out at the rousing climax of Talhaearn's ode, she got up quietly and glided behind the skin curtain hiding the women's door. Another second and she was outside.

The darkness and the chill wind that hit her as soon as she moved from the wall took her by surprise. For a moment she crouched back against the heavy timbers, breathless and blinded. When she opened her eyes again, the sky showed dark grey with pin-points of stars. Buildings made shapes of solid blackness. Bending her head and clasping her arms across her chest, she made for the queen's hall. Another shape moved towards her from around the corner of the feasting hall, then Morien's greasy mouth was breathing mead into her face while his hands grabbed and fumbled for her breasts. She kicked hard at his shin, catching him off balance and, while he staggered, twisted away and ran. Morien was not drunk enough to use force on the king's daughter though he was quite sure she had signalled him to come out to her. Cursing foully, he turned back.

Taniu, hiding behind one of the wooden pillars in the queen's porch, trying to quieten her breath, heard him go.

12

She waited till all was still again; then pushed open the heavy door and caught back the wolfskin curtain. The big room at the front of the building, where the queen and her women gossiped by day over their spindles and loom, and where their maids usually slept, was empty now as she had hoped. All the slave-girls were over at the kitchens and larders for a share in the leavings of the feast and the merry-making that would follow.

She stepped round the banked-down hearth in the centre and sank on a footstool by the queen's chair, pressing her back into the carved wood as if she were a warrior beset by foes, bracing himself against a rock to meet their last charge. She knew that her secret terror was rising out of the forgetfulness where she tried to bury it. She struggled to close her mind against it but it was too strong. Morien had lent the terror his body and his strength; now it came out of the night as he had done and caught her . . .

She was eight years old when it happened. Her mother, dimly remembered as a sickly face and a gentle fretful voice, was dead. Her father had got a new wife out of Pictland; Taniu had to keep out of her way and not anger her.

'She won't want you under her feet!' Old Nurse was sharp, because a new queen meant new ways, and likely new bower-women who would defy her. 'Stepmothers never have much love for the first wife's children, the less so when they haven't got any of their own yet to make them feel secure. Besides,' she added darkly, 'she's a shameless Pictish heathen and best not to meddle with.'

Old Ancarat was a Christian of sorts, because her mistress had been. She always impressed on Taniu that she must take no part in heathen wickedness, though she never explained what that was. The little girl slept with Ancarat and followed her about from the still-room to the herb garden like a dwarf shadow. She did not need any reminders to keep out of the queen's way because she was shy and scared of the newcomer. Drostecca, on her side, had shown no signs of wanting to take a mother's care of her husband's daughter, or even of noticing she existed. Then, one evening, she had sent one of her women to fetch Taniu.

It was Lammas Eve, a day of burning, breathless heat. From the ramparts of Din Pelidr, sea and hills had shimmered under a thin haze. By the evening this had cleared; a golden moon had risen lambent as daylight. Taniu had not been able to keep her eyes away from the moonbeams that shone into her bed-chamber from the window-slits high under the roof. Ancarat was away, tending one of Loth's men who had been schooling a half-broken horse earlier in the day. It had rolled on him, leaving him with cracked ribs and growing signs of fever.

Taniu sat on her bed, staring at the strange golden light that did not send the night away but filled it with uncanny life. The first thing the woman, Lurga, saw as she came in was a small white face turned to her, grey eyes wide with alarm. The woman smiled and held out her hand.

'Come, child. The queen wants you.'

Taniu shrank back, nervous at the unexpected order. She wanted Nurse. The woman came over to her bed and squatted down, bringing her face level with Taniu's. She was thin and brown-skinned, with heavy black braids and thick, almost straight eyebrows over light green eyes. She looked kind.

'Poor little girl, sitting all alone in the dark. Nurse won't be back before dawn. You come along and talk to us, dear. The queen's quite worried about you.'

She put her hands under Taniu's armpits, lifted her off the bed and took her hand. The little girl, bewildered but obedient, came with her down the passageway, past the store-rooms and the door of the royal bed-chamber, into the queen's hall.

Drostecca had given orders not to light the torches; their heat and smoke would be burdensome on that warm evening. The hearth fire was banked down under turfs; the only light was that enchanter's moonlight. At its touch the wall-hangings seemed to open out into eerie landscapes. Shadows gathered in corners; from the shadows women moved and whispered.

Taniu peered across at the carved chair facing the hearth, where the queen sat when she bestowed gifts on the king's guests and sometimes, in the king's absence, heard and judged disputes. It was empty. Lurga led her on

14

past the hearth to a low couch where her stepmother was lolling, hands behind her head. Taniu stiffened and hesitated but Drostecca reached out an arm and gently pulled her stepdaughter towards her. She settled Taniu on the couch beside her, still keeping her in the circle of an arm. With her other hand she caressingly put back the child's hair and cupped her cheek, looking intently in her face.

'So you're Taniu. Little Taniu who sits all alone and never comes to see her new mother. Where have you been hiding from me, my dear?'

Taniu ducked her head shyly and muttered something about Nurse.

'But Nurse has gone away tonight and little girls mustn't be left alone in the dark. So I'll look after you till she comes back, shall I, my lamb? Do little girls like honey cakes?'

She snapped her fingers towards the moving shadows in the corners. Lurga came forward with another woman, who placed a low stool by the couch. Lurga had a silver platter heaped with cakes; she set it on the stool and pushed it towards the child with an inviting smile. Taniu took a cake and nibbled. It was deliciously sweet and sticky with honey. Under her eyelashes she looked warily at this stepmother who seemed so different from Nurse's warnings, so warm and kind.

Drostecca's body was sturdy and rather squat, as usual with Picts. She had full soft breasts, thick hips and thighs. Her face was broad and freckled, with high cheekbones and a wide mouth. Her women had taken off her heavy head-circlet and the silver-tipped pins from her braids; she had pushed her thick, light-red hair back from her face. She had stripped to her shift for the heat; her strong arms were bare. Glancing at the arm cuddling her, Taniu caught her breath to see that it was covered with coiling snakes. Before she could scream or pull away, she realized they were quite flat and still. Cautiously she put her finger on a snake's tail; when she was quite sure it didn't move she ran her finger along it up to its head. It did not seem to be painted but pricked into the skin.

Drostecca felt the soft tickling and peeped down at Taniu's face, smiling. Taniu smiled back; Drostecca drew her closer to her body, rocking gently backwards and forwards, humming under her breath. Taniu relaxed dreamily into this cuddling, snuggling her head against her stepmother's soft breast. Drostecca's humming formed into words, in the same lulling rhythm as the swaying of her body.

'Do you know . . . what tonight . . . is, my love . . . m -m-m . . . ?'

'Full moon?' Taniu hoped she had guessed the right answer. She didn't want her stepmother to find her stupid.

'The Moon of Lugos,' Drostecca went on in the same dreaming voice. 'Lugos the Bright One . . . Lugos of the Shining Spear . . . '

The other women had come noiselessly out of the shadows; they were squatting in a half-circle round the couch. One by one they took up the drowsy, whispering litany, while Drostecca kept on rocking Taniu in the circle of her arm.

'Lugos Kindler . . . '

'Lugos Wakener . . . '

'He burns in the dark places . . . '

'He pierces, he quickens . . . '

'He destroys, he brings to life . . . '

'He pierces, he quickens,' murmured Drostecca. She pressed her right hand hard into her lap and sighed.

Taniu, nibbling her honey cake, soothed by the cuddling and the warmth of Drostecca's body, was not taking much notice of the words that flowed past her ears. She had never had so much attention in her life; she was absorbed in the discovery that her stepmother was kind and loved her.

A clink and the sound of liquid pouring. There was a silver goblet on the stool now, next to the plate of cakes. An unfamiliar smell, pungent yet somehow smoky.

'Usquebaugh.' Drostecca smiled at the child's blank look. 'The Water of Life.'

Water! The honey cake had been very sweet and sticky. Taniu took a generous mouthful, felt a second's cold wetness in her mouth, swallowed—and caught fire inside. Her eyes were streaming; she was choking and coughing helplessly. She turned her blurred gaze towards her stepmother, bewildered. She heard the women laughing.

'Silly one, silly little one!' Drostecca's voice was playful, yet harder. 'Do you think you can swill down the Water of Life like a young pig at the trough? Now, stop coughing and sip slowly—*slowly*. There. That's better. It'll soothe your throat.'

She gripped the child with her left arm and held the goblet firmly to her mouth. Taniu, dazed but used to obeying, made herself sip and swallow several times, though she hated the rough burning taste. The hall began to sway. Moment by moment it dissolved into the moonlight. The wall-hangings stirred, the woven figures stretched themselves, stepped out and began to move towards her. She believed that Drostecca handed the goblet to one of the women and that she had been laid down on the couch . . .

At this point, whenever the secret terror forced itself up in Taniu's mind, her memories—if they were memories —lost all connection and sense. They were not so much memories as a jumble of sensations that stabbed and flashed out of the darkness.

She was being carried in someone's arms, bundled in a cloak. She was shaking with laughter; someone hushed her gently, putting a hand over her mouth. They were out of doors, she could feel the night air on her face. The moonlight washed over them; the moon was swinging and rolling in the sky. They were at the postern gate; it was open—but how would they get through while it whirled round and round them so fast?

Now they were outside the walls and plunging down the cliff, a line of cloaked figures swaying and zigzagging along the narrow path that snaked across the rock face.

They were going through a wood. Leaf-hands tapped at her face; twig-fingers pulled her hair. An owl hooted, floating across a clearing like a ghost.

Now they were out on the open moor. Steps swished through the rough grass. A bird was startled from its nest and flew out almost under their feet. Somewhere a vixen screamed. They were at the top of a slope, looking down on the rim of a bowl-shaped hollow ... In the middle, clearly etched by the moonlight, a circle of stones like broken teeth. Beyond the circle a small pool shining like a polished mirror. In the centre of the circle, a flat-topped stone like a table, with a pillar of rock at its head. Beside the pillar, a white figure standing as still as if it too were stone.

They went down into the hollow near the stones but waited outside the circle. The white figure came outside the ring to meet them. A tall thin old man with wild silvery hair and beard. On his head a wreath of fresh rowan leaves; on his breast the gold lunula of a Druid. Drostecca took Taniu from the woman who had been carrying her and held her out at arms' length. The Druid took her. She felt his beard tickle; then her cheek was jammed against the gold plate on his chest.

He carried her inside the circle and set her down at the foot of the pillar. The cloak slipped as she touched the ground; her back met the cold hardness of the pillar and she realized she had no other clothes on. She heard herself giggling. The stones of the circle kept swelling up and lunging at her, then shrinking back. She shut her eyes to stop seeing the stones but felt herself spinning away into the dark till she opened them again.

A woman was crouched down striking sparks from a flint. The Druid stood a few paces in front of her, holding a strange-looking spear. Its head was made of chipped, polished flint; at the top of the shaft a bush of dried twigs had been woven, with the spear-point sticking out of them. A thin spiral of blue smoke coiled between the woman's hands, then flames leaped. The Druid slowly lowered the spear until its point was in the fire. The tip of a twig kindled; the Druid raised the spear erect. Women's voices screamed and howled. The Druid walked out of the circle towards the pool, carrying the spear with the twigs now well ablaze. A line of women followed in single file with dancing steps. The Druid held the spear over the water, then plunged it point first into the pool with a savage thrust, another, then another. The screaming rose to a frenzy.

Somewhere in the circle a drum began to beat, then a

18

pipe shrilled out in a reel. The Druid was coming back into the circle, carrying the quenched spear, but the women began to dance left-hand-wise, in and out between the stones. They had thrown off their cloaks and were dancing naked in a crazy ecstasy, prancing and flinging their arms, their hair tossing loose. Someone had thrown more fuel on the fire; it blazed up high. Taniu felt that the drummer was beating on her skull and that the pipe-notes had turned into skewers being pushed through her eyes.

The dancers had spiralled inside the circle and were narrowing their reel round the pillar-stone. Drostecca capered in front of it, her red mane swirling, her breasts bouncing, the tattooed snakes on her arms and shoulders wriggling alive.

Suddenly she swooped, snatching Taniu and holding her over her head while she whirled round, laughing. Taniu saw the teeth inside the red gash of her mouth. Then Drostecca threw her to the next woman in the ring and so she was tossed and swung along the whole line, breathless, terrified, but still giggling.

Then she was down on the flat stone. Drostecca knelt on it behind her, holding Taniu against her belly, gripping her with her thighs. Lurga and another woman, laughing hysterically, each caught hold of an ankle and pulled her legs apart. The Druid came to the foot of the stone, carrying the spear. Taniu's drunken eyes focused for one appalled moment on the point, which had been ground and polished to smoothness. She was sure he was going to kill her; she could feel her throat screaming but any sound she made was drowned by inhuman laughter. The Druid stepped towards her, but without lifting the spear to plunge it through her heart. He moved it steadily forward between her legs, she felt a thrust and a prick of pain, then her terror turned to blackness and engulfed her . . .

The next picture was herself, wet and sobbing on the floor by the hearth in the queen's hall. Lurga was rubbing her dry with a piece of linen. There was a bowl of water beside her with a cloth half lying in it. There was a smear of blood on the cloth.

'Oh, you bad child!' Lurga was saying as she rubbed,

though there was a secret laughter in her voice. 'You silly, naughty girl, to make yourself sick like that. Anyone'd think you'd never had a meal in your life!' She gave Taniu a little shake and a slap with the towel; she seemed to be playing at being cross.

'I didn't make myself—I haven't been sick—' She was bewildered by the scolding and trying to gather up some horrible wisps of memory that floated just out of her grasp. Then she justified Lurga's accusation by vomiting over the floor. There was a loathsome, smoky taste in her mouth.

'You wretched child! Haven't I had enough trouble with you tonight? You don't deserve to be asked to sit with the queen!'

A voice spoke from the couch.

'Take that dirty brat out of here. My hall smells like a pigsty.'

Lurga scooped Taniu up and carried her along the passage to Nurse's room. She put the child on her bed and began to pull the coverlet over her, but Taniu caught her wrists, babbling her terror.

'That fire drink—you all went out—you were dancing—and that old man came at me with a spear—oh, what happened, *what happened*?'

She started to scream; Lurga put her hand over Taniu's mouth, firmly but quite gently.

'You gobbled too many honey cakes. Then you went to sleep and the queen laid you down on her couch in case we disturbed you. You had a nightmare, and no wonder with your belly all bloated. And then you were sick, which is just what you deserve if you act like a little pig instead of a king's daughter. But we won't tell Nurse—' she smiled —'because she would be very cross with you and you've punished yourself enough already for your greediness.'

She patted Taniu's tears dry, then stood up. 'And I should keep well out of the queen's way for the time being, if I were you. But don't say anything to Nurse.'

She turned and went out of the room.

Taniu needed no warning not to tell Nurse, she was too frightened of the old woman's anger. Nor did she ever want to go back to the queen's hall. She dreaded meeting

Drostecca; for a time she was haunted by the fear that she would be fetched again. But Drostecca became pregnant quite soon afterwards; the son she bore was the centre of all her care and interest. She never again sent for her stepdaughter at the Moon of Lugos. Nor did she ever again cuddle her or give her honey cakes . . .

Taniu came back to the present, to find herself cramped and cold, her back aching with being pressed against the queen's chair.

The terror had gone for this time, though she knew it would come back. However often she lived through it, she still had no clear idea what had happened to her. If she could ever have spoken freely to Nurse—if Loth had cared enough about her to make it worth the while of any bower-woman to befriend her and share gossip—if Ancarat had ever explained her dark hints about the Old Religion—Taniu might have come to the knowledge that could have saved bitter sorrow and many lives later on. As it was, she could not be sure that the horror had not been a nightmare, brought on by a surfeit of sweet cakes and the usquebaugh that Drostecca had made her drink. A hidden terror that sprang on her from time to time, uneasiness at full moons, a persistent disquiet in Drostecca's presence—what sense did it make?

She got up, stretched her cramped limbs and went into the dark passage that led from the far end of the hall. To her left was the queen's bed-chamber, where she felt sure Loth would not sleep that night. On her right were some store-rooms for weaving-gear, rugs and sheepskins, household vessels; then the still-room. From the far end of the passage came a flickering light from the nursery. Someone had forgotten to pull the curtain right across the door-space. She tiptoed in.

The charcoal in the brazier was down to embers but the draught now and then brushed a flame across them. When this happened, the light round the brazier grew brighter but shadows jumped up and pounced from the corners of the nursery. Snoring came from a pallet where Ancarat was asleep with her mouth open. She was small, bony and frail with age. With her beaky nose and wisps of white hair she looked like a falcon: old, moulting but still fierce and dangerous.

Strangers to the court might have wondered why Drostecca, who had brought women from her own country, should have allowed a foreigner, a servant of the dead queen, to govern her nursery and have charge of her own fiercely adored son. No one in Loth's own household, not even Drostecca now, questioned Ancarat's authority.

The Strathclyde woman was a mistress of herb-lore. There were very few people in Din Pelidr who had no occasion to be grateful for her skill. She knew all the herbs that could brighten eyes, cool the skin or warm a lover; how to ease childbearing or remove an unwanted baby quickly and discreetly. So the women feared, flattered and coaxed her. She could check bleeding, draw the fever from an inflamed wound and set broken bones so that the limb healed strong and straight; therefore the warriors also respected her. Even Loth, who disliked any reminder of his first marriage, valued her usefulness. He had from the first refused Drostecca's raging demands to send her back to her country or, better, throw her over the ramparts of Din Pelidr to feed the crows. During her first pregnancy and labour, however, Drostecca had learned to share Loth's opinion of the old woman's skill. Also it was obvious, even to her jealous eyes, that Ancarat worshipped the new prince and founded much of her own pride on him.

Taniu had never been a cause of pride to Ancarat. The old woman had taken Queen Languoreth's failure as bitterly as Loth, though for different reasons. It was a disgraceful reward for all her efforts and skill as a royal nurse to be given a girl instead of a prince—and with no hope of a prince coming after. She took Taniu's existence as a personal slight, though for her own self-respect she had looked after the child carefully and well.

During the last few years, though, her contempt for Taniu as a person had dwindled. The little girl had always followed her about like a puppy as soon as she could toddle. She spent hours with Ancarat in her herb garden under the ramparts. Of course, she asked questions; though Ancarat was sharp and impatient with her, she answered them. Then Taniu began to play at herb-growing herself, making a little bed of them in the far corner of the garden. Ancarat could not help watching her, if only to see she did no damage. But Taniu's roots and cuttings grew into healthy plants; Ancarat told her when to gather them and added them to her own stores. Soon Taniu was helping her in the main garden. From gathering and drying she progressed to distilling and compounding medicines in the still-room. Grudgingly Ancarat recognized an innate skill equal to her own. She thought Taniu was wasted as a princess; she would have made a superb herb-woman. Therefore, Taniu earned her respect, but no greater show of affection.

As it never occurred to Taniu to expect affection from the sharp-tongued, sharp-beaked old woman, this lack did not make her feel particularly unhappy. She had not come in now looking for comfort from her old nurse. As she paused in the doorway she looked past Ancarat's pallet to a box bed at the other side of the brazier. A round head was poking over its high edge; two big brown eyes were staring fearfully at the jumping shadows. The head jerked and gasped as she stepped out into the fading light.

'Oh-h-h—*Taniu!*' Her stepbrother stood up, gripping the sides of his bed. 'Don't make a noise! The Wild Huntsman's out riding tonight with his hounds. He's trying to get in but I won't let him. I'm staying on guard.'

Taniu looked at him lovingly. Prince Gwalchmai was the pride of everybody in Din Pelidr, from Loth to the kitchen maids. Taniu was the only one who saw he was very nervous. He knew from the hero-tales that princes had to be brave; but he was only six and practically everything in the royal court was bigger than he. When a wolfhound pushed a fanged and hairy face into his, or a gigantic pony stamped close beside him, he would force himself to stand still, then reach out and pat the monster. Loth would laugh to see his own pleasure in horses and hounds showing so early in his son. He boasted that the boy didn't know what fear was. Taniu could see that Gwalchmai knew only too well what fear was, though she would never betray this knowledge to anyone else, least of all to him. When she watched his gallant efforts to rule his terrors, she thought he was the bravest creature in Din Pelidr.

'Come over here, Taniu, so I can keep you safe.'

She crossed the room and knelt by the side of the bed.

'You keep tight hold of me, Gwalchmai—then I'll feel sure the Wild Huntsman won't get me.'

He flung his arms round her in a protecting gesture that turned into a frantic clutch. She slid her arm behind his shoulders and he snuggled up gratefully.

'You're quite safe now, Taniu.'

'Of course I'm safe. Who ever would dare to hurt me now? I couldn't be any safer if I had Culhwch himself to protect me.'

'Who's he?' Gwalchmai was ready to be jealous.

'He was King Arthur's nephew. And one spring morning he went riding out to court the Giant-King's daughter. He rode on a white horse and he wore a purple cloak with an apple of gold in each corner. He had a gold-hilted sword at his belt and a golden shield on his shoulder and two silver spears in his hand. And so he rode and he rode till he came to King Arthur's gate . . .'

Her lulling voice had soothed the little boy. Her warm arms cradled him. His head drooped against her shoulder. The Wild Huntsman and his troop of shadows were blown away and vanished beyond the mountains to the west. It was a spring morning and Gwalchmai in a purple cloak was riding out on his white horse to court the Giant-King's daughter.

Carefully, Taniu lifted a corner of the heavy woollen bed-cover and drew it over herself. Resting her cheek against Gwalchmai's head, she watched the embers die as she drifted with him off to sleep.

CHAPTER
2

There was a good harvest. The bonfires had roared to heaven on Lammas night. Loth's folk swung through the Harvest Dance with light heads and light hearts, or coupled among the stocks as if the fire in their blood would keep them warm beyond Midwinter.

Yet as the year turned to autumn, life in the queen's hall became tense and uneasy. When a chance came to escape from it, Taniu's spirits rose to the skies.

Drostecca's pregnancy was giving her discomfort; she was very big and had lost all pleasure in life. As her comfort lessened, her temper got more vicious. Loth came to her less and less frequently. He rode out hunting most days and slept elsewhere.

Luned had got a pair of showy silver bracelets, inset with red and green enamelled discs, which she was stupid enough to wear in Drostecca's sight. She did not do this in malice; she was proud of her bracelets and never thought of denying herself the pleasure of wearing them.

Drostecca had glanced at the bracelets expressionlessly, then told Lurga in a raised voice to lock up her jewels carefully, away from the paws of thieving bitches. Luned had remarked pertly to no one in particular that kings could give their treasures where they pleased—and where they got their pleasure. Drostecca had tried to claw Luned's face but was slowed down by her bulk; Luned had skipped nimbly out of her way, while Drostecca shrieked abuse and threats and Ancarat came bustling up, scolding everybody.

Taniu, coming in through the side door from the garden with a basket of herbs, heard the outcry and thought Drostecca must be miscarrying. Dropping her basket at the door she hurried along the passage to the queen's chamber in time to see Luned duck into the hall and Drostecca sinking back among her rugs and cushions, red-faced and clutching her belly. Ancarat bent over her; somebody pulled the curtain across.

She looked through into the hall, where Luned was laughing and holding court among a group of bower-women and slave girls.

'—Oh, you should have seen how ridiculous she looked just now, trundling after me like a hogshead of beer!'

Squawks and giggles.

'Did the king—?'

Heads together whispering; gasps and titters, with Luned's voice lilting up in excited pleasure,'—then he called me his *sweet apple*, he says his mouth waters every time he thinks of me!'

Somebody hushed her; when a voice said 'Luned!' into the hush, there was a move away from her as they looked nervously over their shoulders towards the bed-chamber.

'Luned, there's a basket of cut herbs by the side door. Go and bring it into the still-room.'

Luned was so taken aback at getting an order from Taniu that she obeyed at once. Taniu followed her out, leaving a rustle of whispers at her back. She waited by the still-room door as Luned came up with the basket, looking sulky now she had had time to resent that she, the King's Woman, was being made to run errands. Taniu signed to her to go in and put the basket on the heavy oaken work-bench that filled one side wall. Luned set the basket down with a thump and turned to flounce out again but came face to face with Taniu. To her own surprise, she stopped.

'Luned, it would be more prudent if you didn't wear those bracelets when you attend on the queen.' Taniu came to the point at once.

Luned pouted, giving the princess a defiant glance, ready to be insolent. Taniu's face was so earnest and kindly that she found herself answering defensively.

'I don't see why I shouldn't wear what's my own. They were given to me. Nobody has any right to complain.'

As she spoke she lifted her round arms and looked at her bracelets. Remembering how Loth had clasped them on last night, lying across her on the bed, she began to smile. He'd said it was her arms that made the bracelets beautiful. He'd had scope to admire his gift; she'd been wearing nothing else.

Seeing that dreamy, absent-minded smile, Taniu tried again.

'You make the queen very angry. That's not wise. Considering her time, it's not very kind either.'

Luned's pretty upper lip lifted; she looked mischievous.

'She's no right to grumble if others do what she can't manage. I'm not taking anything away from her, not even

26

these bracelets. The king can do what he likes without asking her leave.'

'People don't need a right to be angry. Anger is anger, whether it's right or not—and the queen's anger is fearful.'

'What can she do to me, however angry she gets? She can't get near enough to reach me—her belly's too big.'

She giggled at the memory.

'Besides, the king would never allow anyone to lay a hand on me, even if she ordered it. Now, I could have anybody flogged if I asked him in bed. He comes to my bed, not hers. He doesn't care what she wants, or what she thinks, or anything about her!'

Taniu felt irritated and inclined to leave her to her fate. Then, as she looked at Luned's pretty face, the impulse to anger died away. As well be angry with one of the flowers in the herb garden for blooming and putting out its scent. Luned was like a flower in her blue gown, with her round face framed in dark curls and her merry brown eyes. As delicate, as harmless—and as mindless.

'Drostecca is the queen. Wherever my father lies at night, she's the mother of his heir. And if—and when she gives him another son, he'll give her anything she asks in return—even you.'

Luned shook her curls.

'Loth couldn't live without the pleasure I give him. Poor man, he needs it, wedded to bad temper and sour looks. It's a wonder she doesn't turn his beer in his belly.'

She laughed and admired her bracelets.

It was like watching a child absorbed in picking king-cups at the edge of a marsh, getting nearer and nearer to its black clutch. Luned had no sense of her danger. That scene with Drostecca meant no more to her than a squabble with a girl-companion about hair ribbons or a partner in the Harvest Dance. What it meant to Drostecca, Taniu went cold to think. She had seen the queen's face as she fell back on her bed.

'Luned, Luned, be careful!'

'What have I got to care for? Thank you for warning me; I'm sure you mean to be kind. You've a good heart, princess, but you must admit that I know more about the king's feelings than you do!'

It was not said spitefully.

'Now, by your leave, my lady—' She stepped past Taniu and went almost dancing back along the passage to the hall. Her harebell-blue gown swung round her slim ankles; the silver bracelets flashed.

Taniu let her go and sat down pensively on one of the stools by the bench. Absent-mindedly, she tipped the herbs from the basket. Her hands began to sort them into their kinds for hanging and drying; her mind was still going over the scene that had just passed. Her hands moved slower and slower. At last she gave up, folded her arms on the bench and rested her head on them, enjoying the silence and fragrance.

The still-room had no rich hangings and fur rugs like the queen's rooms; the floor was rough cobbles; two clumsy stools were the only furniture besides the big work-bench. It was Taniu's favourite room in the whole court; she had learned here that healers were greater than kings.

She sighed out a yawn, then craned to pull a sprig of mint between her lips. Chewing the fresh leaves, savouring the clean taste, she set herself to weigh up Luned's danger, as she might have assessed a child's fever symptoms before mixing a cooling brew.

'*What can she do to me however angry she gets?*'

Taniu thought that Drostecca would probably not try to do anything at the moment. If she removed or disabled the king's fancywoman while she herself was unavailable, Loth would just take another.

'*The king would never let anyone lay a hand on me, even if she ordered it.*' Luned's light voice bubbling with laughter, sure she had Loth's heart and body safe under her girdle.

The poor girl would have been safer making her way across quicksand. Loth would take a woman whenever he felt the appetite, but Taniu knew that Drostecca had her father in an unbreakable grip. She was not strikingly beautiful but she had a hot magic in her body, perhaps the gift of the dark gods she worshipped. Her vitality, her lust, even her viciousness made her the most exciting woman Loth had ever possessed. And she was the queen, who had borne him a fine son. As the triumphant mother of another boy she would be crowned with the king's pride and gratitude. When, after that, she took him back into her bed she could ask for Luned's blood to drink in a golden goblet and she would get it. There were plenty of other women in Lothian for the king's pastime.

Between that murderous jealousy and Loth's selfish indifference, was there any escape for a light-hearted creature like Luned, who saw nothing but the moment's pleasure?

Taniu fixed on the time just after the birth for her rescue attempt. Drostecca would be exhausted; Loth would be celebrating; both parents absorbed in the child. In that short respite from jealousy and whoring she would suggest a marriage for Luned. Loth, in high good-humour, would likely be glad of a peaceful riddance from her before Drostecca had recovered enough to make scenes.

Reviewing the warband, she decided that Morien was handsome enough to console Luned. He'd be flattered to have the king's woman in his bed and keep her too busy there for nightly adventures. Perhaps Loth might give—

'Those herbs won't sort and hang themselves with looking at them!'

Ancarat had come briskly enough into the still-room but when she collapsed on to the other stool she looked near to death. Her headrail had slipped; her thin white hair strag-gled in elf-locks round a face that seemed to be turning into a skull, the skin was stretched so tightly across the bones. She had shut her eyes; her lips twitched word-lessly; her hands were shaking so much they scrabbled uselessly for a second before she could get hold of her apron to wipe her face.

Alarmed, Taniu hurried to fill a beaker with cordial and held it to the old woman's mouth. After a sip or two Ancarat jerked the beaker away and drank the rest unaided. This ungraciousness showed she was recover-ing. Taniu went quietly back to her stool. Ancarat banged the empty beaker on the work-bench and puffed.

'Is the queen any easier now?'

'Easy! She won't let herself be easy. She's destroying herself.'

'Is she ill?'

'I can treat illness. But this is something else, I've never known anything like it. She's as sturdy as a hill pony and God knows she goes at it with a will. Yet she's only kindled twice in six years. I think she turns her own strength against herself. She'll tear herself to pieces!'

'Has she taken harm today?'

'If she raises another storm like today, there'll be deadly harm. That half-witted slut, Luned—she's asking to be whipped till her blood runs, stirring up the queen like that.'

Taniu shivered as if a cold hand had touched her.

'She probably will be.'

'And then we'll have another storm. Thank God the king's away off with his bodyguard, so they'll have no need to squabble over whose bed he sleeps in, this many a night.'

'Has my father gone away?' Taniu was startled. 'There can't be war on the borders this late in the year?'

'Don't worry. The only war he's got to fight at the moment is in the queen's rooms—which is why he's taken himself off at the first chance. Word came to the hall last night from one of the western farms that wolves have come down from the hills and taken some sheep. Wolves in September! It'll be a bitter winter, mark my words. Anyway, the king rode out at first light with a hunting party, cheerful as a boy, so we may have some peace for a while. When two bitches fight for a dog, the world's upside down!'

'Do you think the queen will be more at peace with the king away?'

Ancarat sighed.

'I must try to keep her quiet, for the baby's sake as well as her own. She'll need constant watching. I'll not see Nia this year, that's sure.'

She sighed again; the sound was nearly a groan.

Ancarat had suckled Taniu's mother along with her own daughter Nia, her youngest. When Languoreth came as queen to Lothian she had insisted on bringing her old nurse with her to help her through the unknown hazards of bedding and childbirth. Nia came too as a bower-woman; but she had soon married one of Loth's warband. When his father died, she went with him to the family farm away in the southwest, near the Cumbrian border.

30

Luckier than her royal foster-sister, Nia had a child every year and most of them lived. Ancarat always went in state to see each new grandchild, take presents and pounce on Nia's housekeeping like a hawk. When Taniu was little, Ancarat took her as well, since she wouldn't trust her to one of Loth's women. Later, Taniu went of her own choice. She knew the farm as well as the palace and found it a far kinder home.

These yearly expeditions were the high glory of Ancarat's life; she spent months getting her presents ready: blankets and swaddling clothes of her own weaving, salves and cordials for Nia, sweetmeats and herb-cheeses. But Nia, though as tough and vigorous as an apple tree, was now a great age for child-bearing, being in her thirtieth year, almost an old woman herself. This would surely be the last grandchild. As Taniu looked at her old nurse she realized with a shock that in any case there might be no more visits. Ancarat had always been such a mountain torrent of energy—if mountain torrents had voices and could scold all the time—that she seemed immortal. Now she looked just a frail old woman beaten down by life.

Taniu suddenly saw her childhood's tyrant as pitiable. Ancarat's other children had been left behind in Strathclyde; if they lived, if she had grandchildren there, no one had troubled to send word to her. She had been brought to a strange country at the whim of her mistress and here she had to stay, working herself to death for strangers. It was a matter of course that she would have to stay at court now, watching over Drostecca and her unborn child, leaving her own daughter untended.

'Shall I go to Nia for you?'

Ancarat scorned to show pleasure or gratitude.

'You might as well take the things I've put by for her. It'd be a pity to waste them. And while you're there, you can hunt out some roots of wolf's bane to bring back for me—it's good for milk fever—oh yes, and some arnica, it grows down south in the hill pastures, you should find some if you keep your eyes open and don't go round daydreaming as usual. Remember where I showed you last year. Don't go and pester her now. I've had enough trouble getting her to lie down. You can ask her in the morning.'

'Ask her—?'

'Oh, God give me patience, child, do you never listen? The king's away; she'll give hearing till he comes back. You'll have to ask her permission to leave the court.'

Taniu's heart sank; it always did when she had to approach her stepmother. Next morning she slipped into the queen's hall from the rear door and took her place at the back among the other women. They were setting up a loom with as little noise as possible, whispering among themselves. Five or six warriors were grouped in front of the hearth; through the open door she could see many more, crowding and shouldering in the porch.

The carved chair was set beside the hearth, spread with fleeces. Drostecca was throned there, propped with cushions. She looked magnificent in a robe of crimson wool that fell ungirdled from neck to hem, hiding most of her bulk. Her light-red braids shone like fire against its dark glow. A circlet of gilt bronze banded her forehead, a gold torque ringed her throat. Two large saucer-brooches, set with garnets, were pinned on her shoulders, ropes of amber beads strung between them. Across her lap lay a silver rod, with a silver-gilt snake coiled round it, tipped with a beautifully wrought sparrowhawk. This was the Sceptre of Hearing. Gwalchmai was squatting against her skirt, watching everything with intent eyes.

There was only one case for hearing but it threatened to drag down the whole palace on their heads before it finished.

It had begun with a quarrel over dice in the warriors' hall that morning between two of the younger men, bored and resentful that they had not been chosen to go hunting with the king. Marchlew had staked a dagger-sheath, a gaudy object of red and green leather, stamped with gilt patterns and chaped with silver. It was Spanish work, come from Caer Luel in a trader's pack. It was not half so well made as the leatherwork turned out by Loth's saddler but its show-iness and exotic origin made it the envy of every spearman in the hall. Marchlew, the proud owner, had been winning steadily and only staked his treasure to wring an equal stake from Cynon, whose luck was out. That time, however, Cynon won but Marchlew refused to hand over the prize. He accused Cynon of switching to false dice while he himself was drinking. Cynon, furious, hurled back the charge, saying Marchlew was a lying cheat who refused to pay his just debts.

Insults had been exchanged, the families and ancestors of both clans luridly defamed. The question would have been settled bloodily on the spot; Talhaearn the bard stepped in, ordering them to lay the dispute before the royal seat at the hearing. At this point it was discovered that the doubtful dice had fallen—or been thrown—into the fire and were beyond testing.

It was a squalid quarrel. Cynon and Marchlew had described the mating habits of each other's kin with imaginative obscenity. Now the witnesses grimly recited each filthy jibe to Drostecca's impassive face, while the women tittered furtively or gasped in shocked surprise and Gwalchmai looked more and more puzzled.

Terror lay in wait for all of them behind the crude farce. For Cynon and Marchlew the affair had now become a question of personal honour, to be fought out to the death, never mind the consequences. Their kinsmen and foster-brothers would take up the quarrel, creating new quarrels. In no time a heritage of blood-feuds would be amassed that could split the warband, leaving the kingdom helpless before its enemies.

Trying to close her ears to the gross bawdry, Taniu found that her mind was listening to very different words—beautiful, noble words:

> The hall is fallen, the hearth fires are cold;
> Weep for the hero who sleeps in their dust . . .

She was silently reciting the *Lay of the Death of Peredur*, the last British king of Caer Efrog. She always wept whenever Talhaearn performed it after the feasting—and those foul-mouthed louts, now exchanging dunghill abuse, would all weep too.

Peredur and his men had sacked a village of Anglian settlers, descendants of Fraomar's troops who had been granted land by Valentinian, down by Derwennydd. Among the captives was the chief's wife, a woman with silver-fair hair and ice-blue eyes, strange but desirable.

The captain of the warband had dragged her out of her burning hall and raped her first; but a young spearman, wild with the pride of his first battle, had killed the chief. When the spoils were divided he claimed the woman. Peredur listened to both men's stories, then awarded her to the young spearman.

The captain of the warband was Peredur's eldest foster-brother. He listened white-faced to the king's judgement. He watched the woman being led away by her new master, her white skin gleaming through the rags of her dress. He said to Peredur, very quietly, 'You've thanked me, brother, for our mother's milk.' Then he said no more of the matter.

That autumn, when the raiding season was over and the warriors scattered to their farms for the harvest, Anglian warships came up the Great Estuary. Their seamen had kinsfolk in the sacked village; they were out to settle scores. Peredur was hawking in the marshes with some of his household when the ships were sighted. They rode like the wind for Petuaria, the old Roman fort guarding the north bank of the estuary, blocking the road to Caer Efrog. Peredur sent his armour-bearer with the Red Spear of Summons to gather the warband; he couldn't hold Petuaria with his handful of men when the warfleet arrived.

No one came. The messenger rode first to the captain's land, to tell him to send out his riders and gather the army of Efrog. The captain came to the door of his barn to greet the newcomer, looked at his face and recognized the young spearman who had taken his prize—and his honour. He took the Red Spear and drove it point downwards in the ground. Seeing this, his men set upon the young spearman, beating and hacking him to death.

Peredur watched the Roman road to the north for help that never came. He perished when the Angles stormed Petuaria and burned it over the dead and dying. In their laments for him, the bards named it Caer Greu, the Fort of Blood.

It was easy after that to wipe out Peredur's men piecemeal, as each tried to defend his own lands. The Angles were lords of Caer Efrog now. They called it Eoforwic; from it they ruled the whole plain of Deira.

'In all the ages of the world,'' so the Lay ended, 'was there ever a warband that betrayed its lord? The warband of Peredur of Efrog abandoned him when called to fight the Angles at the Fort of Blood. And so their lord was slain.'

The sad dignified words faded from Taniu's mind. She came back into the present just in time to hear what Cynon had said about Marchlew's grandmother and the he-goat. These could be the opening words of the *Lay of the Fall of Lothian*.

Were Peredur's men any different, she wondered bitterly. The bards spoke nobly of honour kept to the death, of courage that earned undying fame for the heroes lying in their grave-mounds or under the burned rafters of their halls. But what sort of *honour* would destroy a whole country for the sake of a grudge—or a scrap of dyed leather? And how much honour went to the peasants slaughtered in their little farms or dying of starvation because their crops and cattle had been looted?

The last witness finished his say. There was a tight silence while everyone waited for Drostecca to make her impossible judgement. The men scowled at her, working up their anger to have it ready if the decision went against their side. Some were already silently wording the abuse they would heap on the Pictish bitch if she insulted their kinsman.

Drostecca gave no sign of hesitation or fear. When her own passions were under control she had considerable courage and shrewdness. She lifted the sceptre.

'This game must be played again.' She sounded aloof from a piece of male childishness. 'It will be done with the king's own dice, under the eyes and judgement of Talhaearn the bard. The winner will keep the dagger-sheath; no one must challenge his right. The loser will take this—'she stretched her hand to Lurga, who had been standing behind her mistress throughout the hearing, gripping the back of her chair. Lurga drew off the heavy ring Drostecca was wearing, set with an emerald, and held it out on her palm. 'A mead-cup will be set ready for the end of the game; the loser will present it to the winner; the two will pledge their friendship.'

There was a pause, while her listeners took in the terms.

Then first one, then another of the men began to grin. Whichever way the game went, neither Cynon nor Marchlew could claim he had been insulted or suffered a loss. These two touched the sceptre in agreement, then went off amicably enough with their supporters. Lurga followed to give the ring and message to Talhaearn. The women burst out chattering; somebody repeated one of the obscener jibes; there was a screech of hysterical laughter.

Drostecca leaned back in relief, yawned and stretched her arms. Then she picked up the sceptre to hand it away. Taniu hurried forward, touched it and whispered her request.

The queen agreed with the generosity of perfect indifference. If Taniu had been a bold, pert girl like Luned, playing for the men's notice, Drostecca would have resented her bitterly. If her stepdaughter had ever tried to compete with her for influence and power over Loth the resentment would have turned murderous. But Taniu was so unassuming there was no amusement to be got from thwarting her. She could go where she liked for all Drostecca cared. As it turned out the highest hurdle in Taniu's way proved to be Gwalchmai, who announced loudly, 'I'm going too!'

'No!' said Drostecca firmly.

'I've got to go! I've got to guard Taniu and keep her safe!'

'I said *no!*'

'But I want to!'

Gwalchmai pushed out his lower lip and looked stubborn. His mother, exhausted and harassed by the warriors' dispute, was fast losing her precarious temper. Another minute and she would forbid the journey and any more mention of it.

'But, Gwalchmai, who's to protect the queen and the hall if you go away now? When the king's absent the prince guards the palace—it's the custom.'

Taniu's charm worked. Gwalchmai stood up straight by his mother's chair, screwing his childish features into a warrior's scowl, and drew his toy dagger. Drostecca laughed delightedly, putting an arm round his shoulders. Over his head she and Taniu smiled at each other in a sudden flash of mutual sympathy. It made a pleasant little memory to carry away from home.

CHAPTER
3

The journey that had started with such good-humoured omens passed off peacefully. The travelling party was made up of Taniu on her shaggy little dun pony Pybyr, three pack-ponies, a couple of boarhounds and two spearmen as escorts.

Drostecca had shrewdly picked Cynon and Marchlew, to get them out of further mischief. Marchlew had won the return match and wore the coveted dagger-sheath; Cynon waved his hands a lot as he spoke so that his emerald ring would catch the light. Mysteriously, the two were now the best of friends; they took fair turns to lead the pack-ponies; their talk was broken by bursts of guffawing all the way southwest as the moors climbed higher and higher into the Cheviots.

Just after noon on the second day their track turned the shoulder of a hill. There below was the farm: a few strip fields and a cluster of round thatched huts, pens, byres and fenced yards, defended by a thick dry-stone wall inside a broad bank and ditch.

As Taniu rode in through the gateway she was nearly swamped in a torrent of children. Nia swung her up in her arms from the pony and carried her over the flood like a friendly giantess.

She was not in the least like her fierce birdlike little mother. Ancarat's long-dead husband had been a big-boned Clydesman; Nia had inherited his large frame and placid temper. After fourteen years of child-bearing and hearty eating she was enormous; though with her wholesome tanned skin, rosy cheeks and glossy brown hair, she was pleasant to look at.

The children were unwrapping the presents and the visitors were admiring the new baby, a little girl placidly asleep with her thumb in her mouth, when Nia's husband Cadwal walked in with his sheepdogs. He was a thin wiry man, his skin leathery from days and nights out in the hills with his flocks. He was usually quiet, almost speechless, greeting his guests now with a smile and a nod.

Taniu congratulated him on the new baby, politely hoping that he didn't mind too much that it was a girl. He was so surprised, it shocked him into speech.

'Mind? No, why should I mind?' With nine sturdy boys Cadwal could welcome a daughter more cheerfully than Loth. 'I'm right blithe o' the lass.'

At this moment a tangle of small boys and puppies crashed against his legs, kicking and biting. Cadwal gently pushed them away with his foot, pretending to scold.

'What's the good o' lads but to eat the house empty and make mischief, till they're old enough to go and make mischief in another man's house?'

His eldest girl, Leucu, rosy and silky-haired like her mother but still girlishly slender, brought him a mug of ale. He put his arm round her and held her close, smiling, '—but a lass that's gentle and handy and sees to her father, that's the treasure, isn't it, my lamb?'

Taniu envied Leucu from her heart; she wished she could have grown up in such a home. She settled in now, quietly and naturally, as another daughter of the house, collecting eggs with Leucu, hushing the baby, taking her turn at bread-making and watching the stew in the cauldron.

Cynon and Marchlew, remembering their dignity as warriors of the royal warband, were lofty and distant at first. They were hardly more than boys, though, and had grown up on farms just like Cadwal's so they soon began giving a hand with the herding, set snares and enjoyed themselves.

The peaceful carefree days slipped by as if they were out of time, but the shortening light of October told them they ought to be on their way home. Taniu had set aside the last day of her visit for getting the roots Ancarat wanted. She remembered going with her to a place some miles to the south, beyond the head of the valley.

'Argoed Llwyfain?' said Cadwal, when she told him this. 'Why, that's away down on the March with Cumbria.'

'Cumbria!' Marchlew scowled. Cynon spat noisily into the fire.

'Nobody comes that way,' said Nia reassuringly. 'The land's too sour and poor for raiding. Cumbrians keep further south.'

Cynon sneered. 'They would. Those scavenging kites find it pleasanter picking dead men's bones. They'd be scared to put a foot on Lothian land, sheep-stealing.'

'If one of them did,' added Marchlew, 'he'd find himself nailed to a barn door as a warning to other vermin.'

When Peredur died in the Fort of Blood, the king of Cumbria had crossed the Long Hills with his horsemen and spearmen. He seized the walled town of Catraeth and built a fortress on the towering cliff above the waterfalls, blocking the Angles from the Roman road over the hills into the Idon valley, the heartland of Cumbria. He had also, of course, blocked the Angles' road north—to Lothian and Eidyn—but he got no thanks for that. The easterners resented the Cumbrians in Catraeth like a sword-splinter lodged in a wound and festering. The Angles were only newcomers and nobody knew who their ancestors were, but there was a long, vivid history of feuding between the British kingdoms east and west of the Hills. By snatching Catraeth, the Cumbrians had proved themselves to be greedy, thieving and treacherous—as if anyone had ever thought them different!

'Perhaps a couple of men ought to go with you, though,' said Nia thoughtfully, looking at Cynon and Marchlew.

Taniu hastily disclaimed. Cynon and Marchlew were planning to round off their visit with some hare-coursing. If she spoiled their sport, she would have to endure their scowling eyes spearing into her back for hours while she grubbed for roots.

'That's nonsense, Nia. I don't need a guard of warriors while I go to dig up a few roots. Nobody's ever been on those hills since the world was made, except your mother and me, last year. I'll be on Pybyr and take a hunting-knife—though I'm not afraid of wild animals. They don't harm folk if they're left well alone. In some ways they've more sense than men!'

She had her way. Next morning found her high above the river valley, heading south across the moors astride Pybyr's shaggy back, her skirt kilted into her belt, a thick woollen cloak pinned on her shoulder and wrapped round her waist.

It was a beautifully fresh morning, bright with pale autumn sunshine under a light blue sky with wisps of white cloud. The heather had faded a little but still laid a purplish haze over the hill slopes. The bracken was golden in the sunlight; the rowan berries gleamed like garnets.

Before noon she turned the shoulder of a high fell and saw that there was a wide grassy hollow in its lee. The little thread of a mountain stream came tinkling down the steep hillside, ran across the hollow and jumped over its edge in a cascade down a low but steepish cliff. At the foot it spread out in a marshy tract, then gathered itself into a rivulet and flowed out of sight into the woodlands beyond.

It was a good place to stop, open to the sun but sheltered from the wind, with grass and water for Pybyr. She slipped off his saddle and bridle, hobbling him to keep him from straying too far while she was at the foot of the cliff. By the side of the waterfall the rocks made something like a flight of irregular steps; she got down without difficulty.

The next hour was wet and messy but successful, as she found enough plants to half-fill her saddle-bag. She got warm from stooping; there were still enough flies and midges to be troublesome. She decided she had gathered enough to please even Ancarat and climbed thankfully up to her hollow, bathing her face and her arms in the stream and drying herself on the edge of her cloak. Then she sat down to look into the other saddle-bag that Nia had packed with food for her: a big hunk of cheese, barley bread, some apples, enough of everything to supply a hunting party. Pybyr had strolled over and was watching her with interest; she cut an apple and gave him pieces on the palm of her hand.

Suddenly he lifted his head, staring towards the wood. Then he snorted and jerked away, trying to kick against his hobble. Taniu put her arm round his neck and a hand on his nose.

'Gently, *gently* now, Pybyr, silly one! There's nothing to be afraid of!'

He was a sensible steady-nerved little beast and he trusted Taniu. He quietened but his eyes and ears were still directed towards the woods. In the stillness, she could hear something crashing through the trees. Some large creature was coming their way, fast.

She glanced round, thinking whether to saddle up and ride away, but decided against it. No stag, boar or wild bull could get up that cliff. A wolf might, but no wolf would make that amount of noise.

While she soothed Pybyr, the creature rushed out of the shadow of the wood. A boar, huge, old and dangerous. It was labouring; she could tell by the foam round its jaws and wicked tusks that it was already hard run; it could not go on much longer. It splashed across the marshy banks of the stream to the rock face a little to her right. There it turned to bay, slashing at the earth with its tusks and pawing the ground as the hunt came out from among the trees.

One hunter only, on a chestnut with two white stockings; she realized with a sick qualm that he had no hounds to bay the boar.

The rider dismounted, looping his horse's reins round an alder stem. Then, carrying his spear loosely underarm, he advanced across the marshy ground towards the boar. Crouched at the rim of the hollow, she saw its bristles standing erect and the great shields of hide on its shoulders that could turn any blade. The hunter's weapon was only a warrior's lance, without the cross-bar of a boar-spear to prevent a stuck animal from hurling itself up the shaft to reach its attacker with its tusks.

At that moment the boar charged. The hunter dropped nimbly to one knee, holding his weapon's haft well forward with his left hand, his right gripping near the butt. He thrust the point unerringly inside the boar's shoulder-blade and through its throat. Taking the haft under his armpit, he pushed with all his might but the boar was struggling so violently that it whirled him round towards the cliff. For one terrible moment it seemed as if it could pull the hunter down and break the shaft.

She didn't know how she got down the cliff so fast, or what she expected to do when she reached the bottom. She had some vague hope that she might come up behind the boar, get beside it and drive her knife into its throat. A poor enough chance, likely to achieve nothing but her own ugly death. Luckily, the hunter kept his balance; his spear-shaft held. As she reached the foot of the cliff, the boar gave one last heave, threshed wildly with its head and legs, then keeled over on its side, dead.

The hunter stood panting, holding the shaft, watching the boar to make sure all the life was out of it. Then he put his foot on its side and pulled the spear out with some effort. He looked up and saw a figure in a grey gown, gold hair streaming across its shoulders, watching him with wide grey eyes.

It was as if sunlight, clear stream and grey stone had shaped themselves into a girl. He had the wild thought that the Goddess herself, the Lady of the hill circles and the holy springs, had risen from the stream to his aid. Then he saw that her gown was muddy and she was gripping a wicked-looking hunting-knife. He relaxed and leaned his spear against the cliff.

'That was very brave of you—and very foolish. People who face wild boars with only a knife don't usually live to be thanked.'

'I wasn't going to face it. Even if I had the courage, I wouldn't be any use at that. I was going to try to cut its throat from behind—you could say I was going to back you.'

He laughed. 'Whatever you like to call it, my thanks. Now, is there any way out of this foul marsh? My horse wants to rest—so do I, but that wood's full of flies.'

'There's a good place at the top of the cliff. You can bring your horse round the shoulder of the hill and up the slope.'

He nodded, turning to fetch the chestnut. She saw his right arm was streaming with blood from the shoulder. When she cried out, he said indifferently, 'The boar swung me against the rock. It's only a scratch, I'll bind it when I've unsaddled.'

'No, wait. She stooped, pulled a handful of sphagnum moss, pushed his torn sleeve off the wound and wiped the blood and dirt away. The 'scratch' was a deep, jagged tear, like a forked twig. When it was clean she took another handful of sphagnum, squeezed it almost dry and, laying the flaps of torn skin flat into place, pressed the moss pad over them.

'Hold that tight.'

When he obeyed, she drew her knife and pulling up her skirt cut a strip off the hem of her shift to make a bandage.

'Don't do that! You might as well have taken a rag of my shirt, it's torn already.'

'And stained with sweat and dirt. Besides being too thick to tie neatly.'

He did not argue and watched her swift fingers tying the bandage. He noted that her hands were not calloused by field work, that the shift was finely woven linen. When she had finished she thanked him briefly, then went to untie his horse while she climbed back up the waterfall. When he reappeared round the hill, she had set out Nia's provisions in the pool of sunlight under the lee of the slope.

The hunter saw first to his horse's comfort; then picked up his saddle-bag and stepped across the little stream to join her. He sat down facing her, opening his bag to add his food to their meal. While he was busy, she had her first chance to study him at her ease. He was a very young man, hardly older than herself.

When she saw his face in her mind afterwards, as she often did, her first thought was always of swiftness in repose, like one of her father's hawks hovering with spread wings for a second before striking down like lightning on its prey.

He had long black hair, with a bluish sheen on it like ravens' feathers, bound back by a leather thong across his forehead; slanting eyebrows almost meeting over a long, straight nose; a finely-cut expressive mouth that was quick to smile. His brilliant smoky-blue eyes fringed with black lashes, illuminated but did not soften the clear-cut sharpness of his face. Their colour and shape would have made an ugly-featured woman beautiful; their look was keen and inclined to be scornful.

He wore a hunter's leather jerkin over a plain shirt of unbleached wool and dark breeches of heavy felted cloth tucked into supple leather boots. All his gear was well made and workmanlike, but had none of the bright colours or ornaments with which nobles and warriors of royal

43

warbands loved to bedeck themselves. She set him down in her mind as a free-born farmer like Cadwal, with enough land and stock to give himself a good horse and a day's hunting from time to time.

The hunter glanced up and caught Taniu gazing at him. Just then, a shadow of wings swept across their hollow, then another. Two dark shapes circled over the marsh, then perched in a tree at the edge of the wood.

'The ravens are gathering to the corpse.' He spoke with a soft lilting accent that was strange to her. 'I suppose I should cut him up.' He smiled at her. 'He's yours, by rights—you deserve him. If I prepare him for you, will you take him home?'

'No thank you! Poor Pybyr wouldn't thank you at all—and Nia's got plenty of meat for the winter.'

'And Nia is—' he considered her, assessing her youth and air of free-born ease, '—your elder sister? Your sister-in-law?'

'No, she's my old nurse's daughter. I've come to visit her for a while, to see her new baby and take news of the family back to her mother.'

'Do you live far from here then?' It seemed important to him.

'About fifty miles or so. I live in Din Pelidr.'

'Din Pelidr!' He looked sharply at her. 'Your family serve King Loth?'

'I'm his daughter.'

He was amused at Lothian's expense, to see its princess looking like that, without one jewel or maid servant, sitting on the ground and cutting up her rough fare with a hunting-knife. Yet he felt some admiration as well. He thought: *She said that as simply as if she were telling me her father's farm was just over the hill.* He noticed too that she had no shadow of awkwardness or fear of him. Most girls who met a hunter alone in the hills were either scared you would rape them or insulted if you didn't try. Indeed, she was so lovely that a man finding her by herself might be forgiven if—But because of that frank sweetness of hers, because she had stood by him in the moment of danger like a young sword-friend—and also for another reason that was beginning to take shape since he had learned she

44

was a princess, he decided against love-play, for that time.

He surprised her by saying, 'After all, it should have been white.'

'White?'

'It's always a white boar or white stag that the hunter follows in the stories, and finds the elf-woman waiting for him by the enchanted spring.'

'And then she takes him to her crystal hall under the water, where he finds a great feast already prepared for him.' Taniu took up the story, laughing as she handed him a rough hunk of bread and cheese. 'And she so beguiles him that when he comes back to middle-earth he finds three hundred years gone by.'

'He might find three hundred years too short to spend with her.'

The hunter stretched back comfortably on the warm grass, ready to entertain and be entertained. Swapping stories was a good game to pass a lazy afternoon when you had already decided against more active sports. When you played it with a new companion you could use it to test his wits and his moods. When you played it with a beautiful girl you could use it to lead her mind the way you chose. 'You like the old stories?'

'I love them! They keep some hope left in life!'

He looked startled. 'What do you mean?'

'I mean,' she said slowly, thinking aloud, 'that in the old stories the heroes are always brave and noble-minded. They never say or do anything stupid or vile. And then you look at the warriors in the royal warband—oh, they're brave enough, but they drink too much and boast and go whoring and looking for quarrels. Think how Peredur's men betrayed him and lost Deira, all for a squabble about a slave-woman! But then you hear the bard singing about Trystan or Geraint or Arthur, and you know that life can still be beautiful!'

He shrugged. 'Don't waste your time dreaming about heroes in old stories. Bards are like swordsmiths and jewellers—they have to make something better out of their raw material or how would they show their skill? If you could call back one of your old heroes—Trystan or Geraint—even Arthur, I suspect—you'd find him as

45

boastful, drunken or stupid as any spearman in your father's warband!'

'But there must have been noble, high-souled heroes once upon a time, or how would the bards know about them?'

She checked herself, feeling that this was wearisome talk for someone who was, in an odd way, her guest. She lightened her voice and face. 'But as for the boar, of course you must take him after baying and killing him single-handed—and such a huge, well-fleshed brute.'

'I didn't follow him for his flesh. I wouldn't have followed him at all if he hadn't killed two of my hounds when they disturbed him.' He smiled. 'You could call it a blood-feud rather than a hunt.'

'Even so, there's too much meat on him just to leave lying in the marsh.'

'My household isn't starving for lack of meat. If you don't want him, he's a gift for the ravens. I've no intention of dragging him all the way south through Argoed Llwyfain.'

'South?' Taniu stiffened. 'Are you a Cumbrian?'

To his ears her tone said: *Are you a leper*? He took offence at once.

'Yes, I'm a Cumbrian. What then? Is King Loth going to charge down on me with all his mighty warband because I've come a few yards into Lothian and killed a boar? And set your mind at rest, it was a Cumbrian boar. So Lothian can sleep tonight without dreading a famine. We're not so poor we have to steal to fill our larders.'

To her ears his tone added: *like Lothian cattle-thieves*! In spite of her disgust at warriors' quarrels, she surprised herself by flaring up just as Cynon or Marchlew would have done.

'You stole Catraeth!'

'Stole it! Who did we steal it from? Peredur's ghost? Who else do you think could hold Catraeth if we didn't?'

'Gwallog of Elmet, of course. Or Eudeyrn of Bernicia.'

His mouth twisted with scorn. 'Those two together haven't the men to face Deira, even if they didn't waste most of their time fighting each other. So who then?'

'My father. The men of Lothian.'

Taniu was daring him to show contempt; but he said with grave courtesy, 'Loth's a great warrior and the men of Lothian are mighty in battle.'

He glanced at the hunting-knife in her belt, then turned his brilliant eyes to her face with a smile. 'I know yours is a brave blood.' Then he returned to the attack. 'But could even Loth keep an army from Lothian as far away as the lands of Efrog, winter and summer, year after year?'

'No.' She knew the difficulty Loth had every year keeping all his men together even up to harvest time.

'If not Loth, who then?'

She saw the answer and was too honest not to admit it. 'Deira.'

'Yes, Deira. And don't delude yourself the Angles will stop in Catraeth if they ever get it! If our men weren't barring the road to the north, there'd have been bloody war on the marches of Lothian years ago! Your folk work their lands and sleep secure at nights behind our shields. For which service we're derided and abused in every hovel from the Weir to the Weryd as interlopers and thieves!'

His voice rose as if he were shouting a challenge to the east. He checked a second; then added with a quiet rage that was all the more frightening for being held down.

'But there's another road from Catraeth, remember, straight to the heart of my country. And we're asking no leave from any eastland chief to protect our own. There'll be no Fort of Blood on Cumbrian land!'

His eyes were fixed on her but he seemed to be gazing right through her with impersonal menace as if she had the army of Lothian at her back. Now more than ever he reminded her of a falcon poised for its death-dealing stoop. Instinctively she caught her breath and tensed to meet a blow.

Then suddenly the threat lifted. He relaxed and lounged back, taking one of her apples and playing with it like a ball as he said lightly, 'So there'd be a cold welcome for me—a cold iron welcome with a spear-pont—if I rode up to Din Pelidr one day?'

'No indeed, never think that!'

Taniu was thankful that she could praise Loth whole-heartedly for some things and this was one: that to men he never failed in royal generosity or honour. 'There's a saying in Lothian: *"A bard with his harp, a craftsman with his skill and a warrior with his spear—they all find a welcome waiting in Din Pelidr."* '

'And would there be a welcome waiting for me from you yourself, princess?'

His voice was respectful, apparently humble but his eyes were teasing. She laughed back at him.

'I always have a dutiful welcome for my father's guests. Besides,' looking gravely at the crumble of cheese-rind, crusts and apple-cores, 'you've already feasted with me.'

'Indeed, then, I've had a lucky day's hunting—to find myself guest-friend of the Princess of Lothian.'

Then the mockery came back into his voice, though without any wounding bitterness. 'And what's the Princess of Lothian doing, all alone in the hills? Has your father sent you to guard the marches against the war-host of Cumbria? Or has Queen Drostecca trained you up to be a woman-warrior, like the Pictish girls?'

'No, you're not in any danger. I'm a woman of peace.'

'Except to wild boars.'

'When they keep their backs to me.'

'Well, then, what are you doing so far from home? If you really are far from it.'

He wasn't smiling now but she couldn't tell whether he was serious or still teasing. 'Do you know, when I first saw you, I thought you were the Lady herself, risen from that stream. Have you really come from Din Pelidr, or are you here for ever, with the stream and the empty hills?'

She lifted her arm in the sunlight. 'Look, I cast a shadow. Ask anyone in Lothian, they'll tell you I'm mortal.'

He watched the long shadow of her arm stretching to the hill, then turned towards the westering sun. She followed his gaze. The short-lived brightness of the October day would soon be over; she heard him sigh. Then he looked up, met her gaze and became as still as the rocks of the cliff beneath them.

Taniu was held speechless, as if she had been caught in a Druid enchantment. The sun-filled hollow could have been Merlin's invisible prison, the walls of which were air. Some parts at least of the bards' old stories were still true.

Then one of the dark watchers in the tree by the marsh stretched and flapped his black wings, breaking the enchanted silence. His mate croaked impatiently.

The hunter stood up. 'My three hundred years are over—it's time to go back to middle-earth.'

He picked up his saddle-bag and began to stow the remains of his food. Taniu shivered as if the black feathers had brushed across her heart. The sunlight felt cold. He reached his hand to help her to her feet and exclaimed in surprise, 'You're trembling!'

'The raven cried over us. That's a black omen.'

He smiled. 'Not to me. The ravens fly on our Cumbrian banner, remember. They've never cried bad luck to us—and they'll never harm you, I promise.'

The evil moment had passed; the sunlight grew warm again. He took up her saddle-bags with his. Together they jumped across the stream. The elegant chestnut stepped towards them, with Pybyr coming behind. The hunter helped her to saddle up before he saw to his own mount. Though she was well able to jump on by herself, he lifted her to the saddle. For a second his arms tightened round her body and she felt as if her blood had taken fire. Then she was on Pybyr's back, breathless and dizzy. He looked up at her.

'Winter will soon be on us. When the spring comes, I'll take the road to Din Pelidr.'

'The sun on your path before you.'

He swung up to his saddle. 'And a good journey to you, princess.' Then he laughed. 'Whenever you see a raven, remember it's bringing my greetings to you from Cumbria.'

He raised his hand in farewell and turned the chestnut's head. Two hours ago he'd been a stranger.

'You haven't told me your name!'

He looked back as the horse rounded the hill slope.

'Owain!' he called and went from her sight. She waited, while Pybyr stamped and shook his head, looking down from the edge of the cliff until she saw him reappear, splash across the marshy ground and make for the track where he had followed the boar through the wood. At the edge of the trees he turned and saw her waving. He waved back; then ducked his head and disappeared into the darkness under the branches.

Taniu turned Pybyr at last and rode slowly northwards. The westering sun no longer reached the empty hollow; it became grey and cold.

Their grimly patient vigil ended, the two ravens flew down and settled happily on the corpse.

CHAPTER
4

Prince Owain of Cumbria was not riding south at the same reckless pace that had carried him after the boar. Still, he urged Seren as fast as it was prudent for the horse to go on the rough track between the trees. He had a long way to go, most of it pathless. Darkness was only a couple of hours away.

If he had checked his angry impulse to take the boar's life in payment for his hounds, he would have been at his journey's end long since—and he would never have met the princess of Lothian.

He drew her face in his mind and set it in front of him over Seren's head to keep him company on his way. He made the dream face gaze at him as she had done while they talked, savouring each changing look at his pleasure. When she smiled or joked her eyes were radiant: she had a sunlit nature. Yet it was strange that one so young could look as sad as she did, when she recalled the lost heroes in the old stories that enchanted her.

Owain was not enchanted by the old stories. When they were offered for his entertainment by a gifted bard, he enjoyed the subtle rhythms, the words chosen and set with a jeweller's care. All the while, he would be sitting in scornful judgement on the old heroes for the blunders they had made—Peredur, making his chief captain the present of a grudge; Trystan, getting caught with another man's wife; Arthur, letting a bastard live who had the will and the intelligence to destroy him.

Still, if the princess loved the hero-tales so much he would make up a new one for her, composed out of the materials of their two lives, and give it to her as a wedding gift.

He was the king's eldest son; soon his father would be debating with the Council what alliance should be made by his marriage. It was unlikely that the name of Lothian would be mentioned. Since the taking of Catraeth there had been more ill-will than usual between Cumbria and the eastern kingdoms. No one would look across the Cheviots for the heir's bride.

Owain was quite willing to marry. It was his clear duty to his family and the kingdom; he did not want to avoid it. His pride in Cumbria was part of his pride in himself: the one would die without the other. That being so, it suited his pride to choose his wife for himself rather than meekly take whatever the old men of the Council thought best for him.

How much more amusing to ride out by himself in quest of a mysterious beast, like those huntsmen in the old tales, find the elf-woman waiting for him by the enchanted spring—and carry out a piece of clever statecraft that even his father had not foreseen!

The track climbed out of the woods; he was coming to the watershed. He gave one last glance back towards Lothian, then turned away southwards on to the moors. He had to watch his way carefully now in the gathering dusk, alone in those untamed stretches of featureless wasteland—heather, rough grass and peat bog—where the few threads of paths were only sheep tracks. He was straining his eyes to pick out the lie of the land when he reached a shallow dip between folds of moorland that could barely have been called a valley. This was the goal of his pilgrimage.

It was a very poor peasant's holding, no more than a wretched living-hut and a few ramshackle sheds inside the stockade of thorn bushes. No one greeted him; he stabled Seren himself in one of the sheds.

Coming out into the yard he saw a woman watching him from the door of the living-hut. She was small, thin and leathery from years of hard work; like most peasant

51

women over thirty she looked sixty at least, her mouth sunken from lost teeth, her thin braids of dust-grey hair twisted into a tight knot. Owain nodded to her; the woman stood aside wordlessly as he went into the hut, following him and pulling the door shut behind her.

The hut was only lit by the cooking fire in the middle of the floor; the air was thick with peat-smoke, greasy stew and unwashed bodies. For a second Owain was blinded and half-choked, peering into the gloom. Then he made out a dim shape of someone lying in a pile of bedding on the far side of the hearth and moved across to it.

The figure in the soiled blankets was a naked girl about fourteen or fifteen years old. The reek inside the hut was almost unbearable; she had pushed the blankets down off her arms and breasts swollen with milk. She was youthfully soft and plump; her unkempt hair was thick and brown. Otherwise she had the same nondescript look as the woman.

When she saw Owain she gave him a wide sleepy smile, stretching her arm to greet him. Owain took her rough little hand, reached inside his jerkin and pulled out a handsome gold bracelet set with garnets and clasped it on her arm.

The older woman bent down to a nest among the blankets, lifted out a very young baby rosy with sleep and warmth, and held it up for Owain to see.

'A fine boy, lord prince,' she said proudly, flicking the tiny penis. The baby woke and realized he wasn't in his warm nest. His face opened into a gaping cavern roaring in protest. The girl reached up, took the baby and plugged the gap with one of her nipples. The roaring stopped; the baby concentrated all his energy on sucking.

Owain looked at the mother and baby kindly but without enthusiasm. Heulwen had been the first girl to bear him a child, but he had not taken her with love or even with any particular intention. He preferred to choose his women with fastidious care, like his hawks and his horses. Casual wenching was not high on his list of sports. Indeed, until recently he'd had little chance to go wenching at all. He'd been sent from home at eight years old to the famous school at St Nynia's monastery, Candida Casa.

His father, King Urien, who was as book-learned as a bishop, held that kings should know as much as their councillors.

'If a councillor knows more than the king of the land,' he used to say, 'he soon rules both king and land.'

Owain had enjoyed his studies, being both keen-witted and inquiring. Even so, when he was brought home to celebrate his sixteenth birthday and begin his weapon-training, his spirits soared up with the joy of freedom.

The other half of his man's training had begun at the same time; it had been perfected more quickly under the teaching of Lady Guendolena, the pretty wife of an elderly councillor.

He had come across Heulwen last winter, after a day's hunting on the northern moors of Argoed Llwyfain—a sharp, diamond-bright day, when the rush of keen air and the echoing sounds of horn and hounds excited the blood like wine. They had kept up the sport until the western sky was a smoky bonfire and the first stars were shining faintly in the east. They were far out in the wasteland and needed shelter for the night. When they came on the little steading, they took possession of it like a triumphant raiding party.

Heulwen had served his food, poured his drink, made up his bed and shared it with him, all with the same good-humoured smiles and giggles. Since then, Owain had slept with her whenever his hounds or his hawks had led him that way but he made no special effort to see her and could scarcely recall what she looked like—small, brown and stocky like all the hill-folk. She was nothing to occupy his mind: a tumble with a willing farm girl was as much a part of a huntsman's evening as the roasting of the kill, the drinking and the songs.

Now, watching her with that sturdy lump of live flesh tugging at her nipple, his chief feeling was pity. She was so desperately poor, so cheerfully unresentful. He racked his brains for something he could say to praise her.

'There's a thirsty little bull-calf. I should think it would take at least twelve milch kine to keep him full and quiet. I'll have them sent up.'

Heulwen opened her brown eyes wide; even the silent

expressionless mother gasped at the magnificence of the gift. It would make a dowry for a rich farmer's daughter.

'The prince has a noble heart,' she muttered.

'Have you got a name for him?' Owain hadn't given the matter a thought.

'I want to call him Dinogat.'

Owain smiled. The baby had stopped sucking and drifted back to sleep. Heulwen was rocking him against her bare breasts, humming the old country lullaby that Owain had heard in his own nursery:

> 'My Dinogat's got a speckled smock,
> Marten's fur to trim his frock,
> Whist, whist, whistle along
> While your mother sings the song:
> Bye, bye, baby bunting
> Daddy's gone away a-hunting,
> All to fetch a marten's skin
> To wrap my baby Dinogat in.'

He picked up the tune from her and was whistling it softly to the baby when the farmer came in. The woman bustled to serve out stew for the evening meal, inviting Owain to a place by the hearth. He had one final inspiration.

'Would you like a husband, Heulwen? I can get one of my spearmen—'

Heulwen smiled sleepily at him; as usual, her mother spoke for her.

'Thank you kindly, lord prince.' She spoke with some pride. 'The smith at Banna has already asked for her.'

'And he'll accept the child?'

Heulwen nodded; the fact that she was bearing a child to the king's son had first drawn the smith's notice to her. He'd been to inspect the baby two days ago and approved of it. He'd pulled the blankets off her, slapped her flank and told her she was a good breeder.

All Heulwen's simple dreams of happiness had come gloriously true. She had enjoyed the prince's love-making without any crazy belief that it would last long. She was pleased with her presents and proud of her fine baby. The smith, as well as being rich, was a big muscular man; she was looking forward to lying with him and having more babies.

His mind at rest about her, Owain took his bowl of stew and later wrapped himself in his cloak on the frowsy bedding the woman made up for him, hoping he would not be bitten too much.

He said no more than 'farewell' to the girl when he left early next morning. There was no more to be said. He did not suppose he would ever see her again.

CHAPTER
5

The same desolate moorlands stretched all round him but his way to the south was blocked by a line of high jagged crags made still higher by the fortifications running along the crest. He had reached the Romans' Wall, riding up to the gateway in one of the milecastles, now gaping open and undefended, its doors long since smashed and rotted away. He passed through, making for the road that ran behind the Wall, the military way, the Legions' Road between the two seas.

Owain found the Wall an eerie place, lonelier than the moors. He tried to imagine what it must have been when the red-cloaked soldiers patrolled the ramparts: the forts crowded with troops, the shouted orders, trumpet calls, chink of harness. He only seemed to call up ghosts, who rustled and whined through every crack and gap in the masonry.

At last to his relief, as the road descended a slope, he saw on the high ground ahead of him a large fort with intact walls. Armed figures could be seen on guard; a group of cavalry was exercising in the field beyond the river; a herd-boy was driving some cows towards the southern gate. Smoke from many cooking-fires rose from inside; even from the distance Owain could hear the murmurs of busy life coming from the place. He could almost believe that the Roman army had never left it—and this, in a way, was true . . .

About a hundred and eighty years ago, before Rome's weakening grip on Britain finally loosened, a German officer of low origins and proved ability brought a detachment of Frisian cavalry up to the Wall. His orders were to relieve the fort of Caer Voran, or reoccupy and hold it if it had been sacked. He found the fort holding out but its commander mortally wounded.

Flavius Constantius Germanus duly cleared the district of invaders and took over Caer Voran. He held it firmly for Rome; then, when orders and pay no longer arrived from the south, he went on holding it firmly for himself. The local farmers paid food-rent to his officers without too much resentment, as those tough hard-riding troopers kept more destructive marauders at bay. The fertile valley of the Tina gave him pasture for his horse-breeding, which he practised with genius and passion. By choosing their wives as carefully as they bred their horses, he and his descendants built up blood-relationships with all the princely families of the North. In fact, the present lord, Garmon, had married a distant and not very well-dowered member of the Cumbrian Royal House and so could call cousins with the great King Urien himself.

This story could have been told about many Roman army officers in Britain who had set up for themselves when the Empire collapsed. Their descendants were now sitting in their halls among their warriors while their bards sang their praises as if they were all come of the high British blood of Cunobelinus himself.

The lords of Caer Voran showed one great difference. They held proudly to their Roman traditions. Above all, they had kept their Latin book-learning.

Old Flavius Germanus had been literate, in the way of orders and supply-lists. The dead commander had left a small library, made up equally of military history and erotic works. In the winter nights, when the snow drifts were piled against the walls of Caer Voran and the wind came shrieking over the Cheviots as if the Waelcyriges were hunting the souls of the slain for Woden, the old German would stretch out on a couch by the glowing brazier with one of the books, moving a stubby finger along the lines and silently mouthing the words as he read:

'In summer's heat and midtime of the day
To rest my limbs upon a bed I lay . . .
Then came Corinna in a long loose gown,
Her white neck hid with tresses hanging down . . .
I ripped her gown; being thin, the harm was small
Yet strived she to be covered therewithal . . .
Stark naked then she stood before mine eye,
Not one flaw in her body I could spy:
What arms and shoulders did I touch and see,
How apt her breasts were to be pressed by me!
How smooth a belly under her waist saw I,
How large a leg and what a lusty thigh!
To leave the rest, all pleased me passing well:
I caught her naked body, down she fell.
Judge you the rest: being tired, she bade me kiss.
Jove send me more such afternoons as this!'

Through a detailed study of such texts the lords of Caer Voran had gained their wide knowledge of Roman life and customs. They always spoke of the Great City with sad pride, as if their roots were deep in the Palatine, rather than in an army brothel in Colognia.

So Owain was sure of a civilized welcome, and comfort for himself and Seren, after the gate guards had respectfully passed him through. Hearing that the Prince of Cumbria had arrived, Lord Garmon's head groom, Wulfric, came himself to hold the prince's bridle and lead Seren away to the well-appointed stables. Quite often the North German strain cropped up in the Caer Voran folk; Wulfric was as Saxon as his name. He was well over six feet tall; his fair skin tanned to bronze. Against this his flaxen hair and pale blue eyes flashed out with startling brilliance. His features were large and rugged but not ugly; in spite of his size he did not move clumsily. Owain gave Seren over to his big sure hands with an easy mind; then made his way on foot to the commander's villa.

If that old Roman commander's ghost had ever come back to visit his fort, it must have flown gibbering back to Hades. Garmon's warriors had their families inside the walls; the old barrack blocks were divided into homesteads overflowing with gossiping women, playing children, crying babies, dogs, chickens and the occasional pig. There was even washing on a line tied to an apple tree in the inner courtyard.

Here Owain was met by a tall woman in a dress of bright scarlet wool and long silver ear-rings. Her black hair was coiled above her handsome, mannish face. This was Ressona, the daughter of one of Garmon's old troop-captains. She had been Garmon's housekeeper since his wife died and his mistress since before he married. She greeted him pleasantly and asked what she could get him.

'A bath first of all, Ressona darling; and a clean shirt if possible. I'm filthy and probably verminous.'

'You can have both in just a few minutes, lord. I've had the bath heating ready for master to come home. I'll go and lay out a shirt for you now.'

She hurried along the colonnade to the bath house, which made a side wing to the courtyard. The household had long ago given up trying to maintain the full ritual of a Roman bath, with rooms of graded temperature and dry as well as damp heat. However, they could always produce a great sunken bath full of hot water as well as a pool for a cold plunge. This bath house was a great wonder to all the chiefs of the North; there was nothing like it outside Caer Luel.

Owain was feeling as well as looking much more like the heir of Cumbria when he made his way back along the colonnade. He turned through the central arch into the small inner courtyard, planted as a garden with grass plot and rose trees. Opening on to this pleasant spot, sheltered from the cruel northeast winds, was Lord Garmon's private dining-room.

It was small but very attractive. There was a mosaic floor with a design of the four seasons; the walls were painted to look like windows opening out on to country landscapes in which all the work—gardening, harvesting and vintage—was being done by cupids. Looking from these pretty painted creatures to the flesh and blood girl who lay on a couch reading, Owain thought that if they could fly down from the wall they would take her for Venus and start waiting on her.

Penarwan, Lord Garmon's only daughter, was sixteen and had the body of a mature woman. She had a mass of auburn curls held on the crown of her head by a pearl diadem and cascading on to her neck and shoulders. Her eyebrows had been carefully plucked to fine arches; as she looked down at her book her long auburn lashes shadowed her creamy cheeks. Her nose was aquiline but small and delicate; her mouth was dark red, beautifully shaped though full-lipped.

She wore a short-sleeved robe of kingfisher-blue silk, heavily embroidered with small pearls and gold thread. Her golden girdle was clasped high under her breasts, underlining their fullness. The linen of her shift was so fine it was almost transparent over her arms. Linen and silk clung to every line and curve of her body, showing what they hid, like the carved robes of Roman goddesses.

He sat down at the foot of her couch. Penarwan raised her eyes. They were very light hazel, brilliant in their frame of dark lashes. She smiled at him without any surprise at his sudden arrival. It was always her way to accept people, however long they had been absent, as if they had just stepped into the next room for a moment.

'Listen to this.' She turned to her book. 'The bard is explaining how you can seduce a woman at the dinner-table while her husband is sitting beside her.'

She began to read the Latin in a soft deep-toned voice:

> 'Watch me, my nods and speaking countenance,
> Take and receive each secret, amorous glance.
> Thy bosom's roseate buds let him not finger,
> Let not his lips on thy lips linger.
> Mingle not thighs, nor to his leg join thine.
> Nor thy soft foot with his hard foot combine.
> Entreat thy husband drink but do not kiss;
> And when he drinks, to add more do not miss.
> If his eyes close, with wine and sleep oppressed
> Then chance and place shall counsel us the rest.'

She looked up, her eyes shimmering with mischief.

'Shall we do it, Owain, at the Nativity Feast? Say you will! It would be such sport to do it under everybody's eyes and no one the wiser.'

He was amused. 'You forget, Penarwan, the old Romans lay down to their meals on couches.'

She leaned back on her cushions, arching her back and lifting her breasts.

'Like this?'

'Exactly like that, I have no doubt, Cleopatra lay down for the Emperor Antony—and so he dropped his sceptre between her thighs. But sitting up to the table in Caer Luel is another matter. A woman could get her husband drunk easily enough and her lover might touch her leg—and her rump too, if it amused him. *Mingling* thighs would be downright impossible—and I'm sorry for anyone who tried fingering breasts, with my father sitting at the High Table!'

'You weren't always so shy, Owain,' she jeered. 'I can remember times at Candida Casa when you'd take up a challenge almost before it was spoken.'

'Do you remember when you bet me I couldn't get into the girls' sleeping-cells for a night without getting caught?'

'And how fetching you looked in that dress and hood you borrowed from the milkmaid!'

Owain and Penarwan had played together childishly at the monastery school; and later not so childishly, though they had never been lovers. Penarwan had the art, by instinct it seemed, helped by her studies of the Bard Ovid, to take play to the limit and then disengage easily and gracefully without maddening her playmate. Owain, intelligent and fastidious, had too much sense to seduce the daughter of his father's most powerful ally when he had no wish to marry her afterwards. He enjoyed her beauty and lively spirits; he didn't desire her. When he thought of her marriage, he felt profoundly sorry for the husband.

'I'll wait till you get married, Penarwan. The game's no fun if you're not deceiving your husband—I shouldn't think we'll have to wait very long!'

Penarwan looked at him for a moment without smiling. 'D'you promise you'll help me deceive my husband—' she began; but at that moment the servants came in to set the table so they had to talk formally.

Soon after, Lord Garmon tramped in, followed by

Meurig his eldest son. Garmon was a short fleshy man with a thick neck and a square reddish face slackening down into his jowls. He had greying-fair hair and small pigs' eyes under beetling brows. Meurig was like him, only younger. So was Padarn, the second son. He was away collecting food-rent, as Garmon told Owain among his boisterous greetings. Penarwan did not get her looks from her father, luckily for her. Nor from her mother; Owain remembered his cousin, a plainish unassuming lady, well aware that her pedigree was her only claim to notice.

As a matter of historical fact, Penarwan's rich beauty was a far-off legacy from her ancestor, old Flavius Germanus's mother, a Syrian dancing-girl who had come north to try her fortune with the Rhine legions and ended her career as a wealthy bawd. Once only, in an active life devoted to profits, she had sacrificed business to romance, being so taken with one of her clients, a big fair Saxon mercenary, that she not only let herself get pregnant by him but went her term and had the child, regardless of the loss of working hours. The hours she put in afterwards earned some influential friends for her son and a nice little fortune to start his way in the army.

Old Flavius Germanus had been fond of his mother and remembered her with grateful affection. He praised her to his high-born British wife and their children as a decent, hard-working woman who had done everything for him. He had her image in his family shrine and set out bread and wine for her on the Night of the Dead, on the unlikely chance that she might come visiting. Never, though, while entertaining the neighbouring chiefs, with their remorseless Celtic memory for pedigrees, did he give any details of her history.

Lord Garmon signed Owain to the place of honour at the handsome marble table. He and his children sat down; after seeing the servants were ready with the courses, Ressona took her seat with them. She and Penarwan had both sense enough to keep on good terms. Ressona, with good soldier's blood in her veins, showed the right amount of respect to the commander's daughter. Penarwan showed the right amount of cordiality to the woman who kept her father happy—and who took most of the wearisome household supervision off her hands.

At first, the meal was silent; Garmon was giving all his energies to a concentrated and merciless assault on the food. Meurig ate speechlessly opposite. If he ever had any thoughts, except about horses, he kept them to himself.

At last, after eating four large fish from a silver tray of grilled trout in oatmeal, followed by a plateful of roast sucking-pig, Garmon had leisure to talk. The Lord of Caer Voran always treated Owain publicly as Prince of Cumbria and young kinsman-by-marriage. Privately, he saw him as his future son-in-law. His manner was a strange mixture of respect and familiarity, touched with jocular affection.

'What brings you to these parts, my boy? Any message from your father?'

'Nothing in particular at the moment. His respects and goodwill, as always. No, I've come on my own account to beg for a night's shelter. I've been chasing a boar up on the northern moors.'

Garmon let out a roar. 'You've been chasing more than a boar up on the northern moors, you young dog. You caught a plump young doe by the tail up there, so I hear!'

Meurig let out the short, hard bark that was his laugh; the women tittered. Owain gave a tight-lipped smile to his host's wit.

Saints, does even the hill wind talk about me? And now, I suppose, every magpie in Caer Voran will be chattering till they can hear it in Cumbria!

Garmon sensed his displeasure but misunderstood the reason.

'I don't hold with men being virgins. There's no use in that, except for monks. It saves poor, tender young girls, like my Puss here, a squeak or two on the wedding night if the man knows what he's doing.'

Meurig barked again; Ressona chuckled reminiscently. Penarwan primmed up her mouth and lowered her lashes to look innocent and shocked. Owain watched this performance with interest, thinking: *I don't imagine your Puss here will get many surprises on her wedding night.*

Meurig spoke into an awkward silence, turning the talk from these trivialities to the one important subject.

'You've had the chestnut out, I saw him in the stables. He's one of ours, by Alarch out of Gwennol. That strain are good goers.'

Owain agreed, praising Seren for his speed, beauty and intelligence. The conversation, having reached the safe ground of horse-breeding, stayed there for the rest of the meal and the wine-drinking. They parted for the night in good humour.

He took his leave next morning with grateful thanks. His clothes came brushed and aired from Ressona's hands; Seren was gleaming like silk from Wulfric's care. He set off westwards in high spirits. He had settled his last debts of duty to Heulwen. He had, he hoped, covered his tracks by his visit to Caer Voran. The way was clear to Caer Luel, where he was going to ask King Urien to get the Princess of Lothian for him as a wife.

CHAPTER
6

Taniu and her companions had a mostly silent ride home; their minds were too busy for talk. Marchlew was thinking about a girl in the palace kitchens, a fat merry creature with a huge mop of greasy curls and a deep, chuckling laugh. Behind his eyes, she was lying naked on the straw in the palace stable; he was running his hands over her thighs and between her legs, listening to her throaty chuckle.

Cynon was deciding that next spring he'd ride back to the farm and ask for Leucu; she'd have a good portion from her father, besides her share of the loot Ancarat had piled up from her love-charms and abortions—the old hag couldn't live for ever. He'd tasted Leucu's cooking and watched her at her household tasks; also, he was very much taken with her warm brown prettiness.

Taniu was also looking forward to the spring, with an excitement she had never felt before. Next spring a young, free-born hunter called Owain was going to ride up to Din

Pelidr and offer Loth his spear as a member of the war band. Her memory was ransacking Talhaearn's treasury of hero-tales to help her imagine the exploits that would make Owain the Champion of Lothian—and earn him the hand of its princess.

Now the great rock of Din Pelidr heaved up like a stranded whale between the hills and the sea. She felt her heart lift with an unusual sense of home-coming. She looked forward to Gwalchmai's shout of joy when he saw her. Then, there was the memory of that smile of understanding between Drostecca and herself at parting. Perhaps now she was a woman, turned fourteen, the queen would no longer see her as a troublesome stepchild but would take her as a friend.

A cold little shudder went over her suddenly as if a drifting ghost had touched her in passing; it was gone in a moment.

The gate-guards told them Loth was still away: Cynon and Marchlew exchanged grins. Taniu hustled Pybyr up the flagged road that wound through the township towards the royal citadel, towering dark over the precipice with the sun behind it.

She said a friendly goodbye to Cynon and Marchlew in the courtyard; they went off to their cronies in the warriors' hall; she waited to see Pybyr stabled. Then she remembered her roots; they'd been in her saddle-bag for three days, it was time they were planted. Once she got back to the nursery and started talking to Gwalchmai, she'd forget them till it was too late; then how Ancarat would scold!

Taking her bag she went behind the stables straight to the herb garden, tucked in behind the orchard and the rampart. She was a careful gardener and became absorbed in her task. It was only when she had finally sprinkled water over her planting and was washing her muddy fingers in the little pool, that she became aware of the noises coming from the orchard.

The swish and cut of a whip, a high-pitched yelp, then whimpering. Someone was beating a dog with prolonged savagery; she realized the sounds had been at the back of her mind for some time. Her mouth tightened. She hated cruelty; brutal whipping did not train a creature, only broke and spoiled it. If they were mistreating one of Loth's half-trained hounds he would do murder when he got home. But why bring the dog to the queen's orchard to beat it? Dear God, it must be Gwalchmai's puppy, that he loved next to herself. It was growing big and boisterous, probably it had worried somebody's best slippers.

She ran into the orchard; no one was there. She turned through the gate into the yard—and stopped, appalled.

Luned had been stripped naked; there were weals across her back and buttocks. Short lengths of rope were knotted round her wrists to pull her arms out at full stretch, so she could not flinch away or try to shield herself. Three of the men round her, Talorg, Nechtan and Brude, were Drostecca's Picts. Holding one of the ropes opposite Brude was Morien, his fleshily-handsome face glowing with ugly pleasure.

Drostecca was wielding the whip, a nightmare horror. Her pregnant belly jutted into her red gown, her face was sweaty with effort, her lips were pulled back from her strong teeth, her eyes seemed to burn. As Taniu came into the yard, Drostecca swung the whip and brought it down on Luned with all her force. Again there was a shrill yelp, followed by whimpering. Luned's legs danced an obscene little jig, while her arms and body were held rigid. Drops of blood rolled down her thighs. The men sniggered.

Sick with fear, Taniu went up to Drostecca and put a hand on her arm.

'Lady—have pity—'

Drostecca whirled round; Taniu expected to have her face laid open with the whiplash and braced herself. But all Drostecca's hate was turned on Luned, she had none to spare. Her eyes stared through Taniu as if the girl were invisible; she answered the words, not the speaker, with horrible mildness.

'Why pity her? She likes it. She's one who likes to have her rump tickled and pricked.'

The men laughed again. Morien and Brude, turning to listen, let the ropes go slack; Luned fell on her face in a blood-splotched heap. Taniu was a little heartened by Drostecca's quiet answer.

'But, my lady, she's so young and not strong. It's cruel to tear her poor flesh like that.'

'Cruel?' Drostecca was looking at her now. 'A bitch is all the better for a touch of the whip. And this bitch,' she looked venomously at Luned's bleeding back, 'has to be taught to keep in her kennel and not come sniffing round my man's legs.'

She half-lifted the whip; Taniu caught her arm.

'If she dies, and it's likely she will, the king will have to ask into it because she's in his household.'

Drostecca laughed. 'Good riddance to the trash. The king'll ask me no questions. I'm carrying his son.'

'It would be a black omen on your son's birth if he came with a death.' She spoke as firmly as she could; then looked at Drostecca's raised belly. The queen, who was very superstitious, paused at that. Taniu seized the moment's respite to put forward her own plan for dealing with Luned. 'If you want to be rid of her, lady, why not marry her off decently to one of the warriors?'

Drostecca widened her eyes in amazement; then smiled.

'An excellent idea, child. With a husband of her own, she might stay in her bed at night and not come wriggling into other folk's. Now, who can we find for her?'

She glanced at the four men. Morien looked scornful. He would have been glad enough of Luned's notice as the pretty, pampered King's Woman. Broken and shamed as she was, he wouldn't touch her. Drostecca was too shrewd to give orders to one of Loth's men which she knew would be refused. Besides, she thought Morien was too good for Luned. So were Talorg and Nechtan, chiefs' sons in Alba, young and quite good-looking. She turned to Brude.

Brude had been Drostecca's bodyguard since she was a baby; he was utterly devoted to her. To a Pict, a royal woman was sacred as a priestess, a goddess even. With the devotion, of course, came deadly hatred of anyone who threatened or wronged his goddess. He could be trusted to make as brutal a husband to Luned as even Drostecca could wish.

He was about forty years old, with a thatch of unkempt reddish-grey hair. He was short but very thickset, with broad shoulders and long, powerful arms furred with red hair. His big mouth seemed to be always grinning, showing yellowish teeth with some gaps between them.

'Brude.'

He looked up quickly like a dog at its mistress's voice.

'Brude, I've got a wife for you.'

He grinned wider than usual, stepped over to Luned, sank his fingers into her tousled black curls and dragged her up on to her knees, pulling her head back roughly.

Taniu's heart ached to see the poor face. Luned's eyelids were swollen, her cheeks were white, streaked with dust and tears. Her pretty mouth hung open as she sobbed; her lips were bruised where she had bitten them in pain. She was shaking so much that her breasts quivered but her eyes were fixed in shock.

'Take good care of her, Brude. Make sure she behaves herself like a good wife and doesn't come night-prowling after other women's husbands.'

'Peg her down,' advised Morien, brutally. 'You've got a good strong stake of your own to do it with.'

Talorg and Nechtan guffawed; Drostecca shrieked with laughter. The hideous skirling broke Taniu's control. The girl's ravaged body, Drostecca's gloating face, the evil laughter, called up her childhood's terror again and merged it into the horror in front of her. She was hardly sure any longer whether it was herself or Luned who lay there naked and bleeding while Drostecca laughed. She had to run away. She bolted past Talorg, dived through the postern gate and hurled herself down the cliff path. Behind her, the laughter rose to screaming pitch and the screams went on and on.

Driven by the horror behind her, she was hardly aware of the sheer rock at the edge of the path or the stones slipping from under her feet. The ground levelled at the foot of the cliff and halted her rush. She stumbled and lost her balance. Somebody clutched her as she fell; she screamed.

'Steady now, my lady! You won't get to the holy man with a broken leg.'

She forced herself to stand quietly and look at the speaker, blinking and trying to catch her breath. She recognized Selyf the jewelsmith, a quiet, self-contained man whose life seemed concentrated in his hands and the beautiful things he made. She was not afraid of him.

'Mercy on us, I thought you were falling to your death!' His wife came bustling up; she began to smooth Taniu's loosened plaits. 'And after all, there was no need to half kill yourself. You won't have missed anything. I've heard he goes on through sunset and moonrise too.'

'Take my daughter's arm, lady,' said Selyf quietly. 'You've hardly got breath to stand.'

She was too bewildered to ask what they were talking about or where they were going. She took the girl's arm and went along with them quite tamely. The path became as familiar as an evil dream but she made no effort to break free and run, even when they breasted the slope and looked down towards the pool in the hollow. Once again, folk had gathered in the circle of stones. Once again a tall figure was waiting for her by the pillar-stone, not white in the moonlight now but black against the westering sun.

He was gaunt; a skeleton dressed in a coarse black robe girt with a cord. His head had been shaved across the forehead as far as the crown, so that a white dome of skull loomed up from a curtain of unkempt black hair. There seemed to be a fire raging inside him: his dark eyes were burning in their sockets; his words were like branding irons.

'Look at your lords riding past you, so proud of their fine weapons and armour, while you trudge in the dust or the mud. Look at their women, glittering with jewels. "*There's glory*," you say. "*There's power, there's happiness!*" You envy them, don't you? You grovel when they speak to you. You're afraid of them, aren't you? Why?'

There was a resentful stir among the listeners clustered round the circle, leaning against the stones or sitting in family groups on the sun-warmed turf. They were mostly farmers and shepherds, with a few craftsmen and servants from Din Pelidr. The monk from Mailros must be a lackwit if he didn't know why they were afraid of their masters.

The monk felt them stir; he smiled, he'd meant to rouse them.

'Yes, I know. They can force you to hand over your stores as food-rent, so that they can feast all winter while

68

you starve. They can put their swords through you if you anger them, or if they're in a bad temper and you're the first one who comes across them. They can burn your roofs over your heads in their feuds. And there's nothing you can do about it, so you think nothing can touch them.'

He startled them by laughing.

'If you saw them as I've done, vomiting and fouling themselves in their sick-beds, shaking with the terrors of death! Look at the stripped corpses on a battlefield when the crows and weasels have been at them—can you pick out the lords from the serfs? And if you could open their grave-mounds, where they've been laid in state with their jewels and weapons around them, what would you see in a week or two, while the worms were doing their work?'

He was making his listeners see it; now they were as quiet as the stones.

'Fools! If you're afraid of these lords and kings, who are all going to die and rot like every slave, how can you face the anger of the King of Kings? He never dies. His servants are plague and famine and storm. His sword is the lightning. No earthly king can stand against him. He knows everything you do, every secret sin. He's coming to judge you. He can open the gates of Heaven to you or throw the damned into his furnace *"where their worm dieth not and their fire is not quenched"*. Are you ready for the Judgement?'

The crowd sighed and shivered, looking down to avoid his eyes. He flung out his arms to embrace them all.

'The gates of Heaven are open—*now*! The kingdom of Heaven can be yours, if only you throw away your sins! The King has invited you all to his feast—serfs, beggars, slaves. You'll never be hungry any more. You'll wear robes of light and be crowned with glory! You are the heirs of the kingdom—come and claim your inheritance! Throw away your sins! Turn your backs on heathen filth and blood and greed and lust!'

His voice lifted to an ecstatic howl. The whole crowd was on its feet now. It was starting to sway with the lift and fall of the chanting.

'Leave idolatry! Leave the crowned whore in her scarlet gown, throned on the hills, drinking the blood of the innocents! Fix your eyes on our Blessed Lady, virgin and mother, pure as the stars, spotless as the dew of morning, chaste as the snow . . . '

The monk's passionate sincerity drove his beliefs at the little congregation like spearheads. He said nothing of God's merciful love; all was sin and endless punishment. Merciless to himself, he had no mercy to teach others.

Yet his grim message came through to Taniu as a revelation of shining beauty. Indeed, to her it was hardly a message. He'd only given words to the loathing and contempt she already felt for the life she saw in her own home. He hadn't taught her anything about filth and lust that she hadn't known long since. She knew all about that crowned whore in the scarlet gown who sat throned on the hills drinking the blood of the innocent. She was up there in Din Pelidr at this moment, laughing at the sight of Luned's blood, just as she had laughed in the stone circle when —when something unspeakable had been done. How lovely to be washed clean from blood and filth—to be like the stars, pure and cold!

The monk ended by saying that he would baptize those who came to him next day, after testing their souls by a night of prayer. He would now lay a blessing on those who were ready to offer themselves to the King of Kings.

A number of his listeners crowded up to him; the rest began to move homeward or stayed hovering in the background to see what others did. Taniu came forward eagerly, forgetting Selyf and his family. A man moved beside her, sun-tanned and stocky, with curly brown hair and beard. The warm evening light gilded a strong plain face and steady eyes that smiled at her as he stepped back respectfully to let the princess go ahead of him.

The man in front rose from his knees; Taniu took his place. The missionary noted the fine wool of her dress, the silver of her belt, her smooth hands.

'Who are you, my child?'

'Taniu, King Loth's daughter. I want to be baptized tomorrow.'

The monk looked at her fair, eager face with gloomy distaste. By woman, sin first came into the world. Also, they were weak and a temptation to men's flesh. On the other hand, it was his duty to save even these frail twigs from the everlasting bonfire.

'Have you got your father's permission?'

'No, I couldn't. He's away from home.'

'I cannot baptize you without his consent.'

Taniu looked crestfallen.

'Patience is a virtue, daughter, that is especially becoming to a Christian woman. When you have spoken to the king, ask him to send to the monastery at Mailros. One of us will come at once. Meanwhile, you can use the time by preparing yourself with prayer and fasting. Keep yourself pure from sin. Turn your heart from fleshly lust. Now, receive the blessing of Heaven.'

His hands clamped on her head. She got up and moved away; the man who had smiled at her took her place. As she left the circle, Selyf and his family came up quietly; the daughter linked arms again. They had been waiting patiently to give her their company across the moor; she felt grateful for their discreet kindness.

When they reached the main gate she slipped in unnoticed as one of Selyf's womenfolk. They walked together to his house, high up by the stockade fencing in the royal citadel. The women went in; Selyf told her he had a gold belt-buckle to return to Talhaearn and came on with her. She guessed he had invented the errand to see her across the courtyard.

The sun was sinking. Over towards Cumbria the south-western sky was turning red as if all the flames of Hell were blazing up for the Last Judgement. Firelight and torchlight gleamed through the open doorway of the great hall. A group of young warriors lounged against the wooden porch-pillars, the gold and bronze of their arm-rings and brooches flaring in the sunset. They were roaring with laughter at some joke.

Selyf murmured farewell and went up to the porch. The warriors called out greetings to him; she glided along the side of the hall towards the women's quarters. Her feet dragged; she moved slower and slower the nearer she got. She was balancing on the edge of running away, bolting back to Selyf's house. While she hesitated she lost her chance. A woman came hurrying

71

out to the porch, saw her and rushed back inside calling, 'Here she is!'

Reluctantly, Taniu entered. The hearth-fire was dying to ashes, untended, the torches unlit. Drostecca's chair and couch were both empty. From the inner room came an animal sound of moaning that lifted to an agonized shriek.

Dear God, they'd got Luned in there!

Ancarat came to the door. There were stains on her dress; her thin hair was wilder than ever; her eyes were almost sunk in her head.

'Where've you been? Cynon said you came back hours ago. You took yourself off again quick enough, didn't you, just when I needed you?'

'I—'

Ancarat swept across her excuses. 'Don't waste any more time chattering. Go and get me the nightshade infusion, quickly! I can't trust any of these whimpering fools with it and I daren't leave her. Count the drops carefully, and mix them with a spoonful of honey—'

The shrieking started again. Ancarat pushed the leather curtain aside; Taniu looked beyond her into the room. Drostecca was writhing on the bed. Her naked body was glistening with sweat; her red hair hung in damp rats' tails across her contorted face. Two of her women were huddled at the foot of the bed gripping her ankles. Lurga crouched behind her, trying to keep the queen's head steady against her breast, reciting charms and prayers to her gods; then breaking off to whisper encouragement and little love-names to her mistress. Her face reflected Drostecca's agony. Every time she twisted in pain, Lurga's face contorted in agony. This was not just tenderness. Lurga was trying with all her might to take the queen's pain into her own body by magic, so that Drostecca might have some ease.

As Ancarat went back to the bedside, Drostecca tore herself free of Lurga's embrace and began to beat her belly, howling like a wolf. Taniu ran in to help; there was a wild struggle for a few seconds until Drostecca sank back exhausted, moaning softly.

'What is it? What's happened to her?'

For once in her life the old woman looked bewildered.

72

'The labour started just after noon. Morien ran in to say that the queen had been taken ill in the orchard—her guards carried her in. But the child won't come!'

'Is it wrongly placed?' Taniu had once seen Ancarat reach in and turn a baby during a difficult labour.

Ancarat twisted her hands in despair. 'No, I've felt for it. The head's there but the child won't come!'

Lurga looked at her, stroking Drostecca's hair and rocking her like a baby. 'Someone has tied witch-knots against her.' The baleful green eyes rested on Taniu. 'There's an evil magic on her, I tell you. You must hunt it out and break it.'

'We've combed her hair again and again!' sobbed one of the women. 'We've taken every thread off her. We can't find any witch-knots!'

'Run and get the nightshade,' muttered Ancarat. 'Now while she's quiet, we can get her to take it.'

'But *nightshade*—'

'There's nothing else I can do for her. I've given her plantain; I've tried poppy-juice as much as I dared. Her body won't let the child go. She can't last much longer —I've got to ease her, to get the child out.'

She gripped Taniu's arm and led her to the door. 'I know it may kill her but she'll die anyway without it. Be quick!'

Taniu ran into the still-room. Her hands were shaking but she forced herself into calmness before she counted out the few drops of deadly liquid and mixed them carefully with honey.

While Lurga held Drostecca's head, Ancarat spooned the drug into her mouth. To their relief she swallowed without resisting. Gradually the wild struggles stopped; the stiffness went from her limbs. Ancarat worked on her desperately, trying to guide and coax her body into natural movements to help the birth.

Far into the night they got the child out of her, looped into the cord. It was the son for whom Loth had waited and planned so eagerly, and he was dead.

CHAPTER
7

As Taniu was passing, unwillingly, into the shadows of Drostecca's hall, Owain was riding out of the great gateway of Petriana, saluted by the royal guards. It was the largest fort on the Wall and had once housed the largest garrison, a thousand-strong cavalry regiment, the famous Ala Petriana. The descendants of those troopers and their fine horses still rode in Urien's warbands. Here was the main source of Cumbria's strength.

Caer Luel lay a mile away at the southern end of Idon Bridge. Its red sandstone walls always seemed to have an inner warmth, even under the grey skies of winter. Now, under that flaming sunset, with the Idon like a river of fire at its feet, it was glowing like a ruby.

Most of the great cities of Roman Britain were dead or dying; Caer Luel was still very much alive. Trading ships still came up the western seaboard; they crossed from Ireland with gold, slaves and fine wolfhounds, or came north from Gaul with wine of Burdigalia and embroidered silks from Constantinople. Scholars and clerics paused on their way to St Nynia's monastery at Candida Casa; many brought priceless books as gifts for the king.

Dusk was falling as Owain entered the north gate. Lights were already shining from the upper gatehouse; torches were beginning to flare out from some of the house fronts. There was the usual grinding and clattering of heavy wooden shutters being dragged into place to protect shop counters. An alehouse doorway opened on to a red gulf of firelight, with the black heads of a group of drinkers leaning together to share a joke, then jerking back with roars of laughter. In an upper room of the brothel at the sign of the Golden Lily, a girl was singing about home-coming to white breasts for a pillow, lips sweet as red wine.

He crossed the forum and rode under the arched gateway into the palace courtyard. The servants who ran up to take Seren told him the king had dined early and retired to his private rooms. Owain declined their atten-

74

dance, shook out his cloak and went eagerly to his father, praying that he would not be closeted with Bishop Viventius or some of the Council.

The anteroom was empty except for a page munching an apple. He jumped up with a quick choke and gulp to clear his mouth; Owain grinned reassuringly. The page tapped on the door, opened it, announced, 'Prince Owain, my lord,' and stood aside.

The room was large; all the objects in it were costly and finely made but they were few, so it looked austere. The floor was plain black and white mosaic; the walls were white plaster. One was almost hidden by a packed book cabinet, scrolls above in their pigeon holes, heavy codices stacked underneath. The only light came from a silver lamp-stand with three lamps hanging from delicate silver chains. They illuminated the massive marble table, the spread parchment and the man who sat in a great high-backed chair studying it.

He wore a long, plainly-made robe of dark, blue-grey wool, with grey fur at wrists and hem. A narrow gold circlet above his brows and a magnificent oval ruby in the ring on his right hand were his only ornaments. This was Urien: *'gold king of the North'*, as the bards called him; but most of his gold was kept for his army and for guest-gifts.

Owain was very like him; it was easy to see they were father and son. They had the same tall, fine-boned bodies; the same long, straight noses and clear-cut expressive mouths. Urien's eyes, though, were so dark under heavy black brows that they seemed to be black as well; his fine, silky hair was silver-grey like frost.

He raised his head, beckoned the page to bring wine from a side table and place a stool for the prince; then dismissed the boy. He filled a goblet himself and handed it to his son.

'I hope you will forgive the lack of a prepared welcome, but you sent no word when I might expect you.'

Owain recognized a rebuke; he described his boar-hunt once again.

'I couldn't let him go after he'd killed my hounds. But, of course, without them it was hard to bring him to bay—he gave me a long chase.'

Urien listened to the recital with his usual grave courtesy; then he asked quietly, 'And what have you called my first grandchild?'

Owain wouldn't condescend to show surprise or embarrassment.

'Dinogat.' He smiled disarmingly. 'A fine lusty boy. Another spearman for the army.'

His father bowed in polite acknowledgement. 'I'm grateful for your help but I must warn you, you're taking a slow and exhausting way of raising a warband.'

Owain chuckled, but was silenced when Urien added, 'Now you have come home, I want to discuss your marriage.'

He was taken aback; to have his father begin the very subject he'd meant to approach as warily as stalking game seemed uncanny. Urien misunderstood his startled look; he said more sternly, 'If you can get bastards on hill-girls you can get me an heir.'

'My brother—'

'A child. And God help any kingdom with a child as an heir. I wasn't young when I married, Owain, though I was young when I inherited the kingdom. So now I'm old, with only one son come to manhood. I won't make the same mistake with you.'

'You're not old!'

Urien smiled sadly. 'I'm not immortal. And death comes to the young as well, especially to huntsmen who go after boar single-handed. It's time you made a suitable alliance. Of all our allies, Caer Voran is the strongest; Lady Penarwan is beautiful and well educated—'

'But not royal.' The last thing Owain wanted was for his father to build up such a favourable idea of the Caer Voran alliance that he wouldn't consider any other.

Urien looked at him sharply. 'They've married into every princely family in the North—including ours. Our cousin didn't find them lacking in birth when she married Garmon.'

'Our cousin wasn't the heir to Cumbria. Whoever the Caer Voran stock mate with—however often they marry into princely families—it's still the blood of a German mercenary. That's hardly a theme for a bard to sing about!

76

We give all the honour in such an alliance, we don't gain any.'

'The blood of that *German mercenary* has been shed for Cumbria often enough. I certainly didn't feel that I was giving any honour while Garmon—like his father before him—was fighting bravely at my side.'

He gave Owain another piercing look. 'What have you got against this match? You and Penarwan used to be good friends.'

'We still are. I like Penarwan very well. I'll praise her beauty and her wit with every bard in the land. But she's not royal blood and she's got no claim on me to make her a queen.'

'Indeed! Can you name any lady you do think royal enough to claim equality with your princely self?'

'I—it's said that Taniu, the daughter of King Loth, is highly praised for her prudence and virtue.'

'Then she doesn't take after her father.'

'Her mother—'

'—was Strathclyde.' Urien could trace the branches of every royal and noble family in Britain as easily as his bards and genealogists. 'A good blood.'

He looked down at the parchment spread on the table. It was an old Roman map of the northern province and the tribes beyond the Wall. Urien had added the British names of the kingdoms and citadels in his fine clerkly script. He gazed thoughtfully at these names, as if he were studying pieces set out for a board game.

'Lothian and Strathclyde united in this princess——Taniu.' He paused over the fact, touching their names on the map. 'Lothian's linked to Eidyn already; Loth and Morcant are cousins. And Loth's queen is Pictish, his boy might have some hold there. And now Cumbria. All the kingdoms of the North joined like a mountain wall against the Irish and the Angles. That for a start. And then to win back the lost lands of the south—restore Britain as it was when Arthur died. We could still do it, if only we can hold together.'

Urien's dreams went beyond the greatness of Cumbria. He wanted to see Britain united, as it had been when it was a province of the empire, peaceful and orderly. Arthur had achieved that miracle two generations ago, before his rule was broken and he himself struck down by family treachery. Urien believed it was still possible.

Watching his father's mind taking the wished-for track, Owain suddenly heard Lothian answering in Taniu's voice—'*You stole Catraeth.*' He felt a cold touch of foreboding.

'Lothian may not be too eager for our alliance. There's still a great deal of ill-feeling about Catraeth. They haven't forgiven us yet for the crime of keeping them safe in their beds.'

'And this marriage would end the ill-feeling!' Urien looked up eagerly. 'Once they were bound to us by a firm alliance, I'd gladly let them hold Catraeth and bring our troops back to the west. Well thought, Owain.'

Owain thought: *If I told you that my mind was full of a golden-haired girl with eyes like stars in lake-water, and none of these wise plans had ever entered my head—would you be angry with your unworthy son?*

He looked at his father's grave, drawn face, wondering about his parents' marriage. Owain's mind, unlike Taniu's, had not been fouled by ugly memories of lust and brutality. His father had been a courteous and entirely faithful husband to the princess of Gwynedd he had chosen for his wife and queen. She had deserved his respect; she was beautiful and gracious, she had given him fine sons. Queen Modron's jewels, the state she had kept, had been the wonder of the North in her lifetime. Now, her pillar-stone in the bishop's churchyard proclaimed her virtues in elegant Latin. Urien had showered the jewels and composed the epitaph; but, reserved and austere as his manners were, it was difficult to guess how much affection had gone with the gifts and the honours. He had not been a young man when he married. Most of his time, possibly most of his love, had been given to Cumbria. Owain assumed that his mother's marriage had been mainly for the sake of the kingdom: to secure the southern border and get heirs.

But doesn't it come to the same thing in the end? The eastern alliance will be secure just the same when I have my golden girl in bed.

Urien's thoughts seem to be taking the same track as Owain's this evening. He rolled up his map, refilled the goblets and leaned back smiling.

'It's good when marriage brings peace and safety to two kingdoms and ends a cankering feud. It was like that when I married your dear mother.'

Owain was always interested in matters of state; besides, he hoped his father would talk for once about his mother.

'I didn't know we'd been at feud with Gwynedd —though I might have guessed. Every kingdom in Britain is at feud with all its neighbours, or has been, or is getting ready to be. What were we feuding about?'

Urien sipped his wine, his dark eyes staring into the past.

'King Maelgwn of Gwynedd—he was your mother's cousin, remember—wanted to marry the daughter of one of his nobles. He didn't mind that she wasn't royal,' his eyes teased Owain, 'she was so beautiful he wouldn't have cared if she'd kept pigs. Maelgwn was already married —so was she, to his own nephew. His wife died. She was found dead in her bed one morning while Maelgwn was away from the court. Then his nephew died. The story went that he'd been speared by the antlers of a stag he was hunting. He was certainly speared. So Maelgwn was free to take the woman he wanted; but because, sacramentally speaking, she was his niece, the Church refused to bless the marriage.'

'Was Maelgwn surprised?' Owain looked amused and inclined to admire.

'I doubt if he thought of it. He was one who cared nothing for the laws of God or man—till the pains of death came on him.'

Urien spoke harshly. He had seen that look of admiration, remembering with a stab of anxiety that this same wild blood was in his son.

'The yellow plague came to Gwynedd, with a cargo ship from Gaul. Maelgwn locked himself in the church at Rhos; he said the sickness was a demon from Hell, it wouldn't be able to touch him there.'

He smiled grimly. 'And then, he couldn't resist, he

looked out through the keyhole and swore he could see it—a yellow monster coming for him. He'd been infected, of course, before he came to hide in the church. He died raving.'

Owain shuddered in spite of himself.

'He had a son, Rhun, by his second wife; he took the kingdom. Those who hated him for Maelgwn's sake said he was a bastard, as the marriage was unhallowed. The first wife had a daughter married to a prince of Eidyn, Elidir was his name. Rhun's enemies offered him the kingdom. He wasn't an ambitious man; they made it sound as if Rhun had been set aside legally. So, thinking no harm, he sailed south from Alclud.'

He sighed. 'Whatever the rights and wrongs of his birth, Rhun was Maelgwn's true son in spirit. Elidir was cut to pieces as soon as he landed and so, soon after, were those who had invited him.'

'So then, everybody accepted Rhun as lawful king?'

'No one in Gwynedd argued the point with him. But Eidyn was furious at the death of a kinsman. Strathclyde took offence because Elidir had sailed in one of their ships and Rhun had seized it. So the kingdoms attacked by sea. Rhun was taken by surprise; though he got away to Môn, the invaders looted and burned his palace at Deganwy before they went home.'

'How did Rhun take that? Of course, he owed an honour-price to Eidyn for their kinsman's blood, but I don't suppose he enjoyed their coming and settling the debt themselves.'

'Rhun took it with a mass-levy of Gwynedd. While the invaders were sailing back to Alclud, gloating over their booty and revenge, Rhun took his army by forced marches up the Long Hills to Eidyn and sacked it very thoroughly before its own troops could get back to defend it.'

Owain smiled his appreciation.

'Then as you can imagine, there was all-out war between Gwynedd and the North, with the lands left ravaged while the Picts and Irish moved in behind. It couldn't go on, so I asked for peace. I had to offer compensation all round and give many hostages to both sides before they would even agree to meet, but—'

'You offered compensation!' Owain forgot all his duty to his father in an outburst of rage. 'You gave Cumbrian hostages! And asked for peace! What concern is it of ours if Gwynedd and the North choose to tear each other apart?'

'If you're going to rule Cumbria one day, you'd better be quite sure where it is.' Urien's voice was cold. He unrolled the map again. The great ruby on his finger shone as bright as a gout of fresh blood while he pointed.

'Here's Gwynedd; there are Strathclyde and Eidyn. When they go to war, which is the shortest road for their armies, can you tell me?'

'I know that very well.' Owain was equally cold. 'But I should have thought a king of Cumbria might at least try to throw intruders back from his borders.'

'We threw them back six times.' Urien looked weary. 'One more victory would have broken us.'

Owain stared.

'When you've seen real warfare, you'll find sometimes that a warrior will fight like a demon all through the battle, then die in the end from quite a feeble blow—if he's been wounded before. A man can only lose so much blood, Owain; it's the same with the kingdom. When most of its warriors are dead—those who should have held the borders and sired the next generation of fighting men— then that kingdom will go down to the next attack. Where's the kingdom of Efrog now?'

Owain wouldn't reply, though he knew the answer. He'd nearly done battle with Taniu over the fate of Pere- dur's kingdom, and the fact that Cumbria was now holding the last fragment of it that the Angles hadn't seized. Even so, his fit of anger hit him like a body-blow, he felt it in his heart and guts: for a second he was afraid he would vomit his wine. He refused to meet his father's eyes. He couldn't face the picture of Urien acting like a defeated king paying tribute to his new overlord—and why, in God's name, when he was unbeaten and vic- torious?

Urien sensed his bewilderment and shame. He laid his hand over Owain's; his voice was gentle.

'No king loses his honour by protecting his land, Owain. Our land is our honour; it mustn't be foolishly lost or

81

thrown away while we live. That's what it means to be king—to be the one who makes the sacrifice. Not the surrender, not even the gift—the sacrifice.'

The word made Owain look up, startled. Urien was not speaking like his father any more—or like any king that Owain had ever met. He sounded like a priest saying Mass, at the moment of consecration.

'What do you mean, lord?'

'There are some things the good monks didn't teach you. Indeed, it's best that such things shouldn't be spoken of too often, even by the heirs of the knowledge.

'Long ago, the king was the sacrifice. His blood was shed by the Druids every year at Calan Gaeaf and his flesh scattered on the fields to make the seeds grow.'

Owain's flesh shivered.

'Well, those rites have ended, since our Lord Jesus Christ made the royal sacrifice once and for all. But it still happens to kings, Owain, that we're called to offer sacrifice for our people. It may be our lives—it usually is, and that's easy. But it may be our hopes, our happiness or our pride—which we selfishly call our honour.'

He looked hard at Owain, tightening his grip on his son's hand. His voice was urgent.

'Remember this. A man who leads his countrymen to certain defeat and destruction to satisfy his pride, or because he's afraid to be called a coward, has lost all right to be a king. To keep the thatch unburned on the peasant's hut; to keep the mother suckling her child unharmed inside it—that's king's honour. Remember this, when I'm not here to remind you.'

'I'll remember.'

Owain made the promise as solemnly as if he were taking a vow on holy relics. His flaring anger had died; he couldn't recall his usual detached mockery. It was impossible to ask himself sardonically why his father, in full health and with his powerful kingdom at peace, should apparently be taking a death-bed leave of him.

Urien seemed satisfied. The tension between them relaxed. He leaned back, sipping his wine.

'And you see, my son, I lost no honour after all. We'd beaten them so often and so soundly, they were grateful to me for offering terms. The peace I made still holds.'

'And both sides were satisfied?' Owain was willing to discuss the matter calmly now, as being of historical interest only.

'There's no reason why not. Instead of certain ruin and probable death, they saved their lives and kept their pride. Elidir's supporters, those that Rhun left alive—or rather didn't get hold of to kill—had to go into exile in the North, of course, but that would have happened anyway. They can't blame me.'

Owain's mouth twisted cynically. 'People have great talents for blaming others. And indeed, if I'd lost my home and lands and the graves of my ancestors to make someone else's peace, I don't think I'd forgive easily. I doubt if they do.'

'I don't lose any sleep over that. My peace has held unbroken for eighteen years. Time enough for passions to cool. Most of those involved are dead now, or too old for feuding, like me.'

He smiled; he could still ride as hard and as far as the toughest warrior in his warband.

'This marriage of yours will keep the peace in the east, as mine has kept it in the west. I'm very pleased with your idea; you're beginning to plan like a king. Winter will soon be on us but as soon as the roads are passable in spring, I'll send envoys to Lothian. It'll need careful handling. I'll send one of the Council to lead the embassy—Lord Custennin will be the best choice, I think. He has a shrewd head and polished manners—'

'But surely, I'm the one to lead the embassy?'

For the first time that evening, Urien looked really irritated.

'Don't be foolish. You're not a farmer's son riding across the hill to ask for a neighbour's daughter. Cumbria is proposing to marry Lothian. Everything will be done in the proper form.'

Owain had an impulse to argue the point but controlled himself. His father had fallen in with his wishes over the marriage, giving up a long-cherished plan of his own. It was just the loss of a week or two—and it would be so amusing to see her face when her father's men brought her to Caer Luel, anxious—perhaps even frightened—at the prospect of having to please a strange bridegroom, and saw him waiting to lift her from her horse.

He bade an affectionate goodnight to his father and went off to his own rooms, well pleased with himself and with life.

CHAPTER
8

As Ancarat had foretold, it was a bitter winter, though the days remained mild and the snow did not fall on the moors till after Midwinter's Day.

Loth rode back from his hunting a few days after Drostecca's agony. He had counted up the queen's time as near as possible to keep away from the women's fuss and screeching. He was ready now for the boasting, the jokes and the celebrations.

When he heard about his dead son he cursed all women. He wasted no words of pity on his wife, flinging away to the great hall and getting noisily drunk. While he remained in Din Pelidr this was the regular close of each day. He avoided the queen's hall for weeks as if it held the yellow plague.

Drostecca kept to her bed, sick and exhausted. She slept long and heavily; when she woke she cried or broke into hideous storms of rage.

For a while Luned hovered around the courtyard like a small unhappy ghost. Any vague hope she had that Loth would save her from her misery vanished under his unseeing eyes. Even when he was in a good humour with womenkind, he only noticed those who were handsome and as cheerfully lustful as himself. There was nothing pretty or desirable about poor Luned now. Her face was white and drawn, with blue shadows like bruises under the eyes; her dark curls were matted into elf-locks; she was dirty and she stank. The horror and bewilderment of what had happened to her seemed to have shocked her into idiocy. She stared dumbly with her mouth open like a crazed beggar-woman, and got as little notice from the royal household.

Brude seemed perfectly satisfied with his new wife. The pleasures he got from women had nothing to do with their faces or their wits. He enjoyed Luned all the more because she was wretched and terrified of him; he grinned at the sight of her.

The queen's women, who had giggled with her and flattered her while she was in favour, now kept away from the sight of her as much as they could. If one of them had to pass close, she would pull her skirts aside, averting her eyes from Luned's dumb, pleading gaze. Some of them were pleased at her downfall; they were all too scared of Lurga to show any fellow-feeling.

It was this dumb endurance that Taniu could not bear. It drove her to brave Ancarat's wrath and raid one of the clothes chests in the nursery. She took a fine linen shift, woollen hose, a warm blue gown that had been made for herself and a pair of soft leather slippers. As she folded them, with a towel and one of her ivory combs, into a bundle to hide under her cloak, she tried to think of an excuse if Ancarat saw and questioned her.

Then she realized, with some surprise, that Ancarat's wrath no longer had any power to disturb her. The visit to Nia, the shock of her home-coming, above all, the harsh creed she had picked up from the monk's sermon had cut the last ties of childish respect for anyone in court. If she met Ancarat, she would tell the exact truth, then go on doing what she intended.

Nobody was about as she passed the great hall and crossed the courtyard. Beyond the stables there was a straggle of bothies and lean-to sheds against the walls. Most of them were used as stores but some of them were lived in. The fighting men slept in the great hall after the feasting was over, or in the warriors' hall close by. However, it sometimes happened that a spearman took up for longer than usual with one of the kitchen servants or a war-captive. Then they would sleep together in one of the bothies and it was here that Brude had taken Luned.

Taniu found her crouched on a frowsy pile of blankets and skins that served as a bed. The remains of a fire were collapsing into ashes on the hearthstone. Placed by it were an empty iron pot and a crock full of water. A wooden chest with Pictish carving stood against one of the walls; Brude probably kept his clothes and weapons in it. A clumsy wooden stool was the only other object in the place.

Luned had not looked up when her visitor came in and stood blinking in the dimly-lit living space. Taniu called her name gently.

'Luned!'

No movement, no answer.

Taniu moved as quietly as possible over to the bed and sat down beside her.

'Luned.' She put her hand on the girl's arm. 'Look what I've brought you.'

She waited for a moment; but as there was still no movement or sound, she set about blowing up the ashes and getting the fire going again. Luckily, someone had made a pile of chopped wood and turfs in the lean-to outside; that would be Brude, of course, it did not seem that Luned lifted a finger to care for her home any more than for herself.

When the fire was well alight, and the bothy all the warmer and brighter for it, Taniu set some of the water to heat in the iron pot. When it was warm enough, she bathed and dried Luned. The girl seemed to feel the comfort of the warm water and the touch of kindly hands; she let Taniu pull off her dirty shift without a struggle and moved obediently as Taniu washed her. While Taniu was dressing her in the clothes she had brought, she kept up a flow of talk about what she was doing, in the simplest words, as if Luned were a child again.

'Smell the lavender on your shift! Isn't it sweet? Now your gown. There's a pretty blue! You like blue, don't you? Hold your arms out while I put it on.'

Luned was watching her face now with an uncertain smile. She silently held out her arms as she was bid; but when the gown was on and Taniu was arranging the folds, she suddenly spoke.

86

'I lost my bracelets.'

Taniu looked up startled to hear her voice after so long. Luned was staring at her mournfully.

'I had such pretty bracelets. Red and green, they were. "*Red and green, fit for a queen.*" But I lost them and the king's angry with me. Somebody took my bracelets.'

The bracelets had not been seen in the women's quarters. They had vanished from the time that Drostecca's Picts had fallen upon Luned and stripped her for flogging. Probably Luned had caused the outburst of savagery by flaunting them again. Most likely they were now in Drostecca's own jewel chest or perhaps she had given them to her faithful Lurga. At any rate Taniu could not come by them; if she could, she certainly would not bring another storm down on Luned by giving them back to her. She was wearing a bracelet herself, a delicate chain of silver triskele medallions. She quickly unclasped it and slipped it round Luned's wrist.

'Why, there's a pretty bracelet! And I'm sure we can find some others—or a brooch perhaps, or a silver belt.'

If trinkets could keep poor Luned happy, she would not grudge some from her own store.

She took the comb and began on Luned's hair, teasing out the knots from each elf-lock and twining it back into curls round her fingers. It was amazing how much of her beauty still remained now she was clean and kempt. She was thinner and paler than before, but her big brown eyes and soft little mouth looked very appealing, framed in a cloud of dark curls. She smiled up at Taniu.

'When I find my bracelets, will the king love me again?'

As she spoke, the door frame darkened and Brude came in. Taniu felt Luned shrink under her hands. She prayed that he had not heard Luned's last hopeful words. Her marriage, dreadful as it was, had probably saved her life; nothing could save her if Brude even suspected that Loth might look at her again.

He had two loaves under his arm; he was carrying a crock of stew in one hand and a leather bottle in the other, fetched from the kitchens. He took in the well-kept fire and the change in Luned's looks, grinning at her.

'You put me to shame, princess,'—he didn't seem in the

least ashamed—'to see you doing for my dirty slut what she's too idle to do for herself.'

'It puts me to shame to hear such words used to a lady from my father's court. Luned was as sweet and clean as anyone could wish, not so long ago.'

'You couldn't be wrong, of course, princess. I'll only say that the bitch doesn't trouble to keep herself sweet and clean for me. A precious wife I've got myself from your father's court!'

'It wasn't her choice to be your wife!'

'What's her choice got to do with it? It was her duty to obey the queen. Now it's her duty to obey me. She's about as much use for the one as the other.'

He pulled the stool to the hearth and with a kind of rough courtesy gestured Taniu towards it, holding out the leather bottle to her. She hated the idea of touching him or taking anything from his hands but she did not want to anger him. She knew who would suffer for that. So she sat down with the best grace she could and touched her lips to the ale bottle before handing it to him. He squatted down by the hearth and took a deep draught himself, before breaking a piece off one of the loaves to hand to her. He tossed another piece into Luned's lap but she did not touch it. She was staring ahead with the same blind stupid look as before. Brude spat towards her in disgust.

'She's moon-touched, crazed. She never does a hand's turn in the place. Everything falls on me. Not that I don't owe you thanks, princess,' the grin broadened, 'for making her sweeter to my taste. I've more of an appetite to her now than I've had for some time!'

He reached over to the bed and ran his thick fingers through Luned's curls, then brought his hand down her shoulder and over her breast. She pushed herself back against the wall with a pitiful whimpering sound. Brude laughed.

Taniu had stood up, clenching her fingers into her palms. There was nothing she could do for Luned. A man had total rights over his woman's body. However, she had to speak, sounding as firm as she could.

'Remember, Brude, though Luned's your wife, she's a Lothian woman. If she's badly treated, she's a right to ask for the king's protection. And if she can't speak for herself, I'll speak for her.'

Brude had turned from Luned and was staring at her. She forced herself to meet his eyes without faltering, hoping that he would not guess her words were mostly bluff. She hadn't the slightest influence with Loth; she couldn't be sure he remembered she was alive.

Brude watched her warily, trying to hide his alarm. Drostecca's Picts had never been much liked by the Lothian men. Now that Loth was angry with the queen, he wouldn't need much persuading to strike at her through her followers. If the princess went to him now, all smiles and fondling, she could coax him easily enough, pretty piece of flesh as she was. Or suppose she didn't trouble the king, but went to one of his spearmen? That young fool, Cynon, who was always singing her praises as if he meant to turn bard? Cynon would see to his death, sure enough, for a smile and a kiss, or whatever else she chose to offer him.

Taniu felt that the silence had lasted for hours while they tried to stare each other out. Then Brude smiled and shrugged placatingly.

'Who's ill-treating her? Is it my fault she won't wash her face or cook me a meal? You see I do what I can—she's got a roof and food.'

There was no answer to that. Taniu bowed her head to him silently then bent and kissed Luned's cheek.

'Goodbye for this time, my dear. I hope I'll see you well, next time I come.'

Luned made no response but Taniu had been speaking for Brude's ears. She hoped that Luned would not have to pay for her visit. As she walked across the courtyard she listened for sounds behind her in the bothy. Once she looked back; Brude had come to his door and was watching her. She turned at once and hurried away.

As it happened she had no chance to see for herself how Luned got on, for after that she was kept fairly close to the queen's hall. She made guarded inquiries of one or two of the women she trusted to some extent. She learned that Brude was kinder to Luned, or at least more prudent.

Luned did not come wandering mazed about the royal halls any more. She stayed, or was kept, at the bothy but she still wore her blue gown and bracelet, and looked decent. Brude had got a woman from the kitchens, a big-boned, tow-headed war-captive, who had been enjoying his favours for some time, to come and wait on Luned and see to the cooking. It was believed that she had taken over most of Luned's bed-work as well as the housework. For poor Luned, that would be a relief.

Taniu was kept to the queen's hall because Gwalchmai and Ancarat needed her. Drostecca did not gain strength. She got thinner and was troubled by heavy sweats; she also began to cough a good deal and complain of pains in her side and chest. Ancarat tried every remedy she knew: coltsfoot for the cough, betony for the wasting, yarrow for women's ills. Taniu was kept busy in the still-room: grating, pounding, infusing, mixing. Nothing seemed to help the queen.

When Loth was not settling disputes or overseeing weapon-practice, he was out hunting. Often he took his meals with one of his farmers and slept with one of their daughters or maidservants. He chose bold, strapping girls who came cheerfully to his bed and did not tire under his riding. Sometimes he looked in on Drostecca, showing all too clearly that he just wanted to see if she were strong enough to make it worth trying to get another son on her. Each meeting turned into an ugly quarrel, which left Drostecca weeping and coughing, and sent Loth storming out to curse her over the mead in the great hall.

It would begin quietly enough.

'Well, then, how are you now?'

'Poorly. I'm weary of my life.'

'You should get up and come into the hall. My men must have forgotten they've got a queen.'

'Why should they remember me when you don't?' The tears would be starting to show. 'You leave me here, you don't care if I live or die, while you go wasting your strength on every whore in Lothian. I know what you do!'

'What's that to you?' Loth's voice rising and his temper with it. 'It's not for you to question what I do. It's for you to give me sons. That's what I married you for. To give me

90

sons. What do you think I brought you here for, you ugly foul-tempered hag? *To give me sons!*'

'I've given you sons!'

'One son. What good is a dead child to me? A queen should bear living sons.'

'How can I give you a son if you don't come to me? Do you think my womb can bear by itself? If you want another son, come to me and give me your seed.'

'When your womb's fit to take my seed I'll come to you and not before. And see you carry it more carefully next time. Why, any hunting bitch of mine, any sow in my herds, knows how to drop her young alive!'

'Then take a bitch or a sow to bed with you! They'd suit you better!'

A bellow of fury from Loth; Drostecca screaming; then Ancarat and Lurga in shrill protest.

Gwalchmai was terrified by these quarrels. He loved Drostecca because she was his mother; he worshipped Loth as the greatest king and warrior who had ever lived. He was puzzled and worried by Loth's demands for another son —wasn't his father pleased with him? His sleep grew more troubled than ever; he was getting pale and hollow-eyed.

Taniu comforted his nights and kept him with her in the still-room and herb garden. She told him stories; but now they were about saints' miracles and brave martyrs defying emperors. She asked Selyf and Ancarat to tell her what they knew about the monks and their teaching. She had no idea how little that was or how garbled it came to her. Ancarat kept the name of Christian because she felt it set her apart from the easterners; it made no difference to her love-spells and abortions. Selyf could not read; he could only teach her a few prayers he had learned by rote.

What she remembered most was the missionary's sermon; his scorn of the warriors' code; his insistence on bodily chastity. She had felt the same scorn growing in her for a long time; as for chastity, could any monk hate bodily defilement as much as she did? The mindless rutting of the spearmen, marriage to Loth or Brude—which was worse?

Taniu was so sickened by life that she forgot the quiet decency of Selyf's and Nia's homes. Anyway, they weren't nobles. And when Owain's face came to her now, as it still did sometimes, she would see the smoke-blue eyes looking at her as Morien and Brude had looked at Luned, imagine his hands dragging off her clothes, clawing at her breasts. She would shudder and try to blank her mind with a prayer.

When Midwinter came, it was hard to work up any real merriment, though the feasting was as heavy as usual and the drinking, if possible, heavier.

Then, with the New Year, the wind turned cruel and the cold bit into their bones. Drostecca's cough got worse. Once, Taniu came to her door with a soothing electuary; she heard voices inside and stopped.

'I tell you, I'll sleep with any woman I like! There isn't one of them who doesn't serve me better than you can—or will!—And I'll tell you another thing. The first one to bear a son who looks like me—I'll bring her here!'

Taniu waited for the outburst of screaming but Drostecca was deathly quiet. Loth paused for a few seconds to hear what she would retort, then came out looking pleased with himself. At last, he'd found a way to shut the bitch's snarling mouth.

Before the New Year was two months old, Luned died. She was found by the river bank where the women did their washing, with her head in the water. She was heavily pregnant; it was supposed she had caught her foot, fallen stunned and so drowned. Only—the bank was as flat and smooth there as a spread blanket. And who would go a-washing at that time of year? And how long was it since Luned had given her mind to any household task?

Luned had no near kin to ask these or any other questions. Two slaves chipped out a shallow grave in the frost-hard earth. She was bundled in, still wearing her blue gown and bracelet, wrapped in a blanket pulled from her bed. They stamped the earth over her and piled stones on top to keep the starving wolves from having her out.

Brude went grinning about the hall as usual. He gave Ancarat a ring-brooch for a few withered sprigs of betony to wear inside his shirt and buried a live black cockerel under the door-slab of his bothy to keep Luned off if she was angry and walked. But she made no sign. She had never had the strength to be angry even while she lived. Perhaps she was glad to go.

Taniu wrapped herself in her cloak of martens' fur and went down to the riverside. Walking along the smooth bank, where a toddler could hardly have fallen, she thought with growing horror of Luned's fate.

'The first one to bear a son who looks like me—I'll bring her here!'

Drostecca had not troubled to answer in words. But if Luned was carrying Loth's child—and the state of her pregnancy made that almost certain—if she had borne a boy and if it looked like Loth—that was a lot of 'ifs' but Drostecca wasn't one to hold back a blow if she thought herself threatened. Luned was young and fertile, that would be enough to make Drostecca hate her. And she looked so pretty when she was well-tended.

She saw Luned's face, with the big brown eyes and the cloud of silky curls that she had combed and twined round her fingers not so long ago.

Did I help to bring Luned to her death?

Taniu shook her head as if her thoughts were angry wasps. She stared at the dark silent river. Only at the Day of Judgement would it be known what had happened there, but she felt she had seen it all. She could see it now: see Lurga come smiling to Luned with the old friendliness back in her voice and face; see Luned, docile as a child, coming with her to the river bank; see Brude waiting, then looming behind her with his great arms and hands outstretched . . .

She paused for a moment before beginning the climb to the postern, pulling her furs tightly round her. The wind flayed her face like a whip. The bulk of Din Pelidr heaved up between her and the clear night sky, pitch-black except for a pin-point of torchlight at the gate and the leaping flames of a bonfire lower down in one of the crofts. Above and around, the sky was washed with moonlight; the stars were sparkling with frosty brilliance.

She suddenly felt that she was looking at Hell far below Heaven. She stared at the cold purity of the stars till her eyes ached. She prayed with all her soul to be taken up to them out of this life, or to be permitted to shut herself away in a house of holy sisters. Anywhere, away from Din Pelidr, from the cruelty and foulness of mankind.

It was indeed a bitter winter.

CHAPTER
9

Spring came at last, though slowly. When the last snows had gone from the moors and the roads were open again, envoys arrived from the king of Cumbria.

They came up the Roman road over the Cheviots, riding slowly to keep their dignity and to show they were not a raiding party. There was time for one of Loth's border guards, racing break-neck across the hills on a sure-footed moorland pony, to give them three days' warning. At once, Din Pelidr buzzed like an overturned hive. Fires were lit in the guest halls, bright tapestries hung round the walls, mattresses and blankets laid out to be aired. Talhaearn the bard hastily altered the ode he was composing in praise of Loth and his invincible warriors into an ode in praise of Urien and his courageous warriors. Luckily, there hadn't been a war with Cumbria during Loth's reign so the words could be sung with good grace.

The kitchens baked, roasted and boiled as if the whole Cumbrian army was coming to besiege them. Loth sent out riders to collect more corn and meat from the surrounding farms. Stocks were low after the winter. More than one child would be belly-pinched and more than one frail old man or woman would die in the little crofts on the plain. No one took much heed of that. The warriors chose their brightest shirts and brought out their gaudiest jewellery—brooches, arm-bands, rings and sword-belts —to receive the visitors with honour. This was all in the name of hospitality but it was for jealousy as well. Cumbria was known to be the richest kingdom of the North. Lothian was eager to show the westerners what royal state really was.

At noon on the third day, while the embassy was reported to be rounding the north of the hills, Loth was walking discontented towards the queen's hall. He was wearing his finest red cloak with the golden fringe. The feast was prepared, the guest chambers warm and ready, the great hall was decked. The silver dinner service was polished and set out on the high table. The envoys would get a welcome suitable in every respect to their rank and Loth's honour.

In every respect but one. When a king's envoys were feasted in a royal hall, the guest cup was offered by the queen. It nagged him like a bad tooth to have to confess that Drostecca was not fit to welcome his guests.

Then it came to him that if they dressed her in her finery—put enough paint on her face and poured enough usquebaugh down her throat—she might keep up well enough to make a decent show at the first night's feast. Once would be sufficient. He could say she was breeding again; that would explain her wan looks and her withdrawal to the women's quarters.

He went hopefully to look at her. One glance told him his plan was useless. She lay shivering and moaning to herself, unaware of him, tossing her head in a tangle of sweat-dank red hair, a trail of bloody spittle at the corner of her mouth. He turned his back on her and went out gloomily.

A door opened at the far end of the passage. A shaft of sunlight came in, and a girl with it. Loth had a glimpse of a tall, lithe figure with a fall of golden hair, before the door closed her into the gloom. For once, his pleasurable interest in a girl's lovely body was dashed with bitterness. Why should he have been chained to two sickly bitches, one after the other, while every slave-girl was bouncing with health? However, this one promised sport.

'Come here.'

The girl started, then came slowly up to him; he saw it was his daughter.

Surprise, pleasure and anger struggled inside him. One of her plaits had come loose, the hair hung gleaming over her shoulder and breast. The fresh air had made her eyes sparkle and touched delicate roses in her cheeks. She was wearing a tunic of thick grey wool, hitched up into a plain leather belt, revealing a pair of clumsy boots made of untreated cow-hide. The boots, and the hem of the tunic, had a generous coating of mud. She was balancing a large trug against one hip; he saw earth on her fingers.

By all the gods, his daughter was a beauty. But, oh gods,

if those high-nosed Cumbrians saw her like this! Anger got the mastery.

'How's this? Don't I keep enough lazy sluts—has Ancarat got to send you to dig up worts for the kitchens?'

'I've only been gathering herbs.' Taniu eyed her father nervously. 'The young leaves are just showing. Ancarat says the maids tear them up like grazing goats.'

Loth was appeased. The healer's art was noble; queens could practise it.

'So Ancarat's teaching you herb-lore?' He sounded jovial, 'Keep to that and you'll grow up a clever woman one day. But put that basket down and come with me. I've got work for you.'

Taniu was speechless with surprise as he went on, 'You know that messengers are coming to greet me from King Urien. They'll be here before sundown and that b— and the queen,' he amended hastily, 'isn't fit to receive them. You'll have to hand the guest cup at the feast.'

He pulled the trug away from her, dropping it carelessly for the maids to find or fall over, and hurried her along to the nursery. Ancarat was nodding by the hearth; Gwalchmai was playing on the floor with his wolfhound puppy.

'Rouse up, old idle-bones!' Loth called out cheerfully, as Ancarat jerked and snorted awake. 'The princess is taking the queen's place at the feast tonight—see she does you credit! Come with me, son,' taking the boy's hand with surprising gentleness. 'When the strangers come, you can sit on Cynon's shoulders and watch me greet them.'

Gwalchmai went off in bliss with the puppy jumping at his heels. Taniu waited for the torrent of scolding for the trouble she was giving. But Ancarat didn't say a cross word. She seemed inspired with a sort of bustling ecstasy. She sent the maids flying to set up a big tub by the hearth and fill it with warm water; then she drove them out and worked on Taniu alone. She stripped her and made her step into the tub while she washed the mud off, then gently bathed and dried every delicate curve of her slender body.

Then she chose new garments from her store chests. Fine white woollen hose, cross-gartered above the knee. Soft green slippers with silver clasps and silver-tipped laces. A shift of finest lawn that hung round Taniu's limbs like summer mist. A long, flowing, tight-sleeved gown of fine wool, dyed with saffron to the golden-yellow of king-cups. Over this, a knee-length tunic of apple-green, with wide sleeves and hem embroidered with gold flag-flowers, silver beads stitched to their petals like drops of dew. Ancarat girdled it with a belt made of silver leaves, catching up one side of the tunic in a graceful drape.

She set Taniu down on a stool, with an abrupt order to keep still and not drag her hem in the hearth-ash. She combed Taniu's hair into a smooth golden stream; then to the girl's surprise, instead of braiding it in two plaits, Ancarat made one thick coil of it, pulling it to the crown of her head.

'What are you doing, Nurse?'

'I'm pinning up your hair. Do you think I'm letting you go into the hall in front of the Cumbrian lords with your hair in two plaits like a cattle-raider's daughter?' She turned to take some silver-headed pins from a box at her side; Taniu thought she heard the muttered words '—even if you are a cattle-raider's daughter!'

When she had woven a golden crown on the top of Taniu's head, she stepped back to admire her handiwork. For the first time, there was a smile on her thin lips. Still she said nothing; she went to the far end of the nursery and unlocked a small chest that stood behind her bed. Taniu had never seen it opened; she supposed it held the trinkets Ancarat had amassed as a price for her spells and cures. The old woman stooped over it and came back carrying an ivory casket, unlocking it with a small key from the bunch at her girdle. Taniu gasped.

Ancarat lifted out a diadem, a circlet of silver filigree rimmed with pearls and set at intervals with square-cut emeralds. It had a cross pendant of pearls in the centre and lappets of pearls on either side, each ending in an emerald and pearl cross. As she fixed the diadem round Taniu's coronet of hair, placed the cross on her brow and arranged the lappets on her shoulders, Ancarat's tongue got loose at last. She was so excited, she sounded drunk.

'Yes, these are your mother's own jewels. She brought them with her from the West, from Alclud. I kept them for her when she got too ill to wear them. Loth never asked me for them after she died. He wouldn't give them to the Pict. *She* wouldn't have let them touch her flesh, anyway, marked with the blessed cross, nasty wicked heathen that she is!'

She clasped a pair of pearl and emerald bracelets on Taniu's wrists.

'Now you really do look like a Christian princess—you look as fine as your mother did when she came here as a bride, before Loth destroyed her!'

Taniu's head jerked round; the pearl lappets clinked.

'Did my father kill my mother?'

'Keep your head still and don't jig about like that! If you get those chains tangled together—'

She was hunting for a ring that would fit Taniu's hand and was trying this one and that one, pulling them from one finger to another as she went on jerkily, between her impatient movements: 'Oh, he was fond of her at first —too fond. He never left her alone, nearly to the end of her time. Mind you, it isn't true that it harms a woman if a man takes her while she's breeding. They do it to the slave-girls and I've never known one of them that was the worse for it, or her child either. But a man usually leaves his own wife to herself at such times, out of respect to the Mothers—I mean Our Blessed Lady. Anyway, a king or a chief can always have another woman while his wife's confined, so he has no cause to complain. But Loth had no appetite for anybody else but her. She was worn out before her labour began, so she couldn't help herself. She was frightened of him, too, and scared of giving birth, so her body fought against it too long—don't clench your fingers like that, how can I fit your rings?'

She looked up crossly and saw Taniu's face. She smiled and patted the girl's hand. 'Don't look so worried, child, it isn't often as bad as that. Your mother was a delicate little thing, as frail as a new-hatched chick. You've got your father's strength—but not his looks, thank God! When your time comes—'

The door curtain was pulled back; one of the queen's women dashed in.

'They've come into the hall! The king's sent to tell the princess to—'

Taniu stood up; the woman broke off, staring. Ancarat gripped Taniu's elbow, talking in her ear as they went down the passage to the queen's hall.

'The steward will be waiting by the women's door to give you the cup. Take it to the man standing nearest the king—he'll be the most important one. You know what to say, you've heard Drostecca enough times. Don't drop the cup and don't trip over your skirt. Hold your head up and speak clearly.'

In the queen's hall a group of bedizened women clustered gossiping by the hearth. They broke off to gaze open-mouthed at Taniu, then fell in behind her in a little procession. Ancarat kept up the flow of instructions into the porch—'and one of the women will be following you with a flagon if the cup needs refilling—'

Taniu stepped out into the mild spring evening. Across the courtyard the women's door seemed about a mile away. She lifted her head, with its crown of plaits and pearls, and walked forward, holding her yellow skirt up out of the dust and stepping carefully.

While Ancarat was preparing Taniu's bath, the Cumbrians were dismounting in front of the great hall. As their horses were led away, they were greeted courteously by Loth, a fair-haired giant in a crimson cloak. After that, they were taken to the guest halls, bright and warm in readiness. Here, their feet were bathed; then they were refreshed with mulled ale and entertained by Loth's harpers until it was time for the feast.

So far, they could not complain of their welcome; there was none of the Roman grace of Caer Luel in this eastern hill-fort but the comfort was lavish.

The great hall was ablaze with hearth-fires and torches that kindled the colours in the hangings and emblazoned shields. The high table was radiant with polished silver. It had been laid out for their admiration so the Cumbrians duly admired it.

'It's Roman stuff,' bragged Loth, glad to show off his luxury to the westerners. He picked up a bowl where Mars and Minerva were presiding over Rome in the form of a she-wolf.

'See here,' he explained, 'the warrior saved the princess from the monster.' He turned the bowl and pointed a thick finger at Venus rising from the sea. 'The Lady of the Lake helped him with her magic.'

Lord Custennin (who had a copy of Ovid's *Fasti* in his well-stocked library in Caer Luel and knew Roman mythology as well as the lives of the saints) murmured politely, taking care not to meet his companions' eyes. The King of Lothian was a gross barbarian, but they'd known that before they set out. Urien didn't want this marriage because of Loth's culture but for his name as a warrior, the strength of his warband and Lothian's place on Cumbria's northeastern flank.

The crudity will have to be taken as part of the dowry, Custennin told himself; then stood transfixed, staring at the tall girl who was walking towards him in a shimmer of gold, green and silver, like sunshine and dew on fresh meadows.

Custennin thought first of Proserpina coming back from the dead with the springtime; but no—this was a British goddess.

' "Her hair was yellower than the blossoming gorse, her skin whiter than foam on the waves. No falcon's gaze was more brilliant than her eyes. Whiter her breasts than the breast of the wild swan, redder her two lips than the reddest foxglove. All who saw her were filled with love." '

He quoted the old story out loud; there was a chorus of approval from the Cumbrians and those Lothian men who were within earshot. At that moment Taniu's cheeks were also redder than the reddest foxglove, but she put her lips to the cup and spoke the ritual words of welcome steadily enough as she presented it to Custennin.

'A welcome before you, lord, to our hall, and rest from your journey at our board and our hearth. Long may you stay to honour us and short may the visit seem to you.'

Lord Custennin bowed over the cup.

'Short and soft the longest journey to such a welcome, lady, and all too short an age would be to enjoy it.'

Taniu bent her pearl-crowned head in thanks. She went with the cup from one to another of the guests; then to Gorthyn and Talhaearn who had a place at the king's table.

Then, as she was not the queen, she took her seat apart among the women. Loth, beaming with family pride, signed for the feast to begin.

Taniu had no idea of the particular interest she held for the Cumbrian envoys; yet if she had deliberately set out to win their approval she could not have done better. She had picked up the notion, among her scraps of Christian ideas, that such feasts were a wicked vanity. No one had told her about a marriage in Cana, and water turned into wine lest a bride should lack her merry-making. Her God was a jealous God. Also, she had always disliked the piggish gluttony of Loth's hospitality—yet her kindheartedness would not let her neglect her visitors' comfort. The tug of these two feelings showed outwardly as an aloof graciousness that would not have been out of place in the Emperor's court at Constantinople.

As the feast went on, Custennin met the eyes of one and another of his party, each time with an imperceptible nod. She would do very well for their prince.

Nothing was said on the first night, of course, about the purpose of their visit. Only once did the talk come to a dangerous edge. Loth mentioned the Cumbrians' journey, asking how easy they had found it; he added laughing, '—but your people have always been quick enough coming over the Long Hills.'

It was clear he meant Catraeth.

Smiling thinly, Lord Custennin remarked that King Urien had no intention of welcoming Angles from Deira at the gates of Caer Luel. He decided to take the opening Loth had given him and went on, 'King Urien came east that time to face his enemies. He'd be much happier to come and meet his own countrymen. He knows there are great British kingdoms in the East, already linked with ties of blood. If the West joined its strength to the East, why shouldn't we win more victories than Arthur?'

'So that's it,' said Loth, meaning: *So that's why you're here*! 'Well, if "*ties of blood*" means Morcant of Eidyn, your king can save his sweat. He'll never follow where another man leads except to look for a good place to put his dagger in.'

His small, bloodshot eyes looked shrewdly at Custennin. 'You think that's the usual family spite, don't you? I

101

love Morcant as little as he loves me. But that's not the whole of it though. Morcant'll never be easy if he thinks he's in second place.'

He stared thoughtfully at his goblet. 'If your king wants to get his plan working, he'd do better to put Morcant at the head of another campaign where the honour and spoils will be all for him. Get him to hold the Picts off. They'll likely come in at your back if you're fighting the Angles.'

Custennin stored this up for Urien. Loth might be illiterate but he was no fool about war. In battle his body thought for him; he was inspired.

The feasting part of the night was over; it was time for carousing and bards' songs. Taniu rose and led her reluctant train of women out of the hall. Custennin sighed regretfully to see her go, then concentrated on his next two objectives: not to show boredom and not to get talking drunk.

The curtain was not quite drawn over the queen's door; the light lay across Taniu's path like a burning spear. Beyond it, Lurga beckoned to her; she hurried in, thinking the woman needed help with Drostecca.

The queen was propped up on her cushions. She seemed to be better, for she was smiling, though her eyes were burning her face.

'Did you enjoy the feast?' she whispered huskily. 'Did the meat taste richer—was the wine sweeter—when you sat in my place?'

Taniu pitied her.

'I didn't take your place, queen. I only went to the hall because my father ordered me to give the guest cup. I sat with the women.'

Drostecca's mouth twisted. 'A dutiful daughter. So you sat with Loth's women on Loth's orders. What else would you do for your father if he ordered you—if he wanted a son by a royal woman, not one of his sluts?'

She was hissing as if the snakes tattooed on her skin had given all their tongues to her. As Taniu recoiled in horror, she reared herself to strike but fell back weakly; her hands clawed the air between them.

'You think my hands can't reach you—but I've got some that can! Make yourself the seed-bed for an heir to Lothian and you'll die before you come to harvest.'

She started to laugh but the coughing took her. After an appalled moment, Taniu turned and went blindly towards the nursery. She was sick and shivering; Ancarat scolded her for taking too much wine when she wasn't used to it.

Lurga cradled her mistress, stroking the lank hair.

'Don't make yourself unhappy about that girl, dearest. She counts for nothing—she's soft and cold like the last snow in a thaw. Besides, she'll never have a man, or a child. She's vowed her body to their White Christ—the women told me.'

Drostecca frowned. 'Why should she do that—she's not a warrior-woman?'

She twisted up restlessly but fell back moaning into Lurga's arms. 'Oh, if I only had my strength! I'd have Loth back, slavering for me. And I'd clear that girl out of my path, as I did the other one. But my life's burning away—'

Lurga caught her to her breast.

'Don't say it, my heart's darling! Your strength'll come back again with the summer sun.'

Drostecca shook her head. 'I'm going to the Mothers. And that girl's the Royal Woman of Lothian. She'll bear an heir to Loth or some other lord—and destroy my Gwalchmai—my flesh—and I not here to stop her—'

'*Never!*' Lurga's face was white with pain. 'By the breasts we sucked, while I live, you'll live in my body—it's yours!' She kissed her foster-sister. 'I'll go to the shrine and make the offering for you. The Lothian girl had better keep her vow to the Nailed God. If her womb kindles, she'll bear her own death!'

Drostecca stared hungrily into Lurga's eyes.

'And death to the seed. And to the sower. Swear it to me, by the Mothers.'

'By the Cup and the Water and the Blood, I swear it.'

CHAPTER
10

It was the last feast. The Cumbrians had thanked Loth for their welcome; Loth had given his good wishes for the journey. Then, as he had expected, the Cumbrians made a formal proposal to keep up the goodwill they had created. King Urien wanted friendship and an alliance with Lothian, sealed by the hand of the fair princess Taniu as bride for his heir.

Loth just managed to hold on to his pride in front of the Cumbrians and accept the offer with decent calm. Custennin opened a casket of what he called a few simple trinkets as a gift for the princess. Loth took the jewels in her name and told them she would come herself in the morning to send her greetings to her bridegroom.

Then he swallowed his rejoicing in great draughts of mead and ale; but even after he had been assisted, staggering, to his bed his mind was busy.

With Cumbria at my back, I won't need the Pictish alliance —that means I don't need that shivering bag of bones in the queen's hall. If she doesn't make haste and die, I'll put a pillow over her face the next time she opens her mouth to me.

He fell asleep on this pleasant thought and woke early in the morning clear-headed enough to remember it. After he had doused his face in cold water, he decided to go himself to tell Taniu her good fortune. He was in high good humour with her; he wanted to see her joy.

Dawn had broken but there were torches burning in the queen's room and the sound of violent coughing. He hurried past to the nursery. Here there was the grey light of morning and grey ash on the hearth. Ancarat's mattress was bare; she would be with Drostecca. Gwalchmai was rolled up in his box bed; Taniu's pallet was nearby. He knelt by her side grasping her shoulders.

'Wake up!'

She woke, startled, and sat up, grey eyes wide, golden hair flowing past her white, rose-tipped breasts. *This is how that prince of Cumbria will see her on her wedding night,* thought Loth, with a pang of envy that he had nothing so fair in his own bed.

'Is the queen worse?'

He smiled. 'No, all's well, my girl. I've got great news for you. King Urien wants you for his son. You must come to the hall to speak to the envoys and send your greetings to the prince.'

'No.'

'*What*?' Then he laughed. A woman's vanity was the strongest feeling she had; it meant more to all of them than their profit, even their lust. 'Not now! You're to come in just before they leave—you've got hours to get into your finery, I'll send Ancarat to you.'

'No. I can't come.'

'What's the matter? Has your monthly bleeding started?' She shook her head; she was very pale.

'Are you ill? You've picked a good time for it! I don't want the Cumbrians thinking you're sickly, like your mother. Get Nurse to give you a draught and put some paint on your face.'

'I'm not sick. I don't mean to marry.'

'Have you gone mad? I've got you the finest match in Britain. Are you waiting for the Emperor to send for you, from Constantinople? What more do you want?'

'I want to keep my maidenhead—to be a holy sister. The monk said I was to be like the Lady Mary Virgin—'

He caught his breath. He gripped her arms above the elbows and pulled her face close to his.

'Have you taken vows? Did he get you to make vows? I'll burn Mailros to the ground and every monk in it—'

She shook her head. 'No, he wouldn't, till you gave your consent.'

'Well, he'll die of old age before he gets it—and you can't keep your maidenhead. I've a use for it. Your maidenhead's my pact with Cumbria.' He grinned. 'Their prince is all ready to stamp his seal on it. Now, get up and get ready.'

'No.'

He shook her till her neck felt like breaking; then threw her down half-suffocated. He wanted to knock the nonsense out of her there and then; but if he marked her, how could he show her to the Cumbrians? And what could he say to them when she didn't appear?

He went to the two he trusted most: Gorthyn for loyalty, Talhaearn for bard's wisdom.

'Beat her,' said Gorthyn simply. 'If any girl of mine defied me, I'd have her into a lump of bloody pulp.'

'Gods, I want to! I'd like to smash her stubborn head against the wall. But I can't see the Prince of Cumbria eager to take a lump of bloody pulp to bed.'

It was Talhaearn who thought of the pretext; Loth sent him first to try it on the Cumbrians. He came to them in the guest hall, making their last preparations for leave-taking. He was in his bardic robes, remote, awesome and holy, come to give them his blessing for the journey.

The Cumbrians bowed. Talhaearn judged he had created the right mood, and began his tale.

The king had gone that morning to tell the princess of the noble marriage that was offered to her. The princess was overjoyed; she said she was proud to be chosen. But her nurse—who had come with her mother at the time of her marriage—had been disturbed. She told them that when the princess was born, her mother, in the agonies of labour, fearing death was on her, had cried out that if she lived and bore a living child, she would devote it to God.

'And did she make such a vow before a priest?' asked Custennin sharply. 'Or on a cross? Or relics?'

The old nurse could not say. The queen had made no vow while she was present; but had been alone with her confessor soon after the birth.

'Send for the priest then. Let him confirm or deny the story.'

The priest had come with Queen Languoreth from Strathclyde and left Lothian within a year. Certainly, messengers would be sent at once to find him. He had been planning a pilgrimage to Rome and the Holy Land but would surely have returned by now, if he lived.

The Cumbrians were watching Talhaearn narrowly, combing his words for an insult, ready to be mortally offended. The bard said gently that it was only an old woman's story, hardly worth a man's notice. But the king had insisted the Cumbrians should be told. If the story should be true there might, to Christians, be some doubt about the validity of the marriage.

Indeed there might. Remembering the troubles that had fallen upon Gwynedd and the North when the Church condemned Maelgwn, the Cumbrians shuddered. They could see no reason why Talhaearn should be lying and decided to believe him.

When they saw the king in the great hall for their leave-taking, their last suspicions faded. Loth, disappointed and angry, repeatedly breaking out into abuse of women's mindless whims, was clearly not acting. Looking at his purple face and furious eyes, the Cumbrians could easily understand why his Christian queen had kept her vow to herself—if she had really made one.

'That such a—a—womanish cobweb should hold two kings back from a treaty!'

'There's nothing holding us back from a treaty,' said Custennin politely. 'And it's no great harm that the marriage should be delayed for a little—they're both very young.'

'Just as soon as the priest can be found—' muttered Loth.

'If he can't be found—or if he's found and confirms the vow, it shouldn't be hard to get a dispensation. The girl didn't know about her mother's intention or give her own consent.'

Loth made a choking sound.

'The princess is heart-broken,' put in Talhaearn smoothly. 'She was so shocked she took to her bed—she couldn't face our guests.'

'I'm truly sorry our proposal should have upset her, even for a moment.'

'Here are the jewels your king sent to my daughter.' Loth spoke with some dignity. 'I regret she can't accept them.'

'I hope the princess will be kind enough to take them as a little token of our gratitude for her welcome. May they be the first heralds of a happy union.' Custennin paused, choosing his words carefully. 'But in case that never happens—if your daughter should prove to be the bride of Christ and our prince must seek a wife elsewhere—then it

107

would be better both for him and the girl if nothing is said abroad about this matter.'

Loth gratefully agreed and the visitors took their leave, not dissatisfied with their mission. He watched them ride out of the courtyard, then strode purposefully towards the queen's hall.

Taniu knew that Loth would be on her in fury as soon as the guests were out of sight. When the threat of marriage had first loomed over her, startled from sleep in her naked bed and ordered to accept the Cumbrian prince, she had not been able to do anything more than refuse, like a stubborn child. The refusal, however, had come from the roots of her being.

The words 'Prince of Cumbria' meant nothing to her. She didn't want to think about this stranger; when a picture came to her mind with the title, she saw someone like Loth or Morien. Someone coming drunk to her bed and taking her like a bull with a cow. Someone whoring with her maidservants, pouring foul abuse on her in childbed if she miscarried or bore a girl.

At times since the Cumbrians' arrival, listening to their soft western voices, noting Lord Custennin's finely-cut features and gracious manners, she recalled the young hunter from Argoed Llwyfain who had promised to come for her in the spring. Strangely, she had dreamed last night that she saw him, leaning on his spear at the far side of the stream in their moorland hollow. He looked eager and longing, his lips moved but she couldn't hear what he was saying. He stretched his arm across the water to reach her—then she had wakened in Loth's grip.

She tried to shut her mind to these thoughts of Owain, as a vanity that had passed out of her life, a wickedness even in memory. Now, as she dressed, she took time to collect her forces, preparing for the struggle with some of Loth's own fighting spirit.

He found her fresh and neat, playing with Gwalchmai and his puppy. His own temper was easier, with the alliance safe for a while and time gained. He was able to face her calmly without alarming his son.

'Come here, Taniu, I want to speak to you.'

108

He led the way into one of the store-closets; only when the heavy oak door shut behind them did he grab her plaits and pull her towards him.

'Now, my girl, what do you mean by defying me? Making me look a fool in front of the Cumbrians!'

'I don't want to defy you, Father.' She looked at him pleadingly. 'I've a vocation for the religious life. I want to go into a sisterhood.'

'Well, you can't go into a sisterhood. Cumbria wants you. I want the Cumbrian alliance. So you're going to marry King Urien's son and put Lothian blood into the Cumbrian royal line.'

'Father, I can't!'

'Why can't you? You've got a womb and breasts, haven't you, like any other woman? The prince'll see to the rest.'

He saw her flush, and laughed. Then he gave her hair a cruel tug; she felt as if her scalp had been ripped.

'I've had enough of this nonsense. I'll hear no more of your "*can'ts*" and your "*won'ts*". You'll do what I say, my daughter, and I say you'll go to Cumbria and marry the king's son if I have to tie you on a horse and drag you to the priest.'

'You can't make me say the words. It's no marriage if I don't take the vows and you couldn't make me open my mouth!'

He twisted her arm behind her so savagely that she shrieked.

'So I can't make you open your mouth? When I've finished with you, you won't be able to shut it. I'll knock every tooth out of your head! I'll smash your stubborn jaw!'

Taniu imagined the face of the Cumbrian prince, confronted with this vision of bridal loveliness. In spite of her pain she screamed with laughter. Loth guessed her thoughts; he threw her down and kicked her.

'I'll kill you!'

'Do! Set me free of you for ever! Do you think I care?'

He started towards her in a red fury, but made a supreme effort and flung himself out of the room. If he wanted this marriage, he couldn't kill her and he couldn't mark her. The cunning little bitch had the mastery.

He sent Ancarat to her. The old woman came hurrying to

the store-room where Taniu was still lying on the floor, breathless and aching. She pulled the girl up on to a wooden chest, smoothing her hair and dress, grumbling and coaxing all at once.

'Stupid child! What are you making all this fuss about? You'll never have a better offer. You'll live in a great city and one day you'll be a queen. Think of that!'

'I have thought of it.' Taniu sounded weary to death. 'I swear to you, Nurse, I'll let the king tie me to one of the standing stones on the moor and leave me to the wolves and ravens, but I'll die a pure virgin. *I'll die* before I let a man have my body!'

Ancarat looked sharply at her. Then she put her hand on Taniu's arm, speaking urgently but in a softer tone.

'You needn't think it's like this everywhere. Don't be afraid you'll end up like Drostecca—or Luned.'

'Or my mother.'

'What do you know about marriage? You've only seen Loth's spearmen like dogs going after bitches. The lords in Caer Luel—they know how to treat women properly. And they've got great pools of hot water—they wash every day and put on clean linen! You take my word—do what your father wants and you'll live happily ever after!'

She led Taniu back to the nursery. It was empty; Gwalchmai had taken his puppy out. Ancarat settled her by the fire; she was white and chilled. Then she went to Loth.

'It's my belief she's scared of marrying. As well she might be, remembering what happened to her mother. It's no good raging at her, she'll only think that's how her husband'll treat her.'

Loth came back, making an effort to sound gentle and fatherly.

'I'm sorry I lost my temper.' He patted her shoulder. 'I've all the cares of the kingdom on my back, it's a heavy burden. You're a grown woman—well past fourteen now, aren't you? I've a right to expect you to help me.'

He pulled a stool across and sat opposite. She could not help shrinking away; he noted that for all her bold words she was scared. It helped his temper, made him sure she was ready to answer the bridle.

'I'm not just thinking of myself.' He looked virtuous. 'I

need every ally I can find. Morcant's got his greedy eyes on Lothian—he'd have his greedy hands on it too if he found a safe chance. What do you think will happen to Gwalchmai if I die before he's a man? You love him, don't you? You could win him a powerful protector—the strongest in Britain.'

He saw that this disturbed her. One more effort and she'd come round. 'But I wouldn't sacrifice *you*,' he said tenderly. 'If it was some grizzled old widower with an eye or an arm missing from the wars, I wouldn't give my little girl to anyone like that, if he was Arthur back from the grave. This prince is young, and surely good-looking. King Urien is a fine man and Queen Modron was famous for her beauty.'

Taniu still said nothing. Loth opened the jewel casket that Custennin had left. 'Look what he sent you.' He picked out a chain of amethysts and gold. 'It's for your betrothal. I should have given it back, but they made me keep it as a gift for you. There's generosity!'

Taniu sighed, remembering the monk's words. She gently put aside the amethysts that Loth was dangling on her breast.

'This is all vanity. How would these jewels look in my grave, lying on my rotting flesh?'

Loth stared at her. She struggled to reach him. It was part of his pride as a warrior-king that he always kept his word. Surely he would want his daughter to keep hers? She had to make him know she was in earnest.

'Do believe me. Rather than be queen in Caer Luel, I'd gladly work in a barn or a cattle-byre if I could only keep my maidenhead.'

Her father guffawed. 'Easy words! You don't know what work is. I've never heard a dairymaid or a fieldwoman talking like that. Ask them. I'll have some of them in here to you, to tell you if they'd be queen in Caer Luel for the price of a maidenhead!'

At that moment the plan came to him, beautiful in its simplicity, by which he could trap her in her own words. He believed she was an honest girl, as women went; she wouldn't go back on herself as easy as most. He jumped to his feet and strode out. Taniu's head dropped to her knees.

She felt battered. When one of the women came to tell her that her father wanted to speak to her in the queen's hall, she dragged herself up, bracing herself for the next onslaught.

The outer door of the hall was open to the porch. Her father was standing at the entry, in talk with a stockily-built man dressed like a well-to-do farmer.

'—hard for you since your wife died,' Loth was saying.

'It is very hard to keep the house, lord.'

As Taniu came up, she recognized the man who had been at the preaching, who had smiled and made way for her. It was Hoel, the royal swineherd, come with fresh supplies for the depleted larder after the Cumbrian embassy.

'I can do my own work well enough, with the two slaves. But at home there's the cooking-pot to tend and my little ones to see to, besides the cows and chickens. And there's not a farm within miles where I can get a woman to give me a hand for more than a day or two. So if you'll give me a strong girl out of the kitchens, lord, it'd be a boon to me.'

He saw Taniu behind Loth's shoulder and sketched out a clumsy bow. Her father swung round and gave her a ferocious smile under hard eyes.

'Well, my girl,' he said jovially, 'have you thought better of your good luck?'

'I can't think better than the best.' Her voice pleaded with Loth not to degrade them both by an ugly quarrel in front of one of his peasants. 'I've already made my choice. I want to take the veil.'

'Yes, you told me.' Loth still had his grin of secret triumph. '"*Rather than be a queen in Caer Luel, you'd happily work in a barn or a cattle-byre if you could only keep your maidenhead.*" That's so?'

She bowed her head.

'And I said you didn't know what you were talking about. So now you can find out. Hoel, here, wants a slave-girl out of the kitchens to keep his house. Well, you're free to choose. Either you agree to marry the Prince of Cumbria, and with a good grace, mind, because it's *your choice*—or you can go and work for Hoel. Now, what do you want?'

She stood in frozen silence. She could hardly believe Loth would do this; not that she trusted in his fatherly love, but that he should be willing to shame himself through her. She searched his eyes and realized why. He had no doubt of her yielding. But the threat meant less to her than to most palace-bred girls. She had been brooding over martyrdom; she had worked herself up to make a grand sacrifice for her faith. This was hardly a sacrifice at all. She had been happy at Nia's farm. She respected shepherds like Cadwal, or craftsmen like Selyf, more than the young nobles in the great hall.

'Very well, Father, I'll go with the swineherd.'

Loth nearly choked. His face went red, the veins in his forehead and neck swelled.

'You think I don't mean it!'

'As you will, Father.'

'You insolent little slut! You think you can defy me now out of a soft bed and a full stomach. You'll be singing a lower tune by the autumn.'

He clenched his fist as if he were going to smash it into her face but pulled back. Gripping his belt, he said hoarsely, 'You're best out of my sight!'

Then turning to Hoel he spoke more calmly, as if the matter were an everyday affair. 'Well, Hoel, you wanted a strong, handy girl, here's one for you. Mind you work her hard and long. You have my leave to strike her, but don't mark her or break her skin—or break anything else of hers, d'you hear? No tampering, or I'll have you flayed!'

He turned to his daughter again but stared across her without meeting her eyes. 'I'll send to you when the Lammas fires have burned. I'll put the same question —you'll have had time to think of the right answer. Now, get out!'

He strode away from them, out of the women's quarters towards the great hall. Taniu and Hoel stared at each other. They heard Drostecca's persistent cough; a woman called for something at the end of the passage; pigeons rose with a clatter from the orchard. Then Hoel turned to go. Taniu followed him. In the porch he stopped.

'Take my cloak. Folk would stare to see us together. Best keep this as quiet as may be.'

She said nothing; standing still as he pulled off his heavy felted cape and wrapped it carefully round her, drawing

113

the hood gently over her bowed head, smoothing back a tendril of hair he had ruffled. His hands were big and calloused but touched her delicately. The cloak was well made, of good quality wool, though like everything of Hoel's it smelt faintly of pig. She clutched it round her, following him to the courtyard where he had left his pony and cart. He put his hands to her waist to lift her in.

'Don't be afraid of me, princess. I'm a Christian like yourself. I honour you for your vow of chastity.'

There were few people about in the township. Nobody, even the gate-guards, had a curious look for them: Hoel the swineherd going back to his steading, giving some farm woman a lift.

A trader was coming up the slope, making for the fortress, riding ahead of the string of pack-ponies. Three couple of Irish wolfhounds loped beside him; two hired spearmen brought up the rear. The trader led his ponies off the path to let the cart come by. Taniu, huddling in her cloak, got a glimpse of tight curly black hair and beard, a pair of bright eyes like jet beads. The eyes darted across the cart and up to Din Pelidr with a look of total unconcern. A peasant farmer and his woman on their way home from the royal township. The eyes noted a slipper of fine green leather with silver-tipped laces under the hem of the woman's cloak; a gleam of silver-braided plait under the rim of her hood.

Hoel rounded the western shoulder of Din Pelidr. The cart splashed across the ford, then picked up the track beside the river, turning southwest towards the forest under the Moorfoot hills.

CHAPTER
11

Taniu relaxed a little once the cart was well away from Din Pelidr. She became aware of the sunlight, larks singing invisible in the high blue sky, the fresh breeze off the sea, the warmth and sweat-smells from Hoel's sturdy body

114

beside her, the brown hairs on his strong arms guiding the reins.

Hoel needed to spare his pony and kept him to a walk. The sun was westering as they drew near to the skirts of the forest, where great oaks and beeches gave mast for Loth's herds of half-wild swine. It had been a silent journey for the most part; Hoel was a quiet man, Taniu was absorbed in her own thoughts.

The steading was not in the depths of the forest; it stood in a wide glade bordered by a stream that ran eastwards to join the river. The royal swineherd was a man of some standing in the kingdom; he had a big, well-built living-hut with a cluster of roomy sheds and barns inside the stockade. It was like enough to Nia's farm to give Taniu almost a sense of home-coming as they drove in. The pony halted of his own accord; Hoel helped her down from the cart. She followed him into the hut still clutching his cloak round her. A shock-headed woman looked up from stirring the cauldron; two little girls made a rush towards Hoel, saw Taniu and drew back, watching her with their thumbs in their mouths.

'Go and unharness the pony, Indeg.' Hoel spoke hurriedly. 'I'll come and help you with the cart in a minute.'

The woman went out, giving Taniu a broad stare as she passed. Hoel went to one of the bed-places behind the roof-posts and opened a wooden chest.

'My wife's clothes are in here. You'd do better to wear them while you stay.'

He came back to Taniu and looked straight at her. 'I borrowed that woman from the farm along the river. She'll go back tomorrow; I promised I'd send her home if the king gave me a housekeeper. Best she shouldn't have too much to talk about.'

He went quickly past her out of the hut. Taniu looked into the chest and pulled out a straight garment of thick russet wool; it seemed to be clean. Quickly she slipped off her green gown, folded it and laid it away. She flung on the russet dress; groping among the other clothes, she found a leather belt to gird it. The little girls were peeping at her from behind one of the roof-posts; their eyes were round as owls' while the newcomer unbound the ribbons from her

115

plaits and hid her silver head-circlet in the chest. At the bottom was a pair of foot-gear, shapeless bags of hide with leather thongs, but stout and comfortable. Her green and silver slippers went back in their place. She was sitting on the chest, rebraiding her hair when Indeg and Hoel came back.

In the storms of the morning she had forgotten her appetite but the smell from the cauldron brought it back. Indeg served their portions in wooden bowls: pork stew with barley, huge chunks of barley bread and mugs of ale. The children crept to their places by the hearth, still staring and keeping close to their father. Taniu didn't force their notice but smiled at them whenever she caught their eyes. At first they looked away and the smaller one, Eirlys, ducked her head against her father's thigh. Little by little, though, they edged nearer; by the time the meal was over, lively brown Collen had scrambled on to her lap; the paler, shyer little sister was crouching against her shin stroking the end of one of her plaits. Hoel looked across at her with quiet pleasure; Indeg was a little sulky. She had been hoping that Hoel would keep her as his woman. She scowled when Collen and Eirlys insisted on sharing Taniu's bed.

While Indeg was there Taniu would not try to meddle with her work. However, Indeg left the next morning to walk the nine miles to her master's farm. Taniu at once set about learning the ways of the place where she was now the woman of the house. Hoel watched her closely for the first day or two, then went back to his herds of swine with a quiet mind. Taniu settled in easily enough, remembering how Nia and Leucu had done things. As her days passed in the simple, lovely rituals of common life—milking, baking, collecting eggs with Collen and Eirlys, serving out food at the hearth—the wounds she had suffered in Din Pelidr began to heal. The little girls had fallen in love with her and were hardly ever out of her sight during the day. Bold Collen would scamper round her, laughing and chattering about everything she saw. Eirlys stayed as close as her shadow, either holding her hand or clutching her skirt as if she were afraid Taniu might vanish as strangely as she had come.

Hoel was often away for days and nights at a time; he and the slaves had a summer bothy of wattles deep in the forest. When he was in the living-hut for the evening meal he said very little but watched Taniu, listening contentedly to the stories she told his daughters. He had hung curtains of hide round the bed-place she shared with his children and slept at the far side of the hut. She had never been afraid of Hoel; now she was living under his roof she took great comfort from his calm strength.

Her only cause of fear was a dread of being snatched away from her homely refuge back to Din Pelidr; but as the spring days lengthened into summer, that fear was forgotten like last winter's frost. She had always wished that she could have been a daughter in a home like Leucu's—and here she was! Something would surely happen to save her from the palace in Caer Luel and marriage to the Cumbrian prince.

CHAPTER
12

There was no pleasing Owain after the envoys returned from Lothian. Under his father's stern gaze he listened quietly to the news that his betrothal must be delayed, perhaps for a year. He even achieved the outward signs of respectful listening, while the old men of the Council agreed with each other about the wisdom of not taking a young bride too soon. Inwardly he was raging with impatience. He was sure that matters would have been different if he had headed the embassy.

He went to Lady Guendolena, who was willing and grateful to have more to do in bed than her elderly husband ever asked of her. But she was not in her first youth; not all the paint she used could hide the folds in her neck or the faint crowsfeet under her eyes. With the memory of Taniu's lithe body always behind his eyes, Guendolena faded like an autumn leaf. He parted courteously from her, rode back to Petriana and took up his weapon-training with passionate concentration.

Twice he came down to Caer Luel under cover of night with a wild group to enjoy the delights offered by the naked nymphs of the Golden Lily. There was one girl, the bastard of a Biscayan seaman, that he picked out for himself. She was small, dark and so hotly avid that for a short while he was able to dull his hunger for Taniu. Not for long.

On his second visit he pulled his girl from the drinking hall up to her cubicle and threw himself on her like a famished wolf. She responded with squeals and wriggles of delight; when at last he slackened, she whispered exciting obscenities and used all her skill with hands, mouth and tongue to rouse him again.

Sleep came; he was back in Argoed Llwyfain, in the sunny hollow on the moors. Taniu was standing on the other side of the stream where it poured over the lip of the cliff. She was looking away from him; though he called her name she did not hear. The stream swelled and deepened—there must have been a cloudburst over its headwaters up in the hills. It was lapping round Taniu's feet but she did not stir. He screamed a warning and started across to her but the waters came down in a deluge and she was swept away out of his reach.

He woke gasping and sweating, with his heart beating like a smith's hammer. In a moment or two he was back in the brothel room, on the pallet with the girl. She was lying asprawl, her legs wide. Under the violet oil she used lavishly, she smelt rank like a vixen.

Owain dressed quietly, stepped cat-footed downstairs and exchanged a word of farewell with the bawd, drowsing over her wine-cup. He went down to the Idon, stripped, plunged and swam till he felt clean.

He did not go back to the Golden Lily, though his comrades-in-arms often wished him there, or further. The demon of longing inside him gave him no rest. He would meet one or other of them in sword-play, attacking as fiercely as if he wanted to take the man's life. Then, after nearly killing his wretched opponent and goading him to the point of doing murder in return, Owain would lose interest, toss his weapon to one of the armourers and walk off the practice field.

Even Madog, his armour-bearer and devoted worshipper, felt his patience starting to fray. When Owain took Milain, his peregrine falcon, on his wrist one morning and called him to come hawking on Idon's sea-marsh, Madog twisted his mouth sourly at the groom. He expected to be back in Caer Luel within the hour.

That day, however, Owain kept his purpose and his temper. The soft, brisk air, the shimmering marshes, the tang of salt and seaweed, the glory of his great falcon soaring and stooping against the blue, lifted his spirits. The sunset light was coming up the estuary with the tide when he dismissed his attendants to return the falcons to the mews. He did not follow them, but still sat his horse, gazing out across the estuary. Madog waited a pace or two behind, resigned to the next whim but lazily content.

The water was still far out; Merin Rheged was a vast tract of sand cut here and there by narrow channels. A child could walk across at such times. Owain's eyes were fixed on the opposite shore. A secret land it looked, a tangle of wild hills slashed by river glens coming down to a deeply indented coast. Even the Romans had left the hills alone. Now it was a patchwork of little lordships, whose chiefs paid a scanty tribute to Strathclyde or Cumbria, whichever kingdom was nearer to extort it. The land was poor; its folk sparse and little thought of, either as useful or menacing.

Yet, as Owain looked at the darkening shore and the silent hills, he felt a sudden cold tension, as if the land had sent out a threat. Who really knew what was lurking in those hidden valleys? In the great Barbarian War, nearly two hundred years ago, the northern Picts had joined with the Irish and with the Angles from over the Eastern sea; the Wall had been overrun. Had all those outlanders gone back to their homes in the north or oversea? Some of the Frisian troops from Aballava had deserted and joined their Anglian kinsmen in the looting. What had become of them? Were their descendants still worshipping Woden and Thunor just beyond the horizon? Would the blood-red tide flow south again over the defences of Cumbria?

Seren, chilly and impatient, stamped and snorted. Owain was brought quickly back to his own side of Merin Rheged again. Madog was whistling softly. He clapped

Seren's neck and swung him round. 'Come on, lad! I'll get you supper at the Star and Anchor!'

It was dark when they came to the harbour township. The fishing boats were all beached; there was only one trading ship waiting for the tide. Lights streamed from the quayside inn; there was a hum of voices from inside and a savoury smell of cooking. The inn was bright, hot and smoky with firelight and candles. There was a good number of sailors and shorefolk on the benches. Owain noticed one man whom he guessed to be the trader, a dark man with curly black hair and eyes like jet beads. He had supped; his lips were greasy and he was swallowing a last mouthful.

In spite of the crowd the place was quiet; it was too early for anyone to be drunk. Finnuala, the Irish tavern-woman, was frying black puddings at a glowing charcoal stove. Her thick blue-black hair was pulled back from her face; sweat was running down her neck; her shift was clinging to her wide buttocks. She took Owain's order with a radiant smile; her hospitality was as famous as her cooking. Most of the merchants and ships' captains along the coast had cast anchor between her friendly thighs.

When she had seen Owain and Madog plentifully supplied, she sat down opposite the trader, with a special twinkle for him that showed remembered intimacy. He poured mead for her; after she had drunk, she grinned at him.

'It's very dull here tonight. Isag, you're a merchant and walk the world. Have you picked up a story for us on your travels?'

'Did I ever tell you the story of *The Princess and the Swineherd*?'

'No indeed, and it's a strange name for a story. What would a princess be doing with a swineherd?'

'Listen then, and I'll tell you.'

The room went quiet as everyone turned and craned. The servant girls perched themselves on table edges or customers' laps. Isag fixed his beady eyes on Owain's face.

'Once upon a time there was a Princess of the East Lands. Her hair was as yellow as gorse; her breasts were whiter than swans' feathers and her eyes were grey like lakes in starlight.'

Owain stopped eating. The black eyes stared into his.

'She was so fair that the King of the West Lands asked for her as his son's bride. But a witch-woman put a spell of cold enchantment on the princess so that she turned against all love.'

Finnuala and the tavern girls sighed for pity of such a terrible fate.

'Her father was angry. He gave the princess a choice: she could either wed the prince or go as bondmaid to his swineherd. So strong and icy was the spell that held her, she chose to be the swineherd's servant. Early one morning he took her away. No one saw her go but a poor pedlar—'

The story rambled on through various magical complications but Owain heard no more of it. His mind was struggling with the suspicion that this man was trying to tell him something about Taniu, so mad and shameful that it could not possibly be true. But why had Isag described her so clearly that he could see her in front of him? And why had he looked so full of meaning?

At last Isag's tale came to an end; his audience clamoured for another one; Finnuala even mentioned free mead. Isag regretfully said no, the tide would be near the flood; he must go.

'I'll see you sail.' Owain got up quickly, signing to Madog to stay where he was. He followed the trader closely to the door amid everyone's good wishes. Outside, it was full dark; a light gleamed down by the quay where Isag's men were loading his cargo. Owain drew him under the deserted arcade, gripping his shirt at the neck.

'What do you know—what have they done to her?'

'I don't know much more than I've already told you. She's sworn an oath not to marry, so Loth gave her to his swineherd. I saw her go.'

'If Loth enjoys putting shame on his own family,' said Owain furiously, but more to himself than Isag, 'he needn't think he can shame us! Does Lothian think we pick our brides—or our allies—out of their pigsties?'

121

'Lothian knows nothing about it. Loth has done all he can to see no word leaks out. The story is that she's gone to stay with her mother's foster-sister, to be out of sight of men till they're sure she isn't a vowed nun.'

He grinned. 'It's a good story and I might never have heard otherwise if Loth kept no women in his court. But I'd seen a silver-braided plait and a silver-trimmed slipper under a peasant's cloak, so of course I asked questions. There's a girl who works in Loth's kitchens—' he chuckled reminiscently—'a fat girl, it does you good to hear her laugh. She sleeps with one of Loth's spearmen, who sleeps with one of the queen's women. She told him about the terrible quarrel Loth had with his daughter, shouting that he'd drag her to Caer Luel tied to her horse. And the princess said nobody could make her take the marriage oath and she'd keep her virginity if she died for it. *"Rather than be queen in Caer Luel, I'd gladly work in a barn or a cattle-byre if I could only keep my maidenhead."* Those were her very words. The woman said she couldn't get them out of her mind, she thought the princess must have been bewitched to call down such a dreadful fate on herself. Then Loth swore he'd give her to the prince or to his swineherd. And she chose the swineherd. The woman said Loth was like a madman after, and he'd kill her if he knew she'd heard and told. But she told for all that—a woman always does.'

Owain listened, stunned. One of Isag's men gave an urgent whistle from the quay.

'I must go, lord.'

Owain began to pull off one of his rings; Isag stepped back.

'No. Cumbria keeps the peace for traders like me to pass in safety. I wouldn't like to see Cumbria cheated. I've only paid a small part of a great debt. Farewell, lord.'

He hurried down to the quayside. Owain stared after him and stood so, long after the ship had gone with the tide.

CHAPTER
13

Thinking of Taniu kept Owain awake all night. Isag's account of her behaviour did not fit with the warm, golden girl he had met in Argoed Llwyfain, who had shared danger and laughter with him, who had promised him a welcome in the spring.

Owain had always found women delightful creatures, as sweet as harp music, as warming as good wine and even more interesting to manage than his falcons or his horses. But Taniu was different; if she refused him now, it was not because she was one of those girls who run like hares in order to be hunted down and caught. She was too honest; also, she had pride and a temper too. That was why he had decided to have her for his wife and future queen as well as his lover. So her refusal would be a real refusal—and she was the only woman whose possession could make joy as sharp as agony to him.

For once in his proud, self-confident life, Owain would have liked a woman's advice. Lady Guendolena might have helped, but he would have scorned himself for asking her, after ending their affair. Then he remembered an old friend, someone he had always been able to talk with as freely as he pleased—and who was certainly well enough experienced in all the intricate wheelings of the female fancy.

It was still early when he reached Caer Voran, so it was no surprise when the guards said that Garmon was away down the Tina valley looking at foals. It was a surprise, though, when he strolled with a groom to see Seren stabled—and give time for Resonna to be warned of his arrival—to find Penarwan in one of the stalls. She was fastening a bit and bridle, not too deftly, under the head groom's unsmiling eyes; she turned a flushed laughing face towards Owain.

'Wulfric is teaching me to ride.'

'Then he has all my pity. I can't imagine how he gets anyone as lazy as you to come as far as the stables, let alone into the saddle.'

He smiled at Wulfric, but the tall fair man was staring gloomily at the waiting mare; he began to unfasten the bridle.

'Don't let me rob you of your lesson.' Owain knew that horses were the chief religion in Caer Voran. Besides, Wulfric was an expert and had the expert's disgust when important matters were interrupted by trivialities such as a prince's visit.

'Oh no, we'd quite finished!' Penarwan caught his arm eagerly. 'Anyway, I want to talk to you! I'm so glad you've come!'

She led him out of the stables without another word or glance at Wulfric.

'What brings you here today?' She looked mischievous. 'Have you been—hunting—again up in the hills? Or is King Urien summoning us all to war?'

'Neither. I was out riding and I thought as I was so near I'd come and visit you.'

'That was a kind thought indeed!' She smiled at him affectionately. *What a lucky escape*! she was thinking. *Thanks be to all the saints we heard him coming—I'd hardly time to get my skirt down—or Wulf to fasten his breeches*!

Ressona was away on some household task; they had the dining-room to themselves once Penarwan had sent a maidservant for wine and cakes. He waited till the girl had gone again and Penarwan was stretched on her favourite couch sipping her wine, before he told her about his father's embassy to Lothian, the evening at the Star and Anchor and the merchant's tale.

'I can't think what to make of it,' he ended. Penarwan looked at him wide-eyed. From Owain, this was a cry for help.

'Perhaps she feels herself bound by her mother's vow.'

'If there ever was one. Anyway, she must know she can't be bound by someone else's vows without her own knowledge and consent.'

'Perhaps she's made a vow herself. There were girls like that at Candida Casa, the only pleasure they could think of was to renounce the world—poor devils!' she added devoutly.

'Taniu isn't like that!'

Penarwan's eyes flashed green as she looked at him keenly.

'You've met her!'

He hesitated, then confessed. 'Yes, I've met her. We met while I was out hunting in Argoed Llwyfain.'

She nearly giggled.

'She's no nun! She's pure like morning dew but warm as the sunlight. And when I asked her should I come for her in the spring, she said she had a welcome for me.'

'She could have changed her mind. Women do.'

'Not she. She's as true as a star. Her truth shines through her.'

Penarwan bit her lips to keep them from smiling. She just stopped herself asking if he'd made that pretty poem up by himself.

'She hasn't turned against me, she's been turned.'

'Unlikely. By that merchant's account, she's not one to be threatened away from any path she's chosen. Even Loth couldn't do it, seemingly.'

'Threats wouldn't do it, but lies could. The easterners have always hated us since we took Catraeth to keep it from the Angles. There'll be folk in Lothian, I don't doubt, who'd do anything to break my marriage. If I knew who'd made this mischief, I'd tear their tongues out and feed them to my hounds!'

He stared into his goblet as if he might see their faces mirrored in the wine. His black brows swept down into a frown that boded no good to anyone who crossed his wishes. Penarwan lounged back on her cushions watching him with amusement. It was agreeable to see Owain, always so loftily self-assured, shaken into uncertainty, wretched for some girl's smile.

She had known for a long time that her father intended her to marry Owain. *Goodbye to that*! she thought, without regret. One day, of course, she would marry some great prince, but though Owain was among the greatest, he was not the only one worthy of her. And, of all possible husbands, he was the one she least wanted. True, he was handsome. He had the fierce beauty of a peregrine at the stoop—and he could be just as dangerous to any woman who couldn't handle him.

Someone must be walking over her grave, wherever it lay waiting for her; she felt the cold shiver for a moment.

Owain would be a skilful, inventive lover; she knew that from the play they had enjoyed together. There was something in his nature, though, that held aloof, even while he played. He would never completely yield up the mastery over himself; and under that detached, smoke-blue gaze she, too, found it difficult to give way completely.

It was different with Wulfric. She leaned back and shifted her thighs discreetly as her memory went pleasantly over the first time she had let him take her . . .

She had gone to the stables with a message about Garmon's favourite horse, simply because Ressona had forgotten it till she was overseeing a dyeing vat with all the maids around her. Penarwan had obligingly taken the message herself rather than face an evening of Garmon's temper.

It had been dark in the empty stall; she'd gone close up to Wulfric before she could see his face, lifting her chin to look up at his great height. He'd stared at her dumbly as he always did, while she was speaking. When she stopped, he went on staring and she had stared back as stupidly as any farm girl.

After a moment he reached out his big hands and laid them on her breasts. She could feel their heat through her clothes; an answering warmth flowed through her and tingled in her loins. She stood passive with pleasure as he cupped and pressed her breasts and tickled her nipples. Her whole body was limp as he slid his hands to her waist and laid her in the straw at the back of the stall. He pulled her skirt up and knelt in front of her for a moment to open his breeches. Then he was on her, thrusting in hard—she nearly betrayed them both by crying out with the sharp ecstasy but saved herself by clamping her mouth to his, gripping him while his great thighs rode her as if he was breaking in one of Garmon's thoroughbred mares.

When they had finished, he helped her to her feet, straightened her clothes and watched her as she pinned up her hair, with the same dumb, respectful devotion as ever . . .

Penarwan had discovered the strange truth that satisfying desire increases appetite. She had slipped back to the stables again and again. Wulfric's body had become a need. He never made demands on her by word or sign—or threat; accepting her visits when she chose to make them as if they were acts of grace.

When I marry I'll make Father send Wulf with me as my bodyguard. I couldn't manage that under Owain's roof, though, his eyes don't miss anything when they're not dazzled with Lothian sunlight or starlight—or moonshine! If I married him there'd be no more sport for me in Caer Luel, except what he chose to give me. Let him marry his Lothian nun, and leave me free to take my own road!

She gave him a resentful glance but he was still staring into his goblet, lost in his own sombre thoughts.

But what if she should become a nun indeed, before they can push her into marriage? It only needs a missionary priest to come past the swineherd's hut. She's not in her father's house any longer—any vow she makes now will stand, even without his consent. And then King Urien will be sending his messengers to Caer Voran!

If I help Owain to this marriage I'll save myself and win Father a grateful ally . . .

She spoke quietly so as not to break suddenly into his thoughts.

'Would you like me to talk to her for you? With a woman of her own age—and rank—she might speak her mind more freely.'

His head jerked up.

'Don't be stupid. How could you talk to her? She's lost somewhere in the wilds of Lothian.'

'She's nothing of the kind. She's staying with the royal swineherd. Everybody in Lothian could tell me where he lives. I'll be riding to Din Eidyn within the month, anyway. My cousin Essyllt's marrying one of Morcant's kinsmen. My father and brothers can't go, they're too busy with the young stock. So I'm taking our greetings and presents. I'll have a strong escort, of course, but they'll go where I tell them. We've got to cross the Lothian border on our way north—it won't be difficult to take a turn out of our direct path. I'll find the princess and sample her mood for you—if you want me to, of course.'

Owain was not too deeply absorbed in his love-thoughts to give her one of his sharp looks at this news. Caer Voran forging a link with Eidyn, neatly out-flanking Cumbria's alliance with Lothian. He wondered if Morcant was trying to encircle Loth—or whether Garmon felt that Urien had deserted him and was showing resentment.

'So your cousin's marrying into Din Eidyn?' He put the faintest tone of sneering into his voice, trying to provoke Penarwan into talking carelessly. 'But indeed, where doesn't your family marry? I've heard it said that Caer Voran folk would marry Picts—or even Angles—if they thought they'd get enough profit from the alliance!'

'If they were worth an alliance, they'd be worth a marriage.' Penarwan was quite unruffled. 'Of course we would.'

Owain had to laugh; she smiled back at him.

'The question at the moment is whether you want an alliance with me? Do you want me fighting on your side? Shall I find your princess for you?'

'If you can do that for me, I'd rather have you for my ally than Arthur and all his cavalry. So come and seal the pact with me, my dear.'

He felt real affection as well as pleasure when he put his mouth to hers.

CHAPTER
14

One bright afternoon in early summer, Taniu was watching Eirlys scattering corn near a broody hen's beak. Collen came racing across the meadow and through the stockade gateway, shrieking that warriors were coming. She felt her heart lurch in her breast, but got up and went slowly towards the gate with Collen dancing in front of her and Eirlys clinging to her skirt.

It was not one of Loth's warriors, as she dreaded, who rode in carrying a green-leaved twig as a sign of peace. He was a very tall man with silver-fair hair and blue eyes pale as ice against his tanned skin.

'Don't be scared, goodwife. We're peaceful folk—from Caer Voran. Our Lady Penarwan is on her way north, she sent me ahead to beg a night's lodging.'

'We're honoured.' She added a swift whisper to Collen, 'Run and tell your father!'

She glanced through the gateway. Riders were coming from the dappled light and shade of the wood into the golden sunshine on the meadow. A dozen warriors on tall grey mounts, carrying shields blazoned with a winged horse; a string of pack-ponies; three women. One of these rode ahead to the gate and smiled down at her, hazel eyes brilliant in a frame of auburn curls under a blue riding hood.

'You're very welcome, my lady.' Taniu's mind made a worried calculation of food, drink, blankets and bed-places. Luckily it was mild enough for the animals to stay overnight in the meadow if the Caer Voran men set a watch—however could she find stabling for twenty-five beasts?

The bright hazel eyes looked through her, reading her thoughts.

'Don't be afraid we'll loot your stores. All we want is a roof for the night. My men don't need waiting on, they're well able to fend for themselves. See to it, Wulfric.'

The tall man lifted Lady Penarwan from her saddle. At that moment Hoel came up breathless. The Caer Voran men were already unloading the ponies and turning the horses into the meadow. Taniu left Hoel to direct them, gave her hand to Penarwan and led her into the house, followed by the two waiting-women. She settled them by the hearth and fetched milk and honey cakes; the evening meal was not ready. Leaving Collen and Eirlys to wait on them, she hurried away to help Hoel make up beds for the men in the largest barn. Wulfric had already set some of his men to spread clean straw; he signed to three of them to help her carry in piles of blankets and rugs. They would sleep soft and warm. There was no shortage of meat—if they liked roast pork—and she had baked the day before. She hoped the supply of ale would hold out; there was plenty of fresh water.

Wulfric had the Caer Voran men quiet and well-controlled; she shuddered to think what it would be like to lodge a dozen of Loth's warriors with Morien or Dunawd among them. She left Hoel showing them where to make their cooking fire. He was going to spend the night with them, leaving the hut for the women.

Penarwan had taken off her cloak; she was sitting on a low stool, her hands clasped round her knees, gazing into the fire. Taniu had never seen anyone so lovely. She looked from her visitor to the hut, worried. It was warm and decent but Lady Penarwan did not look at home in it.

'I hope we can give you a comfortable night's rest, lady. I'm afraid we can't lodge you in luxury.'

Penarwan smiled, stretching her arms. 'Don't trouble your head, child. This place will do very well for me. But the evening's warm and your fire's a trifle smoky.'

She jumped to her feet. 'I'm going to walk in the fresh air for a while.'

Taniu was surprised; her visitor had just had a long ride over rough country.

'Supper's nearly ready.'

'Oh, don't be afraid I'll spoil your cooking—I won't be gone more than a moment—just to clear my head.'

'The horses are loose in the meadow.'

'No matter. There's a little path leading the other way, along the bank of the stream.'

'But that goes into the forest.'

'All the better. It'll be cool and the leaves will make a breeze for me.'

'It's such a narrow path, hardly room to set your feet. The briars will catch your hair—scratch you—tear your gown!'

Penarwan laughed. 'My gown's not made of gossamer—nor am I! My riding cloak and boots are strong enough to protect me from the most savage bush.' She swung her cloak round her as she spoke.

'They wouldn't protect you from a savage wolf or boar! Wait a moment till I get my cloak and I'll come with you. You shouldn't be roaming the forest alone so near nightfall.'

'I've no need to be alone with twelve warriors to guard me. I'll take one of them as escort—will that set your mind

130

at rest while you're getting my supper? I'll take Wulfric himself—the captain of my bodyguard.'

She whisked out of the hut without waiting for an answer. Taniu followed her to the door and saw her striding towards the gate of the stockade with Wulfric at a respectful distance behind. She shrugged. Clearly, Penarwan would have her own way. She went back to her cauldron. Penarwan's women had been unpacking some of the bundles, whispering and giggling together. They were civil to Taniu, thanking her whenever she helped them.

Penarwan was gone for much more than a moment. She must have walked further than she meant and rushed back, because she came into the hut flushed and breathless. The path had been too narrow and the briars spiteful —her hair was tumbled and tangled, leaves and thorns were snagging from the back of her cloak. She was in a good humour in spite of that, said her walk had given her an appetite, praised Taniu's cooking and sat for a long time after the meal, sipping mulled ale and describing Caer Voran to Collen and Eirlys.

At last Taniu went to draw the leather curtains to screen the bed-places. She had made Penarwan's bed wide; she did not know whether her guest would take one of her women to sleep with her for company and greater warmth. However, when she had tucked Collen and Eirlys into her own bed, Penarwan, who had been watching her, said, 'Come and sleep beside me. I want some company in a strange bed.'

Taniu glanced at the serving-women.

'Oh, I'm as tired of Olwen and Creiddylad as they are of me! We've had each other's company all the way from Caer Voran and we'll have it all the way back. I want to hear a new voice.'

Olwen and Creiddylad laughed, not at all put out, and retired to their own bed. Taniu stayed behind, putting turfs on the fire to keep the ashes red till morning, fixing the bar on the door. When she went inside Penarwan's bed-curtain, her guest had already undressed. She was sitting up against her pillow, her curls on her shoulders, her breasts gleaming white above the green plaid blanket. Taniu gave a little cry of dismay.

'Forgive me! I should have helped you!'

'Don't upset yourself. I didn't come all this way to use you as my maidservant, princess.'

Taniu stared at her, wide-eyed and suddenly distrustful.

'Then you know—'

'The whole of Cumbria's talking about you.' Penarwan was a glib liar. 'And crying shame on King Loth for abusing you so. Why punish you because your mother made a vow? It wasn't your fault.'

Taniu looked blank. 'My mother?'

'Didn't she vow you to religion when you were a baby?' Penarwan's eyes bored through her. 'Are you bound by any vows at all?'

She shook her head. 'The holy man wouldn't receive me without my father's consent. And he says he'll never give it.' Her voice trembled.

'Well, time changes most things—even people's minds. Don't fret. Hurry and get into bed, then you can tell me all about it.'

In the close quarters of Din Pelidr, she had undressed in front of Ancarat and Drostecca's women without thinking about it. Yet with Penarwan she felt oddly ill at ease. Penarwan's bright eyes took in every inch of her body. This look of cool appraisal reminded her uncomfortably of Morien's lewd eyes stripping every girl he saw. It seemed strange from another woman. She dropped her dress without folding it and scrambled under the blankets.

'That's right.' Penarwan slid down beside her. 'And now tell me why you won't marry Cumbria, since you're free to do it.'

'I don't want to marry.' Taniu's voice sounded weary; she'd said this so often.

'Not marry? Saints in heaven, what do you mean to do with your life? You surely don't intend to stay here for ever?'

'I want to take the veil.'

'Are you sure?'

'Quite sure.'

'But how long did you try your vocation? Where did you go?'

Once again Taniu looked blank. Penarwan prattled on innocently, her eyes alert.

'I went to school at Candida Casa. My father wanted me to learn Latin, it's a tradition in my family. I liked it well enough; the nuns were kind, but I certainly didn't want to spend all my life there. Where did you get your schooling?'

'I haven't been to a monastery school.' Taniu felt ashamed of her ignorance. 'My father isn't—I don't think he's a Christian, though he lets the holy men live in Lothian—they've got a monastery at Mailros. My mother was a Christian, but she died long ago.'

Penarwan turned on her shoulder, staring.

'Then what do you know about being a nun?'

'A holy man came from Mailros to preach and baptize. Oh, it was wonderful to hear him speak—his words were like tongues of fire! He told us to throw away everything evil—all the lust and filth. I asked him to baptize me but he wouldn't as I hadn't told my father.'

Penarwan gave a little shriek of laughter.

'You're not even *baptized*? Mother of God, girl, you'd better see about becoming a Christian before you start thinking of being a nun!'

Taniu was silent. She felt near to despair, yet inclined to be angry too. The whole world seemed to be against her, barring the way she wanted to go. Facing Loth's simple rage had not been so hard as enduring the arrows of mockery shot at her by this clever young woman from her vantage point of superior knowledge.

Penarwan sensed that she had made a mistake. She slid her arm under Taniu's shoulders and drew her close to her own soft warmth.

'You could be baptized as soon as you like if you were going to be Princess of Cumbria. King Urien's so holy he's nearly a monk himself. He'd be on your side—he'd want you to be able to take communion when you got married. If you sent him word you wanted to be baptized before the wedding, he'd send Bishop Viventius himself to you. And your father wouldn't be able to stop him, if he wants this marriage so badly.'

'I don't want this marriage.'

'Why ever not? Has anyone been brewing poison

133

—carrying tales? I can set your mind at rest—my father's sword-friend to King Urien, I know that family as well as I know my own. I swear to you, I think the prince is as handsome as Apol—as St Michael the Archangel. But perhaps you like fair men best? You'll need a better reason than that for refusing such a good match. Come now, who's set you against him? What have you heard?'

'I've never heard a word of evil against the prince. I don't want any husband, handsome or not. Oh, if only I could make people believe that the one thing in the world I want is to live chaste—to have done with the vileness and cruelty—'

'What's so cruel and vile about being a queen? Look here—' Penarwan held up her left hand. She was wearing a magnificent sapphire ring, set in pearls and gold. 'The kings of Cumbria throw rings like this to beggars. You could hardly dream the beauty of the jewels Urien got for Queen Modron. They'd all be yours.'

'We've got beautiful jewels in Din Pelidr.'

Taniu spoke rather sharply. Her eastern pride was rising; also she did not enjoy being treated by Penarwan as a stupid barbarian who could not understand the value of what she refused. 'And I've shown what I think of them by coming here.'

'And what good do you think you're doing by it? Oh, you make a very neat-handed peasant wife, I admit. You're a good housekeeper to this man and his children. But haven't you thought how much more good you could do as queen of a great kingdom like Cumbria? For you'd be queen of the court there, even before Urien dies—he's a widower.'

Taniu opened her mouth; Penarwan gave her no chance to object.

'I know—you're dreaming about being a nun. Well, as queen you could build churches and found convents. Then, when you were old and had nothing better to—and wished for peace, you could retire to one and rule as abbess. Queens have done that, and are called saints now.'

'You talk about queens doing good,' said Taniu, from the bitterness of her own memories. 'Queens can do as much good as their husbands let them, and that's precious little.'

'You're not paying much honour to your mother, talking like that. After all, she was a queen and had a husband.'

'Yes, indeed, my mother had a husband!' Taniu suddenly went up in flames of anger; she was past trying to control them. 'My stepmother has him now and I can see for myself how much honour she gets by it! Oh, it's a fine thing to be a queen—and serve drunken lust—be abused when you fail in childbirth—and have your waiting-women set over your head!'

Penarwan laughed. 'You're unjust to the Cumbrians. Their manners are better than that, believe me.'

'What difference does it make? There's no real honour or power in being called queen—can't you see? We're still taken from our homes and lands and put into beds we haven't chosen, just like any other slave-woman or war-captive. We might get a few more fine words and trinkets—but they'll hang trinkets on a war-captive if she takes their fancy!'

'I think you'd notice a difference, even so!' Penarwan was highly amused. 'But even if the prince doesn't take your fancy, you don't have to shut yourself away from every other man.'

She brought her face closer, smiling, her eyes glinting in the dusk. Her warm breath caressed Taniu's cheek.

'If you've seen someone—if that's the real reason—if there's a spearman or huntsman in Din Pelidr that you want—you're doing him no good by staying here. Marry the prince and take your man to Caer Luel in your body-guard! That way, everyone will be satisfied. You'll please your father. You'll gain all the privileges of a queen—and you can still enjoy your pleasure, so long as you keep quiet about it!'

Instead of Penarwan's smiling face, Taniu saw Morien grinning at her when he caught her looking at him during a feast. She remembered him coming out after her, grabbing her in the dusk, the hot breath on her flesh, the pawing hands. For the first time, she realized that he thought she had signalled to him, as Loth had signalled to Luned a moment before. She shrank from the memory, shrinking back from Penarwan's embrace very slightly—but Penarwan had quick senses. She drew her arm away, saying

135

coldly, 'Take your own road. It's your concern, not mine. Now, stop chattering and let me sleep. I've a long journey tomorrow.'

She turned on her side. Soon, her even breathing showed that her day's toils were over.

Taniu lay awake much longer. She tried to shut Penarwan's insinuating voice out of her mind, in case it wove a dream-spell against her will and made her spend the night as Princess of Cumbria, coupling furtively meanwhile with one of Loth's warriors. Morien would be at her service.

Suddenly, as if a Druid had held up a magic mirror in front of her eyes, she saw the grassy hollow in Argoed Llwyfain. The little stream sparkled as it jumped down the cliff, the rocks were warm in the sunlight, the turf smelled sweet.

It was only two days' journey to the south; a day and a night if she rode the pony like a cattle-raider. She was homesick for it—and she could no more get back than Eve could return to Eden. Never again would she ride light-heartedly alone on the moors or sit down and share her food with a stranger as one friend with another, thinking no harm. Her innocence had died under the whip that slashed Luned's naked body while the men held her and laughed.

And Owain? He had promised to come to Din Pelidr in the spring. She would never meet him again, whether he came or not. He would be changed, as she was. One week in Loth's warband, with Gorthyn to school him, with Morien and Dunawd as his friends, and he'd soon be fit company for them. Better for him if he stayed at home in Argoed Llwyfain as a decent farmer.

Penarwan had sneered at her for being a good house-keeper to Hoel and his little girls. It would be well for Penarwan if she made such good use of her life! She determined that next morning she would go out of her way to show that she was happy, and proud too, in the choice she had made.

It was doubtful, though, if Penarwan took that much notice of her next morning. Taniu rose quietly to blow up the fire, to have warm water and food ready for the guests. Olwen and Creiddylad got up soon after and helped.

When Penarwan did wake up, it was they who dressed her and served her breakfast.

After she had eaten, she took her cloak and went out into the meadow to watch the horses being brought in, while her women packed the saddle-bags. She was already mounted when Taniu came out of the hut with the women and hardly waited for them to scramble on their horses before she turned to the gate. She called her thanks as she went, with the condescension of a great lady to dutiful peasants. Wulfric was more polite; he thanked Hoel and Taniu with grave ceremony in the name of his men and of Caer Voran.

When the last rider had clattered out and Hoel had already turned to the barn to collect the blankets and rake out the straw, Taniu went to the gate to see the last of the visitors.

Penarwan was riding ahead, her blue cloak glowing like a sapphire in the early morning sun. The rest of the party were straggled across the meadow. Wulfric went past them at a gallop. He caught up with Penarwan as she entered the wood. For a while Taniu could see them, dappled with sunlight; then the forest swallowed them up.

CHAPTER
15

The month passed quickly for Penarwan at Din Eidyn, with the wedding feast, the harping, dancing and other pleasures. For Owain it crawled. He counted the days to Penarwan's likely return, then rode for Caer Voran through a summer rainstorm that blanketed the moors in swirling folds. He cursed himself for the fool he'd be if he arrived before her.

His luck was with him; he learned from the gate-wardens that she was home and that Garmon was away at the horse pastures. He could talk freely with her for as long as he liked.

The rain had kept Penarwan from any plausible errand

137

to the stables, where the grooms would be crowding anyway, busy with tasks that could be done under shelter. She had been trying to charm away her boredom with *The Satyricon* but words were a poor exchange for flesh and blood. She greeted Owain like an answer to prayer and sent her maids racing to dry his cloak and bring some wine. He just managed to cover his impatience with a mask of courtesy while the girls were in the room. Then he put down his goblet and turned eagerly to Penarwan.

'Did you see her?'

Penarwan smiled mischievously, holding the pause for a moment.

'I did indeed. You've a good eye for beauty, Owain; she's very lovely. So you'd better keep her in your mind as a pretty picture, for that's all the good you'll get from her. She's set against marriage—I wish you could have heard her! She makes St Paul sound self-indulgent.'

Owain looked bewildered. 'But why? Surely her father told her—why didn't you explain that she can't be a vowed nun just because her mother said so?'

'Her mother never made a vow, I'd take my oath. When I mentioned it, the girl didn't know what I meant. Loth invented that vow—or somebody with wit invented it for him—to win some time while they break her. But I doubt if they will. She'd let them kill her first.'

Owain was white-faced, as if she had given him a vicious blow and he was determined to show neither pain nor humiliation.

'Even if there hadn't been any friendship between us, I can't see why she should be so desperate against the match, if she's free. She's a king's daughter. She must have known since she was a child that her father would give her to the man who made the highest bid. Put at the very least, I'd make her the richest and greatest lady in the North.'

'And come drunk to her bed—and abuse her if she failed in childbirth—and set her waiting-women over her head—'

'So that's it!' Owain was furious. 'I knew it. Someone's been making mischief, poisoning her mind against me to stop the marriage. Did she say who told her all those filthy lies?'

138

'Calmly now!' Penarwan was watching his face with interest. This was more amusing than any book. 'Nobody's tried to turn her against you. I had it from her own lips that she's never heard a word of evil about you. It isn't you she's taken against, it's the thought of marriage.'

'She's made up her mind to be a nun—it's her own choice?'

'You can't choose what you don't know. She doesn't know what being a nun means. Would you believe it—she isn't even baptized? One day she heard a monk preaching hell-fire and damnation, that's all.'

'And just for that she turned against marriage —against life and love? I won't believe it.'

'From what she said I think she's turned against what she saw of marriage in Din Pelidr. It's hardly surprising. I heard things while I was in Din Eidyn—of course, Morcant hates Loth as only one blood-relation can hate another, but there must be some truth in the stories. If you want to defame a man who likes feasting, you don't call him a miser. You call him a drunken sot, it's a more likely tale.'

'Well?'

'Well, they're saying in Din Eidyn that Loth killed one wife and isn't far off killing another, since she bore him a dead child.'

'Taniu can't believe that all men treat their wives like that.'

'Not all men, possibly—I think she makes some allowance for swineherds and serfs. But certainly all kings. To her, 'queen' means the same as 'war-captive'. You could more easily change stone to flesh than you could budge that girl from her crazy ideas.'

'Crazy?'

Owain called up the image of Taniu that was always waiting just behind his eyes. He tried the word 'crazy' against the memory of her.

In the old stories the heroes are always brave and noble-minded. They never say or do anything stupid or vile. And then you look at the warriors in the royal warband— oh, they're brave enough, but they drink too much, and boast and go whoring . . .

Poor child, is it any wonder you turned away from men in disgust—lost yourself in dreams and old stories—with louts like

139

that to show you what love is, and a savage brute like Loth to show you marriage? I could teach you better. I should have taught you before, in the sunlight on the moors. What a fool I was—to have you in reach of my arms and let you go without making love to you. I wouldn't let a chance go by a second time—

'I should have gone with the embassy. I'd win her to me again if I could only talk to her.'

'If you could only fly to heaven, you could talk to the angels,' said Penarwan flippantly. 'I've watched some of those would-be-holy-virgins listening to the Saints' Lives in the school refectory—imagining themselves spurning crowns, eyes raised to heaven, all set for martyrdom, swearing no prince or emperor in the world could win their maidenheads!'

'Then a prince or an emperor had better not try.' Owain looked at her with gleaming eyes and the beginning of a smile.

'What do you mean?'

'I'll be an outcast—wounded, fugitive. She wouldn't run away from me then because I'd be the one in danger. She'd spring to my aid at once.'

As she did when the boar charged. That time—the scent of the moors, the splash of the waterfall, the autumn sunlight caught in her bright hair—came to him so clearly that he could not call it a memory.

'Have you really come from Din Pelidr, or are you here for ever, with the stream and the empty hills?'

She was there, waiting for him by the sparkling water; he only had to come to her.

'And how are you going to account for the Prince of Cumbria as a wounded fugitive?' asked Penarwan's mocking voice. 'Tell her that Guendolena's husband is after you with all his clan? That'd be a sure key to unlock her sympathy!'

Owain was too deep in his dream to be provoked.

'I'll have been hunting, of course.'

'In the *Moorfoots*?'

'We'd followed the chase north into the Forest of Celidon and went across the Strathclyde border unawares. They thought we were a band of cattle-raiders and attacked us without warning.'

He was beginning to feel a bard's pleasure in the making of a good story. 'They harried us northwards to cut off our escape and killed or took my companions.' He looked at her in triumph. 'That's why I'm making my way round the Lothian border—circling back to Cumbria—and that's why I have to hide my name and beg her secrecy: I'd be too valuable as a hostage.'

'So she'd send the swineherd hot-foot to her father and Loth would have you escorted back to Cumbria with royal honours by his warband. And Strathclyde would be sure that Urien was making a pretext for war. A fine cauldron of hell-broth you'd have set boiling to scald us all—even if she believed your story, which she never would.'

'Have you forgotten when we were at Candida Casa and you bet me I couldn't get into the girls' sleeping cells?'

'Have you forgotten you were thirteen years old when you did it? The time for child's play is past, Owain. It's impossible—anyone less like a frightened, wounded fugitive—wait! I'll prove it to you. You'd be a laughing-stock.'

She jumped up and ran out of the room, to the closet where soiled garments and linen were dumped until the weather was warm and dry enough to have a laundering. She rummaged till she found the clothes of a stable-hand who had been thrown and trampled during horse-breaking. They were torn and fouled with blood and dust.

On her way back she stopped at Ressona's room, left her bundle outside and went in. Ressona was bending over her embroidery-frame, making a border for one of Garmon's shirts.

'Oh, Ressona,' she said casually.' Tell the maids not to come into the dining-room till I call. Prince Owain says we're losing our Latin since we left Candida Casa, so we're going to read to each other for practice. He's chosen a rather difficult text—we particularly don't want to be disturbed.'

Ressona smiled and nodded without raising her eyes. She thought she knew what Owain and Penarwan would be practising while they were shut up together and was quite sure they wouldn't be using a book. She saw no reason to interfere. Garmon intended his daughter to

141

marry the heir of Cumbria and would not be at all vexed if Owain arrived before the priest. With King Urien's high notions of honour that would only settle the matter more quickly.

Meanwhile, in the dining-room the magical shape-shifting of the Prince of Cumbria into a blood-stained, dishevelled fugitive was merrily in progress, slowed at moments by bursts of helpless laughter. Finally, after he had staggered up to Penarwan's couch, gasped out his plea for help and collapsed at her feet, he lay smiling up at her and challenged, 'Well, did you believe me?'

She stared down at him critically. 'Oh, you look pitiful enough to melt a heart of ice, I grant you that. But if I were planning a seduction, I'd still want a better story to be quite sure of tricking her. For one thing, you haven't got a wound under your bloodstain.'

He looked shocked. 'I am not trying to seduce Taniu! And I haven't the least wish to trick her. The story won't have to stand up to inspection, any more than the blood-stain. I only want the chance to talk to her quietly—to show her I'm ready to trust myself to her, so she can trust herself to me.'

Penarwan's lips curved in a wicked smile. She began to say, 'Yes, but can you trust—?' then saw he was lost in his dream again and checked herself with a shrug. This jest could turn out in a way to surprise the jester but what odds? That, if it happened, would only make the jest more laughable—and successful, from her point of view.

'So be it.' She tossed her ivory comb down on to his chest. 'Now get up and put your clothes on. If the maids see you like that, they'll think I've raped you.'

The rags were safely packed. Owain settled down to enjoy Ressona's good dinner and Penarwan's good company. She was in her liveliest spirits. He watched her vivid face with warm appreciation and some tenderness. He didn't love Penarwan; he did not feel that strange mingling of dream and desire that almost made Taniu a goddess in his memory. Penarwan was all-too-earthly flesh and blood —but how lovely she was! And what a quick sympathetic intelligence she had, to enter into a man's purposes and

142

plans. She was his dearest friend; he must find a way to return her kindness.

When he said goodnight he said goodbye as well. He meant to ride at dawn; lazy Penarwan would not be out of bed for hours after that. He pressed her hand and murmured out of Ressona's earshot, 'I could say *thank you* for ever.'

She turned her cheek to his kiss, whispering, 'Be sure to come and tell me all about it. It's the best joke in the world!'

CHAPTER
16

The early sun had cleared the dawn mists, there were only a few wisps of vapour melting from the higher slopes. Owain struck north over the bare moors. Ahead, the lower ground looked as if it was covered with a shaggy green blanket. This was Coed Celidon, the ancient forest, stretching almost unbroken to the highland mountains. The trees were in their early summer foliage; they spread a whispering roof over his head.

When the shadows told him it was nearly noon, he decided to rest Seren. The forest floor was rising steeply; he came out on a bare slope and listened. In that hill country, a stream was never very far away. Sure enough, his quick ear caught the sound of water falling somewhere to his right. Over the brow of the slope the ground fell steeply into a narrow gully; he could just catch a glint of water in the bottom. A thin cascade fell down the rock face, looking like a grey horse-tail.

Near the foot of the waterfall, the gully widened into a little dell; the slope was gentler, making it possible to get Seren down. As he got nearer to the cascade he found a narrow but well-marked path. Someone must come there often enough to keep it beaten out.

Leaving Seren with his nose plunged in the stream, he strolled towards the waterfall. It had scoured out an almost circular pool; a few straggling hawthorn bushes were rooted in the cliff beside it. They were decorated with strips of coloured rag and bits of ribbon. On the stones at the pool's edge lay an odd little collection of objects: a bunch of wild flowers, some oatcakes, a bronze hairpin. It was a shrine to one of the old gods, that the country folk still worshipped behind the hills. Looking up to the rock face, he saw them watching him.

They sat side by side in a niche, squat and shapeless. They had been carved clumsily but there was power in their blank faces and huge eyes. In their laps they carried the signs of their fruitfulness: one had apples, one a sheaf, the third a lamb. With a gentle pricking at the nape of his neck, he realized that this place belonged to the Mothers, the three-fold Goddess of the earth, whose womb brought forth all living things and took them back for their long sleep.

In spite of his monastic training, he made a slight gesture of reverence before turning to cup his hands in the pool and quench his thirst.

'You're making very free in the house of the Goddess.'

The words came from behind. He spun round and saw a woman watching him. She was standing so close to the fall that the spray misted her hair. She was thin and brown, with black hair falling in elf-locks round her face. Light greenish eyes like a cat's glinted at him under thick straight brows. A green plaid was thrown round her, pinned on one shoulder; her necklace of moon discs and crescents looked to be of pure silver. She must be a priestess; her face was bold and arrogant.

He smiled at her. 'If she is the Mother of us all, I'm at home. Surely, she wouldn't grudge her poor son a drink of water.'

The woman walked round the rim of the pool.

'When a son comes to visit his Mother, he should bring a gift.' Her green eyes stared him up and down. 'What have you got to give her in return for her kind welcome?'

Before he could answer, she took a small silver cup from the breastfolds of her plaid and filled it in the pool.

'She asks so little.' She handed him the cup. 'So little for all she gives us—a flower contents her, or a seed.'

He took a sip. There were herbs in the cup, she must

have had them ready. His tongue recognized vervain; they used it at the Golden Lily.

'Or a seed,' the woman repeated meaningly. She had shaken the edges of her plaid apart; he could see her bare side, the line of her ribs and jutting hip-bone, the shadow hair inside her thigh.

For a moment he was tempted. She was so wild and strange, unlike any woman he had ever had. Then a mocking voice inside his mind commented that this was an odd way of preparing himself to persuade a Christian virgin into the delights of holy wedlock. He nearly burst out laughing; though he compressed his lips firmly his eyes were sparkling at the jest.

Lurga's senses were quick as a wild animal's; she felt his suppressed laughter and thought he was jeering at herself. And nothing can break the strongest spell so easily as laughter; her magic for Drostecca was threatened. Her green eyes narrowed to slits; she showed her teeth like an angry cat-a-mountain.

'Insolent fool! How dare you mock the Goddess in her holy place?'

She snatched the cup from his hand and held it up over the pool.

'If you're too proud for her love, you can have her hate!'

She tipped the drugged water into the pool. 'May all your joy in life be poured away like this! May you be empty, empty, empty!'

She ran away along the rim of the pool, turning back to scream at him, 'The Goddess will be angry!'

Then she vanished into the waterfall. For a moment he went cold and hastily crossed himself. Then he realized there was probably a cave behind the water-curtain. He wondered cynically how often she had played that trick; worshippers at the shrine would think they had seen the Goddess and be terrified.

Rather vexed, he got Seren and toiled up the side of the gully. At the top he looked back. The pool and hawthorn bushes were out of sight; the hills were empty but he still seemed to hear the echoes repeating:

The Goddess will be angry!'

He shrugged off the memory and continued his way

north. The day was oppressively hot; even the sunset brought little relief. Sleep did not come for a long time; when it did he had no peace.

He seemed to be back with Taniu by the stream where he met her. She was warm and willing, but when he took her in his arms she turned into the cat-faced priestess under the waterfall. Then he knew that it was neither Taniu nor the priestess who had come to him but the Goddess herself, the Lady of the hill shrines and the holy springs. She had come to claim her tribute—and she was very angry.

It was better in the morning, still sunny but with a cool breeze and white flecks of cloud. At last he looked from a mountain-spur across a forested plain to the line of the Moorfoot hills. He had learned from Penarwan that Hoel's steading was somewhere under their eastern slopes. He worked his way warily in that direction and chose his camping place with care. He found a craggy knoll among the oaks, with brambles growing from the rocks. There was a hollow at the top, with room for Seren to graze and a deep pool in one corner.

It was St John's Eve. The summer nights were short; he still had an hour or so of daylight. It was impossible to stay idle; he wanted to explore. He'd better wear his disguise in case he was seen. He took the rags from his bundle and began to change himself into a haggard fugitive. His restless night in the wilds had done some of the work for him; by the time he had crawled across the ground and pushed his way through the brambles, he was dirty and scratched enough to pass muster.

He followed the downward slope of the land, picking up a streamlet that led him to a meadow where three or four cows were grazing. Beyond lay a farmstead protected by a stockade. The sun was low in the west, turning the grass as golden as the buttercups. The cows' shadows lay long and black behind them. Someone came out of the stockade and walked over to them, someone with a slim, lithe figure and shining braids. His heart began to beat violently.

Three of the cows had swollen udders; they wanted to be milked and went into the yard at once. The fourth was a young heifer; she had no intention of leaving sun and grass

146

for a narrow byre. She frisked away from the gate and led Taniu a merry dance all round the meadow. She was very agile; Taniu found it impossible to drive her single-handed. She didn't want to leave the silly creature out all night; even in summer a wolf might come questing. She kept up the chase, half-vexed, half-amused, hoping the heifer would get tired or bored and go to join the other cows, now lowing impatiently for her.

Suddenly she realized that her quarry was going in the right direction because she was being driven by a tattered figure that had come out of the forest. Together they chivvied the heifer neatly into the yard. Taniu leaned on the wall by the gate, blinking and trying to get her breath, but having some difficulty between panting and laughter. Her cheeks were rosy after the frantic scramble; her hair had tumbled loose from its plaits. She looked so warm and merry that Owain was very near to catching her in his arms there and then and begging her to marry him. But he was interested in the situation and enjoying the joke too much.

While he hesitated, she swept her hand across her face to brush the sweat and hair out of her eyes. Then the hand dropped and she was staring at him.

'*Owain*!' she gasped; and stopped, horrified.

His clothes were filthy, the shirt nearly torn off his back. His raven hair had lost its sheen, tangled with dust and twigs as if he had needed to break his way through pathless country; his hands and face were oozing blood from dozens of tiny scratches. More dreadful was the dark-brown stain over the ribs—that looked to be some days old. At once, her hands reached out to draw him into the steading; he caught them but pulled her back from the gateway.

'Quietly!' he muttered, with a quick, wary glance round. 'Is there anyone about?'

She shook her head. 'Only two little girls and they're minding the cooking-pot.' Yet she was whispering too. 'Owain, what's the matter? Come in, and I'll see to your hurts.'

Weary to death as he looked, he could still smile.

'I'm not so bad as I look. I'm not dying—just yet—but I daren't be seen by anyone else.'

'What happened? Where's your horse—were you thrown?'

'We were hunting north of the Idon; we chased a stag west through Coed Celidon. How could we know when we crossed into Strathclyde? They must have thought we were cattle-raiders and set on us without warning.'

The prepared words were coming out glibly enough but he was afraid the laughter would show in his face and voice. He sighed, closed his eyes and went on in the flat tones of weariness.

'We had no body armour—they were too many for us—we were scattered and cut down—'

He felt her hand on his shoulder, touching gently in case his flesh was bruised.

'You're in Lothian now. The whole war-host of Strathclyde wouldn't dare to touch you. Come in. When you've had food and rest, I'll get Hoel—'

His eyes flashed open.

'Don't do that—you'd destroy me! No one must know I'm here, it could start a war. I've got to get back quietly. Will you help me?'

'How can I, if you won't come and be helped?'

'Would you bring me some food tomorrow?'

'But what will you do tonight?'

'Don't worry about me—I'm a skilled hunter. I didn't lose all my gear. I've got a camping place in the forest, well hidden. I'd only slipped down here to scout around, when I saw you.'

'I open the gate at sunrise to let the cows out. Wait for me by the edge of the trees and I'll come to you. But are you sure you won't come in for supper and a bed in the byre? I could tell the children you were a beggar—if you didn't mind pretending.'

He smiled; she was glad to see his spirit had come back.

'I can wait till sunrise. Dawn comes early on Midsummer's Day. Now, go and get on with your milking or those cows will burst!'

He set off across the meadow at a swinging stride, turned at the edge of the trees as he had done once before, waved and disappeared.

Taniu went in to the impatient cows. While she milked,

then went in to supper with Collen and Eirlys and lay for long hours awake in her warm bed, her mind was away with Owain, shelterless on the cold ground.

Back in his camp, Owain was lounging comfortably by his fire, enjoying Ressona's lavish provisions. Suddenly he threw back his head and laughed, thinking of the scene that had passed, the still more amusing one that was to come. His wooing would make a fine tale for a bard; tomorrow he'd compose the last episode. Then he could end the nonsense, take her back to her father and set about ordering his wedding feast.

There must be a blessing on me, it's all being made so easy. A flash of unwanted memory showed him the priestess at the waterfall, spitting curses at him like an angry cat. He shut her out of his mind and rolled himself in his cloak. Sleep came soon and dreamless.

Cautiously, Taniu opened the hut door and stepped out, carrying her bundle of provisions. She let the cows into the meadow, barring the gate behind her in case Collen and Eirlys should wake and follow her. Owain was waiting for her just within the trees; he had washed away the grime and looked refreshed. His eyes were uncannily bright but he showed no signs of wound fever and greeted her cheerfully.

'Do you feel better? Are you sure you can get back to Cumbria?'

'Perfectly sure.' He laughed. 'I can do anything.'

He seemed almost light-headed; she laid her fingertips on the bloodstained shirt.

'You must let me look at that before you go.'

'Gladly. But not in front of the farm gate. Come to my camp—it's well hidden.'

He turned as he spoke; she followed him under the trees along a faint track close to the stream. A branch grew low; he held it up to make room for her. She brushed against him as she passed, smiling her thanks. She had got up from bed and gone straight to milk the cows and let them out. Her bright hair was hanging loose down her back; like most country girls on a hot summer day she was wearing nothing but her shift, strings untied at the neck. She would have worn her gown in the presence of an ordinary stranger but she was too concerned for Owain's plight to be shy.

The light touch of her body scorched him worse than a Midsummer bonfire. Since he had taken a disgust to the whores at the Golden Lily he had lived chaste as a monk for two months, obsessed by memories of Taniu. To have these memories made flesh and blood again, within reach of his hands was a disturbing pleasure, close to pain. His heart was hammering as if it would break through his ribs and his blood was stirring his flesh.

A bramble bush straggled across their path, reaching out to the stream. He stepped across, neat-footed as a cat, then turned to help her. He put his arm round her waist, swinging her up and over, her toes just skimming the rim of the brook. She landed laughing, still within the circle of his arm, pleased for him that he had recovered from the defeated weariness of yesterday. The tips of her breasts brushed his shirt; he forgot why he had brought her there, all he had meant to say.

He tightened his grip and pulled her against his body, sliding his hand down her back till he could cup his fingers in the cleft. She looked up, her lips parting in surprise; he pressed his mouth on hers, his tongue probing to taste and possess the sweetness she had locked inside her.

She pulled away frantically, her struggle to escape inciting him to grasp her still more firmly and master her. She was strong and lithe; it was not easy to hold her. She tried to writhe out behind him to get out of reach of one arm while she used both hands to break his other wrist. She moved so fast that he, in turn, was taken by surprise and almost let go of her. He whirled round on her; she became still, he felt her muscles go slack.

He was smiling, as he smiled at sword-play or in the hunt when he moved in for the kill. As she stared at his fierce, hawk's face it seemed to blur and she saw other faces, other smiles. Brude gloating over Luned's body; Morien's greasy mouth leering at her across the feast; Drostecca fondling her that Lammas Eve before the horror began. It was the same smile.

He saw the knowledge in her eyes as she went limp. He

thought it was consent, swung her up in his arms and carried her a little way long the path, looking for a place wide enough to lay her down. He had a strange feeling that he was drowning in waves of his own hot blood. He could hear the witch-priestess laughing. Even at this last moment, one part of his reason, not yet overwhelmed, seemed to stand apart and cry out in his mind: *Stop it, you fool! This isn't what I meant—*

Then the blood-red tide surged over him. The Goddess had come, demanding his service. There was no mind left, no choice, no Owain. Nothing but a desperate drive and a hunger that could only be appeased inside the soft flesh that offered no bar against him.

Taniu was trapped inside her own shock; swung up in that falcon's grip she could not even struggle. Out of the bewilderment of Owain's sudden attack, her childhood terror had caught her at last, not in dreams now, or wisps of memory, but in truth. And that earlier time had been a mere ritual preparation: the old Druid had only mimed the god he summoned, with spearshaft and polished flint and the flames of kindled twigs.

Now Lugos himself had come to claim her, with the stoop of a hawk on his prey, and the Spear that drove into her was alive with its own fire. *'Lugos Kindler, Lugos Wakener, Who burns in dark places, Who pierces and quickens, Who destroys and brings to life—'*

The dark litany drummed in her pulses as the spear moved inside her, kindling her own flesh into an answering flame that swept up from her loins and burned through her. It was for this, then, that women bared their bodies, leaped and danced and cried out under the moon, for Lugos the midsummer falcon, Lugos the fire of Lammas, the Lord of the Burning Spear. Just so, Taniu's blood danced, her flesh leaped and her mouth called in soft moans and high-pitched cries.

She had been taken as ruthlessly as a plover or leveret gripped in the claws of a bird of prey and carried soaring—until the raptor chooses to let it fall on the rocks, then glut itself on the smashed flesh and bones. When it was over at last, Owain drew away from her body and slowly got to his feet, staring down at her. His desire had died of what it fed on. There was always a weariness after such a coupling, the little death that follows the spending of so much life. But if he had found Taniu a virgin, her swift wakening to passion would have left him exultant and gentle. He could have lain beside her, flesh cradled against flesh, drenched in the sunlight, till the tide of desire flowed back again.

Now, behind the weariness and melancholy of coition, there was disgust at her and a dreadful cold anger. She was lying sprawled where he had thrown her down, her shift rucked up above her waist. Her hair was tangled with fragments of twigs and dead leaves; her face and limbs were smeared with dust. A trickle of blood ran down her leg from a graze on her shin. No other blood, of course. She kept her eyes shut but she was sobbing convulsively, so he knew she was conscious. She looked soiled, defiled.

The little slut, no wonder she was scared of coming to Cumbria as a royal bride. A nice surprise she had ready for her bridegroom on the wedding night! Which of Loth's spearmen got there before me? How many? Do they boast to each other, compare times? What names have they got for her—and for the Cumbrian fool who was going to take the leavings of Lothian? You lying bitch, making out you're too pure even for marriage! The cheapest whore in the Golden Lily's clean compared to you!

Yet even while he lashed himself into a fury with the words 'whore' and 'slut', he waited with a strange kind of hope that she would say something, excuse herself, explain.

But Taniu had gone beyond speech, even if she had known what he wanted her to say. She had even gone beyond the shock of the attack she had just suffered, back into an older, darker grief. It was her eight-year-old self that lay shivering and bleeding on the floor of the queen's hall, weeping for a wrong she couldn't even put a name to.

The sobbing began to grate on Owain's nerves. 'Don't cry, dear,' he said coldly. 'There's no harm done, how could there be? And surely, nothing's happened to surprise you? It's stupid to weep over a few moments of sport.'

He turned and left her lying there. He went back to his

camp, stripped off his disguise and got into his own clothes. He collected the rags Penarwan had lent him, weighted them with a stone and sank them in the pool. Then he took Seren and rode away southwards.

He rode easily, taking care of his horse's legs and wind. His trained hunter's senses noted the sky, the taste of the air, a wolf's tracks in a muddy bank. It was as pleasant a ride as ever he had under the midsummer sun. Somewhere behind his eyes, a wasteland stretched away to the ends of the world. There was nothing there but dry rock and a cold wind and a woman's voice calling, '*May you be empty, empty, empty!*'

Taniu lay on the path a long while. For a time, her body sobbed of its own accord; then she was quiet, dozing. Finally, she got up, took off her shift, then washed her hair and skin with furious thoroughness. She dried herself with the shift, put it on, carefully plaited her hair. Then she walked quietly back to the steading. The little girls had been looking for her anxiously and ran to greet her. Eirlys cried out at the sight of the angry graze on her leg.

'I tripped and fell,' she said calmly. 'Don't fret—it's nothing.'

CHAPTER
17

Owain went back to Petriana and took up his weapon-training. If he had been away on one of his solitary hunting trips that annoyed his father so much, it proved to be his last. His restlessness had vanished. Now he practised each new method of death-dealing that the weapon-masters could teach him with a single-mindedness that was frightening to watch.

He did not make any more visits to the Golden Lily. He said men were fools to pay women for what they would do fast enough for nothing but lust. He had a lashing tongue for any of his friends who were unwise enough to mention their marriage plans.

In spite of this, he was popular, thanks to his skill with weapons and his total recklessness. He had his own following: noblemen's sons who would risk their necks trying to match him and would have followed him without question if he had promised a raid on Hell.

Urien was away over the Long Hills, seeing to the defences of Catraeth. There had been trouble between Elmet and Bernicia; more trouble between both and the Angles of Deira. It was all too likely that the British kingdoms might smash each other, leaving Deira to collect the wreckage and become all-powerful in the east. It was equally probable, however, that the enemies might ally for a while to hurl themselves at Catraeth. Whatever their other quarrels, every eastern kingdom would have liked to see the Cumbrians driven out of it.

One late afternoon in August, Owain and some of his cronies were riding north through the forest, making for the Roman road that went past Guasmoric to Caer Luel, on their way home from hunting. They were riding with loose reins, letting the horses set their own pace. They would probably be benighted but that did not matter. It would be a fine sunset evening; later there would be a full moon.

They were content with life and pleased with themselves, even Iarddur, who had taken a toss during the chase, straining his left shoulder and earning himself a good deal of friendly jibing. He was just starting a song when Owain, who was leading with his cousin Llywarch and Madog in close attendance, saw a dark shape crouched under the bushes at the far end of the glade.

He thought it was a wolf that had scented the blood of their kill and was now trying to lie low. He readied his spear. The dark shape crawled into the open and lay still. It was a farm boy, his clothes torn and scorched, a very ugly wound across his brow. Blood was caked with ash on the torn flesh but a trickle was still oozing over his eye.

Llywarch and Madog dismounted. Llywarch knelt and lifted the boy's head gently against his thigh; Madog took his flask and got a few drops of barley spirit between his cracked lips. The boy licked his mouth, then sucked and swallowed till Madog pulled the flask away. The boy opened his eyes and stared up into Owain's face. He looked mazed.

'What's happened to you?'

The boy opened his mouth but made no sound. Owain looked at the scorched rags, then sniffed the wind.

'Is your home on fire? Where d'you come from?'

'Caermollt.' The boy's voice was hoarse. 'They burned it. They came on us so suddenly. They took our cattle. They took my sister.'

He started to cry, great wrenching sobs that seemed likely to tear his ribs apart.

'Stop that!' Owain needed to know what had happened before the boy collapsed completely as he seemed about to do. Caermollt was a large, prosperous village inside the walls of a Roman fort. If the men from another village had attacked it in the course of a local feud, Urien would have every one of them hanged and raze their homesteads. If forest outlaws had done it, Urien would want the forest swept from end to end till they were caught. Everyone in Cumbria knew that; he could not believe any native Cumbrian would dare to commit such an outrage. Irish raiders? Not very likely these days, with the Isle of Manau friendly to Cumbria; in any case, why had there been no warning from Alauna on the coast? He frowned over the puzzle while the boy was quietening down.

Llywarch had been cleaning the head wound with barley spirit and was binding it with a strip cut from his own shirt. The boy sensed that he was being cared for and relaxed against Llywarch's knees. When Llywarch questioned him, he answered clearly enough, though jerkily, as if ready to shy and bolt from his memories.

'Try to tell us what happened. Don't be scared, no one's going to hurt you. What happened? Who are you?'

'Gwion of Caermollt. It was this morning. The cattle were down in the meadow. The gates were all open. We thought no harm. Wolves don't come near us in summer. And when we saw them riding out of the forest we still thought no harm. And then they started rounding up our cattle. And my father ran to tell them to stop. And they speared him.'

155

He started to shake but made himself keep talking.

'Then we tried to run for our weapons but they came at us—and I ran to our house to get Teleri—my sister—away—but one of them came after me—a big man—he stood in the doorway and we couldn't get out—he was laughing—I put her behind me and he came at me—he had an axe— he was lifting it to hit me—Teleri pushed me aside—she screamed and my head was hit—when I woke up the house was on fire—I got out and all the houses were burning—and everyone was dead—and I couldn't find Teleri. So I'm going to find the king.'

He struggled to get up but Llywarch put an arm round his shoulder.

'The king's son is here. He'll see you get justice.'

Owain stooped from the saddle. 'Who did it? Outlaws from the hills?'

Gwion shook his head.

'I don't know. They weren't our people.'

'Irish?'

'No. I've been in Alauna. I've seen Irishmen in the port there and heard them talking. These weren't Irish. They weren't like any men I've ever seen.'

'What were they like?'

'Some of them were very tall. They were young but they had white hair. And some of them were blue! When I saw the man close—the man who tried to kill me—he had blue pictures on the skin of his face and arms!'

'They were Picts,' said Owain. 'And probably some Frisians or Angles with them.'

'*Picts!*' His companions were unbelieving. Picts lived beyond the Northern Wall, beyond Strathclyde and Eidyn. It was nearly two hundred years since they had mounted a raid so deep into Britain.

'How would Picts get here to burn Caermollt?' asked Iarddur. It was what everyone else was thinking.

'They came over Merin Rheged.' He spoke with complete certainty, as if he were watching the raiders on their journey. In his memory he was looking across the estuary at low tide, the hills opposite black against a blood-red sunset.

I knew it then. I knew this was coming. The land spoke to me.

Why didn't I keep it in mind? I was hawking with Madog, I remember; then we went down to the harbour tavern and that trader told me how she—

He shut his mind on the memory before it could get to Taniu.

'There'll be a wasps' nest of them over there in the hills. They came over Merin Rheged at low tide, that would be about the second hour after midnight. Then a merry morning raiding our cattle and away on the next ebb.'

Madog swore; Llywarch thought of the quiet homesteads tucked into the forest between the sea-marsh and the fells, prosperous and secure from raiding these many years.

'How many?'

Gwion shook his head miserably. 'They seemed to be everywhere.'

'Think!' Owain stared straight into the boy's pupils as if he would swoop into them and claw the memory out. Gwion stared back, forced by the stronger will to look at the horror again.

'There would be fifteen at least. Perhaps two dozen. I can't tell. They came so fast.'

'Iarddur, get to Guasmoric as quick as possible. Make the headman send a rider to Caer Luel on the best horse he's got and tell the fort commander to bring a troop west along the shore. Then he must raise as many spearmen as he can from Guasmoric and meet me at—' he thought a moment—'at Maia. Off with you—oh, and take the boy up in front of you, get some woman there to tend him.'

He gathered Seren's reins and turned towards the north.

'Where are you going, lord?' asked Madog.

'After them, of course.'

Llywarch, being his kinsman, could dare to argue.

'Owain, they went hours ago and who knows which way they went? It's madness, trying to find them.'

It was indeed and Owain knew it. The raiders had the whole forest to hide in and a long start. And if hunting them was madness, the wish to catch them was madder still. He had a dozen in his party—eleven without Iarddur, whose shoulder would stop him using weapons for days. They had their hunters' spears and knives against a larger

157

band in full war-gear. At best, they would be mauled; likely they would be killed, a far greater loss to Cumbria than a few head of cattle and some peasant girls. They knew it; he could see the knowledge in their faces, though they would follow him without hesitating for a moment. He knew it too; but knew also that he could not let the raiders get away after attacking his land if he had to track them through the fires of hell to deal with them.

He rounded on Iarddur. 'What are you waiting for? Take the boy and go! Help him up, one of you.'

Gwion had got to his feet but backed away.

'I'll come with you, lord.'

'Nonsense. We can't be burdened with you. Go with Iarddur—or stay here in the forest if you like it better. You're no use to us.'

Gwion was stubborn. 'I can kill one of them. They've got Teleri. I promised Father I'd always look after her if he wasn't here. I won't be a burden to you. I'll walk after your tracks.'

Iarddur laughed; he pulled out his hunting-knife and threw it into the turf at Gwion's feet.

'I won't be needing that. Kill one of them for me while you're about it, little hero.'

Llywarch reached Gwion a hand. 'You can ride with me. We're both light in the saddle.'

'As you please.' Owain was impatient to be gone. 'Away with you, Iarddur—and don't fall off again, there'll be nobody to pick you up.'

Iarddur turned away; the rest of them rode after Owain. He set a course somewhere north of where Caermollt had been. They went ahead for about an hour; then Owain swung westwards, with the idea of cutting across the raiders' tracks and getting some notion of the direction in which they had gone.

There were three main fords across Merin Rheged; two of them were much nearer to Caer Luel. They were shorter to cross but lay under the notice of the garrison at Petriana. Maia, the last fort of the Wall, long derelict, had guarded the lowest ford. That was why he had told the reinforcements to meet him there. Of course, with light ponies, it was possible to cross further down the estuary at low tide.

Their quarry could be anywhere. However, he had to fix some point to make for. Maia was the best he could think of.

Madog gave a shout. He pointed to a ride that led northwards. The turf was pitted with many hoof prints, spattered with cowpats and the rounded mounds of horsedroppings. They were cool but not stale. Cattle had been driven that way not long before. They turned up the ride; his companions were for urging their horses to gallop but Owain held Seren in and waved them back. They were startled and ready to object.

'But, lord—'

'There's no need to hurry.' Owain kept Seren to the same easy pace. 'They've got the cattle and the prisoners to slow them down. They don't know anyone's on their track and they've got a long road ahead. They won't be riding a race. But if they hear us coming after them, they'll scatter in the forest and lie low. Oh, we'd round up most of the cattle and get some of the girls, maybe, if the Picts didn't cut their throats to keep them quiet. But they'd be over Merin Rheged at the next ebb, boasting to all the cattle-thieves of the North, that the coast of Cumbria is wide open.'

He thought of Urien, struggling to block the passes over the Long Hills into Cumbria, while the kingdoms along his eastern border tore each other apart. He was angry and bitter.

'We're not the Roman Empire. We can't keep an army on patrol along the coast, twenty-four hours a day, every day of the year. Not one of those raiders is to get away, do you hear?'

Llywarch looked doubtful.

'If we don't catch them in time, they'll be over Merin Rheged on this ebb. Even our whole war-host couldn't flush them out after that.'

The others muttered agreement.

'Think!'

They had come out on to the bare crest of a ridge and could see a wide stretch of treetops and sky ahead. The west was burning with a clear gold, while the ghost of a full moon floated low in the east. Owain turned to face the rest, his black hair caught by the wind. A west wind, and freshening rapidly. He was smiling triumphantly.

'Think. It's full moon tonight, and a high tide about the eighth hour. *Think.*'

Llywarch saw it. 'A spring tide!'

'A spring tide, with a west wind driving it. They may think they've got three hours or so in hand for crossing, but with a spring tide coming in fast, it could already be too late. But they're hill-men out of the North, they don't know our Merin Rheged as we do. And as it's their first raid across, they've no way of telling how much slower they'll be with the loot. I don't want them starting to worry too soon.'

There was a laugh.

'You'll take them on the shore, then, Owain?'

'On the shore, and Merin Rheged fighting for us, with luck.'

An hour later, as they came out of the northern fringe of the woodland and saw the track of their quarry, quite fresh now, heading for the ford over the sea-marsh, he was quite sure of their luck. There was no sign of burning farms on the open plain, so far as they could see. The raiders had headed straight for Merin Rheged, ignoring the ruins of Maia on its bluff over the estuary.

He made for the old fort, to keep his men out of sight if any of the raiders looked back. They came quietly through the gap of the south gateway and down the cracked weedy road to the north gate, where some rotting timbers still hung.

He dismounted with Madog and Llywarch and climbed the gate turret to the parapet. Below them, the estuary was about two miles across. At this moment it was a stretch of gleaming sands cut by trough-like channels of running water, one of which curved close under the bluff where Maia stood. The water was running east, inland, very fast. To Owain's experienced eyes it was deepening every minute. Both the sands and the water were fire and blood under the setting sun; the moon hung golden in the east.

He looked across the sands to the north and pointed. About half a mile out he could see the black dots of cattle circled by raiders on ponies as small as scuttling beetles. A short way behind was a line of travellers on foot, looking at this distance like the stick-dolls that little girls made for playthings. They were moving as jerkily as stick-dolls come to life; he realized that their arms were bound and their necks linked by ropes to keep them together. They were finding it hard to keep their balance as they waded across the fast-flowing channels with their skirts dragging. Every so often one would stumble; then a rider, doubling back round the group, would jab at her with a spear-point to get her on her feet and thwack her with the shaft to keep her moving.

But the riders were finding it harder to control the cattle. The beasts had a sense of their danger and were trying to break back towards the nearer shore. Looking towards the west, Owain could see the bore coming, the waves racing three abreast with their crests tossing.

'*Ride!*'

He raced down the turret steps and jumped on to Seren's back. The others cantered after him back through the southern gate and round towards the shore. He halted them under the shelter of the bluff.

'The cattle will bolt for the shore. Keep out of their way while they go past, then take up a line on the beach. Don't go beyond the high-water mark and get taken by the tide yourselves. Don't throw your spears—think of boar-hunting, keep them at spears' length and try to pitch them into the water. We're not equipped for close combat and we've no numbers to spare. I want some of them alive, if possible, but kill them rather than let them get away. Ready now, and hold the horses!'

Water came swirling up the inner channel and licked at the foot of the bluff. From out in the estuary came a thin high screaming like seagulls. Llywarch glanced anxiously at Gwion, standing by his bridle with Iarddur's knife ready in his hand. The boy's face was calm; he seemed to have no idea what was happening out there. Llywarch thanked God they could not see it. The horses shook their heads and snorted; one or two danced a little but their good training and trust in their riders held them firm.

Now the cattle came splashing ashore and lumbering up the slope from the sea-marsh, ones and twos, then a dense knot almost crazy with terror. Owain let the main rush go by, then raised his spear and swung Seren out along the shore with the rest in line behind, then wheeled to face the tide.

The first of the raiders was near the shore, fighting his terrified pony. He saw Owain waiting for him, tried to swing his shield round from his back, nearly lost his balance and clutched at the pony's mane. He was yelling; the spear took him under the throat. The spear-point jarred on bone, the man's eyes looked amazed, he spewed red and keeled over. He was under the hoofs and the breaking waves before Owain realized that he had killed his first man in war.

It was more like a hunt than a battle. As he had said, Merin Rheged was fighting for them. The raiders' ponies were out of control with the terror of the waves; some had been bumped or gored by the stampeding cattle. It was almost impossible to ride them while trying to handle weapons, but if they were unseated the water took them and the Cumbrians on their tall horses were able to spear them or club them down, laughing at the sport. Gwion had fought like a small demon, venturing out waist deep by Llywarch's saddle-girth, slashing at ponies' necks and bellies. Four or five of the raiders did get their mounts ashore and clustered together trying to make some sort of stand. Exhausted and outnumbered, they were easy enough to pen into a galloping circle and overpower.

When it was over, they took eight prisoners back to Maia. The sun had set but the harvest moon was almost as bright as daylight, clear enough for Madog, Riwallon and Idris, who were still feeling active, to round up some of the cattle. The poor beasts were already tired with their long drive and once they felt firm ground under their feet and the terror of the tide had left them, were glad to stop by the rivulet south of the fort. One of them was so badly injured that it could hardly drag itself, so Madog slit its throat and they hauled it up to the fort. The others had already got a fire going with some broken timbers, so there would be roast meat for supper after they had washed and tended their cuts and bruises. No one was seriously hurt and the horses were unharmed.

Owain and Llywarch, in wordless understanding, made

a last patrol up and down the tide line but they did not find what they were looking for. They found five more cows and three ponies, tired out and docile, but the stick-dolls they had seen trudging over the sands had vanished. Llywarch was distressed for Gwion; Owain was in a cold rage. They turned back to Maia.

A shout from the south gateway; a group of well-armed men was waiting for them there. They had just arrived; their ponies were in a lather. Their leader raised his spear in salute, panting.

'Anthun, headman of Guasmoric. We came as fast as we could. I'm sorry we're too late.'

He looked crestfallen.

'You've come in excellent time.' Owain forced himself to sound hearty; it would be churlish to throw his own burden of anger and pain on them. 'I'm very grateful to you. Welcome to the victory feast.'

He waved them into the fort which was beginning to smell pleasantly of roast beef. When he had dismounted he went over to look at the prisoners, huddled together where they had been bound and thrown down near the pile of their war-gear. Everyone who wasn't seeing to the horses or the meat gathered round.

Six of them looked to be fighting men in the prime of youth. Two were tall, with flaxen hair and beards. They had some faint likeness to Caer Voran folk, though Garmon would never have let any of his household be so filthy and unkempt. There was an older man with greying hair in braids, a gilt bronze torque and an arm-ring that marked him as chief of the band. Like most of the others, he had patterns tattooed on his cheeks and forearms. Beside him crouched a boy about twelve years old with a broad smooth face between braids of coppery-brown hair. He, too, wore a torque; his jacket was of fine stamped leather. Owain guessed he was the chief's son, out on his first manly exploit. Well, it would be his last.

Riwallon pulled off the boy's torque and knelt over him to unlace the handsome jacket. The thongs were wet and tight-knotted; he drew his dagger. The boy turned terrified eyes towards his father. The old chief made a guttural sound; he was struggling to find words of British.

'Ransom. We—give—ransom.'

Owain looked at him coldly, thinking of the women of
Caermollt; thinking also that this man had led a raid
twenty miles and more into Cumbria and nearly got away
with his booty. If he hadn't gone hunting south today
instead of up into Argoed Llwyfain—if they'd killed
Gwion as well—if there hadn't been a westerly gale and a
spring tide, the whole gang could have been over Merin
Rheged, boasting to whoever else was lurking in the
wastelands how easy it had been.

'There isn't treasure enough in the North to pay your
ransom. You're going to spend the rest of your lives
working for it.'

'Owain, that's hardly wise,' whispered Llywarch.
'They're savages. No one would be safe with one of them
as a slave. They'd need an armed guard to watch them.'

Madog backed him. 'It's true, lord. They're not worth
their keep. Best slit their throats here and now.'

Owain shook his head smiling. 'Bulls are killers but you
can get a hard day's work out of an ox without any trouble.'
He looked round at the men from Guasmoric. 'Does any
one of you know the farrier's craft?'

'I do, lord.'

Gwion had come up. His hands were playing with
Iarddur's knife but his eyes were fixed on the prisoners
with dreadful interest. Llywarch felt cold. It would not
have been so bad if Gwion had been angry or weeping for
Teleri. He merely looked as if he were coming to a meal
with a good appetite. He had not once asked about his
sister after the fight or even mentioned her name.

'I know how to do it. I used to help my father. He was the
first one they killed.'

'See to it then. Ask the men for any help you want to
hold them down.'

The Guasmoric men crowded round Gwion, glad to be
useful and pleased at the chance of some fun.

Owain had spoken rather absently, his eyes on one of
the prisoners. The Picts and the Angles had not been able
to follow what the Cumbrians had been saying. Though at
least one knew some British words, the quick low-voiced
exchange had been beyond them. All but one man, who

looked up suddenly when Owain mentioned the farrier's craft, met his eyes, then turned away and wriggled behind the others. It was the withdrawal that caught Owain's attention. He stepped over and grabbed the man's shoulder, wrenching him round. He was small and wiry with no tattoo marks on his face or arms.

'You're British, aren't you?'

The man looked away uneasily.

'You're British.' Owain put the tip of his dagger to the man's throat and jerked his chin up. Riwallon let out a yell.

'It's Dunwal!'

He rushed over to Owain. 'He's a horse-coper. He comes up to Petriana quite often, trading pack-animals. I've seen him hanging about in the stables, cadging beer from the grooms.'

And picking up news. Learning how many men we've got and where they go on patrol. Learning that the king's away across the hills with his warband. Learning where the rich villages are.

He could see Dunwal walking through the markets in Caer Luel, sitting in Finnuala's tavern sipping his drink and listening, always listening. Just another upland farmer or horse-trader, going quietly about his business, harmless and unnoticed.

Dunwal suddenly threw himself on the ground and writhed forwards to Owain's feet. He was glad the man's arms were tied, he couldn't have borne his touch. A Cumbrian who sold Cumbrians.

'Which brings in the best profits—horse-trading or spying?'

'I was forced!'

'Who forced you? Where do they come from?'

'Caer Ehedydd.'

The Cumbrians exclaimed in surprise. Caer Ehedydd was a little lordship that held the lower valleys of the Ned and Llwchwr. It had come into being after the Pict wars when the Frisians who garrisoned the fort there had mutinied and deserted. Both Strathclyde and Cumbria had claimed overlordship and indeed had fought bloodily for it more than once. Since Urien's peace it had drifted into independence by a kind of unspoken consent. Strathclyde's honour was satisfied so long as Cumbria did not hold it. Urien was too busy building up friendship with Strathclyde to squabble over it. So neither kingdom would be concerned over missing tribute—

'—but Caer Ehedydd is a strong place. How could it fall into the hands of an outlaw pack like this?'

'The chief died. They were keeping his wake—'

'You mean they were all drunk.'

'They didn't know there was an outlaw pack up in the hills. Nobody did. They were taken by surprise. That's how I got captured—I came in with my stock just as usual—'

'And bought your freedom by selling your country.'

There was such a noise of screaming coming from among Gwion and his helpers that Owain had to shout. There was only one other prisoner left to deal with besides Dunwal. He had risen to his knees; he looked round in terror, then flung himself down again, screaming too.

'Lord, I was forced! I don't belong with them! I'm a Cumbrian—I don't deserve to be treated like that!'

'No, you don't. Get up. Madog! Riwallon!'

He led the way to the turret at the north gate. His companions followed, gripping Dunwal's bound arms. They climbed to the parapet where Owain had first sighted the raiders. He stared out across the estuary, remembering what had happened far out on the sands. No one dared to break his silence.

The sands had vanished now; the tide water was well up the cliff, much more than the height of a man. A few stunted hawthorns were growing near the top, by the ruined walls. He beckoned to Madog.

'Tie the rope to one of those. Make sure it's long enough and that the noose won't tighten—I don't want him hanged or strangled. You'll have to wait till the ebb before you put him there—keep him in the guard chamber down below and get the others to take their turns watching him. I don't suppose he'll be very good company.'

He turned towards Dunwal, who tried to pull away from Riwallon's grip, thinking they were going to pitch him down from the walls. Owain pointed to the foot of the cliff.

'That's Cumbria—yet it's not Cumbria, the sea takes it back twice a day. You're a Cumbrian and not a Cumbrian,

166

you sold your own people's lives. So I'm going to kill you and not kill you. But you're going to die like a Cumbrian —like some Cumbrians, anyway—with your hands tied, drowning when the next tide comes in.'

Dunwal said nothing; he was dead yet not dead. They came down again. Madog pushed Dunwal into the guard room; Riwallon went off promising to bring him some roast beef when it was ready. Owain paused for a few minutes in the shadow of the gateway.

Dusk had fallen. More fires had been lit, they blazed brightly in the gloom. The air was scented with wood-smoke, roasting beef and salt sea-wind. The little ruined fort was as busy as a fair. A detachment of horsemen had come along the coast road from Caer Luel, alerted by a rider from Guasmoric. Folk from Aballava, the little fishing township to the east, had followed the horsemen to see the fun and hunt for pickings. One generous soul had driven up in a cart loaded with barrels. Farm girls had appeared from the hinterland, so many Heulwens, all willing and eager to thank the prince and his gallant band for defending them. Llywarch was sprawled by one of the fires having his drink poured by a dimpling little creature who was listening to the tale of his exploits with flattering interest. She was so anxious not to miss a word that she was pressed tight against his flank. It promised to be a merry night.

Owain could no more join in the merry-making than the gelded captives, who were crouching with their heads on their knees, broken with shame and misery. It was his own victory they were celebrating; they would want him to have the chief share of the praises and the jokes. But Dunwal's treachery had drowned joy and good-fellowship as surely as it had drowned the girls from Caermollt. He had been cut off from his people's warmth and simple loyalty by Dunwal, who was no more a Cumbrian than Taniu had been a virgin. He had no words to say what they were except blasphemies.

'And the Lie was made flesh and dwelt among us.'

He got Seren and sent word by Riwallon to the captain of the horsemen to take charge until the fort was cleared, to see that no one started a brawl or burned the place over their heads. Then he turned his back on Maia, the lights

167

and singing and laughter. He went out into the dusk of the salt-marsh, the whisper of the tide and the cold fingers of the sea-wind.

The gates of Caer Luel were still open, its streets busy. He felt a mood of excitement, caught snatches of talk that made him ready to find the palace courtyard bright with torches and the red cloaks of the royal bodyguard, to see the Raven standard. Urien had returned; he went straight to his father's room to report, though all he wanted was to be lying on his own bed in the quiet darkness.

Urien was sitting in his high-backed chair as if he had never left it. Someone must have raced back from Maia with the news of the raid; he had wine ready to greet his son's victory.

'I'm very pleased with you. You've done very well. The enemy totally routed and the booty recaptured. You can be proud of your first campaign.'

He smiled but it was pleasant teasing not sarcasm.

'By the way, if you'll take a word of advice from someone who's been campaigning rather longer, don't forget this—men who have nothing to hope for can fight like demons. If everyone who faces you knows he'll be castrated if he loses, you're going to have some desperate encounters, my son.'

'I taught a lesson to a pack of scavenging mongrels to keep off our land.'

'Oh, as a lesson, yes.' Urien looked rather anxiously at his son's tense, masked face. Did Owain think he was finding fault? He had done so very well. The fight, indeed, had been little more than a skirmish. But the way of the fight promised a brilliant future. The quick decision, the hunter's instinct for the enemy's movements, the use of the land to fight on his side—all signs of a born war-leader. For a moment, his pride in his son was shadowed with melancholy.

A war-leader has to be something of a bard—only he turns his dreams into corpses, not songs.

The silence dragged; Owain forced himself to keep up his side of the talk.

'They came from Caer Ehedydd. We'd better send troops over there to clear the country.'

'I'm going to take Caer Ehedydd into Cumbria, keep a garrison there.'

'Strathclyde won't like that.'

'If Strathclyde wanted to keep Caer Ehedydd, they should have held it firmly. We've got Candida Casa to guard. We'll be safe-guarding their pilgrims as well as ours.'

Owain was too weary of life to argue. His father believed that when you saw what was best to be done, you did it at once, quite openly. If you couldn't do it for yourself, you would be sincerely grateful to those who did it for you. He was too honest. Dunwal could have deceived him, just as Taniu would have deceived him with her show of purity and virtue if she had ever become his daughter-in-law. Well, neither of them would be getting the chance—and what did it matter? There were plenty of others. Blessed are the hypocrites for they shall inherit the earth.

Looking at his son, Urien blamed himself. What a dreary home-coming for the boy after his first triumph.

'I'm very pleased with you. I'd already decided it's time you had a lordship of your own to rule. I'm going to give you Llwyfenydd. It'll be announced tomorrow at the Council, but you can have the prospect to sleep on!'

He waited for Owain to take it in; to see him come alive with excitement and pleasure but was faced with the same blank mask. Of course, he told himself, the boy must be deathly tired. There had been the pursuit, the fight, the ride back to Caer Luel, all at the end of a day's hunting.

'Go to bed, Owain, and have a good sleep. We'll talk about it in the morning.'

Owain got up, made a dutiful reverence to his father and went out without a word.

CHAPTER
18

The first time Taniu was sick she blamed fat pork and the sultry weather. It was easy to keep on believing this the second time and even the third, as the weather stayed very hot. But she had spent too long with Ancarat; seen and heard too much around the women's quarters in Din Pelidr. Soon, too soon, she was sure.

Yet, childlike, she pushed the knowledge away, even while her mind noted each one of Ancarat's signs as if her body were some other woman's she was watching. Deep inside her being, she felt there was some wound she dare not probe in case she stirred up a pain she could not bear.

Indeed, she was so shocked and bewildered she could hardly think at all about what had happened, still less about what fate might be coming to her now. Owain had appeared so suddenly, then called up all the terrors of her past. Yet for a short time he had made her feel that behind the terror was ecstasy, if she could only reach it; unbelievable beauty in what she had only seen as ugliness. Caught in his arms she had soared into freedom.

Then, as suddenly, he had left her, throwing a few words at her like stones. She had not understood what he was saying but she could feel the total rejection. The falcon had opened its claws with indifference, dropped its unwanted kill and lifted up its pinions over the mountains. She had fallen crushed in the dirt.

'Take that dirty brat out of here. My hall smells like a pigsty.'

That time too, there had been smiles and warmth and cradling arms; then disgust.

Because her pain and shock had its roots deep in her childhood, she could only deal with it at the moment like a child. Turn her back on it. Refuse to think about it. Fail to remember. It didn't really happen.

She went about her usual household tasks, played and chattered with Collen and Eirlys just as usual. The little girls noticed nothing amiss; she got a strange comfort from that. The rest of life was the same, so she could still hide from the fact that she herself was changed.

Lammas came and went but Loth did not send for her. Hoel learned in Din Pelidr that there had been cattle-raiding from Bernicia. Loth was zestfully engaged in reprisals in the south.

As the leaves began to fall and the days shortened, Hoel left the bothy and spent more time around the homestead.

One evening he came in quietly from the byre and stood looking at Taniu. She had put the little girls to bed and was sitting on a stool facing the hearth, leaning back against one of the roof-posts with her eyes closed. The firelight caressed the curve of her belly and stroked the shadowed hollows in her face.

'What have you done, Taniu?'

Her eyes opened on him, wide and startled.

'Done? What should I have done?' But her cheeks were burning.

'You've been with a man.'

She lifted her hand as if to push the words away.

'You've been with a man and you're with child.'

He was cold with fear, yet bitterly jealous. All the months that Taniu had lived in his hut he had desired her, till his body became his torment. Yet it was not only fear of Loth that had kept him off her. He had loved her for her gentleness with his children and almost worshipped her for her vow of chastity. And now she had let someone else taste the sweetness of her body. Loth would spill his heart's blood for that, and all for nothing.

She licked her dry lips.

'I didn't go with a man.'

'You mean you were raped?'

She bowed her head.

'Who was it? Did anyone follow you from Din Pelidr?'

She shook her head. 'He was a stranger. I don't believe he belonged to Lothian. He took me in the forest.'

'Why didn't you say?'

'I didn't want to talk about it. And I thought—I hoped—that nothing—'

She looked so wretched that pity overcame his fear and anger.

'You must get away from here, out of Lothian. You can take the pony. I'll say you ran away to join a sisterhood.'

She looked horrified. 'I can't do that, Hoel. The king would be furious and all his anger would fall on you.'

Seeing that she was worried and frightened for him, not herself, he hadn't the heart to say: Loth will be furious anyway. He'll flog the skin off my bones. But if he sees you like that, he'll kill you.

171

'You must get away. Best make for Strathclyde and go to a nunnery. You can't take the veil now, of course, but you could offer yourself as a lay servant. You'd be safe enough with the nuns, even if Loth did come after you. They say the young king in Alclud is very pious. If the worst happened and Loth tracked you down, you could claim his protection. He's your mother's kin.'

'And whose protection could you claim, Hoel, when Loth asked you where I was? He's angry with me already, it can't be any worse, but I'll tell him you're not to blame.'

Nothing Hoel could say would budge her from that. She would not go, she told him; and soon she could not go even if she would. The wind shifted to the north. For a few days there was a biting cold that froze the marrow in their bones and made their eyeballs ache, while great clouds banked up behind the mountains. Then everything outside the walls was lost in a blinding, suffocating whirl of snowflakes. When that ended they found themselves alone in a world of white and crystal.

The stock was safe in pens and byres; their barn and woodshed were full; they didn't go short of food and warmth. Hoel took over all the heavy tasks, indoors as well as out. He treated Taniu like a careful, kindly husband whose wife was nearing her time.

She herself never thought of the coming child as her baby. She felt none of the protecting tenderness she had for Gwalchmai. This was an invader; a stranger that had taken a place in her body and used it for its own purposes, that had nothing agreeable to do with her. She drowsed by the fire like a sleepy cat, with the little girls snuggled beside her, while the new life grew and stirred. She had drifted into a state of untroubled calm, as if she were living in the Land under the Hills, beyond mortal time and space.

Even Hoel let himself enjoy those last months of peace that the Great Winter brought upon them. Anxiety and fear moved at the back of his mind, like wolves in the forest, but they kept their distance.

When the wind turned southwest at last, and a few days' rain had washed away the snow, setting all the forest brooks flowing brimful, Loth's men rode into the homestead. Hoel glimpsed them splashing along by the riverside and had time to warn Taniu.

'They're coming!'

For the first time she seemed to realize her danger and turned deathly white.

'Is my father—?'

'No, just three of the warband. Get your own clothes out of the chest—hurry!'

She caught up the garments in a flurry and ran behind the curtains of the bed-place. Hoel stood in the doorway, watching the gate, willing her to be quick. When she came out, he took his heavy cloak and wrapped it round her, drawing the hood close to her face.

'Keep yourself covered till you reach Din Pelidr. Get into the women's quarters and stay among the women if you can.'

She nodded. They might be some protection against the worst savagery.

They heard the horsemen ride into the yard. Hoel went out to meet them; Taniu followed and stood in the doorway looking at the newcomers: Brychan, followed by Dunawd, with Morien leading Pybyr.

'Your father wants to know if you're ready to come home,' said Brychan curtly.

Morien looked at Taniu's cloak and grinned. 'She's been ready this long while. Sorry to keep you waiting, princess, we couldn't come before.'

She stepped forward, painfully aware that she couldn't jump nimbly on Pybyr's back as they were used to seeing her. Luckily, Collen and Eirlys burst out crying to see her go and hung on to her. Pybyr pulled towards her, nearly jerking Morien out of his saddle. In the confusion, Hoel was able to pick her up and set her on her pony out of the little girls' clutches. Then he took their hands and stepped back respectfully. She made herself smile down at them.

'Don't cry, darlings, I'll come back,' she lied to comfort them. 'Goodbye, Hoel.' She raised her voice for the warriors to hear. 'Be sure I'll tell the king you kept his orders faithfully.'

He tried to say goodbye with his eyes.

'Farewell, princess. May God guard and comfort you in life and death.'

Brychan swung his horse with an impatient order to get started. Morien closed up to her bridle rein; Dunawd followed. She had no chance for another word or look of farewell as they set off at a brisk trot.

Hoel watched them till they disappeared; he still stood gazing after them, though Collen was pulling at his hand and dancing while Eirlys was sobbing against his knee. He wondered if he should run for it now and lie low in the forest. But he couldn't move fast enough or stay quiet enough with the little girls. Loth's men would flush him out like a hunted hare and the running would look like guilt. Taniu had promised to swear to his innocence; he trusted utterly in her loyalty and truth. He crossed himself and offered a prayer for her soul.

'God have mercy on her!'

He hoped Loth would kill her quickly.

Taniu had no wish to talk to her escorts. She was near her time; her size made Pybyr's hard trot into a torment. Brychan was silent by nature; Dunawd was surly at being dragged out on an errand that promised no sport; but Morien was playing for her notice. He made his horse curvet; whistled or sang by snatches; tried to beguile words out of her by compliments. She answered as civilly as she could, so as not to provoke even closer attention.

Perhaps he saw her increasing pain and weariness; perhaps he wanted to ingratiate himself by showing more thought for her comfort than the others. After all, she was the future queen of Cumbria, her favour was worth something.

They had been travelling for about an hour and were passing a small farm when he rode up to Brychan and spoke. Brychan sounded impatient when he answered, but turned his horse in at the gate. A woman appeared; Brychan yelled to her for food, drink and a seat by the fire for the king's daughter. Dunawd and Morien dismounted; Morien threw his reins to Dunawd and hurried to lift Taniu down before she could dismount by herself. He was grinning with pleasure at his little scheme as he put his arms round her and drew her close. His face changed; he tightened his grip and, as he set her on the ground, drew his hand down the front of her body, feeling for her shape under the cloak. He said nothing; she went silently past him, pulling her cloak even closer as she entered the hut and sat down on the stool the woman placed for her.

Morien tied Pybyr by the other horses; then came and beckoned to Brychan. They spoke for a while, too quietly for her to hear. Then Morien withdrew; a few seconds later she heard hoofs going away at a gallop. Brychan came back and stood staring at her. This would have made her uncomfortable but she could not heed him. The pains in her back and loins were almost unbearable. She could not eat and could hardly force herself to drink some milk.

When the men walked out she dragged herself after them. Brychan got Pybyr, then watched grimly while she tried to pull herself on to his back. Dunawd stared. Finally, Brychan hauled her up roughly, took her bridle rein and they set off. No one spoke to her on this half of the journey.

At the gatehouse they were passed through by Talorg and Nechtan, two of Drostecca's Picts. Morien was lounging inside the gate; he laughed when he saw her and let his eyes wander insolently over her body, but he said nothing. A horse was waiting nearby, saddled and bridled. She noticed, without understanding the meaning of what she saw, that it was a fresh horse, not the one he had been riding before.

She went on with her escort up the flagged road to the citadel. There were few people about at that hour; nobody paid any attention. Through the palace gateway, across the empty courtyard, round to the queen's hall. Gorthyn was waiting in the porch, looking worried and angry. Brychan dismounted and pulled Taniu down; Dunawd took the horses off to the stables. Gorthyn and Brychan each grasped one of Taniu's arms and led her into the hall.

The place seemed deserted. Nowhere in the whole building could Taniu hear the chattering, laughing and scurrying that usually told the presence of women. Then a shadow moved from one of the hall pillars. Lurga had been waiting for her. Gorthyn pulled Taniu's cloak from her shoulders; both men stepped back. She was left exposed to Lurga's cold green eyes. Her gown was too tight and short now over the lifting curve of her great womb. Lurga pressed her hands on it, taking in every line of Taniu's body. She nodded, tight-lipped, to the men; Brychan went out; Gorthyn gripped Taniu's arm and dragged her into the passage, past the heavily-curtained doorway of the queen's room. Lurga opened the door of a store-closet; Gorthyn pushed Taniu inside, throwing the cloak after her. A key turned in the lock. She staggered a few steps, then tripped over something soft and warm, a pile of unspun fleeces. Thankfully she let herself sink down on them, half-fainting, half-exhausted, and went into merciful blackness.

When she was roused by the grating of the key in the lock, it was getting dusk, Ancarat came in, carrying a plate of oatcakes and a beaker smelling of one of her famous possets—hot milk, ale and spices. She set the food on the ground and stooped over Taniu.

'You must say he raped you.'

'He—?' murmured Taniu, her mind still cloudy.

'Hoel. You must say he raped you. It's Loth's fault, sending a lovely young woman to live with a peasant. He should have known what would happen.'

'Hoel didn't rape me.'

Ancarat gripped her shoulder. 'You little fool, do you want to die? Loth will kill you if he thinks you were willing.'

'So I'm to let Hoel die instead?'

'Hoel's dead already, or will be by tomorrow.'

Taniu stared, horrified.

'Morien set off at once, as soon as Lurga saw you. Loth said if it was true, he'd burn the whole place and everybody in it—'

Everybody. Strong, gentle Hoel. Laughing, fearless Collen and little Eirlys who had held her hand for comfort. The slaves, who couldn't help themselves. All dead, or dying now in pain and fear, thinking she'd betrayed them to save herself.

'—so you can't hurt Hoel whatever you say. You'd better start thinking how to save yourself.'

'Hoel didn't rape me. He was a kind, decent man. I won't throw dirt on him now he can't clear himself.'

'And what good will that do? Loth will kill you, just as he killed Hoel, that's all.'

'Loth didn't kill Hoel. I killed him, and his dear little girls, and the poor slaves. I killed them all, the day I refused to marry. Oh God, if only I'd taken the Cumbrian prince none of this would have happened.'

'You can still marry, child.' Ancarat spoke eagerly, misunderstanding her grief. 'There's no hope of Cumbria, now, of course. They won't take anyone's leavings. But you've got royal blood and beauty, and at least you're proved fertile. Many a great lord would be glad to have you. Once we've calmed Loth down and got rid of the child—'

'Got rid—? I'm in my ninth month.'

'God, do you think I can't see? You'll have to bear it, but Loth won't let it live.'

Seeing Taniu's face, she went on more gently, 'It won't feel anything. Nor will you, I promise. I'll mix you a sleepy drink; it'll be gone when you wake up.'

Her scrawny throat jerked; for a moment she couldn't speak. She touched Taniu's hair lightly with her claw-like fingers.

'It's not the end of the world. You're not the first high-born girl it's happened to, and their fathers got over their anger. You can still have a good life—don't throw it away!'

Taniu struggled to sit up. The courage of her fighting ancestors was coming back; she lifted her head as Loth would have done, seeing his death coming across a battlefield.

'I've cost too many other lives. Let mine pay for all and make an end.'

'Don't be too sure of that!' Ancarat was fighting desperately for some hold on Taniu. 'Somebody fathered your child. If it wasn't Hoel, it was some other man. Loth will want to know who.'

She looked sharply at Taniu. 'So if there's somebody you don't want hurt—some young spearman from the body-guard, perhaps?—Or a shepherd from one of the farms?—Or a hunter from the hills?'—her look stabbed with each question—'Loth will take the land apart to the last blade of grass, but he'll find him and kill him. So you might as well say it was Hoel.'

She knew Ancarat was right. And if Loth ever knew that the man who had damaged his property and his family pride was a Cumbrian, he would take his warband over the border and smash everything in his path. Fighting-mad with anger, Loth was a great enough warrior to cut a swathe of destruction through their land before the Cumbrian army came up and wiped him out.

She saw a black-haired hunter going down under Loth's mighty spear: Owain lying under the charred beams of his farm in Argoed Llwyfain, his supple limbs stiff in death, his bright eyes dull and blind as stones. That should have been a sweet thought to lick her lips over, but she found it bitter.

Then the Cumbrians would take their revenge in turn; the blood-red tide would flow back over Lothian. She thought of Peredur's last stand, the Fort of Blood, the fall of the eastern kingdom.

'There'll be no Fort of Blood on Cumbrian land!'

Owain's voice and his eyes.

Nor in Lothian, she answered silently, neither you nor anyone else shall die for me.

Into the waiting quiet, they heard a raven calling, winging its way home in the gathering dusk from the lambing country. Ancarat shivered, crossing herself and muttering a charm to the Mothers all at once. Taniu was listening.

'Whenever you see a raven, remember it's bringing my greetings to you from Cumbria.'

A dark greeting you brought me, Owain. You brought my death as surely as if you had come riding in with Urien's warband behind your Raven banner. Your life in me is my death. Tomorrow your ravens will be tearing my flesh. And still, I can't hate you, or send you a death-curse in return.

'I've a blood-debt to pay to Hoel and his family, Ancarat. The sooner it's paid the better.'

The door creaked ajar; Lurga's voice called angrily, 'Ancarat! Come out of there! The king said no one was to speak to her! If you don't come out this minute, I'll have you whipped!'

The old woman got up painfully. Taniu reached for her hand.

'Thank you, Ancarat.'

'Say it was Hoel,' Ancarat repeated in despair. 'You can't harm the dead.'

The door was shut and locked. She dragged the food nearer. The oatcake made her stomach heave but she made herself drink the posset. It was comfortingly warm; Ancarat had laced it with something stronger than ale.

I must keep up my strength to die with, she thought, and laughed a little. She tried to imagine death, but her mind had begun to float. She lay back staring into the patch of blue that was the window-slit. She watched it deepen, flush with pink, fade to grey. By and by there was the faint blink of a star; then she slept.

In the morning she was cold; most of her courage was in ashes. She managed to be standing when Loth's men came for her. She wrapped Hoel's cloak round her to keep from shivering; also, she hated their eyes on her body.

Loth was waiting for her in the queen's hall. The maids and slave-women were out of sight; Loth's men held the outer door and passageway: Gorthyn, Brychan, Dunawd, the ones he trusted most. She glimpsed young Cynon's distressed face looking through from the porch; he turned away when she saw him. And Morien had been sent to Hoel's steading with Drostecca's Picts. That was to be expected. What did surprise her was that Drostecca was waiting for her too; the queen had seemed to be bedridden long before she left Din Pelidr a year ago.

Drostecca, in all her regalia, was being held up by her cushions in her chair of state, with Lurga standing behind gripping the chair-back. Lurga had decked her mistress's hair and tried to paint her face into some show of health, but there seemed to be only bones under the red robe, the face was a skull. There was a trail of blood-flecked spittle at the corner of her mouth. Only her eyes seemed to be alive; they fastened on Taniu's belly with a dreadful look of greed, triumph and envy. That look drained most of Taniu's remaining strength.

Oh God, why should she hate me so much? I can understand Father—but surely a woman could pity me now?

Drostecca was too frightened for pity now, if she had ever felt it. Picts followed the ancient custom: their kings were sons of the royal women who mated as they chose. As Drostecca saw it, if Taniu bore a son, he would be the heir of Lothian. She knew that Loth and his men had some ridiculous whim about kingship coming by the male seed. But Gwalchmai was so young; Taniu was a grown woman, strong and fertile, well able to fight for her child, while her own time, she knew it, was now so short. It would be long enough, though, to see Taniu dead, with the child dead in her womb. She had dragged herself up in agony to see it done.

Loth had been staring at his daughter, fighting for speech. In spite of Morien's report, confirmed by Lurga with bitter malice, he had not quite believed it till he saw her.

'You filthy cheat! Even the Prince of Cumbria wasn't good enough for you, so you told me. But you can wallow in a pigsty and let any rutting swineherd take up your skirt.'

'That's a lie!'

'So you cry rape?' Loth's voice was bitter. 'Well, you would. Every woman does. I hope Morien roasts Hoel slowly, that's all.'

'Hoel was faithful to you.' To make this clear before she died was the only thing that mattered now. 'You never had a better servant. And he was as innocent—' her voice shook—'as his poor children.'

Loth cared nothing for that.

'If it wasn't Hoel, then who's to blame?'

'I blame no man.'

He stared at her. 'How did you get yourself with child, then? Are you having another virgin birth for your Christian friends?'

She felt sick.

'Whatever happened, I'm ready to pay for it. You've already killed the innocent. If you want more blood, take mine and make an end.'

'Oh, I'll do that. You'll get what you're asking for, never fear. Can't you even trouble yourself to make up a lie for me, you insolent whore?'

Taniu looked at him: at the red face beginning to slacken with drink and indulgence, the veins swollen at the temples. She looked at the dying wreck beside him, remembered Luned—and many others. Lifting her chin, she stared straight into his eyes.

'How dare you call me a whore? I'm—cleaner—than your mind knows how to think.'

She thought her death was coming then but he held himself back.

'Get her out of my sight! Take her away and get rid of her! Put her over the rampart—let the wolves eat what the ravens leave. She's none of mine—she'll get nothing of mine—not even a grave—I don't want a bone or a hair of her left on my land—' His voice choked.

Gorthyn gripped her arm. She felt crushed with loneliness. She had accepted death but it was still dreadful to go out alone into the dark without one word of pity or fellowship.

She did not go alone.

There was a sudden shriek—'Taniu! *Taniu*! Stop! I won't let them hurt you!'

Gwalchmai hurled himself at the warriors, clutching their legs, kicking, biting, jabbing with his toy dagger. The men were taken aback; they halted, uncertain what to do. They couldn't tear the little prince off without injuring him; but he was battle-mad, well able to cripple one of them for life if nobody stopped him.

Then Loth, cursing, pounced on his son from his great height and dragged him away, muffling him in the folds of his cloak. She saw him stride off with the heaving bundle in his arms, saw Drostecca falling back on her cushions with a stream of blood gushing from her mouth. Then Gorthyn pulled her through the doorway, the other men closed up and she was hustled from the queen's hall.

Gorthyn led them out by the back door, making for the guest halls. Here, the precipice was steepest under the ramparts; as there were no guests at present, no eyes would see what they were going to do. On their way, their pace slackened under the shadow of increasing uneasiness. Taniu, nearly unconscious, moving like a sleep-walker, was probably the least caring. Loth's men were tough, brutal fighters who thought little of killing a captive woman in the excitement of a raid or a sack. It was a different matter to destroy a woman of their own royal race, without any preparation of bloodshed or lust to make them feel drunk and happy.

Though Taniu had never flaunted herself for the war-band's admiration, they had always been more aware of her than she knew, and had set her apart from the other women in the court. They weren't blinded by rage, like Loth; each one was sure that she was neither a whore nor a liar. Also, she had not acted like a frightened girl trying to shield a lover. If she blamed no man, there might well be no man to blame. If one of the old gods—the powers that haunted the hills, the stone circles and the hollow mounds of the dead—had come upon Taniu and put his seed in her, then anyone who harmed her could expect a hideous vengeance.

Their walk slowed to a halt. Gorthyn turned on them.

'Get on! Let's get it done with.'

'I don't like it,' said Dunawd.

'What a shame. Then go and tell Loth you don't feel like carrying out his orders. He'll deal with you—and if there's anything left when he's finished, then I'll deal with you. Well, are you going or not?'

Nobody moved. Gorthyn's furious eyes went from one sullen face to another. Even Brychan was disturbed.

'She said she didn't blame any man.'

'Suppose it was one of *Them*?' Cynon sounded scared. 'One of the Lords of the Hollow Hills? He'd never let us kill her.'

Dunawd and Brychan looked more worried than ever; Gorthyn laughed.

'He's left it mighty late to stop us! Why did he let her be dragged back to Din Pelidr and shamed? Why hasn't he wrapped his cloak of mist round her and carried her off to his magic palace? You lot waste too much time listening to bards and storytellers.'

Gorthyn believed in Loth and in his own sword-arm—and in very little else. 'I don't care who or what had her. Loth wants her dead, that's enough for me.'

Brychan looked uneasy. 'He could change his mind when he calms down.'

This was too true for argument, so Gorthyn let his temper slip.

'That's his affair. He gives the orders, we do what he says. If he doesn't like the results, he can blame himself not us.'

He glared at them suspiciously. 'Why are you making all this fuss about a girl and her bastard? Drivelling about a god having her! Which of you went sleep-walking down the path to Hoel's place last summer? What about you, young Cynon? You went traipsing down south with her the year before—is that when you got the taste for it?'

Cynon's face was white but he met Gorthyn's eyes steadily enough.

'I know nothing more about it than you, Gorthyn. But whoever or whatever fathered it, while she's carrying it she's under the power of the Mothers.'

There was a chill silence. Even Gorthyn felt the skin of his neck prickling. A man might defy the other powers; at least in the daylight with his comrades around him, or in the hall when he was pot-valiant, but no man tempted the vengeance of the Goddess. Her anger was deadly.

Gorthyn thought of the tree-roots that could clutch a man's ankle and bring him down the moment the boar charged; the sword that could break in the hour of need as the foe drew close around. Worst dread of all, the manhood weakening and shrivelling, leaving the wretched victim helpless to the pity and mockery of all, even the slaves.

He saw the others thinking about it too; he knew they would not obey him if he dared to give the order. Yet if he did not give the order he would have lost command and they would know it. And there would still be Loth to face.

Puzzled and angry, he stared across the ramparts at the sweep of country below; at the river winding away northeast; at the sword-grey line on the horizon. The sight made up his mind.

'Right. Run and fetch that hand-cart, Cynon—there, against the wall.'

'What are we going to do with her?' asked Brychan.

'Loth said he didn't want her on his land.' Gorthyn sounded highly satisfied. 'So we'll put her in the sea. Then, if any god wants her, he can come and take her. Either way, she won't have a grave in Lothian, but we won't have killed her. Now, get her into that cart, we've wasted enough time.'

CHAPTER
19

The man who held Llwyfenydd was the shield guarding Cumbria's heart. The valleys of Idon and Llwyfenydd were the richest pastureland in the country. The great road from Caer Luel to the south ran through it; coming across the fords was another road over the Long Hills to the east. At its other end stood Catraeth, which was why Urien had seized it. If Catraeth fell, the Roman road would bring enemies straight to the Cumbrian heartland.

By the road junction there had once been a flourishing town round the fort of Brocavum. Its folk no longer found it pleasant to be near a Roman road, especially that Roman road. They had moved northwards to the hill, where they felt safer. It commanded the fords; they could see enemies coming and give warning to the countryside by lighting a beacon on top of the fell.

Owain agreed with their choice. He too settled at Penrhyd, founding his chief court and stronghold there. Urien had allowed him to choose his warband from the younger warriors at Petriana, so he had his friends with him, veterans of the skirmish at Maia, including Gwion. Llywarch had taken the boy as his page.

He found that this new lordship demanded as much time and thought as a new mistress. He was glad enough to give it, riding far and wide till he knew the remotest valley, the loneliest farm in all Llwyfenydd. The ceaseless moving from place to place, the constant arguing over food-rent and lawsuits, the endless procession of new faces, each one with a name he had to learn and feelings he had to manage—all helped him to hide from the knowledge that he was alone in a wasteland.

Sometimes, crossing the high fells on a fresh autumn morning after rain, he would see Taniu in the sunlight and the crystal-clear moorland streams. He could drive her away in the daylight, but she would return in the night, befouled and weeping as he had last seen her. In his dreams he would shout at her to be quiet; it was stupid to weep over a few moments of sport. Then she would lift her face and he would see cat's eyes, white teeth snarling, the gleam of moon-silver.

Better to tire his body beyond the reach of dreams. So he rode furiously while daylight lasted and his nights were blank as death.

Once, briefly, he enjoyed a respite of gentle pleasure. He had ridden up to Caer Luel to report to Urien and spend a few days in the palace. The shorelands of Cumbria, facing westwards round the great estuary, had escaped the worst ravages of the severest winter in living memory. Now, there was a feel of spring in the air, the birds were busy and talkative, bare twigs were greening.

Owain, striding along the garden colonnade, did not see the girl in the shadow of a column and almost knocked her down. She glided aside with a murmured apology. He saw it was Heledd, a young orphan of good family whose lands were in the king's wardship. Lady Guendolena was her guardian. Owain had been carelessly kind to the child whenever he saw her on his visits to his mistress; she was a grown woman now, past fourteen, and her breasts had budded. She was very pretty, with her light silky hair and great golden-brown eyes, but she looked as desolate as when she had first come to the palace after her parents' death.

'Why, child, what's wrong with you?'

She stared at him forlornly.

'Has Lady Guendolena been unkind?'

She shook her head, her eyes brimful.

'What then?'

She stared at her feet. He could hardly hear her.

'You don't live here now—you were so good to me—you never come to see us—it's so long—and—'

It was so clear what was wrong with her that he had to smile. He brushed his fingers across her cheek. 'Suppose

185

you come to my room and tell me all about it. Come after nightfall, so we can be private and knock like this—' he tapped out a rhythm on her palm. 'Will you come?'

She bowed her head.

'Till night, then.'

He sent Madog off to amuse himself in the city; then undressed and stretched out on his bed, sipping wine, enjoying the warmth of it inside him, the glow of the charcoal brazier, the soft touch of the fur coverlet against his naked limbs.

A tapping at the door; Heledd entered, closing it quietly behind her. She tried to take off her dress but her hands were shaking so that she could not unfasten her brooches. He laughed at her and jumped up to help, letting the unpinned dress drop to her ankles, sliding her shift down her shoulders.

She was shaking like a reed in the wind as he lifted her on to the bed but she lay back submissively, spreading her arms and parting her legs. Because he neither loved nor hated her, but was only thinking of pleasure, he took care of her pleasure as well, soothing and fondling her with his long, fine fingers and entering her gently. Though she cried out and quivered as he took her, she embraced him at once, stroking his back and covering his face and neck with soft little kisses as if asking his pardon even for that.

She had no knowledge or skill in love-making but her gentleness and docility delighted him. After their play he drew the fur coverlet round them and lay back satisfied into a dreamless sleep.

He woke in the grey dawn. Heledd was curled in the crook of his arm, her warm breath brushing his skin. It had been a sweet night; he thought about taking her back to Llwyfenydd and enjoying more of her sweetness, like spring violets or new milk.

But I couldn't live on sweetmeats, he said to himself, half-bitterly. I'd get sick and weary; then I'd hurt her, and she's got no strength to fight back. If Taniu had been what I dreamed she was—*she* could have held me, mind and heart and body. Best say goodbye to this child while she can still remember me kindly.

Heledd stirred and opened her eyes. He smiled at her

and drew her close, brushing his lips tenderly across her mouth.

'Morning's here, sweetheart. You must be off before anyone sees you or you'll get a scolding from Lady Guendolena.'

She sat up and reached for her shift but he cupped his hands at each side of her slim waist and turned her to look down at him.

'I may see you again in the great hall when I take leave of the king—' he spoke with careful lightness— 'but we'll say our own goodbyes properly, here. Kiss me, darling and wish me a good journey.'

She looked at him wistfully. 'Are you going away today, lord?'

'I must. I've a troop of young spearmen to take back to Penrhyd and three lawsuits to settle when I get there.'

Her lips quivered; he expected an offer to come with him, tears, pleadings. His black brows drew together in an angry frown. She said nothing, though, and began to dress. This time her hands were quite steady. He was touched; he reached for a casket on the chest by the bed and groped till he found a small sapphire ring he sometimes wore on his little finger.

'If—' he had been going to say *If I've got you with child* but found he could not— 'If you're ever in trouble, or sickness, or grief, you must tell me at once, and me only. And if ever anyone is cruel to you—frightens you or treats you badly—just show this ring and say who gave it to you. It's a sign between us, our own special bond.'

He put the ring on her finger as he spoke. Heledd kissed it as if it were a holy relic; then knelt and kissed his hands. He felt her cheeks were wet but she glided away without a sound.

So that ended satisfactorily and was pleasant to remember when he had time. This was not often, for the cares and interests of his lordship absorbed him.

All this while he kept away from Caer Voran. He knew Penarwan would be avid for details of his Lothian adventure. He would have died by torture rather than serve them up to the mockery of her bright eyes and sharp tongue. When he had to go to Garmon's horse-runs in March to select mounts for his warband, he came up Tinadale from the south by the road over the fells.

Then courtesy trapped him. Garmon took it for granted that he would be going on to Caer Voran. He was busy with foaling, so he asked Owain to take up some messages for his household. Owain meant to give the messages to Ressona and not see Penarwan out of her company; luck was against him.

Penarwan was having her monthly bleeding. This was always a bad time for her and her temper suffered. Ressona took care to find herself employment at the other end of the house, leaving the maids to bear the brunt. That day, Penarwan had already harried most of them into tears. Owain's arrival made a welcome diversion; Ressona thankfully sent him to the south room.

Penarwan was on her couch, her feet propped on cushions; her eyes brightened when she saw Owain. He delivered her father's messages and began a detailed account of his horse-dealing. When he paused for breath, she asked eagerly, 'And what happened in Lothian? I've been dying to know. Did your scheme work?'

'No matter. That's a very fine grey stallion your father's got—will he sell him or keep him for the stud?'

Penarwan's eyes gleamed maliciously.

'So it didn't work! And all your famous love-craft left standing outside the magic circle of her chastity. What did she do to you?'

'Let be, Penarwan!' He spoke sharply but she took that as a challenge. She had been edgy and spiteful all day and was ready to enjoy tormenting. Owain promised better sport than the wretched maids.

'What happened, Owain? Does the smell of pig put you off? Couldn't you keep your—interest—up when it came to the point?'

He gave her a murderous look; she laughed in his face. He knew she'd keep up the teasing till she got an answer; she'd keep it up in front of Ressona and the maids at dinner till all Caer Voran rang with it. Fighting his temper, he reminded himself that he had taken her so far into his confidence that she had some right to be curious.

'Listen, Penarwan. You've helped me; I owe you an

answer. So I'll speak of it once and no more. If you ever ask me again, or tell anyone else, that will be the end of our friendship. I mean that.'

His tone sobered her; she laid her hand on his.

'I didn't mean to hurt you. Don't take it so hard. You went to her too soon after she defied her father—I thought of that after you'd gone. A girl says "No" once and then feels ashamed to unsay it. But she can't refuse you for ever.'

She patted his hand. 'She's had all winter to think better of it—and what a winter! I'm sure by now she couldn't get to Caer Luel quick enough if she could only think how to get there without making herself look a fool.'

She thought it over; then looked up, her face alive with an idea.

'Suppose we get Bishop Viventius to work on her? He'd find a way for her to back down gracefully, make it look like her religious duty.' She laughed. 'I'll wager we have her smiling by your side at King Urien's high table before midsummer—come, what'll you bet me?'

'I'll never have her by my side!' Owain's temper flared. 'And my father's house is no place for drabs. If she ever comes to Caer Luel she can get a lodging in some brothel where she belongs.'

Penarwan stared. He curbed himself, thinking bitterly that Taniu wasn't worth a show of feeling.

'I tried her. As others had done before me. She wasn't a virgin.'

'I don't believe it!'

'Penarwan, for God's sake, let be!'

But Penarwan would not let be. She surprised herself by the strength of her determination to fight the point; she was not quite sure why. There was the pleasure of setting her own judgement against Owain's; she was ready for a little velvet-pawed tormenting by the way. There was the instinct to defend another woman against a charge that could have been thrown in her own face. Deeper than all, there was a strange impulse of loyalty to the truth of her own knowledge of Taniu.

'She's not a drab. A woman can cheat her father or her husband; she can even cheat her lover. But she can't cheat

189

another woman about that. I've shared her bed, I know what I'm talking about.'

'And do you think I don't know the feel of a maidenhead? Oh, I give her credit, she took a very cunning way to cover her loss. She's not the first cheating whore to act virtue; she won't be the last.'

Penarwan shook her head.

'It would be such a stupid lie. If they forced her into marriage, the truth would come out and it'd be a hundred times worse for her. She could only keep the story up by becoming a nun in the end—and if she were that sort of woman it would be even worse than death.'

She spoke with conviction; Owain was unconvinced.

'Din Pelidr's never been sacked since the Pictish wars. She's never been carried off. None of Loth's men would dare to take her against her will. So can you explain how she could give her virginity away without being "*that sort of woman*"?'

'Perhaps she gave it to Lugos,' said Penarwan lightly.

'She what—?' He broke off to stare at Penarwan who had begun to shake with laughter. Her face flushed, her eyes streamed, her hair fell over her cheeks, she clawed at her cushions—and still she laughed.

He put his long fingers round her neck.

'Stop it, or I'll kill you.'

She blinked her wet eyelids and shook her curls back, still chuckling.

'I wasn't laughing at you. I was just remembering Pluma's wedding.'

'Pluma?'

'Ressona's daughter. My half-sister, of course. I don't think you ever met her, she's five years older than me; she married just after I came home from Candida Casa. A rich farmer down in Tinadale, who gives himself the airs of a chief. Father gave them a fine wedding to please Ressona and because he's fond of the girl—indeed, she's a pleasant enough, well-meaning creature. We bedded them in one of the houses under the north wall, where nobody would disturb them; then came back to finish the celebrations, or be finished by them, because by that time most of us could hardly stand. Things had got quieter, and those of us who weren't under the tables had our heads down on them, when there came such a howling and screeching you'd have thought the Picts had come south again. So we all staggered back to where we'd left Pluma and her man, because that's where the outcry was.'

She started to laugh again.

'There was Pluma, hanging on the guttering, trying to pull herself up to the roof, and her bridegroom standing underneath, trying to hit her with a hay-rake. You've never seen anything so funny!'

She sniffed and mopped her eyes.

'They were mother-naked, both of them, just as we'd left them in the marriage bed. Pluma's a big girl, she couldn't pull herself over the guttering—her fat rump looked like the full moon at Lammas just hanging there on the edge. He couldn't quite get at her because the rake was short-handled—lucky for her, or we could have used her back-side for a colander. All the while he was lashing out he was yelling about damaged goods, and we'd sold him a broken pot, and I don't know what all. She was screaming like all the devils in hell. My brothers got the rake off him and threw him in the horse-trough to cool down, then locked him in a shed for the night. Then we had to get Pluma down. She was nearly out of her mind. Ressona had to sit up with her.

'In the morning my father wanted to know what it was all about. He was in a foul temper, I can tell you, what with the wedding being spoiled, and having a thick head and Ressona upset. The man said he hadn't had fair play, being let think she was a virgin when someone else had had her first. The insolence! How many farm girls keep their maidenheads for their marriage nights? But Pluma swore by every saint in the calendar that no man but him had ever come between her legs. Then Ressona said that five years before, when there was sickness and the mares were dropping dead foals, she'd given her maidenhead to Lugos. So Father had him flogged for insulting our family and made him apologize to Pluma. He was very willing—when he knew Lugos had had her, he was scared for his life.'

'What do you mean?'

To Owain the phrase meant nothing. Though Urien was too wise and compassionate to tear his people from their old faith before they had found a new one, he was sternly orthodox himself and saw that his household was likewise. Owain had heard of the old gods mainly in the poetic tales of the bards. He knew that the country folk had their rites at the four seasons' ends; as far as he had ever seen they consisted of harmless drinking, love-making and dancing round bonfires. Only his meeting with the witch-priestess had shown him the darker face of the Old Religion.

'He's the Lord of the Burning Spear—so of course he can destroy the marsh-demons who bring the sickness. And if the land, or stock, or women's wombs are barren and can't bear, he can kindle them into life. It's *that* sort of spear, you see. And if he does these favours for mortals, he expects a thank-offering.'

'And so—?'

'They give him a maidenhead. And because he's Lord of the Spear—in fact, he *is* the Spear—they do it with a spear.'

She lowered her voice to a whisper. 'Ressona told me. The Druids do it, they use a spear with a flint head that they get out of the fairy hills, you know, the sort they call elf-bolts.'

She tittered nervously.

'Only women are allowed to see it, apart from the Druids. They all go up to one of the holy circles and dance naked for the god—I'd give anything to go, just once! Only my father came in while I was asking Ressona, and he told her if he ever heard her speaking to me about such things again, he'd take every inch of skin off her with his horse-whip. So she never has. Ressona will always obey Father rather than me.'

Owain had been listening intently.

'But, Penarwan, just because your father's mistress gave her bastard's maidenhead to a heathen god, it doesn't follow that a Christian king would do the same with his daughter, especially if he planned to offer her to a Christian prince in marriage. He'd feel the same as your father did.'

She laughed. 'Loth's a queer kind of Christian. He'll

worship anything and everything he thinks will give him success in battle or in bed. As for that Pictish she-devil he married, she's no kind of Christian at all. And she doesn't bear easily. I've heard Morcant laughing about it in Din Eidyn.'

'But would she do that to her husband's daughter, even to get a child?'

'From what I heard in Din Eidyn, there's nothing she wouldn't do. There was a dreadful story about a girl Loth had and a child she was going to bear him.'

Owain was struggling against a terrible conviction, as if he was trying to swim against a river that was taking him slowly and inescapably towards the lip of a waterfall.

'But if such a thing happened to Taniu, how could she ever claim that she wanted to dedicate her virginity to Christ?'

'She needn't know about it.' By now, Penarwan had fallen in love with her own theory. 'Pluma didn't. After all, a god expects his brides to be joyful and willing, but it isn't so easy to act joyful when you're stretched on a slab having a spear put into your—Ressona told me they filled Pluma so full of barley spirit the Druid could have slit her up to the navel and she wouldn't have noticed.'

She saw Owain's face and added hastily, 'I only said what might have happened. I've no proof that it did.'

He stood up.

'Give my excuses to Ressona and the dinner she's getting for me. I've a journey to make.'

He wanted speed above all things, without foundering Seren. He went east along the Wall to Onnum, then up the great Northern Road that led from Deira.

I'll go quite openly, he told himself. No more nonsense about disguise. I'll make her talk to me and if I find Penarwan was right—or if she tells me any other believable story—I'll believe her, and ask her pardon, poor darling! At any rate—he smiled at the thought—she won't be able to claim any longer that she's refusing marriage to keep her maidenhead intact. I'll just put her up on Seren, take her to her father and tell him I've found the quickest and simplest way over that fence!

He could picture Loth bellowing with laughter and slapping him on the back. Taniu might not be so delighted with him; he could imagine she might be rather offended. He looked forward with interest and pleasure to coaxing her round; he'd need all his falconer's skill before he had her coming tame to his hand.

The wind was from the west as he came to the Moorfoots. It brought some quality to his nose and palate that made him remember Gwion crawling from the ruins of Caermollt.

He was recognizing landmarks now, the curve of the river bank, the stream where he had led Taniu, the faint path going up to his camping place. And all the while, the reek of burning grew stronger.

He turned the bend in the river. There was the meadow where Taniu had chased her cow, the stockade at the crest of the slope. The gate hung open, giving a glimpse of black ruin inside. Yet he rode on, as if in a nightmare. Smoke was still rising but everything seemed dead, even the flames.

Inside the courtyard, though, life was going on quite merrily. There was a good fire blazing, broken stools and bits of household furniture. Over it, on a makeshift spit, a piglet was roasting. It was being watched by a young man with curly black hair and a floridly handsome face. He was sprawling across a barrel, one of several that had been rolled up to the fire; he had some of their contents in a stone jug, but was shifting them as fast as possible into his mouth.

It was so like the scene after a sack that Owain would have thought a robber band had come down on the steading, if he hadn't seen the man's shield propped against a barrel. It showed the Black Bull's Head of Lothian; this was one of Loth's warriors. He dismounted and walked slowly towards the fire.

The warrior waved his jug hospitably. 'Greetings, hunter!'

'Greetings.' Owain spoke like a sleepwalker, his eyes searching the ruins.

Perhaps a spark caught in the thatch, or a lamp overturned in the milking-shed or woodstore. There was a charred stump lying in a gap that had been a door; it had a

194

twisted bough with some blackened twigs. Lucky for them one of Loth's men was here to help them deal with the blaze. She must have taken the children to one of the farms down the river.

The Lothian man noticed Owain's western accent; he grinned.

'What brings you east, Cumbrian? Come to pay your respects to your future queen? You've left it a bit too late—have a drink instead.' He handed the jug.

Owain bit his lips to keep them from trembling. 'There's been an accident?' he said huskily, still staring at the little bough with the blackened twigs. He had just realized it was a child's arm.

Morien had reached the jovial stage of drunkenness. He chuckled.

'Yes, an accident . . .' He tried the word carefully in his mouth. 'The swineherd was careless, very careless. What else can you expect when a man doesn't stick to his job? Hoel's job was keeping pigs. But he would go ploughing. He ploughed up the king's private meadow, virgin soil, and sowed his seed in it.'

He paused to savour his own wit; he laughed. 'Sowed his seed in it.' He shook his head and became owlishly solemn. 'The king was angry, very angry. Can't have such doings. Have to stamp them all out. Slaves ran away though. Talorg and Nechtan are off hunting 'em in the woods.'

'Do you mean he burned her?'

'Not her. He's very just, our king. He had her up to Din Pelidr, for the women to look at her. But there wasn't any doubt. I had her in my arms when I helped her down from her horse and she was as round as a cheese. I heard Loth say, if it was true he'd throw her over the walls for the crows. It's a long drop.'

He lifted his hand high over his head and brought it down with a smack against his knee.

'Splat!' he said, and giggled. He was still giggling when Owain brought the jug down on his skull and he crashed forward with his face in the fire.

Owain remounted and rode westwards into the wind. The reek of burning was blown behind him but he could not get away from Taniu's face. She was looking from among the trees, sometimes fresh and smiling; sometimes with her face blotched with dust and tears; sometimes with her skull smashed, the jagged bone sticking through the skin, the bright hair clotted with blood. She watched him hour after hour, mile after mile.

To get away from the face he dug his heels into Seren, urging him faster and faster. The horse caught his master's mood and began to panic, dashing blindly forward. Twigs and branches whipped Owain as he was hurled past, clawing and striking like arms. They were arms. They were black because they had been burned. And always Taniu staring at him.

A violent blow smashed across his forehead; he fell down into darkness where a witch voice screamed at him that all his joy in life had been poured away under the walls of Din Pelidr and he would be empty, empty, empty . . .

CHAPTER
20

For Taniu, huddled on the bare boards of the cart, the journey to the river-mouth meant no more than that the pain was battering her from outside as well as inside her body. As far as she could hold on to her mind, she was praying for a quick death.

At last, the river wound into the marsh; the track veered away over the salting pasture and came out on to the sands. Here, upturned among the dunes, they found a coracle; Gorthyn pointed; Dunawd and Cynon righted it and dragged it to the water's edge. Gorthyn and Brychan lifted Taniu out of the cart. She made herself stand and walk between them unaided.

All her senses were sharpened in these last moments. She was keenly aware of the sand under her feet, soft and dry above the tide-line, then hard, damp and ridged into ripples; the crunch of shells; the smell of dulse and bladder-wrack; the high pure cry of a gull. The sun was setting to the northwest; the sea was a sheet of shimmering gold; she was moving out into the heart of the brightness.

The coracle began to lift with the waves. Dunawd held it as they put her in; she lay down on her side with her head pillowed on her arms as if ready for sleep. Cynon, biting his lips, tucked the cloak round her. Then he and Dunawd waded out to sea, pushing as hard as they could. The coracle wavered; then the ebb took it and it moved steadily out to sea.

Gorthyn led the way back across the beach. They went in silence; when they had climbed the first slope above the river, they turned with one impulse to look back. The light on the sea was deepening to rose; in the eastern sky the first stars were showing. Far out, they could just discern a bobbing black dot, getting further and further away.

'Well, I don't see Lugos swooping down as a falcon to rescue her,' said Brychan sourly, ashamed of his earlier fear.

Dunawd sniggered. 'Or Llyr driving his chariot over the waves to invite her to his sea-palace!'

'It's a pity she had to die.' Cynon glared defiantly at Gorthyn.

'A great pity,' agreed Gorthyn unexpectedly. 'A fine upstanding lass, with more courage than most. I've seen hardened warriors break, faced with a death-sentence in cold blood—she kept her head up and her mouth shut. But pity or not, there's the end of her!'

They turned their backs on the sea.

The coracle, rocking on the waves, was like a cradle. Its sides kept the sea-wind away from her; she was snug under her cloak. The pain had changed; it moved down her back and came in moments of griping intensity.

Between whiles, she dozed fitfully, or gazed up into the vault of deepening blue, brilliant with stars. The coracle drifted on as the tide ebbed, slackened, turned.

There was an unwelcome change. The pains were getting more violent, the intervals shorter, when the coracle itself began to shake and batter her. This reminded her body so dreadfully of its torture in the cart that she forced herself to sit up. The waves had brought the coracle against a shelf of smooth flat-topped rocks; beyond was a beach backed by dunes. The coracle swayed with the receding wave; the next one slapped it against the rocks again, jarring her unbearably. She got shakily to her feet, nerving herself to get out next time the coracle came against the shore. If she slipped into the water or fell on the rocks, she wouldn't be able to get up again.

She made the step, stumbled but managed to keep on her feet, though she lost her cloak and her skirt got soaked. Free of her weight, the coracle swung clear and was carried up the Weryd on the incoming tide. With painful care she picked her steps over the slippery ledge and at last reached the sands.

Now she was shivering with cold as well as pain. The sea-wind cut through her bones; her wet skirt was icy to her legs. The damp sands below the tide-line had a chill gleam under the moon. She longed to lie down out of the wind and that cold pitiless light. Looking desperately along the beach she saw something that glowed red instead of silver-blue. Every nerve in her body yearned towards it, forcing her limbs into tottering movement.

It had been a large fire of driftwood; the ashes were still giving out a fair amount of heat. When the breeze swept across it, the embers woke to a light, wavering flame. There was a pile of unburned wood stacked nearby; she clawed at one or two smaller bits and dragged them on to the hot ashes. They kindled; the flame shot higher.

She collapsed beside it as the birth-pangs took her body and bent it to their needs. With the last of her fading mind she tried to remember what she had seen Ancarat do, but all she could think was: *I haven't got a knife—I can't cut the cord—no knife—no knife—*

Then she began to scream.

Coming back to life was hard because he had to rise up through waves of pain. Owain struggled to sink back into darkness but each wave was stronger; the last one rolled him up into light that hurt his eyes.

The light showed a bed where he was lying, covered with blue and brown blankets. When he stirred and moaned, someone leaned over and put a beaker to his lips;

he swallowed a mouthful of ale. Then his head was touched gently with a wet cloth. Turning painfully, he saw a broad rosy face, round dog-like brown eyes gazing at him with concern and pity. He recognized Heulwen but was too weary for surprise.

'What's this place? How did I get here?'

'It was your horse, my lord. My man went to get it.'

Heulwen rarely talked much and was not used to giving clear explanations. 'My man said there was a stray horse in the forest, it looked like good stock and he was going to get it. So he went out with the boy who blows the bellows. And the horse was dead weary and they got it easily and brought it back. And I went out to look and said, "That's Prince Owain's horse, he thinks the world of it. He'd never part with it or let it run wild like that. There must be something wrong. Go out and look for him." And so we all went out to look and there wasn't a sign of you anywhere. Then when the horse was fed and rested my man said, "I'll take the horse and see where he goes." And he went northeast and my man was away for a day and a night and part of another day and then he came back with you laid over the horse and oh! my dear lord, we thought you were dying. So my man went off to Caer Luel to tell the king and—'

She broke off and lifted her head. There was a clattering of hoofs and jingling of harness some way off. Heulwen scurried out. Voices sounded; steps came nearer. The door opened; his father entered followed by a man in black robes, Mavorius, the palace doctor.

Urien waited in controlled silence while the doctor examined Owain.

'How is my son?'

The doctor nodded slightly. 'The prince is blessed with a strong constitution. There has been concussion and some fever but his body has overcome it.'

'Will he be able to travel to Caer Luel in the litter?'

'There is no reason why not.'

'Then will you be so good, Mavorius, as to tell the men we'll set out as soon as they've taken refreshment and rested the horses.'

Mavorius bowed and withdrew. As he went out,

Heulwen came in with a jug of mead and a platter of oatcakes and sliced meat for the King. Dinogat, a big sturdy toddler, came in after her and made straight for the gold fringe on Urien's cloak to grab and finger it. Heulwen hissed, 'Oh bad, *bad*!' with an appalled look at the king. She wanted to pounce on Dinogat but her hands were full.

While she dithered, Urien, who like all truly strong men was very gentle with the young and the weak, had stooped to lift the little fellow and give him to his mother. Dinogat grinned happily into his grandfather's face. Heulwen put her things down and hurried up to collect her son, but Urien held him a moment looking at the two of them.

Dinogat was his mother's child entirely; he had her stocky build, broad snub face and round, guileless brown eyes. Urien smiled kindly and handed the little boy to her. She scuttled out thankfully; Urien turned to his son at last. The smile had vanished.

'Will you never leave your folly, Owain? You could have died out there in the wilds and we might never have found your body to give it a grave!'

In spite of his control his voice shook.

'Does the lordship I trusted you with mean less to you than a day's hunting?'

Owain said nothing.

'If my peace of mind counts for nothing to you—if you won't learn prudence for my sake, perhaps the care of a wife and child may teach you.'

Between two heartbeats, Owain had time to picture Loth softening at the sight of his daughter and smuggling her away to Nia to bear her baby in secret. He had just decided that he would send for the child and own it as his before the wedding, when Urien's voice broke in.

'There will be no marriage with Lothian now—though the alliance, I trust, will stand. The sickness was heavy there this cruel winter. Loth lost his wife and daughter; they died within a day of each other and were buried together. I had the news out of Lothian just before the smith came to fetch me. It's a grievous loss for the king. I've sent mass-offerings to Mailros in your name and mine. As for your marriage, we'll have to arrange something else.'

He waited for Owain to comment but his son's face

showed nothing but the utmost stony indifference. He watched more sharply as he said, 'The woman here, who has your son—she's a decent, faithful creature, we both owe her a great deal. I've seen that the smith is rewarded and you will, of course, provide for the boy—but in the name of heaven, Owain,' his voice showed his exasperation, 'there's surely nothing about her to make you turn from lawful marriage with a beautiful girl of your own rank!'

In spite of his misery, the idea of poor simple Heulwen, with her plain, honest face, as his fatal lover, made Owain's mouth twitch. His father saw the smile; it relieved his anxiety but increased his irritation. His tone hardened to a command.

'I've sent messengers to Lord Garmon, but as we already know each other's minds, I've no doubt of his answer. At midsummer, you marry the Lady Penarwan.'

CHAPTER 21

The fishers of Culenros had made a big haul that night; it took a long time to land the catch. Last and slowest was Bran; he was only thirteen and had no man to help him with the boat since the sea took his father. For a while he had been afraid he would have to give up the boat and with it all claim to a share in the nets. Then he would have had to scratch a living along the foreshore; it would have gone hard with his grandmother and cousin Rigan, a sea-orphan like himself, who lived with them. But Rigan had offered to come out with him; she was twelve, as tough and wiry as a boy, and she hero-worshipped Bran.

Between them, they had not done so badly; Bran was feeling more hopeful about the future. They finally hauled their coracle under the shelter of the dunes beside the others, sorted and creeled their share of the catch and stowed it in the fish-sheds for gutting and salting. At last, they turned up the track towards the huts that clustered beyond the dunes; they were tired and walked in companionable silence. Suddenly, two points of green fire shone down at them from the crest of the ridge.

This was Brith their brindled collie bitch, who could take a wolf by the throat, come to see why they were late. When the nights were fine and the boats put out, Brith would patrol outside her hut and wait to welcome her people back. There was never any leaping, barking or tail-thumping; Brith was not an effusive dog, even her attacks were as silent as they were deadly. A touch of her cold nose, a sniff at their legs, then she would fall in behind them and see them to their door.

Tonight, though, she stayed gazing down the beach, her hackles rising, growling softly.

'What is it, Brith?'

They turned to follow her gaze. Far down the beach, they saw the dying fire spring into flames.

'Who's down there? The boats are all in, I counted them.'

'Pirates?' Rigan gasped between excitement and alarm.

'More likely those poaching swine over from Eidyn, making free with our waters and our beach!'

Bran set off towards the flames, keeping to the landward side of the dunes. Rigan and Brith padded silently behind him, Rigan feeling for the handle of the knife in her belt. She was ready and willing to use it on anybody who tried to rob Bran of his rights.

Arriving level with the fire, they raised their heads cautiously over the ridge. There were no boats in sight; the beach seemed deserted. The firelight showed nothing but a dark heap or bundle. While they craned, Rigan felt something brush against her legs, bare under her rolled-up breeches. Glancing down, she saw with surprise that it was Brith's feathery tail waving gently. The dog was talking to herself; not growling but making a soft crooning noise in her throat that was only heard when she was suckling her puppies.

'Look at Brith.'

At that moment the bitch went streaking towards the heap by the fire. Rigan ran after her, followed by Bran, then stopped in amazement. The heap was a young woman, lying with her arms flung wide, hands clawing the

202

sand, her knees drawn up. Brith was lying beside her, licking her face.

'What's the matter?' Bran was taken aback. 'What's she doing?'

Rigan had seen three little brothers born and die; her mother had gone with the last. She knew only too well what the strange woman was doing.

'Quick! Run and tell Grandmother there's a woman having a baby on the beach. Then tell some men to come with a hurdle. Go on, run!'

As Bran, totally bewildered, showed no sign of doing anything but gape, she swung him round, giving him a violent shove. Then she turned to the stranger, drawing her knife. There was going to be a use for it after all.

Some hours later, when Father Servanus came out of his little oratory, the stars were fading though they still showed as points of light towards the west. He had been saying the Dawn Office; he stood for a moment breathing the dew-fresh air, thanking God for the creation. Since childhood, his thoughts had always turned to the love of God with answering love; so for him the veil between the Two Worlds would sometimes grow thin and almost melt away.

'*Laudarent simul astra matutina*—when the morning stars sang together and all the sons of God shouted for joy . . . ' It seemed for a moment that he could hear them singing, high, clear and far away.

A robin flew up from the grass, startled; Servanus came back into this world, saw the little group waiting by the fence and went to meet them. They were fisherfolk from Culenros; he blessed them, then asked, 'What brings you here so early, my sons?'

Several voices told him.

'There's a woman—she's had a child—a son—'

Father Servanus thought over the village women.

'Annis? She's well before her time—no mischance, I hope?'

They were excited; the story came at him from every side.

'Not Annis—a stranger!'

203

'She came from the sea!'

'Bran found her on the beach!'

'She's got a green gown and slippers—and a shift as fine as a spider's web—and silver brooches—'

Servanus held up his hand.

'One at a time! Now, let me be clear. A high-born woman having a baby on the beach. Alone? Was there any sign of a wreck? Did you say she's come from over the sea?'

There was a moment's silence; one of the men said, 'We think she came from under the sea.'

'There wasn't a boat but we found her footprints in the sand, coming up out of the water.'

'And she's as white as foam, her hair's golden like the sands in sunlight.' This was Bran, blushing to his ears.

'And we want you to come and put holy water on her,' said the oldest fisherman, 'and see if she changes shape.'

Taniu was lying in Bran's hut on a bed of bracken and rough blankets. She had been in a deep sleep and wakened to a wonderful feeling of lightness and freedom from pain. The horror of the night had become vague —there had been voices and flaring lights, women had handled her. They spoke strangely, with a harsh northern accent reminding her unpleasantly of Drostecca, but they were kind and the old one was very skilful. She had been washed, dressed in somebody's shift, coarse but reasonably clean, and bedded down snugly.

The innocent cause of all the trouble was sound asleep in the crook of her arm. He was no longer an unknown creature that had invaded her body against her will; he was a person, miraculous and very dear; not all that had happened to her, or her totally destitute state, could check the almost light-hearted happiness she felt while he sucked.

She turned her head carefully to take stock of her surroundings. The hut was desperately poor. The women who had helped with the birth had gone, except the old one, crouched on a stool by the fire stirring something in a crock. The only other creature in the hut was a brindled collie lying by her bed, nose in the blanket, staring at the baby. It looked a wolfish, dangerous animal but when Taniu half-fearfully stroked its head, it waved its tail.

There were steps and men's voices outside. The wild-looking girl in boy's clothes dashed in, shouting, 'Father Servanus has come to look at her!'

The old woman got up; Taniu shrank back nervously into her blankets, her heart thumping unpleasantly. The dog raised its head and stared for a second at the figure following the girl into the hut, then turned back to the bed, burrowing its nose in towards the baby, wagging its tail again.

'Oh, look at Brith!' Rigan clapped her hands. 'She's as pleased as if he's a puppy she's had herself.'

'A princely little hound,' said the stranger in a pleasant Irish voice. 'You've said the name-word, Rigan. Kentigern, Hound-Prince, shall be his name.'

Taniu ventured a look. She saw a small thin man in a monk's robe of coarse homespun. The hair left by the tonsure was mouse-brown and wispy; his eyes were a pale shade between brown and grey. There was nothing impressive or distinguished about his looks, yet he had a remarkable air of authority. To Taniu, his appearance was dreadful; remembering the monk from Mailros, she expected to be denounced as a whore; she would be outcast.

The old woman brought the stool across; the monk sat down by her bed looking at her cheerfully.

'How are you now, daughter? I'm sorry for the bad time you had, but—' he glanced at the swaddled bundle, his eyelids crinkled—'there's no need to ask if it was worth while, to get such a beautiful boy—what do you ask for your child?'

'Baptism.' Taniu answered promptly. She had been at several christenings at Nia's; she had heard the ritual question and gave the ritual answer. She heard the old woman draw in her breath. The priest nodded; she felt she had answered some other question as well as the one in words.

'You're a baptized Christian yourself?'

She shook her head. 'My mother was, and I wanted to be but my father wouldn't let me.'

'Well, well. That's two christenings I'll have to be doing, then. And the child's father—is he a Christian?'

Her throat felt suddenly tight.

'I don't know.'

'Are you married, my dear?'

Now it was coming—the anger, the disgust, the cursing. Her lips moved, no sound came; her eyes were blind with tears. Servanus looked at her face and made a sign to the old woman. She went out, beckoning Rigan to come with her. He leaned over and took Taniu's hand.

'Poor child. Then it's a father that both of you are needing. That'll be myself. Father Servanus, that's who I am. Now, suppose you tell me all about it.'

Strange, how much strength flowed from such an insignificant man. She gripped the thin brown hand tight and began her story.

CHAPTER 22

Taniu's eyes were shining at him, wide and clear, rimmed by her bright hair. Then her face splintered into fragments as she hit the rock. The eyes stared unblinking, reproachful, as the blood welled up and drowned them. Only her hair stayed unsoiled, golden.

Owain realized that he had been staring at the goblet for some time and hastily drank the blood-red wine. An arm, stiff with jewels like a mosaic from Constantinople, beckoned at his shoulder; his wine-cup was refilled. He remembered that this jewelled mosaic at his side was Penarwan, that some hours ago he had married her, and hastily emptied the goblet again.

King Urien, watching him, frowned slightly while his mouth kept smiling politely at the compliments Bishop Viventius was paying him on the splendour of the festivity. Wedding feasts, by custom, ended in a general carousal but he himself had not gone intoxicated to his marriage-bed and he had not expected that his son would do so.

Owain was too proud to get pig-drunk in public; also he was too skilled in pleasure to lose the fastidious enjoyment of his young bride's body while he groped for it in a haze of wine.

Of course, a girl brought up in Caer Voran would be used to drinking bouts; she'd be expecting this. If her bridegroom wasn't thoroughly drunk by the time he came to her bed she'd think she wasn't welcome. One of the Caer Voran men had already gone down at the other end of the feasting-hall, crashing to the floor amid derisive cheers and applause from the Cumbrians. A big fair man with a Saxon look about him like so many of the Caer Voran stock; Urien had noticed him leading Penarwan's bodyguard when the bridal procession rode into Caer Luel.

Garmon, with Meurig and Padarn drinking neck-and-neck beside him on the dais, had joined in the shouts and laughter when their man went down. Owain had taken no notice; Penarwan had gone on smiling. Urien concluded thankfully that she was quite happy but he wished she wouldn't keep pouring wine down Owain's throat.

Under her splendour it was difficult to tell if Penarwan was happy—or even if she was human. Garmon had been looking forward to his daughter's wedding feast as one of the great days of his life. Every time merchants or jewel-smiths came to Caer Voran he had bought lavishly to add to his collection of treasures for her. Also, he had some vague inkling that his old ally had once looked for royal blood to mate with his heir. He was determined to show Cumbria that a Roman lady could outshine any hilltop cattle-thief's daughter, though he called himself a king.

Penarwan's under-tunic was heavy rose-coloured silk, its tight cuffs and hem stiff with bands of jewelled embroidery. Her wide-sleeved over-tunic was purple, so heavily couched with gold thread in patterns of roses and palm-leaves that it might have served for armour. Her shoulders were covered by a great collar, made from bands of elaborately wrought gold plaques, each set with a huge square amethyst, and fringed with egg-shaped pearls. There were more amethysts in her coronet; from each side there was a cascade of pearl pendants. Even her body seemed to be jewelsmith's work; her fingers were stiff with rings, her unruly auburn curls were imprisoned in a net of silver wires; her face had been painted like an enamel.

Only her eyes were alive and they were wary. Penarwan had a difficult task in hand; she couldn't afford to miscalculate. She had to get Owain so drunk he would be incapable of noticing or remembering certain details, but not so drunk that he would be incapable of action. If that happened, it would be all to do again the following night, with Owain sober and in a foul temper, very likely. Remembering how he had looked when he told her Taniu wasn't a virgin, her stomach tightened.

Would he kill me? her mind was asking, while her mouth smiled and she let her warm breath brush Owain's cheek as she put the wine-cup to his lips.

Or denounce the marriage? But my father wouldn't let anyone hurt me. And I don't suppose Urien would want to lose our alliance. We're too strong to insult and Cumbria's got enough enemies. If he keeps the alliance he won't want my name in the sewer. But could even Urien—could anybody—stop Owain when he's angry? And they'd kill Wulf for sure.

She had seen Wulfric go under the table and knew why. For the moment, though she was worried sick for him, she had no pity to spare.

It's all very well for him! I wish I had nothing to do but fuddle myself. What a stupid fuss men make over a little bit of flesh. I wonder what would happen if we refused to marry except with a guaranteed male virgin. Most of us would have to look for a place in a nunnery—or a brothel. Shall I give him another cupful? He's pretty far gone but he's got a strong head. It won't be easy to over-reach him.

In spite of the richness and outward gaiety of the feast there were some strange undercurrents; if the thoughts and feelings of all the revellers had taken visible shape, some eerie ghosts would have walked in the banquet hall. Wulfric had already put himself out of his misery; Owain had gone a good way along the same road. Urien was uneasy; Penarwan was as tense as a warrior waiting to ambush an enemy.

At one of the lower tables little Heledd was laughing with feverish excitement; half the time she couldn't see the wedding party on the dais for the tears that filled her eyes.

Of course, it was right that Prince Owain should marry a great lady with jewels and warriors as her dowry. She herself would never have been so stupid as to hope—But he had talked about a special bond between them and kissed her as he spoke—and then, he had never been near her again. She had his ring under her dress, on a chain between her breasts, but now her worst fear had proved true beyond doubt, how could she ever claim his promise to help her when she needed him?

Her laughter grew shrill. Madog, pressing close beside her on the bench, watched her hopefully. A wedding-night was a good time, when the girls were already excited with drink and the thought of what was happening in the marriage-bed. He decided he would try tonight.

Penarwan judged her moment. She stood up, wine-cup in hand, glancing along the tables. Smiling delightfully, she raised the cup in a farewell greeting and drank to the guests. The hall resounded with cheers. She stepped down from the dais, making a deep reverence to the king and the bishop. Urien smiled kindly; Viventius blessed her. The minstrels struck their harps and led her round the hall, while the men pulled roses from the garlands and showered her with petals, calling out good wishes.

The bride's procession was met with torchlight at the hall door. It wound across the great courtyard, where Urien's bodyguard was feasting in the open air, turned under an archway and along the colonnade into the stillness and fragrance of the garden courts. When they reached Owain's door, Penarwan entered with the noblewomen of highest rank; the rest stayed outside with the harpers, singing wedding songs.

The room had been carefully prepared, the bed made up with lavendered sheets, roses and honeysuckle garlanding the walls, scented candles lit. The women set to work to turn Penarwan from a glittering icon back to a flesh-and-blood girl, stripping off her armoury of jewels and brocaded robes, letting her auburn curls tumble free. Lady Guendolena broke the seal off a phial of costly perfume for them to anoint every curve and fold of Penarwan's soft body. At last, they brought her to the bed and laid her on it, putting out all the candles except one by the bedside.

In the banquet hall the drinking got deeper after the women left, though Urien was glad to see that Owain was not taking part any more. At last Garmon thumped his son-in-law across the shoulders, shouting, 'Don't keep her waiting, lad!' and he got to his feet. To Urien's relief he seemed quite steady on them. The pipers blew up a cheerful march tune; he went off with the younger men in a much noisier and less decorous procession than the bride's had been.

The women were waiting outside his door. They fell upon him and began to pull off his clothes, while the men cheered and incited them. Though they were laughing, there was an edge of savagery to the women's play. They were seeing themselves in Penarwan, laid out ready for a man to have his will of her; there was a fierce pleasure in having a man for a moment or two at their mercy. When the man was their proud young prince to be stripped like a war-captive, it was a rare treat.

He was soon naked; they dragged him up to the door while his comrades yelled cavalry jokes: 'Keep your lance straight!' 'Don't let your spear-point drop!' 'Ride straight for the breach!' and so on. One laughing girl held the door just ajar; he was pushed through; his clothes, rolled in a bundle, were thrown in after him and the door was slammed.

Outside, the pipers and harpers began to play a reel, loud enough to drown any sounds from the bedroom. The bride-folk linked hands and began to dance along the colonnade. It was a chain-dance and would go all round the palace, but its links showed a tendency to break and fly off at tangents. Reaching a corner, Madog tightened his arm round Heledd's waist and tried swinging her into a dark passage that led to the knot-garden, where there was an arbour. She let herself go with him. Madog had black hair too, though in the dusk that hardly mattered; she could shut her eyes and pretend he was Owain.

Leaning against the door, Owain looked across at Penarwan. The soft candle-light brought out the deep glow of her hair, put a sheen on her full breasts and plump haunches, the delicate little curls between her thighs. A ninety-year-old hermit, starved with fasting, would have desired her; Owain was young and heated with wine. He felt the blood stir in his loins; his flesh rose to greet her. He started towards the bed.

Watching him, Penarwan had a thrill of fear that had nothing to do with her virginity—or lack of it. Her love-making with Wulfric was simple pleasure, taken quickly with carefree enjoyment. Also, for all his male strength, Wulfric was only a servant; she had the choice and the mastery with him. Now, ever since the women had stripped her, she felt strangely weak and helpless. In spite of her hard, frivolous nature, she kept thinking of the chosen Bride of Lugos lying on the altar waiting for the spear.

She couldn't see Owain any longer as her half-drunk husband, to be coaxed and cheated; nor as the childhood friend who had shared jokes and secrets. This lithe form standing over her, gold-bronze in the candle-light; this wild, fine-boned face framed in black hair; these winged brows and smoke-blue eyes that seemed to glitter with an inner flame—this was a terrible stranger with a power in him as tameless as the Cheviot winds, as cruel as the ancient Druid stones.

Yet for all her terror she desired him, then. She felt her loins and her breasts tingle and throb; she called to him to come quickly, as she reached to claw him down into her.

When the young people had gone, the banquet hall seemed empty and quiet. Meurig and Padarn had gone whooping after Owain; Garmon and a few other hard-heads were toping with a steady concentration; several guests had followed Wulfric to the floor. Most of the older Cumbrian nobles were just waiting for Urien to give the signal to depart, though some of them sat huddled and speechless till they might be removed by discreet servants.

Bishop Viventius cast an experienced eye down the hall and began to take his leave to give the king an excuse to come away. Urien escorted him to the courtyard with the deference due to a prince of the church, then made his way to his private rooms. In the distance he could hear the music of the wedding-dance; they would keep it up most of the night but wouldn't come near his apartments.

He dismissed his weary attendants and sat for a while in

his high-backed chair, thinking of the wedding; thinking too of that other wedding twenty years ago, when Modron of Gwynedd had come to his palace and his bed. Proud and wild, like all Maelgwn's race, yet with a high-born courtesy and tenderness that had wakened to lasting love. And how beautiful she had been, with her black silk hair and luminous smoke-blue eyes. Now she was gone those eyes still looked at him from the face of her son, who had her beauty and depth of passion, and the promise of greatness for good or evil.

His heart was very heavy. This must have come from his memories of past joy and lost love, for what was there to grieve about? Penarwan was beautiful and clever, the daughter of his faithful sword-friend. Owain had always liked her and took pleasure in her company. Why, then, did he have this sense of some nameless wrong done, some irreparable loss suffered?

With a deep sigh, he got up and went to his oratory, where he spent the rest of the night on his knees in prayer and vigil for Owain's happiness.

Owain woke lying on his face, with what seemed to be a burning spear through his skull and a mouth into which all the sewers of Caer Luel had been emptied. He groaned a curse and rolled over; the spear-point twisted inside his brains. It took courage and effort to open his eyes.

Penarwan was already awake. She was sitting up against the pillows, her hands clasped round her knees. Her hair was a tangled mass; her paint was smeared all over her face; marks of bites and bruises were beginning to show on her pale skin. She was looking at him sourly.

'Did you enjoy yourself? Have you had pleasant dreams? What did you think you were doing—sacking an Anglian township?'

'Be quiet.'

'Or wrestling with a Pictish warrior-woman? That would be just the sport for you—and any girl you had would do better with military training.'

'Be quiet!'

But Penarwan would not be quiet. She was suffering a

savage recoil; she was not used to fear or to being mastered. She had to punish Owain on both accounts.

'Of course, a man who practises his love-making behind a sty with a pig-woman can't be very choice.'

With difficulty, he focused his agonized eyes on her mouth and hit it with all his force. His stomach heaved; he dragged himself off the bed away from her and staggered out into the colonnade.

The sun was already up, throwing shadows of the columns in black bands across the turf, where the dew and the fountain glittered like diamonds. He leaned with an arm flung round one of the pillars, pressing his forehead against the cool stone. The air was fresh and sweet with the calling of blackbirds and thrushes. Then a human voice was raised over the birdsong:

> 'All night by the rose, the rose,
> All night by the rose I lay—
> I dared not steal the rose-tree,
> But I stole a flower away.'

Madog was coming in, announcing his triumph for all to hear, while Heledd flitted away like a ghost, clutching her torn gown around her. The wedding night was over.

CHAPTER
23

It was a cool greyish day, like most days that summer, the sun's disc blanched behind thin, high clouds. The air was refreshing after stooping so long over the hearth. Taniu set her girdle-cakes to cool and gave a last sniff and stir to the contents of her cauldron. She had taken over the whole care of the cottage since Grandmother died last winter. Rigan still went out with the boat and had quite enough to do.

She peeped into the cradle behind the hearth, smiling at what she saw. Kentigern's stomach was as hearty as the rest of his sturdy eighteen-month self; after a good helping of broth he would sleep for hours.

213

The time had passed when she tried to deny to herself that whenever she looked at her son she looked for Owain in him. He was big for his age and would probably be tall, but so was she for a woman and her father was a giant. He had her colouring, and Loth's, fair and grey-eyed. There seemed to be nothing in him that could call up the wild dark huntsman who had shared a few hours of happiness with her on the southern moors and then came back with passion, betrayal and death as his love-gifts. Then, sometimes, Kentigern would stop his play on the sands, alert as a hunter to watch a bird or a creature of the shore; he would turn his head and smile at her as if they were sharing a secret, and her heart would check for a second.

After making sure that the fire was safely banked down with turfs, she went out. Brith, who had been sleeping against the wall, got up and shook herself, then came with her usual quiet deliberation to lie across the doorway.

Taniu strolled across the beach, enjoying the sea-wind on her cheeks, gazing across the firth but still seeing Kentigern's face behind her eyes. How would Owain look, what would he say, if he knew he had such a fine son? He had left her so cruelly after getting her with child, that she might have thought it meant no more than any other outbreak of violence and lust that happened somewhere every day. But the cold scorn in his voice had told a different story.

'There's no harm done, how could there be? And surely nothing's happened to surprise you?'

At the time the words had made no sense. Since then, she had told her story to Father Servanus and had learned exactly what the terror was that had haunted her childhood.

Drostecca set her mark in my flesh as surely as in Luned's —and she mated both of us against our wish.

Her sense of justice still asked angrily how a man who had decoyed a woman away from shelter with a plea for help, and then set on her like a hungry wolf, could dare to demand virginity from anyone else. He should be worrying about his own honour. She was too honest, though, and too proud to make other folk her scapegoats. After the first moments of surprise and struggle, she hadn't been held against her will. Will had nothing to do with it; the midsummer fires had blazed in both of them, he might have been as much taken by surprise as herself. Whatever else he had done, he hadn't raped a nun in the forest; she'd learned that much about her nature.

But if he thought she was a hypocrite, mouthing about her chastity while coupling furtively with one of her father's household—hadn't Lady Penarwan hinted that was what she was doing?—then no wonder he was disgusted. But if he cared enough to be angry—

A shadow fell across her; looking round, she saw Bran. At fifteen he had come into his man's strength; though he was not very tall his shoulders were massively powerful. His shirt sleeves and breeches were rolled up high; salt was dried and caked in the hair of his arms and legs.

'Welcome back, Bran! You must have had a good catch, you've been so long. Where's Rigan? You must be hungry—dinner's ready.'

He grinned at her, rather sheepishly as usual. 'Did you come out to look for me?' He seemed pleased. 'Look, I've got something for you.'

He held out his hand; she bent to look. He pressed so close to her side that his legs were almost gripping her thigh; her nostrils were filled with the stink of fish-guts and sweat. He was holding a freshwater mussel; its valves had been pulled apart to show a large pink pearl.

'Oh, how pretty!'

He pressed tighter.

'I found it up the burn,' he mumbled. 'I kept it for you.'

A foot crunched on the shells at the tide-mark. Rigan came up; her back bent under a creel. She was thin, tough and weather-beaten; in her man's shirt and breeches she looked no more like a woman than she had at twelve. She was scowling balefully.

'It was an unlucky day when I was born. Now, if I'd been a chance-come beggar with a bastard, maybe I could sit at home taking my ease and get pearls for presents instead of slaving my guts out in other people's boats.'

'An unlucky day indeed!' Bran was furious that his carefully chosen moment had been spoiled. 'It's a pity you weren't taken out and drowned then, for a poison-toothed, yapping bitch!'

Rigan gasped as if he had hit her. Then she turned on Taniu, screaming, 'Very well, then, let's see how you handle the boat!'

She threw the creel from her back and kicked it; the fish poured out across the beach. Then, tears streaming down her face, she turned and ran back to where the boats were drawn up in the dunes. Bran raced after her, cursing, afraid she would drag theirs down to the water and set it adrift; she was quite crazy enough when she got angry.

Taniu set the creel upright and collected the fish. She left it on the sands for the other two to find; Bran could manage Rigan but it would be better if she kept out of their sight for a while. She went away to the other end of the beach. Here the burn came down to the sea; trees grew to the edge of the dunes. She splashed across the shallow water and took shelter under their branches.

Her heart was jumping unpleasantly. Rigan had a fierce temper and a sharp tongue. Since the old grandmother's death her rages had got more frequent and more violent, though without any obvious cause. This last attack on Taniu had been quite unjust; she had always been eager to repay the household that had sheltered her. When she first came, she had made Bran take her brooches and buckles to trade up at the chief's hall. He had got a second coracle which he hired out, for a share in the catch, to a family with a newly-married son. He could have worked his own boat with some of his new partners, so Rigan needn't go out at all if she hadn't chosen. Taniu hoped she would have remembered this and calmed down before they met again.

All the while she strolled and thought, her eyes were busy, on the watch for useful herbs. She had taken up her healing again; it was another way to make some return to the fisherfolk. She did not realize it added to the awe in which they held her. Though she had let Father Servanus baptize her without turning into a salmon or seal at the touch of holy water, they still felt there was something uncanny about her and her strange arrival out of the sea.

Another thing that had come back to her, as life and hope began to have meaning again, was her old habit of telling herself stories. In a few years, when Kentigern was big enough to take round with her, she planned to set up as

216

a travelling healer. Healers were welcome everywhere, like harpers, because they harmed nobody but made life more bearable. She would get a pony and travel freely from kingdom to kingdom exchanging lore with other herbalists. She might travel to Cumbria—if she met Owain again she would ask no favours, but she would justify herself and let him know about his son. That was her right, and Kentigern's.

She had come to a standstill, leaning her back against a tree, when she heard someone coming through the wood behind her. It was Bran, looking heated and angry. He was so furious that he had lost his usual shyness and came straight up to her.

'Don't be angry, Taniu. Don't mind her.'

'I'm not angry. She's tired; up all night and half the morning.'

He put his hand on the tree trunk over her shoulder, staring at her with hot eyes.

'You are angry. You won't come in and eat with me. But don't mind her—I'll throw her out.'

'Bran! You couldn't! Think of all she does, how hard she works for you.'

'We don't need her. She makes you angry, you keep away from me. I don't want her.'

He pressed himself against her, so that the knots and bark of the trunk drove into her back, while one hand fumbled for the cord at the neck of her shift.

'I want you. Lovely, lovely Taniu, I want you.'

No! she thought, *not again*, *never again*! Never again would she let her body be invaded and used against her will. Drostecca's power was broken—ghosts and childhood terrors couldn't scare her any more. Instead of struggling in blind panic she kept still and wary, alert to defend herself.

He thought her stillness was consent; he moved back, glancing round for somewhere to lie down. She clenched her fist and slammed a punch with all her force under his ribs. As he doubled up, gasping, she dodged round him and raced for the edge of the wood, trying to decide where to flee. She could run faster over the firm sand of the beach but there was no refuge. The village offered shelter but her feet would be cumbered by the loose sand of the dunes —suppose he caught her in one of the hollows? Her blow had not stopped him for long; she could hear him coming after her.

The trees thinned out nearer the shore. Someone blocked the path; she stopped in panic until she saw it was Father Servanus. Bran came crashing out after her; then stopped dead.

'Bless you, daughter—and you, too, my son,' said the priest calmly. 'I see you're in a hurry to get to your dinner, and no wonder after a night's fishing! I've a word to say to you, Taniu; but I won't keep you from your meal, Bran my boy.'

Bran pushed by them, head averted. Servanus watched him tramp across the burn, then disappear upstream towards the village. Then he seated himself on a fallen tree trunk. She waited in silence, her cheeks flaming. What must the priest think of her, romping in the woods like a peasant girl on May Eve, with her shift off her shoulders. She pulled it up and tied the strings, wondering uncomfortably what he had to say.

To her great relief he began, 'Kentigern's growing like the bracken in summer. He must be well past his weaning now—'

She glowed. 'All the women say they've never seen a baby like him. Annis told me he was like a little prince out of the Fairy Hills!'

She stopped, fearing this was heathen talk to give to a priest but he went on gently—'and so it will do him no harm to come away out of Bran's cottage.'

She gasped. 'Come away?'

He took her hand and made her sit down beside him. 'If you stay here much longer, Bran will take you for his woman and Rigan will kill you. She's not far off it now—nor is he, by what I've just seen.'

'But why? I've never done her any harm.'

'My dear, if you weren't here, Bran would have married Rigan months ago.'

She remembered Bran's words and the scene just past. 'But he doesn't want her.'

'They've always been close. She's shared the hard times

218

when their fathers were drowned, she faces the same death at his side every time they take the boat out. He loves her, as a man loves his right hand, his daily bread.'

He sighed. 'He loves you as a man loves a dream-woman out of an old tale told by a bard. He'll never look at Rigan with you in front of his eyes.'

'We'll go away at once! I'll make a little hut of wattles up near the church. I don't want much—I can easily keep us by herb-growing and cures.'

'The church isn't so far that Bran won't come after you, and the other men too, once you're on your own. They've only kept off because they think you're Bran's woman. They know you gave him your silver dowry.'

'Do you mean, Father, that Bran thinks I'm his promised wife?'

'So it seems. Would you marry him? If so, I'll do my best. I'll ask the chief to find Rigan a husband down the coast—though I dread it's herself she'd be killing then.'

She shook her head. She felt nothing for Bran but the affection of gratitude and habit; and she couldn't smash Rigan so cruelly.

Servanus spoke more sternly. 'Then you must go. Taniu, you are my very dear daughter-in-God, but Bran and Rigan are my children too. If things go on like this, they'll be destroyed.'

'As I destroyed Hoel and his children, you mean.'

'I didn't say that.'

'You don't need to say it, Father, I've said it for you and it's true. Hoel begged me to go and I wouldn't. I'll go now. I'll take Kentigern and we'll go right away. I'm a healer, I can get a living anywhere.'

'My poor child, how long do you think you'd be let alone to do it? There's no road in this world that a lovely young woman can go walking on her own. And the man who'd take you would have no use for your child. You'd likely see him killed before you were raped; and then what would your life be—captive drudge to some brute—or brutes?'

He watched her anxiously. She looked white and sick, yet there was a reckless stubbornness in her face that frightened him. He spoke more urgently.

'The very best fate you could hope for—and it would be

219

almost unimaginably good fortune—would be for some petty chief to take you as a concubine and let you have Kentigern with you to keep you good-humoured. And then, what would his prospects be? Half-brother to the chief's bastards, picking up a living round the stables, bedding with some slave-girl if he's lucky enough to get one to himself. Is that the sort of future you want for your son?'

Taniu's feelings had been bruised enough by Rigan's and Bran's assaults; she couldn't bear any more.

'So what do you expect me to do?' She was almost screaming at him. 'You've told me I can't go and I can't stay! Do you want me to put myself in the sea?'

She jumped up with a wild look as if she were going to do so at once. He caught her hands and made her sit down, looking into her eyes until he made her look back at him. Still holding her hands, he went on quietly, 'There's only one place where a woman can go if she wants to stay unmated. My countrywoman, Monenna, is abbess in Din Eidyn. Two of the brothers are taking a boat across the firth next week with some manuscripts I've copied for her. You can go with them. I'll write you a letter to give her, she'll take you in.'

His hands were warm but she felt them like the clutch of death. Of all the vicious tricks life had played on her, this seemed the cruellest: that the blessing she had once prayed for and sacrificed everything to gain should be given to her now without her asking and come like a death sentence. She hunted for an escape, or at least a reprieve.

'How could I take Kentigern into a nunnery?'

'I'll take charge of Kentigern. He's my spiritual son. I'll see he's well fostered till he's old enough to come into the monastery school.'

Sentence had been passed.

Eighteen months ago I thought my death was on me but this is worse. How many times have I got to die before I come to my last rest? And how could I bear to go on living in a strange place with not even a memory of Kentigern it it? Won't my soul leave my body just to fly back here and look for him?

Servanus, looking at her with deep pity, seemed to follow her thoughts.

'If it makes it any easier for you to go, I shan't be staying here much longer myself; I've nearly done the work I came for. When Brother Dyfrig is ordained, I'll go back to Mailros for a while and take Kentigern with me. There's a fine library there; I'll want him to have the use of the books.'

She flared out in rebellion.

'You want to steal Kentigern! You've always wanted him for a son, haven't you, ever since you saw him! You can't have a son out of your own body so you're going to rob me of mine. That's why you're driving me out—and it's why you're going to rob him of his man's life, shut up in a monastery, so you can have him all to yourself!'

It was her pain talking; she knew it wasn't true. She broke out crying and slid to her knees on the ground by his feet. Servanus stroked her bright hair.

'It's hard for you. Each parting is a little death, especially a mother's parting with her child. But every prince has to leave the queen's hall and go to join the warriors. Kentigern's got your royal blood in him—our Pictish folk back in the hills would say he was true prince of Lothian—'

He felt her whole body jerk as she raised her head to stare at him.

He was glad to have pulled her attention away from her own grief and went on persuasively—'but I'm offering him a kingdom greater than Lothian. It's already wider than the old empire of Rome and growing greater every day. Kentigern is going to be very great in that kingdom. When he was born I heard the stars singing for him. And in that kingdom, Taniu, a woman can work—and fight —and rule, as well as a man. You could be a great abbess, you've got the brains and the strength.'

She was listening intently, but not to the priest, though some part of her mind heard the words dimly and far off. Another voice spoke close, hissing at her ear.

'Make yourself the seed-bed for an heir to Lothian and you'll die before you come to harvest.'

For herself death hardly mattered any more; but what about Kentigern, with her blood in his veins, her looks stamped on his face like a death-warrant?

221

'You think my hands can't reach you—but I've got some that can!'

Those hands could reach out and kill a child in a Pictish village as easily as they killed a broken child-brained girl in Din Pelidr. Besides—and in spite of her Christian teaching her skin crawled—Drostecca served the dark gods. The hands she used need not be flesh and blood. Let Servanus take Kentigern on to holy ground where Drostecca's curse could not hunt him down. She would never again lay her cheek against his, for evil eyes to see the likeness.

'Very well.' She closed her eyes. 'I'll go to Din Eidyn.'

He patted her shoulder. 'That's brave, my daughter, worthy of a princess of your blood. You're no more suited than Kentigern to live out your days in a little fishing village. It's time you moved on, there's a great destiny waiting for you.'

The reminder about her blood steadied her; the thought came to her that she still had something of her own. She pushed the hair from her face, looking up with proud dignity.

'I have a brother in Lothian, Prince Gwalchmai. He always loved me, he fought for me at the end when they took me out to kill me. But he thinks I'm dead. When you're at Mailros you won't be far away. He's too young now, it would be cruel and foolish to tell him. But in a year or two, when he's a man, would you let him know he has a sister who loves him?'

'That's a promise. Now, wash your face in the stream. You must go back—don't let Bran see you cry.'

Taniu dreaded going back to the cottage; this made leaving easier to bear. Bran was sullen when he heard she was going but he made no further attempt to molest her. Servanus spoke to him; quiet as he was, the little Irishman had his flock under firm control. When the villagers sent off a cartload of salted fish as tax to the chief's hall, Bran offered to take it and stayed away.

Rigan, on the other hand, was good-tempered and as far as her dour nature allowed, friendly. When Taniu took Kentigern to Annis's cottage and came back white and shaking, Rigan had food ready for her and helped her pack her bundle. She even went to her own chest for a green-checked plaid of her dead mother's weaving, which she offered to Taniu for a cloak. Taniu needed kindness; she thanked Rigan from her heart. Remembering what she had made the girl suffer, though unknowingly, she said, 'I hope you and Bran—' then stopped, afraid of rousing Rigan's temper.

'Oh, we will. Just as soon as you're out of the way, he'll turn to me.'

Rigan had shut her chest again and was sitting on the lid, her trousered legs sprawled out, thumbs in her belt. She looked at Taniu thoughtfully but without hostility.

'He'll always dream about you, of course, but I'll be in his bed, bearing his children. Anyway,' she added with cheerful brutality, 'I'd rather have him dreaming about a holy sister walled up in Din Eidyn than some good-looking slut down the coast, where his legs and his prick can follow his mind. I'm not beautiful like you.'

Rigan's words *walled up in Din Eidyn* were echoing in Taniu's mind next day, sitting in the boat with Rigan's plaid wrapped round her, being rowed downstream to the opposite bank of the firth. It was a grey overcast day, with the fangs of a bitter east wind biting at her. The plaid gave no warmth against her chilly thoughts as she watched the great rock of Eidyn drawing nearer. It looked like a huge beast crouched on the southern horizon; she wondered what new unwelcome fate was waiting for her there, ready to spring and maul her.

However, they were not going up to the mountain-city, towering above its wall of sheer crags. There was a house of religion at its foot, a very sacred place with a relic of the Holy Rood, but this was a house of monks.

West from the monastery, the ground rose in a long thin spine to another outcrop of rock about a mile away, much smaller but sheer over a marshy loch. There had been a stronghold on it since before the Romans; Morcant had given this to Monenna when she arrived from Ireland. Morcant was not noticeably pious; but all the great western kingdoms were famous for their houses of religion, mostly royal foundations. In Morcant's religion the first and greatest commandment was *'Thou shalt not be outdone.'* Since the nuns' arrival the Eidyn folk had renamed the old fortress 'Caer y Morynion', the Castle of Maidens.

All this while, Taniu's fear had been growing. This climb up to the gate, escorted by the silent monks, was too like the last time she came back to Din Pelidr. She had the crazy certainty that all the last year and a half had only been a dream; she was going to find herself in Drostecca's hall facing Lurga.

Instead, she found herself in a bright, simply furnished room facing Abbess Monenna.

She had prayed that Monenna might be like Servanus; she was more like his pet robin: round, neat and rosy, with very bright black eyes and a clear sweet voice.

'Sit down, my dear. Why, how cold you are! Sure, you must have nearly frozen to death coming over the firth!'

A shy, fresh-faced novice brought a platter of oatcakes and a mug of hot milk, but it was the abbess herself who placed Taniu on a stool near the brazier and chafed her hands till she could hold her mug. She left her to eat and drink while she read Servanus's letter; when Taniu looked up, the robin's eyes were fixed on her.

'Father Servanus says you've been wanting to take the veil since you were a young girl.'

'I wanted to, yes.' She braced herself. 'But now it's impossible.'

'And why?'

'I'm not a maiden. Didn't Father write that? How could I take a vow of virginity?'

'Virginity's more a matter of the spirit than the body. All sorts of things can happen to us, that we didn't plan for, or grow to regret. There's no reason why you shouldn't follow your vocation.'

Taniu swallowed. 'I have a son.'

'Whom you love. And why wouldn't you?'

She saw the tears in Taniu's eyes and said gently, 'Are you afraid I'll tell you to be ashamed of loving him? That you'll never be allowed to speak about him? Ah, never be ashamed of loving. All true love comes from God, you can offer it back to him as your most precious treasure. And any other love you're keeping in your heart.' She was smiling.

224

Taniu hesitated. It would be so easy to take what the abbess was offering. It would set the seal of peace on her past as well as her future. And yet, it would be a living lie, to Monenna as well as herself, and she was already liking Monenna too much to take her friendship in exchange for a lie.

'If I'd really loved,' she said painfully, 'I mean, if I'd given myself to a lover and he'd died, or left me, I'd willingly be a nun if you'd have me. Or if I'd just been raped, through bad luck, the way a man can get thrown by his horse, then I suppose I'd come in time to see it wasn't so important —that I hadn't changed. But it wasn't like that.'

'How was it, then?'

She stared at the glowing brazier, frowning a little, trying to see the real truth.

'I think it was pride. Disgust, too—I hated what I saw men and women doing to each other in my father's house. But mostly it was pride. I wanted to be better than the rest of them—' she thought of Hoel and his children; her voice shook—'and I ended up doing so much worse!'

'Don't we all? The cock crows in everybody's life—lucky for us if it's only once. You can start your novitiate now, if that's your wish.'

She shook her head.

'What do you want me to do for you, then? If you're skilled with your needle, I could get one of the chiefs' wives to take you as a bower-woman.'

'Couldn't I stay here as a lay servant? I'd love to work for you.'

'We're glad of all the hands God sends to help us. What can you do?'

'Milk, make cheese, tend fowls. I can cook. And I've some practice in healing, my nurse was a skilled herb-woman.'

'Then God did send you! Sister Agatha, our infirmarian, is telling me every day that picking herbs will kill her. She doesn't bend very easily. Have you finished your bread and milk? I'll send you to her.'

Sister Agatha was as different from Ancarat as she well could be. She was a large puffy woman with a face like unbaked dough and pale watery grey eyes. Her breathing

225

sounded like a creaky bellows. The pale eyes gave her Ancarat's sharp appraising glance, though, when the novice brought her into the still-room and explained why the abbess had sent her.

'You say you understand herbs? What would you use for marsh-cramps?'

'To drink: infusion of young silver birch leaves or restharrow root; ointment of oil of juniper to rub in.'

'Good. And for wounds?'

After half an hour of this, Taniu felt that Sister Agatha had taken out all her carefully stored knowledge of cures, spread it on her work-bench and sorted it as neatly as her bundles of herbs. Under the nun's pale eyes it seemed a pitifully small store. Just when her head seemed empty, Sister Agatha gasped to a halt.

'You'll do. Come along, I'll show you our herb garden. Better wrap that plaid tight, the wind can break your bones up here.'

She wheezed out; Taniu, following, paused for a backward glance. The still-room was larger and neater than Ancarat's; there were some utensils—retorts and alembics—that she couldn't recognize or name, but she'd make it her business to find out. Then, there was that mysterious writing to be mastered, the signs on the drawers, that row of big dark books. Work, healing and knowledge were being offered to her; they were great gifts.

Grief and loss were still too raw inside her for happiness but she felt the stirring of life in her, like the herbs that were cut down year after year and still grew again.

She wrapped her cloak tightly about her and followed Sister Agatha out into the bitter wind.

CHAPTER
24

While Taniu was being rowed, shivering, across the firth, eighty miles to the south of her Owain was staring at the same grey eastern sea and sky. His spirits were sinking closer to despair as each long wave crashed on the bleak shore.

There was no reason for despair. He'd just taken a notable part in a great victory; a dream that had faded when Arthur died on Medraut's spear was coming back into brilliant reality.

Urien had at last succeeded in forming an alliance of the northern kingdoms. This was not because the northern kings had suddenly seen the light of British unity but because Angles had suddenly won a stronghold on the coast of Bernicia.

It had not started as an invasion. A battle-hardened sea-rover, Ida Eobbasson, Woden-born, had come coasting north with a couple of ship-loads of like-minded adventurers, to see what they could find. They found the great sea-fort of Din Guayroi almost unmanned, as Eudeyrn was away raiding his southern neighbours. The guards were disgracefully slack; it was easy to surprise and cut them down. Rejoicing in their luck, the raiders swarmed in. The fort was well stocked; they decided to give themselves a victory feast before they shipped their loot and set fire to what they left. Before that happened, however, Ida had given the place a long, loving survey and changed his mind.

The fort stood on almost sheer rock, the sea lapped it at high tide. There was a deep well of pure water in the rock; a little to the north a small river ran into a sheltered bay that would make a good harbour. With ample stores and guards who kept their eyes open, the place could stand against a war-host. It was the kind of stronghold a warrior dreamed of; a man could live like a king with such a fort—and if the rest of the country was held so slackly, the kingdom itself wouldn't be long in coming. He told his men they were staying and sent one of the ships south to Lindesse, where he had kin, to bring up reinforcements.

Ida was right about the kingdom. Eudeyrn, greedy and drunken, believing that cruelty was a proof of strength, had not been loved and was not regretted. Before long a powerful chief from Gefrin above the Glein, who was at blood-feud with him over the rape and death of a foster-sister, sent to Ida, offering his friendship and his own sister as a wife.

King Ida had consorts all round the North Sea coasts. Three of his crewmen claimed to be his sons and may well have been, though his memory was hazy over their mothers. He was ready to settle down and marry Bernicia. He ordered his bride-ale to be brewed and sent for the bride.

She was a tough, handsome hill-girl; whatever her name was, it sounded like 'Bebban' in Anglian ears. She had never dreamed of becoming a queen but took to it with zest; like most seamen ashore, Ida was cheerful to women and free-handed with his loot. Cattle-raiders and pirates could see each other's point of view; she was soon at home in her palace and Ida saw he could trust her to hold it firmly whenever the sea called him away. His men had been struggling for some time to say 'Din Guayroi'; now they gave up and called the place 'Bebban's Burh' among themselves.

The country people took their change of king with stolid indifference. Warriors were warriors; whatever their race and speech, they took what they wanted. So the farmers handed over their dues of food and cattle to the new lords with the old grumbles; their prettiest daughters bedded contentedly enough with the big fair strangers, and life went on.

Eudeyrn, of course, did not see it like that; he went shouting his wrongs to his neighbours. They shed no tears for him; remembering the fall of Caer Efrog, they were worried about their own lands. Lothian and Elmet, to the north and south, felt most threatened. If Lothian went, Eidyn would be open to attack. Strathclyde usually followed where Eidyn led, because of a marriage alliance and because the young king, Riderec, was very much under Morcant's influence. He was also pious and thought of a holy war against the heathen. The North had never been so united since Arthur ruled as High King. Urien saw the chance to save what was left of Britain and offered Cumbrian support.

Left to themselves the kings would have wasted their time remembering old feuds and starting new ones, throwing away their strength in pointless attacks on the high cliffs under the Anglian stronghold. Controlled by Urien's wise advice, they worked together to a plan.

A small force came down temptingly from Lothian. They straggled as they marched, boasting and drinking. The Anglian war-leader, Theodric Idasson, Flame-Bearer, had good warning of their approach; he had a hearty contempt of Britons as fighters and went to wipe them out. As he expected, they broke when they saw him. The Anglian warriors surged ahead to hunt and cut them down—and found themselves faced by the main war-hosts of Strathclyde and Eidyn, coming up behind.

Theodric was a fine leader; his men were well trained. He rallied them and fought a rearguard action in good order towards his stronghold. Once inside, he could laugh at them, stuck on their backsides under the cliffs and starving—if they didn't cut each other's throats first in their endless quarrelling.

Urien had got there first. The Cumbrian horsemen had moved up from the Wall, following a Roman road that came along the coast behind a range of low hills. Seeing them between him and his fort, Theodric stood at bay. Even at that desperate moment there was no rout and no panic. The Angles kept their shield-wall unbroken while they were driven back towards the sea. As one fell, another stepped into the gap, unflurried as if they were at weapon-training. They had taken a heavy toll of their attackers.

In the end, Theodric got all that were left on to a little off-shore island a few miles north of Din Guayroi. At low tide it could be reached from the mainland over the sands but it would be an ugly place for the attackers to be caught as the sea came in. It was excellent for a last stand; Theodric had known what he was doing.

The garrison in Din Guayroi had also kept their heads; they had held the landward cliffs while some of them tried to get the ships out to bring their men off the island. They might have done it, too; but it was low water; the ships were beached and Owain, with his uncanny battle sense, foresaw their attempt. He led the last wild charge down the river and across the bay, with bloodstained water splashing round their horses' fetlocks, as the tide came in while they fought round the ships. Every one had been smashed and burned.

So there was ample reason for self-satisfaction; and all the while, as Owain watched the waves beat and recoil, they seemed to beat despair into his mind.

It must be this accursed coast; grey sky, grey sea. No colour anywhere. The wind coming straight from the eternal snows. And those sea-birds screaming and wailing northwards, like lost souls in torment!

'Wail for the Flame-Bearer, then!' he suddenly shouted at them, up to the blank, dead sky. 'Go and scream death in his ears, tell him we're coming!'

My father won't let this alliance break up, once the Angles are gone. He'll lead us south—we'll win Efrog back—we'll sweep across the lowlands like a mountain torrent. We'll ride into Londinium. We'll make the High Kingdom of Britain again as it used to be in Arthur's time. And then—

And then, Arthur's kingdom will need a High King to hold it together. Who would that be but Urien? And I am Urien's heir.

Despair . . . despair . . . despair, said the waves.

Why did he feel so hopeless? He wondered if he was getting a warning of some disaster in Cumbria. But Urien had not made the mistake of leaving the kingdom unmanned while he went campaigning on the other side of Britain; he had not called out the whole war-host, just his household troop of picked horsemen. Cumbria was well guarded, watched by the Council under Penarwan's very capable regency. There could be no firmer hands than hers to hold the reins. Inside her soft luxurious flesh there was a clear mind and a very strong will.

After their disastrous wedding-night, Owain and Penarwan had practised the most icily rigid courtesy to each other for a few days; then gone back with mutual relief to their usual easy friendliness. She was a delightful wife; a warm, responsive lover and most intelligent companion. Urien was very fond of her; some of their best moments were when the three of them were in Urien's room, bending over his map, discussing alliances and policies. Penarwan's comments were always acute; more than once they had followed her advice and found it valuable.

It was an excellent marriage; it didn't reach the heights and depths of passion, but perhaps those feelings only came once in a lifetime. His had died under the walls of Din Pelidr.

Despair, said the waves.

Damn this place! We should have left it to the Angles. They deserve it. A little more time and they'd be throwing themselves over the cliffs—Custennin told me the sea's on the horizon at Din Pelidr. Was this the last thing she saw—this cold grey desolation—when Loth's men lifted her and threw her over?

Well, he wouldn't have to look at it much longer. The Angles were holed up in their island—what was it called? Metcaud. Tomorrow the four armies would follow the tide across the sands to Metcaud; Urien was with the other kings now, making plans for the final assault. Old Loth would have smashed his way straight in after Theodric and finished them at once.

Not for the first time he wished that Loth had been leading the eastern hosts; but Loth was dead. He had crashed to the floor of his hall during a drinking bout; when they picked him up he was purple-faced with his mouth drawn up to one side. He breathed for another two days but never spoke again.

As soon as the death was known in Eidyn, Morcant came south with his warband 'to protect the kingdom for his poor young cousin'. Gorthyn, with those of Loth's men he could trust, took Gwalchmai to his own stronghold, Segloes in the Eildon Hills, to protect him from cousin Morcant. Ancarat went with them because Gwalchmai clung to her as the last security of his childhood; they would have had to break her arms to tear him from her.

Morcant considered the position—especially the position of Segloes manned by tough hill-men who didn't ask who was king because they only took orders from Gorthyn. He decided to let things be. Gwalchmai was too young to threaten his rule; if he stayed on friendly terms for a year or two, till they got careless, he could easily arrange a hunting accident.

Owain knew nothing of these undercurrents, or he might have seen some reason for his depression and uneasiness. There was nothing suspicious about Morcant leading Lothian as well as Eidyn. A ten-year-old couldn't lead a war-host; it was only right that the elder kinsman should hold the boy's kingdom for him till he was old enough to rule.

There was nothing suspicious about Morcant either, or about the warmth and courtesy of his welcome to Urien when the two kings met after the battle. Morcant had ridden up attended by his armour-bearer and a group of his nobles; thanked Urien for his help; complimented the bravery of his horsemen; praised Owain's victorious charge. He spoke heartily but without fawning; here was a man they could like and respect. He was a fine-looking man, tall and stately with light-brown hair and pale-blue eyes.

No one would guess from Morcant's pleasant, dignified bearing that he was eaten inside by the envy felt by one who had always taken second place when he thought he should be first. Eidyn was a strong and wealthy kingdom, but Cumbria and Strathclyde were far richer. He was a brave and skilful fighter, but it was that drunken bull, Loth, that the bards still sang about and the warriors remembered. He spoke wisely in council, and knew as he spoke that they were waiting to hear what Urien would say.

No shadow of this having appeared in Morcant's opening speeches, he then presented his armour-bearer, a man called Lovan.

'He, too, has an interest in Cumbrian victories.' Morcant smiled. 'I may say he's a connection of yours, since he's a kinsman of your most noble queen, Modron of Gwynedd.'

'Indeed?' Urien was immediately interested. 'Then I'm even more happy to meet you, Lovan, and greet you as my kinsman.'

'I don't claim that honour.' Lovan was modest and quiet-spoken. 'It's true, my mother was distantly related to Princess Modron, but her fate took her from Gwynedd before her marriage. I was born in the North, far from her home.'

'Where are her family lands?' To Urien every detail about Modron, even her most distant cousin, was precious.

'Oh, my family have no lands in Gwynedd. We're not rich or powerful. My mother came from Aber Menai, I think she left her heart there. I've never seen it, but she often described her old home to me, so it seems I knew it. Gwynedd folk are very loyal to our loves as you know. We don't forget easily.' He smiled.

Urien was pleased at this delicate praise of Modron. He took a liking to Lovan, all the more because he could trace, or fancied he could, some slight resemblance to his dead wife. Lovan was fine-boned, with smooth black hair and grey-green eyes that seemed to be always changing colour like the sea.

Morcant must have sensed this liking; whenever messages were sent between the kings, Lovan was always the messenger; he was in and out of Urien's tent as if he were one of the Cumbrians.

Owain stamped his feet to keep the blood flowing. It was hours to sundown; after dark most of the Cumbrians were riding north to join the other forces for the all-out attack on Metcaud. The garrison in Din Guayroi must not know that the siege had been lifted.

He decided to take a canter northwards over the sands; there were very few troubles he could not out-distance on horseback. Madog came with him, of course, and one or two others of his own following; also Meurig who had joined Urien with a contingent from Caer Voran.

They were going easily when Owain's quick eyes caught something dark moving furtively among the straggling brambles that edged the beach.

'Spying.' Meurig reached for his dagger.

'Probably just one of the farm folk looking for a strayed beast,' objected Madog.

Owain frowned. 'They're not over-friendly, I've noticed. I wonder how many of them are up in Din Guayroi with the Angles.'

'Be fair,' Madog laughed. 'If you'd had Eudeyrn ruling you, would you want him back?'

All this while, they had been swinging their horses towards the bushes, alert for the stranger to break cover. Their quarry did not wait to be flushed out; to their surprise he came on to the sands and moved slowly towards them.

His left arm was dangling; he was holding his right hand bundled in his cloak in front of his body. It looked disagreeably as if he had a belly-wound and was holding his guts in.

They closed round him; then Owain kicked his horse forward and jumped down.

'Llywarch! What's happened? Where are you hurt? Stay still now and let me look. I'll bind it tighter—we'll get a litter from the camp. *Ride*, Madog!'

Llywarch clutched his cloak tighter but shook his head. His eyes stared blankly in his white face.

'It's just my arm.' His voice was a dead whisper. 'The horse fell on me. It broke its leg—I couldn't get up. That's why I wasn't killed.'

This was nonsense; the fall had made him light-headed. Owain passed his hand through his cousin's hair, feeling for a skull injury.

'Urien must have sent him back with a message.' Meurig sounded impatient. 'Young idiot, coming so fast he lets his horse step in a rabbit hole. Well, what did he say—do they want us to ride at once?'

Llywarch shook his head again, still staring. Owain frowned at Meurig.

'Go easy, he's in a bad way. Come on, Llywarch, I know you're hurt, I can see the blood. You've got to let me look, so we know how to carry you.'

He began to disentangle the blood-soaked wrappings. Llywarch pulled back screaming, 'Don't look, Owain! Let Madog—' but it was too late. Something fell out of the bundle and rolled to Owain's feet.

The blood had slopped out from the hacked flesh around the splintered bone and gristle. Twisted with shock and pain, his father's face stared at him with dead eyes from a tangle of grey matted hair.

The agony came into Owain like a spear driven straight into his heart; he wondered why he hadn't fallen.

'The Angles have broken out of Metcaud!' shouted Meurig. 'Those stupid eastern bastards have let Flame-Bearer loose!'

They turned to the north. Nothing broke the stillness but the screaming gulls. Llywarch's dry whisper went on.

'Lovan struck him first, in the back. Even then, he drew his dagger and would have fought, but Lovan caught his arm and Morcant put his sword through him. He fell across my horse's neck—I'd been riding at his left side—it panicked and fell with me. I was half-stunned—I think the others tried to fight—but we were taken unawares—we only had our daggers. The others were all dead, they even killed the horses.'

'But why—?' Madog could not finish his question; words no longer made sense.

They were dazed by the horror in front of them. Owain crouched on the sand with Urien's head across his knees, stroking the blood-clotted hair away from the face as if his fingers could draw the life back into it: the wise dark eyes, the mouth that had smiled at his exploits with pride and tender irony, the high, thoughtful brow. Urien had gone. This was just a lump of bloody carrion. Yet still his hands went on seeking.

'They stooped over him to see if he was quite dead. Morcant said, "You won't fly over our heads any more, Raven, or dig your claws into Catraeth!" And Lovan said, "You'll buy no more marriages, Cumbria, with other folk's lands!" And he laughed and spat on the king's face.'

Meurig swore. 'And then the cowardly swine hacked his head off. They couldn't face him in battle.'

'I did that,' whispered Llywarch. 'They left the bodies in a little hollow down by the edge of the sands. They didn't want even their own men to know, till they'd trapped you. They were going to kill you tonight, when you go to their camp. Then they're going to put Urien's head on a stake to watch over your corpses. I heard them laughing about it while I was lying under the horse. It took me a while to crawl free, my shoulder's broken, I think.'

He swallowed. 'The gulls were coming—some of them had begun to settle. I couldn't carry his body. So I took his head; they can't dishonour him. And I brought you this.'

He held out the Cumbrian ruby on his blood-caked palm. Owain picked it up, and with it the kingship—his father's legacies. He sneered as he put it on, in case he wept in front of them.

'My father was a fool, for all his wisdom. He expected

faith, honour and concord from the British. He would have given them unity. They'd rather wallow in the muck of their own dirty little grudges. *You should have left them alone!*' he screamed at the head. 'Let them eat their own dung till the Picts or the Angles destroy them one by one!'

Meurig loosened his sword in the scabbard. 'Well, we won't leave them all for the Picts and the Angles.'

The others murmured assent; even Llywarch struggled to his feet. They were all looking at Owain. When your kindred's blood was shed, you slew the slayers. That was the time-honoured commandment; his highest duty as Urien's heir.

And he longed to do it: to rip flesh, smash bones, soak the ground with blood. His heart leaped with joy at the foretaste: to ride into the easterners' camp; see Morcant come smiling to greet the unwary victims who had put themselves in his trap; bring his sword down on Morcant's skull and see it splinter among the brains. Then one last bloody charge, killing as many as they could before they were cut down by the three armies. Darkness and peace.

He took one last intense look at Urien's face, so that he could see it in his mind while he killed and died, calling up his father's spirit to ride with him and see himself avenged.

And it seemed that his father came to him, was standing by his side, so that he looked up from the dead thing in his hands, expecting to see Urien alive.

'It still happens to kings, Owain, that we're called to offer sacrifice for our people. It may be our lives—it usually is, and that's easy. But it may be our hopes, our happiness or our pride—which we selfishly call our honour.'

No! Owain's soul cried out in protest. *You couldn't ask me to do that—dishonour you and myself for ever—*

'A man who leads his countrymen to certain defeat and destruction to satisfy his pride, or because he's afraid to be called a coward, has lost all right to be a king.'

'Well,' demanded Meurig, 'what are we waiting for?'

'Remember this, when I'm not here to remind you.'

Owain got to his feet.

236

'Give the orders to saddle up at once—no horn calls or shouting, pass the word along quietly by word of mouth. As little noise as possible.'

They nodded.

'They're to file off in separate detachments, from the western side of the camp first, and so on, group by group. Follow the hill-tracks, keep below the skyline, till we get to the Roman road.'

Again they nodded, Meurig smiling grimly. Owain was going to fall on the easterners in one of his famous surprise attacks.

'At the road they're to close up and ride south for the Wall as fast as possible without foundering the horses.'

They stared, shocked, not quite believing what they'd heard.

'South? *South*!' roared Meurig. He drew his sword and pointed north. 'Your father's body's lying there, remember? And the filth who struck him down are alive and gloating. I'm ready to go and kill as many as I can—can't you do that much for your own father's sake?'

'Oh, I can do much more than that for my father's sake.'

Owain was smiling.

'For my father's sake I'll leave his body unburied to feed the gulls. I'll leave my honour here to rot with it. I'll get our men home before Morcant can strike. I'm going to make Cumbria so strong that no enemy will ever dare to cross our borders. When I see my chance, I'll take revenge. And always, as long as I live, I'll see him lying on the shore with the gulls tearing him and remember I turned my back and left him. That's what I can do for my father's sake.'

They avoided his eyes; even Meurig kept quiet. Owain mounted.

'Give Llywarch a lift, one of you. Remember orders, no noise when we break camp.'

He turned his back on the sea. The others followed. The loose sand of the dunes muffled the sound of the hoofs. From the north they could still hear the gulls screaming.

CHAPTER
25

The Cumbrians had been expecting orders to leave camp silently. They melted away into the landscape in the gathering dusk. Even their southerly ride did not make them wonder at first; there could have been a sudden change of plan; perhaps a new enemy coming up from Deira.

After the news was broken next day, in a few icy words from Owain to the troop commanders and passed down the ranks, they were kept together by discipline and the driving force of Owain's will. Something else had taken over his body and used his voice to give orders, while he stayed apart in his cold hell. He still carried his father's head, wrapped in one of Urien's cloaks. Once Madog, desperate with pity, offered to take it. Owain turned on him, snarling; Madog recoiled; from then on he kept away.

They came to Caer Voran; there was the ordeal of telling Garmon. Meurig began to bluster about what should have been done and what he would have done. Garmon stopped him curtly. He said quietly to Owain, 'I was fighting beside your father before you were born. I knew him as one sword-friend knows another. If he'd been in your place, he'd have done just the same.'

Ressona said nothing; she went up to Owain and lifted the ghastly bundle out of his arms. He let her. She took the head away, washed it, combed out the silver-grey hair and crowned it with Garmon's coronet. Then she wrapped it in an embroidered cloth and laid it, strewn with herbs, in a casket which she put on the altar of the household chapel. In the morning she handed the casket to Owain, again without a word.

Garmon rode with them the first part of the way; he was going to call out his fighting men. When their roads parted, he touched Owain's hand.

'Don't worry about your eastern border; we'll hold it for you. Give my love to Penarwan—this'll be a sad homecoming for her.'

During the last day's ride along the Wall, the thought of

this home-coming, of being with Penarwan again, grew brighter. It was like a gleam of firelight in the distance to a traveller lost on the wintry moors, promising warmth, shelter and food for his hunger. Next to himself, she had been closest to Urien; she loved his father and had shared his mind. She, of all people, would know the greatness of the loss and measure the depths of his grief.

More than that, he wanted Penarwan as a woman, wanted her arms round him, the touch of her lips, her soft breasts, the deep warmth of her body.

I never really knew Taniu. Whatever she was in real life, she's never been more to me than a dream, like one of those mist-wraiths that take the form of a woman and suck a man's life away. I've finished with dreams.

But Penarwan was real flesh and blood, warm and lovely.

If I could only rest my head against her breasts I could let myself weep and then I should be healed.

He held on to this comfort during the arrival at Petriana and the long conference with the grim-faced fort commander. Owain was adamant that news of the murder should be kept secret till he gave it to the Council; above all, that no word of the warband's return should reach Caer Luel before the morning. He wanted no overnight panic, with people bolting in all directions for the country, spreading rumours and confusion as they went.

He entered the city at dusk, just before the gates were shut, riding through unnoticed in his plain horseman's leathers and weather-stained cloak. As usual on a summer's evening, there were plenty of people about; lights were glowing through the shutters of the Golden Lily; there was singing in the taverns.

There was one thing to be done before he was free to go to Penarwan. He made his way to the bishop's house and asked for an audience, keeping his cloak over his face till they were alone. He told his tale briefly, handing over the casket with its grim burden into the keeping of the Church, for vigil, prayers and masses.

Viventius had the strength and compassion to hide his own shock and grief. He listened with his wise eyes on Owain's face, letting him go with a short blessing and a

239

promise to come in the morning. The new king's best comfort would come from his wife.

Owain felt the same; his steps quickened as he turned at last towards his home.

The palace was strangely quiet; even when the king was away there was usually a great deal of coming and going; the servants were always busy. Neither the fort commander nor the bishop had mentioned Penarwan's absence.

'Where are all the folk?' he asked the gate-porter. 'Is Lady Penarwan away?'

'No, my lord, she's in her apartments. She's been very anxious about you away at the war, though she wouldn't make a show of it in case the folk lost heart. Tomorrow's the feast of St Nynia; so my lady ordered everyone of the household who could be spared to go out and keep a torchlight vigil by his holy well, while she spent the night in prayer for your return. Forgive the poor attendance, lord, we didn't expect you. I'll go now and announce you.'

'No, don't disturb her. I'll go myself.'

He felt strangely touched. Penarwan was not ardently religious; if she had ordered a vigil she must be really worried. Perhaps her spirit had been troubled by the same forebodings as he had felt just before the murder. People who loved each other often got these unspoken messages.

He turned under the archway, going softly along the colonnade towards the garden-courts and paused outside his room. The diamond lattices, high up by the roof, were glowing; she must be still at her prayer-book. Not to startle her, he opened the door gently and so was able to stand for a moment watching the bodies on the bed before they noticed him.

Wulfric was on top, his great back and thigh muscles working between Penarwan's drawn-up knees. Her hands were clawing at his back; she was gasping and moaning with pleasure. Owain watched, while the last glow of human warmth flickered out of him and died. Then he drew his sword.

The sound, and a draught of cool air from the doorway, disturbed them. Wulfric turned over; for a heartbeat or two they stared at each other. Then Wulfric came at him. Perhaps he was intending a desperate attack, trusting to his height and strength; though naked and unarmed as he was, he must have known it was hopeless. Or perhaps he just wanted to defend her by letting Owain spend the first anger on his body.

Owain watched him come; choosing the place with the unhurried deliberation of weapon-practice he put his long cavalry sword neatly between two ribs and drove home. Wulfric lifted one of his hands and touched the blade, then looked at Owain. His eyes widened; he seemed surprised; his lips moved as if he had something to say. Then the eyes went blank; he collapsed over the sword and sank to the ground.

Owain looked across the body at Penarwan. She was curled up against the pillows, her arms clutched round her breasts, staring at him. He sheathed his sword.

'You filthy, adulterous bitch. I'll have you burned.'

It was pleasant to see the panic in her eyes. He had spoken of burning because it was the death given to wives taken in adultery; he remembered now that Penarwan had a special dread of fire. He knew that it was the destruction of her beauty she dreaded even more than death: to be exposed to men's gaze as a twisting blackened horror. Good.

She started to laugh, a high-pitched grating noise.

'How wonderful! Prince Owain the Virtuous rebuking sin! Who are you to talk about adultery? If you want to strike a blow for chastity, take your sword again and geld yourself! Do you think I don't know about your women? Madog's wife, that prim-faced chit—she keeps away from court but I've seen her daughter. They say she could be Queen Modron born again. And there's a boy up at the forge in Banna, isn't there? And that carrion, Guendolena—how did her old lord get his heir at last? How many husbands in Cumbria are bringing up your bastards?'

'It's no good, Penarwan.' Owain spoke with a kind of weary patience. 'You won't goad me into putting my sword through you. And I can tell you one husband in Cumbria who won't be bringing up a bastard.'

For a moment her anger and fear vanished in surprise. 'You don't think I'd be such a fool as to let that happen? I took good care.'

'You took good care, did you? Is there a whore in all the brothels of Caer Luel who could teach you anything?' He laughed without amusement. 'It'll be a wicked waste to burn you; I should trade you to the Golden Lily.'

'Don't you dare insult me. Your father made our marriage because he wanted the Caer Voran alliance, he won't let you throw it away in a fit of rage. He's your king as well as your father—and he loves me, remember!'

'My father's dead. I'm King of Cumbria.'

Of all the ways he had imagined telling the news to Penarwan, he had never foreseen using it to strike her.

'Dead?'

She searched his eyes to see if he were trying to scare her. He lifted his hand into the candle-light and the ruby took fire.

'There's been a battle? The Angles were too strong?'

'He was murdered. By Morcant, his ally whom he trusted. It's easy to fool people who trust you, isn't it, Penarwan?'

Now at last he saw in her face the pity and warm concern he longed for.

'Oh, my poor Owain.' Her eyes misted with tears. 'What a terrible thing—to lose him, and like that. My dear, how you must be grieving.'

And she stretched out her arms to him across Wulfric's body as if she would draw him to her and lay his head against her breasts. He stepped back as if he had trod on an adder.

'Yes, you're right!' She jumped up briskly, reaching for her shift. 'We haven't time to mourn, we'll have to act fast.'

She pulled her gown round her and began to pin her brooches. 'You'll be calling up the war-host, of course? You'll find them ready to ride. I thought you might be needing reinforcements, so I told the Council to send word to all the chiefs.'

She fastened her slippers; then took up the mirror, frowning a little at her reflection as she smoothed her curls and twisted them into shape round her fingers. He stared at her, fascinated.

'Do you think Morcant will attack at once? We mustn't

leave the southern border unguarded if you take the army north—I don't trust Elmet.'

Suddenly she put the mirror down and turned to him with sparkling eyes.

'I think we should try to separate Strathclyde from Eidyn. They were angry when you took Caer Ehedydd, you should have foreseen that, but Riderec doesn't go in for murder. It shouldn't be impossible to come to terms with them. Suppose I go myself with an embassy—he's young and impressionable. We could put it to the Council, I've already arranged a meeting for tomorrow. It would be easier for a woman to win him over than a Cumbrian war-chief, he wouldn't seem to be yielding out of fear.'

She laughed at him, wanting to share the joke of her seducing the pious young Riderec. When he kept silent, she said rather impatiently, 'It's urgent, Owain. Dawn's coming, we've got to discuss what we're going to do.'

'We're discussing your adultery.'

'God above, man—our whole power's in danger! You're not going to waste precious time over a little thing like that?'

A little thing like that. He looked from her to Wulfric's body, remembering that the man had put himself between her and the sword. He saw that to her it was indeed a little thing, too small for his rage or jealousy. She hadn't robbed him of love or honour, as a man; there'd been nothing to lose. But he was also King of Cumbria, the country's honour was his own.

Penarwan followed the direction of his glance and looked down at Wulfric for a moment.

'He loved me better than you did—he didn't bring a dead woman with him every time he came to my bed. So I let him love me and you've killed him for it. At least, I've never killed any of your mistresses. Why keep on quarrelling?'

'It's no good, Penarwan. I've finished with you.'

She gasped and clenched her hands.

'Oh, have you? You'll find it's not so easy to finish with me. The time's coming, Owain, it's coming fast, when your precious Cumbria's going to need strong, reliable allies. Well, Caer Voran's all you've got and *I'm* Caer Voran.

D'you think my father will stand idly by while you burn me for a whore?'

'No, I don't think he'll stand idly by. If he'd seen what I have tonight he'd light the fire under you with his own hands. But it would grieve and shame him, and I don't want him grieved and shamed. He's a brave, decent man, my father's sword-friend. Which is why, Penarwan, you're going to ask me tomorrow, in the presence of the bishop and the Council, for permission to leave me and take the veil. Your grief for Urien has made you turn from the world, to spend your days praying for his soul in perpetual chastity.'

To a creature like Penarwan that would be an agony almost as dreadful as burning—and it would last much longer.

'I won't do it. You can't make me.'

'You'll do it, because if you don't I'll burn you.' He smiled at her. 'There'll be no need to shame your father, I can do it myself. I'm stronger than you, and you've arranged for nobody to be within earshot. All I have to do is muffle your head and tie you up in a tangle of bedclothes, then overturn the candles you left burning when you fell asleep, exhausted by your pious orisons. Then I leave you to your prayers and go to my father's room on the other side of the palace, to plan the morning's Council. What a tragedy you'd sent all your servants to St Nynia's Well on a holy vigil! So no one noticed the fire till it was too late. Wulfric, your bodyguard, tried bravely to reach you, but died at your side.'

She was shivering; he saw her glance at him furtively.

'And it's no use promising now, thinking you can back out later. Because if I don't do it tonight, I can do it any night of your life. And if you go round telling people I'm planning to burn you in your bed, the palace doctors will send you to a convent anyway for treatment, but you'll go chained as a maniac.'

He had been watching her with enjoyment and saw she was beaten. Being Penarwan, she wouldn't grovel. She lifted her chin and stared back defiantly.

'Give my loyal bodyguard decent burial and I'll do it.'

'Very well. Now get his clothes on before he stiffens.'

He stood aside while she pulled on Wulfric's shirt and breeches, fastened his shoes and his belt. Then he put his sword point over the wound and stabbed him again through the clothes. He hadn't bled much.

'Give me a hand to throw him out.'

'You promised him decent burial!'

'He's got to be found before he can be buried. He'd better not be found in your bedroom, or what becomes of your pure and virtuous name? We'll put him over the wall at the bottom of the gardens; he'll fall into the alley. He'll have been coming back from a brothel and got stabbed in a quarrel over some whore. Let's tell as much of the truth as possible.'

She said nothing but stooped to pick up Wulfric's legs by the ankles, while Owain lifted him under the armpits. In silence, they went along the colonnades that led from one garden-court to the next. Penarwan was quite steady; when they got to the end, she held Wulfric propped upright against the wall while Owain climbed to the top; then raised the arms so that he could catch hold of the wrists. He hauled the body up, then pitched it into the darkened alley. Side by side they made their way back, Owain scanning the flag-stones for any drops of blood.

There was a small pool of it on the mosaic floor of the bedroom. She filled a bowl with water from her ewer and picked up a sheet. He unbuckled his cloak and threw it to her.

'Better use that. I'll deal with it after.'

He watched her get on her knees, washing the floor. When she took the bloody water to pour into the garden mould, he brought the cloak and wrung out as much moisture as possible. Once dried, there would be nothing surprising about bloodstains on a cloak he'd worn on campaign.

He turned to leave her at the bedroom door but she stayed a moment staring at him.

'Goodbye,' he said.

Her lips moved; he waited politely.

'Whoever else burns, Owain, you will. For ever.'

He smiled. 'Hell's dark, Penarwan, and it should be quite crowded by now. With luck, we won't see each other there.'

245

He went away to Urien's room, where his father was waiting for him in every familiar object—his chair, his books, his map—in everything except his beloved presence. Owain sat in the king's chair and unrolled the map, staring at the names of the land he had to keep safe, picking them out with his ringed finger—Caer Luel, Penrhyd, Llwyfenydd, set out for him in his father's hand. After a time he bowed his head on the map. His black hair fell over Cumbria like a mourning pall. But still he could not weep.

CHAPTER
26

The novice told Taniu there was a man at the gate saying something about his wife. She went there and found a very young man, tanned to leather by sea and wind, smelling of salt and fish. He reminded her of Bran; he was carrying a basket with a fine, fresh-caught salmon wrapped in dock leaves.

He was shy at having to talk face to face with the famous Healer of Eidyn, shyer still of having to talk about women's matters which he didn't understand anyway. The birth had gone well; it was a fine boy; his wife had seemed quite all right. Then she started talking wildly; she was burning; she didn't know any of them; she didn't want her baby. Witches had surely put her image in a fire, trying to melt her spirit out of her body. He offered his basket; all the while his eyes were saying: *You're a wise-woman, help her, do something.*

Taniu ran back for a word with Sister Agatha, busy with a class of novices, while she made up a bag with whatever she guessed might be needed: ground ivy, if it was the afterbirth; plantain for haemorrhage; yarrow to take down the fever—what else? It was a pity they could never tell you clearly what was the matter.

She tied her veil over her head, hitched up her robe and got the convent pony. They went in silence—the boy was tongue-tied in awe of her—north to the fishers' huts, curing-sheds, nets, creels and boats that clustered where the burn came into the firth. The young husband pointed out a cottage but stayed outside. She found the sick mother hardly more than a child, surrounded by womenfolk of all ages, from little sisters to crones, and a deadly choking reek. The old women had been burning some foul compound mixed with dung to keep hostile witches away. They were quite willing to stop now that Taniu had come with her stronger magic.

At last she got a fresher, cooler air into the hut; the yarrow infusion took down the poor child's fever. There was nothing seriously wrong, though her devoted family might have killed her. Taniu watched her through the rest of the day and the night, while a sister-in-law nursed the baby with her own child. The girl slept peacefully. It was good to see her next morning, sitting up with her baby in her arms, holding court among her kinswomen. The young husband had ventured into the hut at last; the girl held up his son, smiling, but it had been her face he kissed first.

Taniu turned and stared out of the open door, unable to see the sparkling water or the gulls wheeling bright against the sky, because her eyes were flooded with tears. She wiped them away with her veil, not to spoil the happiness around her, and managed to be smiling as she took her leave.

There were children playing on the beach; a group of idlers lounged on a rough bench and a few balks of timber round the door of a brew-house. She paused to exchange friendly greetings. Behind her a bold child dashed up on tip-toe, touched her shadow for luck and bolted. Taniu rode on, hearing the voices talking away more vigorously than ever. They would be interested in the young mother and her baby; they were probably all her relations.

'That's a lovely woman,' said an inland man, who had come for some barrels of salt fish for his chief's stores.

'She's a water-elf.' Eurnaid the net-maker spoke with local pride. 'The man of God, Servanus, found her by her spring on St John's Eve and threw holy water over her. So she couldn't escape but she can still do magic.'

247

'No, you're wrong.' Dumna the alewife had come to the door and was leaning there nursing her elbows as she listened. 'My sister's husband's cousin married a man over on the north shore and he said she was King Under-Waves' daughter. She came up out of the sea at full moon—her father'd banished her because she was with child. Father Servanus baptized them both but the child turned into a salmon and swam away down the firth.'

'What nonsense you folk talk!' Elcu the pedlar was scornful. 'That comes of sitting at home telling old stories. Men who travel the world know better.'

In his daring youth, Elcu had once made his way all along the Northernmost Wall to Alclud and shipped to Nendrum with a trader who was short-handed. On the Irish side he had drunk with the crew of a Gaulish ship who regaled him with yarns about the wonderful south. As a widely-travelled man, he despised local legends.

'She isn't an elf-woman, she's a Greek doctor. She reads books. The Greeks live in a city at the end of the world, called Constantinople. All the books are written there. It's a very great city, ten miles across. Its walls are made of jewels and the whole city is covered with a bowl of pure gold.'

This was reasonable; they'd heard of such things in the old stories. They were quite willing to believe in Elcu's city, but it was impossible that Taniu had come from there, as Arthgal the fisher triumphantly pointed out.

'If she'd come from the end of the world she'd be an old, old woman.'

'And if she'd read all the books in the world,' added Dumna, 'she'd have been old before she started out.'

'But you can see she doesn't get any older, year after year. That proves she's from the Land of Youth!'

'She doesn't stay young because she's an elf-woman.' Elcu fought on gallantly for science. 'That's because she's a holy sister. They don't have anything to do with men or child-bearing, so their skin stays smooth and their eyes don't sink into their heads. They're all like that in the Castle of Maidens, even the fat one who breathes out loud.'

'But they're not all beautiful, like her,' objected Arthgal.

They could all agree with that, even Elcu.

Taniu would have been amused to hear them; a laugh would have done her good. However often she helped at a birth, the sight of a baby in its mother's arms could still tear her. She decided to treat herself tonight and reread her letters from Servanus in Mailros, describing Kentigern's growth, health and brightness. She had four now; he wrote every year. There was also other news for her to consider; this had not come by letter but was written on her memory.

She glanced up at the cliff-wall of Eidyn to the city above the crags; it was quieter than usual, indeed the whole land seemed almost deserted. Morcant was away with all the war-host. Thinking of Morcant, her lips tightened. Loth's daughter could never think of Morcant kindly while Loth's son and heir was shut out of his own palace in Din Pelidr, forced to skulk in a remote corner of his own kingdom. Gwalchmai was safe enough in Segloes; whatever else could be said against Gorthyn, anyone living in his hall under his protection could sleep without fear. Still, she was worried about her brother's up-bringing. Gorthyn would be teaching Gwalchmai to handle his weapons skilfully, to hunt any creature worth taking, to strike before he was hit and to take bloody vengeance for any insult. He could not imagine anything else needed to make a complete man and king; Taniu could. Also, she had not lost her Lothian pride. She felt that her house was belittled while the kingdom was under Morcant's rule and the rightful heir had to be thankful that Morcant had not troubled to deal with him—yet.

Besides the wrong done to Gwalchmai, she hated all she knew about Morcant. There was that ugly business of King Urien, who might have been her father-in-law, and had been a brave just man by all accounts. Morcant had put out a story after the slaughter at Metcaud, about finding Urien plotting treachery with the Angles in exchange for eastern land, but not even his own men had believed that.

Strathclyde fell to Morcant next. There was a rebellion, ably fostered by Lovan, who had kin there among the exiles from Gwynedd. Morcant had marched in 'to help his kinsman'. It was intended that Riderec should die in the rebellion before Morcant arrived with the help; but his bodyguard died where they fought while he and his sisters were smuggled aboard an Ulster ship. They sailed to Nendrum, where the abbot sheltered them. By all accounts Riderec was quite happy, which is more than could be said for Strathclyde.

Now Morcant had gone north with his host to crush the Picts. He was at peace with Alba; the Picts were celebrating the Midsummer solstice, a time of sacred truce among them. Once the Pictish warriors were defeated— massacred, since they would be taken unarmed and unawares, Morcant would be supreme in the north. Only Cumbria remained, unsubdued and defiant, on the southwestern border.

Well, Morcant wasn't going to have it all his own way much longer. Taniu's mind went back with a lift of excitement to those messages she had been getting by word of mouth.

Servanus had kept his promise. Soon after he reached Mailros he went up to Gorthyn's stronghold where there were Christians, including Ancarat. He told Gwalchmai that his sister was alive though for her sake, as she was on Morcant's land, this was to be kept the darkest of secrets even from Gorthyn, till Gwalchmai was a man.

Gwalchmai had kept the secret nobly, but his ideas about his manhood were more generous than Gorthyn's. Last year, a visitor had come to the Castle of Maidens, bringing a gift for the convent—a Gospel-cover, splendid with goldwork and jewels—and a request to speak to the lay sister Taniu. Surprised, she went to the gatehouse and found Selyf the jewelsmith. He had a message from Gwalchmai: the prince was overjoyed that his sister was still alive. When he had his kingdom back, he'd found a convent bigger and richer than Mailros and she should be its abbess. Gwalchmai's ideas about lay sisters were as hazy as the fisherfolks' of Eidyn.

Selyf was the royal jewelsmith; he worked for the king and his warband, so he had to live at the king's court. Now that Morcant had taken Lothian into his kingdom, the court was in Din Eidyn, so Selyf had moved there with his family. However, as a free craftsman, he had the right to travel where and when he chose. Being a pious man, he often chose to go to Mailros with offerings he had made. He was quiet and unwarlike, seemingly taken up by his work and his faith. No one from Eidyn thought to spy on him. No word came to Morcant that, instructed by Father Servanus, he lengthened his journeys with visits to Segloes in the Eildon Hills above Mailros. Gwalchmai and Taniu spoke to each other through his mouth every time he journeyed there and back.

Gwalchmai was a man now, turned fourteen; Gorthyn was ready to march. While Morcant was looting Pictland, the Cheviot spearmen would come up to Din Pelidr and Gwalchmai would claim his inheritance. Taniu had no doubt he would succeed. He was Loth's son; anyway, all Lothian despised Morcant as much as they hated him. They would welcome Gwalchmai as their king, and then—

And then I'll take the veil and found that house he wants to endow for me. He'll need another counsellor besides that old fighting boar Gorthyn, brave and loyal as he is. I can do it; Servanus said I'd got the brains and strength; as a royal abbess I'd have the authority. There'd be no Lovans on Gwalchmai's Council if I'm one of his advisers. That's why I was sent to Din Eidyn—I can see it now—to get the book-learning. As Servanus said, it's time I moved on.

She rode up to the convent in high spirits. The portress was looking out for her, anxious and flurried.

'Reverend Mother wants you at once.'

She hurried in. There were some men in the courtyard, a couple of palace guards standing over a man in tattered bloodstained rags, crouched with his head bowed on his knees. Agatha came past, moving faster than she had ever seen, making for the still-room. She went on into Monenna's apartments. The abbess was standing on one side of her bed; opposite her was an elderly councillor from the palace. They were both looking down at what was on the bed; Taniu looked too; in spite of her experience her stomach heaved.

They had already got as much of his clothing off as they could. It had been rich; he was a nobleman. But round the burns on his side the cloth had stuck; when they tried to lift it, the flesh had come too. He'd gone untended too long, the burns were suppurating.

Monenna raised a troubled face.

'We must do what we can.' She kept her voice low. 'He's far gone. The Picts set fire to the heather where they were hiding; I don't know how his armour-bearer got him out alive.'

'Can you make him talk?' said the councillor. 'His man's out of his mind with grief—he's his foster-brother, it seems—and he wouldn't understand much anyway.'

Taniu gave him a look of furious disgust; Monenna put a hand on her shoulder.

'Indeed, it seems cruel, but it's a cruel need that's on us. We've got to know what's happened.'

Her voice sank to a whisper.

'There's been a terrible disaster in the North. The king's taken—and God knows what's left of our army.'

CHAPTER
27

The horsemen made a brilliant splash of colour on the summer moorland. They were a royal warband, their cloaks and armour were of the richest. They were riding easily, carrying their helmets on their saddle-bows in the heat of the glorious midsummer day; but they were not riding carelessly. There were scouts ahead, outriders on their flanks; their king was one whose vigilance never slept. His own eyes were as alert as the scouts' to read the land, brilliant smoke-blue eyes under winged brows, their glance as keen and swift as a falcon's flight.

People said Owain was growing more and more like Urien; the cares and defence of his kingdom had given a sharper chiselling to his face, now edged with a neatly-trimmed black beard. He was not worn out by these cares, though; his figure was as upright and as lithe, his zest for hawks and fine horseflesh as great as ever.

He had little cause for care at the moment. During his

short reign he had taught enemies to avoid him; Cumbria was strong and prosperous. He still rode the marches himself, to keep in fighting trim and have the whole land under his eyes, not because of the desperate need there had been at first.

He had a fine kingdom to leave when he died—and no son to come after him. For Cumbria, that was no matter: there was his younger brother Rhun, and no one could want a better successor. Rhun had Urien's seriousness and strength of purpose; his little son Rhoyth was a promising lad.

For himself, it was a matter of regret. If the boy at Banna had shown any sign of leadership, Owain might have been tempted to own him publicly. But Dinogat was Heulwen's son in mind as well as body. He was strong and healthy; in a year or two he'd be taken into the bodyguard. Sleep would be safe with Dinogat at the door, he was as faithful as a good hound, with rather less initiative. He was no heir for Cumbria; it would have to be Rhun.

Heulwen was perfectly happy with her son's prospects; she'd never expected anything more. She had six other children and looked nearer to fifty than twenty-two, but thoroughly contented. Her life was just what she wanted.

Glancing at Madog riding as usual at his side, Owain hoped that Heledd was equally satisfied with her lot—she had reason to be. He remembered with wry amusement the day when his page had brought a little sapphire ring to him with a message that a veiled woman was asking for a private audience. Then he'd had Heledd weeping at his feet, sobbing that the women were making life at court unbearable with their sneers about her daughter's looks. And what would she do—what could she say—if Madog ever knew? How carefully he'd had to pick his words as he explained that Madog knew already, had always known. That he was as fond and proud of the lovely little girl as of the sturdy son she'd borne him.

Heledd had looked taken aback, but swallowed the truth quietly and went away without more fuss. She stayed away from court, mostly on her own estate near Guasmoric, but this was her own choice of a peaceful family life. Madog always spoke of her easily, with cheerful affection.

Fate is strange, thought Owain, with a touch of bitterness. *I never cared much for those two, hardly noticed them even while I was making love. Yet I've never brought them anything but good luck—it had to be Taniu and Penarwan, with their beauty and bright spirits, that I destroyed.*

Then he nearly laughed aloud at himself. He hadn't destroyed Penarwan—could anybody? Royal ladies who entered religion didn't stay as lowly handmaids of the Lord unless they chose. With haughty generosity, Owain had paid back her dowry; Penarwan had founded her house. She was learned and clever; on the Day of Judgement she would never be charged with hiding her light under a bushel. Her letters on church policy were already famous and much copied; she had presided over a synod. Perhaps she might come to be a saint—Owain's mouth twitched at the thought—there was no doubt she was a very great abbess.

He had never seen her since they acted their prepared farce of dignified parting in front of the Council; not because he hated her, hatred had long since given way to bitter compassion. But she was still quite a young woman; remembering her, he could not believe the fires in her body had died down. It might hurt her to see him; he no longer wanted to hurt her.

Perhaps when I'm old—if I live to be old—and I've resigned the kingdom to Rhun or young Rhoyth, when I feel death coming I'll ask to see her and we can forgive each other.

This was a dreary thought to take riding on the moors on a bright midsummer day. But the night he'd just spent in Caer Voran was a memory to darken the sun; he should have known better than to go to Garmon's house.

Garmon was dead; he had fallen with his sons defending the border in that dreadful year after Urien's death, when all Cumbria's enemies had fallen on her at once. He himself seemed to have spent every hour of it awake and in the saddle.

The Angles had come out of Metcaud and Din Guayroi just as soon as the besieging forces broke up. With their Bernician allies they had come pouring over the Cheviots to take reprisals. Owain was away in the south, fighting Gwallog of Elmet for Catraeth. It looked like the end of

Cumbria, but the Caer Voran men had fought the Angles to a standstill between Brewyn and the Wall. Led by Garmon's master of horse, they had got back to their fortress in good order, bringing the bodies of their lords.

Ressona received them, washing and laying them out herself, seeing them carried to the chapel where the Roman troops had once kept their standards. She insisted on keeping the dead-watch herself, saying with pathetic gallantry that Garmon would never believe he was home if he didn't spend the first night with her.

So she took her place at Garmon's side and never left it. They found her next morning with Garmon's dagger placed, very neat and soldierly as befitted a soldier's daughter, between her ribs. They buried her with him; she had earned the right to be treated as his wife.

Owain had brought his horsemen racing up from the south and smashed the invaders at Brewyn, while they were still in disarray from the drubbing Garmon had given them. He himself had killed Theodric Flame-Bearer in hand-to-hand combat; whenever he recalled the fight, he still felt surprised to be alive. The Angles had kept away from Cumbria ever since.

He took Caer Voran into Cumbria; its lords were gone, it could not stand alone. He put the master of horse in command, the man had shown himself competent and loyal; and ordered that the king's share of the rents should be paid to Abbess Penarwan, as Garmon's last heir.

Old habit had drawn him to Garmon's deserted house when the warband halted there last night. Even the feast the fort commander gave for them had not been loud or bright enough to drive away the desolation that had come on his spirit.

Along the colonnade, the dead leaves of five autumns pattered and whispered behind him like the tap of Penarwan's sandals and the rustle of her silk gown. He came to the south room, where he had laughed with her so often; he remembered her disguising him before he set out on that mad, that fatal adventure in Lothian.

'Be sure to come and tell me all about it! It's the best joke in the world!'

The fort commander had moved into the old headquarters building; he liked to live in the basilica with his men around him like a chief with his warriors in his hall. His womenfolk were quartered in the orderlies' offices behind. They had cleared out the costly dining-room furniture; damp was stealing the painted landscapes on the walls, the Cupids looked forlorn. There were some things, though, that they had not cared to take. Some books were tumbled on the floor, as if somebody had taken them up to look, seen nothing but meaningless black marks and then dropped them.

They were too valuable to be left as rubbish; he picked one up, thinking he would send them to Penarwan, and glanced at the writing:

> Thy bosom's roseate buds let him not finger,
> Let not his lips on thy lips linger,
> Mingle not thighs . . .

but it brought Penarwan herself too vividly before his eyes; he hurriedly laid the scroll aside. It was not, anyway, a book to send to a respected abbess.

Rome had died in Caer Voran. It was still a stronghold and could keep its enemies at bay; but something—some southern grace, some breadth of mind—had gone for ever. The old world, or a memory of it, still lingered in Cumbria but how long would even that memory last after he was dead? Rhun was serious and learned, but all his interest was in the church.

He felt a sudden chill; his muscles tightened, so that Ferlas, his big grey war-horse, halted in his stride and twitched one ear back to ask what was wrong.

Why is it that every thought I have today ends in my death?

Perhaps he was fated; the raven might have called today over Caer Luel; the Washer at the Ford might be dipping his bloody shirt even now. It didn't matter very much; he'd done the work he meant to do. He'd always known that death in battle was coming to him as it came to most warrior-kings. By all the laws of likelihood, it should have come years ago.

All the while these thoughts and memories flowed through his mind, his eyes were alert over the surrounding country; he saw what was coming as the scouts gave warning. A sight that meant war, just as seagulls inland meant storm.

The newcomers were not threatening in themselves: a few hill-folk. The ominous fact was that they were carrying all their possessions with them, bundled on their backs or piled into a crazy cart, where an old woman lay, shaking with fever, and a girl nursing a sickly baby.

Seeing the path blocked, the wretched little procession halted. The scouts closed in; Owain rode forward to question the strangers.

'What's amiss? What brings you here?'

'Raiders, lord,' said the ragged, tousle-headed man leading the cart.

'What raiders?'

'We don't know. We saw the smoke in the north and we were frightened.'

'Where in the north?'

'Calchfynedd.'

Owain heard his men murmuring; he was furious.

'Calchfynedd! Then get back north where you belong! Go to Din Eidyn and tell your king Morcant to protect you.'

'Lord, we can't go back.' An old man driving a few bony cattle spoke up desperately. He was such a feeble creature he should have been on the cart himself, though it would probably have broken down under any more weight. 'My wife's sick—and my grandson. They'll die on the road back.'

'You'll all die on the road here if you don't get off it. Do you think Cumbria's a bolting-hole for Eidyn's rats?'

'Lord—'

The nearest riders lowered their spears; one point touched the old man's throat. The fugitives stared at Owain's men and saw no pity. With a sighing groan, the younger man dragged the exhausted horse into movement; the cattle were goaded; the forlorn group turned off the track. The child began crying, a thin hopeless wail.

A call from one of the scouts drew Owain's attention to the hill-slope ahead. A second band of fugitives was coming. His mouth tightened as he saw them standing firm when the scouts barred their way. He brought Ferlas up at a canter, ready to deal harshly with their insolence. Then he saw that the newcomers were monks, half a dozen brothers, one carrying a child, with some younger novices and schoolboys grouped behind a priest holding a preaching-cross.

The peasants halted their cart and beasts, emboldened by the presence of the holy men. This did not improve Owain's temper. The priest turned towards him; a small man, mild-eyed and wispy-haired.

'The Lord be with you, my son.'

'And with your spirit, Father.'

Owain had no quarrel with the Church; besides, he could tell from the priest's voice he was an Irishman. He could ask for news; churchmen were usually well informed.

'The roads from the North are busy today, I see.' He looked grimly towards the country folk. 'Is there any trouble in Eidyn?'

'Great trouble. The Anglian war-host has come out of Din Guayroi. They're harrying the coastlands to the north.'

'I wish Morcant joy in dealing with them. He may find himself wanting allies—he should have taken more care to keep those he had, once.'

'King Morcant is dead, please God.'

Owain looked at the priest with a mocking smile. 'What a pious prayer, Father. Do you hate him too?'

'I am praying that God will have had mercy on him. His army was trapped in Alba; it's said he was taken alive.'

Owain laughed heartily.

'And I'd promised myself the pleasure of killing him. But we mustn't be selfish, must we, Father? I hope the Picts keep him alive as long as possible.'

The priest looked at him gravely.

'Well, you were wise not to stay and preach to your Anglian visitors. I'm sure they're too busy to listen carefully. Have you come far?'

'From Mailros.'

In spite of himself, Owain was shocked. 'Mailros! Is that all that's left of you?'

'I hope not. Abbot Boisil divided our numbers and shared out the holy vessels and books among us. He hoped

258

that some of us at least would reach Cumbria or Strath-clyde to beg for help.'

Owain felt his anger welling up. He deliberately mis-understood, saying coldly, 'Any holy brother or sister is sure of a safe refuge in Cumbria. Abbot Boisil might have known without asking.'

The priest smiled into Owain's stony face.

'Help for our Christian brothers and sisters in Din Eidyn, who are in sore distress and grave danger.'

'And you're asking me, of all people, to go to the rescue of Morcant's folk? You think that's such a little thing to ask of Urien's son?'

'It's a very great thing. Great enough to ask of Urien's son—for *he* was great, and it's what he would have done.'

'It's what he did. That's why he rode east, that last time. He could be alive now—' Owain's voice shook; it only made him angrier—'he came to help them and they killed him. So let them burn, or rot.'

'They killed my Lord and all his first followers. But the work goes on.'

The little man was planted beside his preaching-cross. He was as insignificant as a dusty brown sparrow, as unbudgeable as Helvellyn.

'Listen, Father—?'

'Servanus.'

'You say, "*The work goes on.*" I've got my work too, I'm King of Cumbria. You can save your breath. Not for anything—even if Eidyn hadn't killed my father—am I going to call my people from their farms at the start of the harvest and take the war-host up north just because Picts or Angles might be raiding there.'

'Even if you could get the war-host together in time, I wouldn't be asking that of you. It's swift riders we need to get to Din Eidyn. It's a strong city; barbarians don't come to attack cities. But when they realize the city has no king and few defenders, they'll come in like hungry wolves and destroy it. Think what that will be like.'

'Do you imagine I haven't thought?' Owain's voice was bitter. 'If Morcant's folk had got their wish, my people would have been in that very plight, leaderless, their warriors dead, waiting for destruction or slavery. I bought my people's safety at the price of my own honour. Every-thing has a price, Father Servanus; if we want something we pay for it. Din Eidyn bought its own destruction with my father's blood. It's time they took delivery.'

'You keep saying Din Eidyn killed your father. Morcant killed him, with some handful of others, who will be dead now, God be merciful to them. Most of the folk there are as innocent as this child.'

He put his hand on the head of the little boy perched on the monk's shoulder. He was sitting up straight, watching the king on the grey stallion with alert eyes, quite unafraid.

'Kentigern's mother is in Eidyn.'

Owain glanced at him: a fine well-grown child with the light eastern colouring. For a moment he had an image of the mother: she would be tall, fair, grey-eyed; he shut his mind hurriedly to the picture.

I should have a child like that; but those damned easterners gave him for food to the crows. Like my father.

'If blood is the price of your father's death,' the priest's voice was sorrowful, 'if that is what you want, surely you've been paid. There isn't a family in Eidyn that isn't mourning its dear ones.'

'As I am mourning mine. Who also died in the East.'

' "*Vengeance is mine, says the Lord, I will repay.*" '

'It seems He's repaying now.' Owain spoke with bitter satisfaction. 'Five years my father's been waiting in the sands by Metcaud.'

Staring down at the turf, he forced himself to see his father's face as it had been the last time he saw it: the dead eyes, the clotted hair, the bloody pulp of the neck round the splintered bone. That face was always there, waiting behind his eyes.

But now, it would not come. It was Taniu's face that looked up from the ground where he had thrown her, blotched with tears, the golden hair tangled with dust and twigs.

There were other faces too: Penarwan alone on her narrow nun's bed, her auburn curls cropped away; Heledd weeping at his feet, terrified and ashamed. Of these, it might also have been said that they had paid for what they willingly bought. But what had Taniu ever done that he should destroy her?

I came to her like Morcant, disguised in smiles and friendship. She followed me like Urien, helpless because she trusted me.

So that's why she's haunted me all these years. She wants the price of her blood. I'll pay it; then she can rest.

He drew the royal ring from his hand and gave it to Llywarch. There was no need for such a precious token, a message brought by Llywarch would be believed. But Rhun was his heir; he wanted to make sure the ring was safe with his successor, and a cousin he could trust while his son was a child.

'Ride as fast as you can to Prince Rhun. Tell him to warn the chiefs they may have to call out the war-host, and man the borders, especially to the north and east. Then wait till he hears from me.'

Llywarch was away like the wind. Owain gathered Ferlas's reins. Kentigern had reached from his perch and was stroking the grey's nose; Owain touched the bright hair for a moment as he passed. The child glanced up and smiled.

Owain rode to the head of his troops; they took the way northwards to Eidyn.

CHAPTER
28

The wounded chief died without speaking. His armour-bearer, struggling with grief and remembered horror, told brokenly of a narrow glen, an enemy host that came up suddenly out of a summer fog, terror, slaughter, a deadly remorseless hunting.

Then the country people began to come in from the north, driving their beasts into the grassy spaces inside the ramparts, squatting in byres and outhouses, camping in huddles against the walls. Monenna brought the nuns over from the Castle of Maidens, into a nobleman's hall whose lord would never return to claim it. The convent, isolated on its spur of rock, was too dangerous. If the Picts attacked, nobody could have come to their help.

The Picts did not attack at once; they were far too busy. They had their sacred Midsummer festival to finish, now enriched by splendid offerings to the gods and watched by the agonized eyes of Morcant and Lovan whom they had impaled as oath-breakers. There was the usual quarrelling over spoils; it nearly caused a clan war. Many of their warriors were still away hunting fugitives; it was excellent sport, too good to miss.

Gorthyn had taken Din Pelidr. The news of Morcant's disaster travelled south; he knew what Loth would have done, given such a perfect chance. Leaving Brychan in charge, he marched north with Gwalchmai to claim Eidyn for him, as Morcant's cousin. The news went on its way southwards and crossed the Bernician border. It reached Bebban's Burh, where its listeners also saw a perfect chance. The young war-leader, Ethelric Idasson, remembered how his father had found the great Bernician sea-fort almost unguarded because its king was away fighting his neighbours. Now the Lothian fighting-men had gone north and would likely be embroiled soon with the Picts. It seemed that the whole kingdom of Lothian was likewise a treasure for warriors' taking.

A land without a king is like a hive without a queen bee. The folk in Eidyn accepted Gwalchmai, there was nobody else. Also, the arrival of Gorthyn's tough hill-men made them feel safer.

Someone started the idea, which swept through the crowded hilltop like stubble fire, that Morcant's many treacheries had brought a curse on Eidyn and only the hands of holy women could lift it. Monenna must crown Gwalchmai at his hallowing; Taniu, the Healer of Eidyn, must buckle on his sword and keep him safe from wounds and death by her magic.

Taniu was appalled; if she consented she would be guilty of presumption as well as heathenism. Monenna told her not to worry.

'The poor creatures are half out of their minds with fear. Anything that can help them face death with a bit better heart is an act of blessed charity.'

Taniu looked into the robin-bright eyes.

'Are we facing death, Mother?'

'I'm thinking so, my dear.'

She tried out the idea in her mind and on the nerves of her body and found that it did not disturb her unduly. She had faced death before; in a way she could say that she had already died more than once. The company of women who saw death as a joyful birth was a strong cordial against the chills of fear. However she left her body, it could hardly hurt more than any other birth-pangs.

So she went with Monenna to the hallowing.

Gwalchmai was coming up to Loth's height but had not yet grown to Loth's strength. His father's well-known mail-shirt and baldric, adapted by Gorthyn's weapon-smith, made him look more spindly than he really was. He reminded Taniu so much of the nervous baby brother she had left in Din Pelidr, trying hard to be a warrior with his toy dagger, she wanted to give him a hug and tell him not to mind.

This would have been the last shame for Gwalchmai, as she well knew. So she helped him instead by playing her allotted part as the Healer of Eidyn, remote, mysterious and powerful, as if she really had come from the fairy hills to put a spell of safe-keeping on him. She made a private vow to get to his side if possible when the end came to Din Eidyn and die fighting. She had the knife she used in her work and was prepared to use it on herself if need be.

'What would your life be like—captive drudge to some brute—or brutes?'

She wasn't a vowed nun; surely God would forgive any woman for defending herself against an evil she had no share in.

She tried to imagine what the Lothian men made of her sudden reappearance among them from the dead. She wondered still more painfully what sort of stories about her might be going round at the coronation feast. Doubtless Lothian had been alive with rumours eight years ago about her lost maidenhead and her father's deadly rage. The sight of her now must be calling the old scandals into everyone's mind.

She need not have worried. Loth's family pride had kept

the truth to the few he could trust. Most of Lothian believed that she had died in the Great Winter. The old stories of magic they heard from the bards, the newer stories of miracles they heard from the missionary priests prepared them to accept marvels. Whether Taniu had been protected by angels or hidden in the Hollow Hills, her return was taken as a good omen for Lothian: Loth's blood was lucky, unlike Morcant's.

'I told you God was guarding her.' Cynon, now Gorthyn's second-in-command, fingered the crucifix at his neck. Fixed by Ancarat's beady eyes, Cynon had been ordered to become a Christian before he was allowed to marry her grand-daughter Leucu. He had forgotten he once committed Taniu to the care of other gods.

Gorthyn grunted. 'It's lucky she's got this hold over the Eidyn rabble. She'll stop them making trouble for Gwalchmai. And we'll need all the cures she can do when the Picts come.'

The coronation rejoicing faltered, then died, when it was heard that the Angles were raiding to the south. They were cut off now and no help would come. Morcant had seen to that for them. To their west was Strathclyde, torn by civil war and bitterly resentful of Morcant's recent overlordship. No one in Strathclyde would lift a finger to help Din Eidyn. Beyond was Cumbria and Urien's unappeased ghost.

A few survivors struggled back from Morcant's war-host. Some had been horribly wounded; only a comrade's loyalty or their dread of the hunters had got them along; they reached Eidyn only to die. Others had whole skins but no shields or weapons. They told long detailed stories about how they had got separated from the war-host in the Highland mist and lost their way, repeating themselves defiantly, glaring at their hearers for signs of disbelief. Gorthyn listened to their sagas without comment and told them to get new weapons from the war-chests. Gwalchmai was shocked; he was still young enough to believe in honour.

'Why soil good spears by giving them to cowards?'

'Because they've got hands to hold them. Don't worry, they won't run away again. There's nowhere they can run.'

Most of these newcomers seemed to believe, for reasons they were not eager to explain, that Morcant and Lovan had been taken alive. In which case, however short a time they lived after that, it would seem too long to them.

These stories, whispered through Din Eidyn, strengthened the belief that the city was already lost. Fear spread like summer fever, though outwardly the place was as lively as a Midsummer fair with children, pigs, chickens and dogs playing, scrabbling, rooting and fighting between the camping family groups. And as happens at fairs, there were outbreaks of violence, all the uglier because they sprang from fear and grief not drunken high spirits.

Late one afternoon Taniu came out of a peat-store behind one of the halls, where she had been tending a sickly half-starved baby. The mother, nearly in the last stages of lung-disease, had no milk.

She stood easing her back and blinking in the bright sunlight; the lean-to had been dark, and crowded to suffocation with fugitives. Some sort of argument was going on in front of the hall; an angry voice was raised in passionate denunciation; there was an outcry of women like gulls round a dead fish; a shriek.

Her own anger rose; she was overworked and strained by the suffering she had to watch while she kept outwardly calm and smiling. It would be pleasant to let her temper free in a good cause; these shrews would disturb the dying mother; if they had energy spare for fighting, she'd soon find them work.

She was angrier when she turned the corner of the hall and saw that the screeching group a few yards in front of the porch were noblewomen, resplendent with fine clothes and jewellery, though some of them were in mourning veils.

'Stop that disgusting noise. Can't you find anything better to do with your time than squabble like drunken whores in an alehouse?'

They swung round like spitting cats; when they saw the Healer of Eidyn, they backed away in respect and some fear. One girl took no notice. Unlike the others, she was in a plain black robe with not a single jewel or one gleam of gold or silver. Her dark hair hung unbraided under a mourning veil, her pale face looked like a corpse against the blackness. She was stooping over a huddled figure; as Taniu arrived she twisted her fingers in its light auburn curls and dragged it by the hair a few more steps towards the porch. There was another shriek.

Taniu rushed forward to stop her.

'In the name of God! What are you doing to her?'

The girl glanced at her, then stood up to confront her.

'I'm taking my sister-in-law back to my brother's hall.'

She shut her lips tight as if she had said all that was needed. The other women crowded round, eager to justify themselves.

'Lady Nefyn caught her coming out of the stable—she thought she could slink back without being seen.'

'She'd been down in the straw with one of Gorthyn's men.'

'Not a noble, holy sister, just a common spearman,' explained the gaudiest woman self-righteously. In her eyes this was clearly the unforgivable sin.

'A stinking bitch she is, that Essyllt!'

'Lord Alawn's wife.'

'One of the royal kin.'

'And he's dead, isn't he!'

Essyllt had raised her head from the ground. She was a pretty little thing, plump and rich-coloured, though her auburn curls had been clawed into elf-locks and her face was streaked with dirt. She knelt up, glancing round the circle of threatening faces with a strange blend of hatred, fear and defiance. Her dress had been torn and pulled half off her shoulder; suddenly she wrenched at the neck and ripped it down to bare her breasts, screaming at them.

'He's dead! What harm can I do him? And what good can he ever do to me now? They're all dead! I'm nineteen —have I got to wait till the children in the cradles grow into men?'

'That's all she thinks about,' said the bejewelled woman. 'Just because she's got no kinsmen left to punish her she thinks she can do as she likes. She can't spare time to mourn her husband like a decent widow, she's too busy lifting up her skirt for a Cheviot sheep-stealer!'

Essyllt winced; then snapped back viciously.

'If I did lift up my skirt, at least I took a man in under it! Not like that running cur of yours, Ceinwen, that brought a whole skin back from the north. The only spear he's ever used is the one he puts between your legs.'

Ceinwen gave a screech of anger and pulled a knife from her belt. The others closed up to back her; their numbers and their shared rage made them forget the respect they owed to the Healer. She knew they were not far off slashing her as well as Essyllt, but still she moved in front of the girl, trying to hold the others by her unbroken calm.

Surprisingly Nefyn moved to her side. The last words seemed to have shifted her hatred from her sister-in-law. She stared at Ceinwen with loathing, though she spoke to Essyllt.

'Get out of my sight. The spearmen's whores stay down in the camp by the north gate. Go and join them, it's where you belong. And don't ever come back into my brother's house. He's still got kin to guard his honour. If you come here again I'll kill you.'

Taniu broke in, though Nefyn might turn on her next.

'You don't have to go there, Essyllt. Come with me to the abbess, she'll take you in. And remember, you've got other ways of doing good to the living. There's a sick woman in the peat-shed behind your husband's hall, with a baby she can't feed. And that's not the only child in Eidyn that's going to die soon if it gets no tending.'

Essyllt had got to her feet. She stood for a heartbeat, staring at Taniu. Then she shrugged, pulled her tattered dress up to the neck and turned down the path to the north gate.

Ceinwen's pack began baying.

'Slut!'

'Filth!'

'She needs her whore's face laid open!' Ceinwen waved her knife, 'Make sure even a Lothian spearman wouldn't stoop to pick her up.'

The pack started after Essyllt like farm dogs going for a vixen.

'Even a Lothian spearman?'

The sheer rage in Taniu's voice halted them; she had never felt so close to Loth in all her life.

'Even a Lothian spearman would be good enough to stand between you and the Picts! But you don't have to suffer our protection if it shames you so much. Come down with me, now, this minute, to the north gate. I'll see you're passed through it! I can explain to my brother, King Gwalchmai, that you're too proud to have any truck with Lothian.'

Ceinwen backed away in horror, then retreated behind the porch pillars and round the corner of the hall, followed by her allies. Nefyn watched them go with a cheerless smile, then turned to Taniu.

'You despise us, don't you? *'The Eidyn rabble'*, that's what your men call us. Oh, don't trouble to deny it. Gorthyn's got a loud voice and he doesn't keep it down to spare our feelings. That's why I—' her mouth twisted—'I can imagine what the Lothian men say about *her*—and every word well-earned, only it shames my brother too. *'Rabble'*, that's all that's left. The best of us are dead.'

Taniu reached out to hold and comfort her. Nefyn swung up her hand; Taniu expected a blow but she only put her knuckles to her mouth and bit them hard. Then she sighed.

'So you're Gwalchmai's sister. We're cousins, far off. Morcant's kin, though I don't suppose you boast about it. Now, where's this sick woman you were talking about?'

Since the news of the attack from Bernicia, they had wondered which of their enemies would arrive first to destroy them. Dust on the southern road and the gleam of spear-points in the morning sunlight answered that question. It would be the Angles.

But those who were coming so swiftly were horsemen and carried the Raven banner.

Of course, they should have expected this. These warriors had been on their way since Urien fell under Morcant's sword. The Cumbrians were not going to have their goblet of blood snatched from their lips. They were riding hard to get in first.

However, when they came to Eidyn, they halted on the

plain, all but one rider who came up to the gate carrying a green branch in sign of peace. Then they knew that their exorcism had worked; the hands of holy women had lifted the curse. King Owain had come to offer his help against the heathen.

After midsummer the days had got hotter. Even on the open hilltop, there were moments when Taniu felt as if she were shut inside an oven. Whenever she could get a moment's respite from her work, she would climb up to the peak of Eidyn, a jumble of rocks that thrust up through the turf above the highest rampart of the citadel. There were grassy hollows among the crags where rock plants could be found. This made a good excuse for the climb, though she went there just as much for the quietness and a sense of freedom. She took off her veil and let sun and air wash her clean of the human squalor that was piling up in the city. The scene with Ceinwen and Essyllt had been like falling into cowpats; it left a stink.

Moments like that filled her with grief and disgust. They had grown more frequent as the days of waiting dragged on. It wanted very little for Lothian and Eidyn to be at each other's throats. She asked herself bitterly if the enemy would even arrive in time to keep the peace between them.

Then the Cumbrians came, cutting through the jealousy and tension like a spear of sunlight breaking through thunderclouds. Their generosity was so simple and reckless that it made nonsense of feuds and squalid resentments. Both Eidyn and Lothian felt the contrast and dropped their bickering for a while.

Taniu was sitting on the peak waiting for sunset on the day the Cumbrians arrived. From her point of vantage she could look right over Eidyn and across the firth. Far below, a valley opened out on to the plain; she could see the tiny brilliant figures of some of the horsemen. Her mind went out to them and to their King Owain, who had tossed away his revenge as carelessly as throwing a pebble into the sea.

This was so like her own ideas of honour that she felt as if she knew him. His name, too, was familiar in her thoughts, it came easily—though there was nothing strange in the coincidence. Owain—Eugenius,

Well-Born—had always been a favourite name among the Romanized westerners; no doubt a whole crop of boys had been named after King Urien's heir.

She was sorry for this king. Probably only Monenna's nuns and the brothers of the Holy Rood truly understood and valued what he had just done. The rest were glad to take his help while they were in danger; if the threat was lifted the old feuds would break out again. She felt sick when she thought there were even some of the Eidyn and Lothian men who would be capable, when blind with drink or temper, of throwing in his face that he'd left his father unavenged. And if he were as true-hearted and free from suspicion as his father, he could well end in the same way.

She felt a surge of generous anger for his sake, as if he were a kinsman. He might have been her husband; he had wanted her once and offered good terms. It hadn't been herself he wanted, of course, and his father had done the offering, to get an alliance with Lothian and make peace with the east. The need was even more urgent, now that Bernicia had fallen and Morcant had infuriated the Picts.

There was no reason why the alliance should not be reforged. She was a lay woman; King Owain's wife had taken the veil years ago with his consent, so leaving him free to marry again if he chose. Gwalchmai would do what she asked him; she could get him to offer her again.

And King Owain could say no.

Even sitting alone, she felt herself flushing with shame. There need be no offence; he could have vowed chastity when his queen entered religion; he could be betrothed to some baby princess in Manau or Ireland and be waiting till she grew to womanhood.

But if word got out—and it would!—that he'd refused me, our hot-headed fools would say that Cumbria had insulted Lothian and we'd have the old feud back again, worse than ever.

If only women could speak for themselves, without this deadly nonsense about warriors' honour.

What am I thinking of? A woman offer herself to a man —wouldn't everyone say I was no better than that poor little slut Essyllt, running out like a bitch on heat?

That's not true. Lust has nothing to do with it. A warrior can go to a foreign king and offer his strength and skill as a member of his warband, without any shame. Well, I've got strength and skill too, and if I choose to offer them to the King of Cumbria, he can only thank me whether he accepts or not.

The sun was low now; it would soon be dusk. She picked up her veil to cover her head. As she wound the folds around her neck and breast, she realized that she could go to King Owain before the eyes of the whole army because in their eyes, she wasn't a woman. She lived in a house of nuns, they looked on her as a holy sister, she was the Healer of Eidyn. If she asked to speak to the king alone, they'd think she'd come to describe a vision or give a heavenly message.

I'll just tell him simply who I am. I'll say, 'I'm the Princess of Lothian, Loth's daughter. Nobody knows what I'm saying to you and nobody will ever hear about it from me. Once, you wanted to marry me. If you still think that a marriage between us will help to keep the peace, I'm willing.' And if he says no, I'll get Gwalchmai to help me found my house in Lothian and work for peace that way.

Suddenly she began to laugh.

Tomorrow or the next day, we could all be dead.

The turf was still warm from the sunlight, larks were still singing. It was hard to think of the world, and herself not alive in it.

There's nothing to be done about death except to take it as bravely as possible when it comes. But while I'm alive there's so much for me to do!

She jumped up and ran down the rocky slope, as light-footed as a girl for all her twenty-two years.

Gorthyn had taken Owain to examine the city and its defences.

'It's a fine strong place.' Owain looked at the sheer wall of rock round the western side. Above and beyond, the smoke of many hearth-fires was rising.

'It's too big. You'd need a whole war-host to hold it.' Gorthyn pointed along a ridge to the west. 'See that rock? There's a fort up there, the nuns had a convent inside it but the walls are still sound. With your men and mine in it we could draw our ranks a good bit closer.'

'But we'd lose the advantage of our horses. We'd just be

a few extra footmen—with the numbers coming against us that wouldn't be enough.'

'Will they be enough on horseback?'

'Perhaps. It depends if the Picts and the Angles link up—they've done that before.'

'If they do?'

'We can kill enough to weaken them. They won't get much further south. If they do, my war-host will deal with them; I've told my brother to send out the summons. And I think Strathclyde will help. They'll have Riderec back now Morcant's gone.'

Gorthyn snorted. 'If he comes back with a boatload of chanting monks he won't be much use.'

'If he comes back with some boatloads of Ulster warriors he'll be a great deal of use. Don't be too hard on Riderec. He's not the only one who trusted Morcant too far—we weren't all wise before the event, like you.'

Gorthyn looked pleased but embarrassed; they were getting near dangerous ground. Groping round in his mind for another subject, he decided to try statecraft, as he understood it.

'Suppose we try for terms with the Picts, just while we see the Angles off? Morcant was our enemy, as much as theirs. Young Gwalchmai's half-Pictish through his mother—and if there are many more like her up there in Alba, I could even be sorry for Morcant. I've got some of her people with me—Brude, Talorg, Nechtan—I'll point them out to you.'

Seeing that the Cumbrian was listening with flattering interest, he went on expansively: 'They came with me when Morcant took Din Pelidr. I can't say that for every-one; there were Lothian men who joined Morcant because he had more to offer, but not these Picts. They're ugly fighters, too; useful to have beside you. Can't say I like them much. Sullen devils; and Brude's woman Lurga —she was the queen's foster-sister—is a blood-sucking witch if ever I saw one. But I'll say this for them, they'd let themselves be skinned alive for young Gwalchmai. Suppose I send them over the firth, to find out what's going on?'

'It's an idea.' Owain thought it over. 'Yes, if nothing

happens in a day or two—and you can trust them not to go straight to the Pictish king and tell him all our numbers and plans.'

'For myself, I don't trust them an inch, even when I can see what they're doing. But they belong to Gwalchmai, body and soul, for Drostecca's sake. Picts always make more account of the mother than the father, even when they know who he is. Queer folk.'

Owain smiled.

'Will you come up to the city now? They'll have got the palace ready for you.'

'Thank you, but I'll stay with the men, in case we have to move quickly. They're camping down there by the loch beyond that monastery—there's more room for the horses. I'll come up later when I've ridden over the ground, seen what it's like for cavalry.'

Gorthyn nodded and turned to climb up to the citadel. Owain's skin had crawled with disgust at the thought of eating and sleeping in Morcant's hall; it would be as foul as wearing the creature's clothes or finding him by his side at a feast.

He thanked God he had the Lothian men to deal with and not some survivor of Morcant's blood. He'd taken Gorthyn's measure at once, he wasn't hard to understand: the typical captain of a warband, a brave fighting animal, within his limits totally loyal. A sound but not a brilliant commander; he wouldn't do anything stupid and he was willing to take advice from someone with more skill and not resent it. He could deal with Gorthyn; and he very much liked the tall gawky young king who listened so earnestly to everything he said—and who might have been his own marriage-kin.

Gwalchmai had none of Taniu's haunting beauty; there was nothing about him even like her except his broad forehead and the clear integrity of his manner. After Morcant, this was refreshing; though it had its dangers, as Owain discovered that very evening.

He had ridden round the mountain. Its crest was nearly ringed by sheer cliffs. Only to the north, facing the estuary, the ground fell away in a long narrow valley, widening as it met the plain. The man-made defences of Eidyn were strongest here; the way up was blocked by a stout rampart. West of the valley, there was a fold in the ground, hiding a broad shallow trough of peaty turf. In wet weather it would be a bog; after a hot dry June it was firm enough under Ferlas's hoofs. The ridge was high enough to hide his horsemen from anyone coming on foot up the valley, but not too steep to come over the crest in a charge, taking the enemy in the flank on their unshielded side.

'Horses can't perform miracles,' he explained that evening to Gorthyn and Gwalchmai. They were sitting round the hearth in one of the guest halls; he noted with bitter amusement that the Lothian men also avoided Morcant's palace as if it housed the yellow plague.

'They're not much use against determined footmen—an Anglian shield-wall, for instance. If a footman has the nerve and skill to run in under your spear, he's only got to smash your horse's leg or slit its belly open, and you're down. Believe me, if you've just come off a horse at full gallop, you're far less able to make a fight of it than if you'd started out on foot.'

'But if our spearmen came out with you—' said Gwalchmai, eagerly. To fight under the eyes of the famous King Owain and earn his praise were Gwalchmai's highest ambitions at the moment.

'We'll need the spearmen to man the rampart,' objected Gorthyn. 'We've got few enough to do it too, even with the Eidyn rabble, whatever use they'll be. All we know about them is that they can move faster than your horses at full gallop, give them half a chance.'

They had settled the last details of the defence; Owain moved to go, when Gwalchmai called him back in a high excited voice.

'King Owain!'

Owain paused, smiling kindly at him. Gwalchmai swallowed hard.

'It was very good of you to come to our help. You needn't have come, your own land's not in danger. And it's especially generous of you because—'

Owain had a foreboding of what was coming and tried to interrupt but Gwalchmai rushed on:

'—because your own father was murdered—here in the

east—and it was a foul shame—he was our ally—we're all shamed by it—and—I ask your pardon!'

Owain was appalled. The boy's generosity and honesty touched him. He himself could never have said such words; indeed, they should never have been spoken. Gwalchmai had done something unheard of—committed the unforgivable crime, as Lothian would see it—of asking pardon of another king, and a westerner at that.

Gorthyn's face was turning purple; his second-in-command, a youngish, decent-looking man called Cynon, was white with temper. And if their spearmen ever heard what Gwalchmai had just said there would be the devil to pay.

I could end like my father, with an ally's dagger in my back and the enemy unfought. What an evil jest that would be!

He tried to think of something he could say. If he accepted the apology he would be setting his seal to the insult; if he ignored it, they would take that as an insult as well.

Then he remembered that there was something he could say—he had come to her people to say it—and since he was ever more certain that he would not live through the fighting, best say it now.

'You may not remember, you were very young,' he said formally, with Urien's own grave courtesy, 'that I once asked for the honour of your sister's hand in marriage. She died before I had that happiness, but I still consider myself pledged to her. Bringing my warband here—think of it as her bridal gift.'

They stared at him. In the silence the door had opened; servants brought logs in for the hearth. Through the open doorway, Owain glimpsed one of the Lothian spearmen. As soon as the servants had gone, Gorthyn said hurriedly, 'Ah yes, well, you know best what your horsemen can do. So we'll follow your plan: we'll hold the ramparts, you'll ambush them from the flank. If they break, we'll come down to you.'

He got up. 'I hope you've got comfortable quarters in your camp. Is there anything we can send down to you? We're well stocked up here.'

He was walking towards the door as he spoke; Owain

went with him. The boy looked as if he was going to speak again but Gorthyn swept determinedly past and Owain deliberately didn't see him. He had reined back from one precipice; he didn't want Gwalchmai bolting with him over another.

Gorthyn saw Owain mount and ride down the valley, a vivid figure in the sunset light with his black hair streaming above his crimson cloak. As he turned back he saw Drostecca's Picts sitting by the rampart. Brude was cutting the turf with his dagger, seemingly marking out a board for a game of dice. The three looked up scowling as he passed, then bent their heads over Brude's dagger again. Gorthyn's normal and immediate response was to put his sword through anyone who looked at him like that, but he reminded himself of their devotion to Gwalchmai. Sullen devils; but too useful to get rid of—not before the battle anyway.

When he got back to the hall, Gwalchmai nearly sprang at his throat.

'Have you told him?'

'No.' Gorthyn dropped on a stool, reaching for his mead-cup.

'But we'll have to tell him. He thinks she's dead.'

'Good.' Gorthyn took a long gulp and wiped his mouth with the back of his hand.

'What do you mean?' Gwalchmai looked bewildered. 'You heard him say he still thinks of himself as pledged to her.'

'Very pretty. A bard could make a song about it. And it's certainly useful for us!'

He nodded across at Cynon and grinned, as if he'd just seen the answer to a riddle. 'So that's why he came rushing to our help! I've been wondering, as I couldn't see what he expected to gain and he must hate our guts. But who'd have thought of that?'

He guffawed. Even Cynon was smiling. Gwalchmai looked at them, shocked.

'But we can't take his help and not tell him! It would be shameful. Do you think I'll cheat a man who's just said he's bound in honour to my sister?'

Gorthyn took the prospect coolly.

'It hasn't hurt him. Being bound in honour to your sister hasn't kept him off other women, from all I've heard. Of course, he thinks about her most, just as you always think about the prize wager you lost, or the stag that outran your hounds. They're always the best, because you didn't have them. She's the woman he didn't have, because she died young and untouched.'

He took another drink and went on bitterly, 'So now we tell him she isn't dead after all. Her father threw her out when he found she was having a bastard and she's been lying low.'

'Don't you say a word against my sister!' shouted Gwalchmai, his face flaming.

'I'm not saying a word against your sister. She's a very fine woman. There aren't many I'd sooner have at my back than her, if I was making my last stand. D'you think you're doing her a favour, letting the Cumbrians have her story to rake up with their horses' dung?'

'But—'

Gorthyn slammed his great fist on the table. 'No, Gwalchmai, I won't have it! Don't you think we've been shamed enough?'

His strong coarse face was twisted with pain he would never have shown for the cruellest body-wound.

'The Cumbrians have got enough to jeer at in Eidyn—a king who stabs his sword-friend in the back—warriors who run like hares the minute they hear a curlew calling because they think it's the enemy war-cry—do you want them saying it's no wonder our women are whores?'

Gwalchmai was silenced, staring at his feet, red and shamefaced. Cynon looked thoughtful.

'Suppose he finds out?'

'How would he do that? It's lucky he's chosen to camp down on the plain. But even when he comes up here, he won't get a sight of her. She's a nun, isn't she?'

Outside, in the warm evening sunlight, the three Picts were still bent over Brude's dagger.

'I tell you, I heard him,' said Nechtan. 'I was outside the door when the servants went in with the logs. He was telling them he'd brought his warriors to fight for them as a bride-gift to their Royal Woman.'

Brude was frowning as he carefully drew his dagger round a perfect curve. He was cutting Drostecca's snake-emblem out of the turf.

'Gorthyn lied to our queen. He only pretended to kill Loth's daughter. He told the queen she was dead and all the time he was hiding her, till she was ready to take the kingdom.'

Talorg looked puzzled.

'She put the king's sword on Gwalchmai, that day he was hallowed. I've heard the folk here say she'd put a spell of safe-keeping on it, that way he couldn't be wounded in battle.'

'And why wouldn't she?' demanded Nechtan fiercely. 'She needs a royal warrior to lead her armies. But now, she'll take this Cumbrian to be her man and put seed in her and he'll give her the kingdom. And then they'll kill our king.'

Brude had finished carving his snake. He balanced his dagger over the creature's open jaws, then slammed the point down on the tip of its tongue.

'If he lives.'

Two other dirks flashed down beside his into the snake's mouth.

CHAPTER
29

The time of waiting was over at last. Smoke to the west and the arrival of a last few terrified herdsmen told them that the Picts were on their way. Owain's men broke camp and moved to the hollow flanking the valley. Gorthyn drew up his men by the rampart. His front rank was made up of Din Eidyn palace guards and those warriors from local chiefs' warbands who had been left behind from Morcant's fatal hosting, to protect their own halls. These were untainted by Morcant's defeat but Gorthyn had no idea what account they would give of themselves in battle. Then came his

Lothian spearmen, the only ones he really trusted. Last of all came what he called '*the Eidyn rabble*': deserters from the defeat, with boys and old men from the farms and fishers' huts, carrying knives and sticks. Gorthyn thought them useless, but if the enemy got that far it would not matter.

Smoke and flame a mile to the north: the fishers' huts had gone.

Owain was standing at Ferlas's shoulder, his arm across the grey's neck. It was going to be another day of burning heat; he was sweating already with the warmth of his chain-mail lorica over a padded leather tunic. He waited for a few more minutes before putting on his helmet, savouring the lightest touch of air against his skin, the flawless blue sky, the scent of turf and furze, little sounds that would soon be drowned by the roar of battle: the clink of a bit, a hoof-stamp, the whine of a midge past his ear. Somewhere, high above, a lark was singing; his own spirits were as high and bright. Some burden of grief seemed to have been lifted since he had spoken Taniu's name in front of her own people and affirmed his faith to her. He felt as light-hearted as if he were off on one of his boyhood exploits.

Madog was waiting at his side with the Raven standard; Owain caught his eye and grinned; it was all he could do not to laugh aloud. Behind him, the warband waited beside their horses; like all warriors who have fought together for years, they were quick to catch their leader's mood, his exultation came flowing through them like a full river.

Hoofs drummed on the turf to his left; the scout urged his horse at a gallop up the slope and reined in at his side.

'They're at the mouth of the valley!'

'Many?'

'A large host, but not well-ordered.'

Owain swung up to the saddle and rode towards the crest of the ridge till he could see down the valley without showing himself on the skyline. The valley-mouth was filled with a dark mass that might have been muddy flood-water, only it flowed upwards. He nodded to Madog, who gave the signal to mount. There was the clink and clatter of mail and shields; then almost complete silence again except for some restless movements among the horses.

The enemy were making so much noise themselves that if the Cumbrians had been blowing horns and shouting orders they would hardly have been noticed. The high cliffs of Eidyn echoed and re-echoed the clamour over their heads; the air in the valley shook with war-cries mixed with wordless wolfish howling, the deep blare of battle-horns and above all, the high skirling of pipes.

The first ragged lines were coming up the track almost abreast of the Cumbrians' hiding-place. Remembering how steeply the ground rose to the rampart, Owain thought with grim amusement: if they keep on yelling like that, they won't have breath to fight when they get there.

But this horde had not come to fight; for them, the battle had been over days ago when they smashed Morcant's war-host; they were making their way to the spoils. They were racing each other to be first; each one's enemy, for the moment, was the man who might outrun him and grab a richer prize. There were gaps in the ranks as the swifter-footed drew ahead; then a packed, jostling mass, where one warband overtook another and tried to push through; another space with a scatter of stragglers and the next wave coming shrieking at their heels.

For all the disorder, they were a fearful sight: tattooed faces snarling or grinning under mats of hair that served instead of helmets; knives and spear-points blazing in the sunlight. Lightly armed and bare-legged, they were as swift and sure-footed as mountain cats. Ugly fighters, as Gorthyn said—and there were so many of them.

Owain took in all these details as he waited for the moment to signal his attack. His mind and battle-experience were coolly assessing the enemy's numbers and position but, as always, some other sense was speaking through his nerves and muscles. He felt the Pictish host as he would feel the weight and poise of a spear before he threw it.

The moment of perfect balance came. He put Ferlas to the crest of the ridge. Madog raised the standard; the ranks of cavalrymen moved forward. Owain gave a great cry: '*Taniu!*' With the deadly speed and precision of a well-aimed javelin, the Cumbrian horsemen struck into the unprotected flank of the raiders.

When the assault came skirling up the valley, Monenna called the sisterhood to prayer. This was the help they were expected to give. The brothers of the Holy Rood had been giving the warriors such doctoring and godly care as they needed. Even they had no part to play at the start of the attack. The wounded lay where they fell; their comrades stepped over them or drew back and left them under the enemies' feet as the fighting line swayed backwards and forwards round the gate.

Little by little, though, the battle moved away from Din Eidyn. Though the first rush had been so savage that the Picts nearly broke through, Owain's charge had smashed the back of the enemy host further down the valley. The fighters at the gate sensed some danger in their rear; their impetus slackened.

Then the Eidyn men went into the attack. These high-born warriors of the palace guard had been smarting too long under the contempt of the Lothian men. They were wild to show their courage, to win back the honour that Morcant had lost. They crashed down on the Picts like a landslide. Seeing the enemy breaking, Gorthyn threw in the Lothian men; the fighting surged back down the valley. Behind came the local levies, with the survivors of Morcant's war-host who had their own scores to pay.

Round the city's rampart a wrack of bodies and broken weapons remained, like a red tide-mark. Here and there a man staggered to his feet; others were trying to crawl; some only showed they were alive by their moaning.

Now some of the folk inside came up to the gate; seeing the fighting had moved away for the time they ventured out to help the wounded or look for their kin. Most of the Eidyn women had knives or axes at their belts, carried for a last desperate defence. Those who had been widowed or bereaved in Morcant's disaster made the enemy wounded their special task and went about it with quiet grim relish.

The brethren of the Holy Rood were there, doing what they could for the wounded and dying, trying to restrain the worst savageries. At last, when she got word how things were at the gate, Monenna sent Taniu with some of the novices to help.

Taniu had never seen the deeds of war so close before; no sickness or accident she had ever tended had prepared her for what men could do to each other's bodies when they deliberately set out to maim and kill. She had been used to take time over healing; now she was hurriedly staunching blood, splinting shattered bones, lapping and binding torn flesh for strangers who moaned under her hands or bit their mouths but asked no questions, even with their eyes.

Tomorrow, she kept telling herself, *if there is a tomorrow, I can give more care to the ones who live through the night.*

Soon, she stopped thinking about the men and only saw the wounds.

The battle was neither swift nor easy. Owain needed all his battle-skills to keep his men together as they wheeled and reformed. The Picts were fighting with the courage of total recklessness. More than once, when a Cumbrian had been carried too far by his enthusiasm, or his mount, they had run in under his guard and killed his horse, bringing him crashing to death on their dirks. Owain even saw some of them jumping like wild cats on to a horse's back, attacking the rider in the saddle.

At long last, his instinct sensed the heart go out of them. They were fighting to escape now, not to kill. If one of a group was attacked, the others would take their chance to get away, leaving him to his fate. The knots of resistance grew smaller, like sandbanks disappearing under a rising tide, and Owain saw Gorthyn advancing down the valley with the Lothian spearmen. 'That's finished them,' was his greeting.

'Are you going after them? Because I can't get much more out of the horses.'

Gorthyn shook his head. 'Leave that to the Eidyn folk.' He grinned sourly. 'They know all about hunting fugitives. Will you be bringing your men up to the city?'

'No, we'll go back to our camp by the loch, it's better for the horses. And we don't want to be cooped up on that hilltop if the Angles are on their way.'

'Right. I'll get some of the carts loaded with supplies for you, and ask some of the brothers to come down and help with your wounded.'

'My thanks.'

Owain wheeled Ferlas, then reined in again.

'Look!'

Gorthyn followed the line of Owain's spear and swore. A group of Picts was heading along the ridge towards the Castle of Maidens. They were keeping together, hurrying, not fleeing. They were probably a clan group, held by loyalty to their chief.

'May the crows take their eyes out! Once they're inside that fort they can hold it for ever. The nuns only brought out what they could carry. I'll take my oath the place is stuffed with stores for an army.'

Owain laughed. 'I doubt that. And once they're in, they won't get out. The place is easy enough to besiege, they'll be trapped.'

'And if we're on our backsides round it when the Angles arrive, we'll be trapped. I said we should have left a garrison.'

'It's not desperate. Most of the horses are good for one more canter, to round off the day. We'll ride them down before they get to the fort. Leave it to me.'

Gorthyn nodded; then broke away with a roar of fury. Two of his men were fighting over a gold torque on a dead chief's neck; the fight was spreading. Most of the others were gathering to watch. Three figures slipped away towards the edge of the valley and went cat-footed down the cliff. No one saw them go. Owain had ordered the muster call blown so that he could pick the men and mounts for his last ride and send the others to camp.

'I'll come with you, King Owain.'

He turned; Gwalchmai was at his shoulder. The young king had fleshed his spear thoroughly and was wild with triumph. At last, he had laid the two besetting fears of his life: that in battle he would find out he was unskilful and cowardly. Even Gorthyn had said, grudgingly, that he'd be greater than Loth; he felt in his bones it was true.

Owain was about to refuse; the pleading look in Gwalchmai's eyes softened him. There was no real danger; let the boy say he'd charged with the Cumbrian horsemen and helped to win the final victory. If it stopped Gwalchmai's terrifying bent towards asking his pardon in public, it would indeed be a victory.

He smiled and nodded. Gwalchmai, bursting with pride, turned to order up his pony. Owain took the chance of passing the word that the boy must be covered all during the fighting.

The pause had given the horses a chance to breathe; they were tired but not foundered. They had enough strength and spirit for one more effort and moved off quite briskly. As they came out of the valley, Owain raised their pace to a trot; they were soon catching up with their quarry.

They were heard; faces were turned back; then the Picts tried to run. They were exhausted; they had been fighting all day since the first wild charge uphill towards Eidyn. Now, as the track before them steepened, they could not make the extra effort.

The Cumbrians rose to a canter. Their wings began to fan out, drawing alongside and ahead of the fugitives to get them inside a ring. Owain drew slightly ahead of the centre to lead the charge. Behind him, the riders of second rank closed in on Gwalchmai to keep him back. Some of their quarry were blown and staggering; they would not be able to make much of a fight. A few had already fallen; perhaps they had been wounded in the battle; one or two bodies were lying on the track.

Owain rode straight across them; but as Ferlas lifted his forefeet to leap over one of the corpses, it suddenly turned like a crouching wolf and sprang up under the horse's belly, slashing it open with a dirk. Ferlas screamed and reared as his guts fell to the ground. Owain struggled to hold the poor creature while he jumped free, but was attacked by two other Picts who came clawing at each side. Even in that last second he tried to fight, striking out with his shield and spear-butt. Then Ferlas crashed down on him, rolling and lashing with his hoofs in his last agony. A snarling mask loomed over Owain, eyes gleaming hate amid a tangle of blue serpents; then the sun died.

Taniu had lost all sense of time. She looked like a butcher's apprentice. Her arms were red to the elbows; blood had seeped through the front of her habit, so that the skirt stuck uncomfortably to her legs. She straightened her back for a moment and yelped at the sudden stab of pain. As she looked up, her brother's face met her eyes. It was twisted with such agony that she forgot all care for his dignity and cried out, 'Oh, my love, what have they done to you?'

'Taniu, you've got to come at once.' Gwalchmai could hardly speak. 'King Owain—he's badly hurt.'

'How dreadful!' she exclaimed with quick sympathy.

'I've got a horse ready for you.'

'I don't need a horse, they're wanted for the carts bringing up the wounded. I'll just get some things and run down the valley in a moment.'

'He's in the Castle of Maidens—we didn't dare carry him far.' He dragged at her arm, 'Hurry!'

She tried to think what medical stores had been left behind at the convent when they took refuge in Eidyn but her mind was a blank. Gwalchmai had already pulled her some steps towards the gate. She turned to Nefyn, who had been working calmly and tirelessly at her side, calling, 'Tell Sister Agatha where I've gone—beg her to send what's needed!'

Gwalchmai hustled her into a run. A man was waiting by the gate with a horse; Gwalchmai jumped to the saddle; she put her foot on his, he pulled her up in front of him and set off at a canter. As she struggled to clear her mind, she realized he was sobbing, terrible dry sobs that seemed to tear his body.

'Try not to grieve too much, my dear. He's been given the brave man's choice. A warrior makes it every time he goes into battle.'

The boy groaned. 'It's worse than that. It was our own people who did it.'

'*Our own people?*'

'Brude, Nechtan and Talorg. They'd joined a band of Picts trying to get up to the Castle of Maidens. King Owain was riding to stop them—he let me ride with him—I was so happy—'

He was crying now; she could feel the tears on her neck.

'Those three—they were shamming dead. And then, as he rode by, they cut his horse's belly open and dragged him down. He was crushed. They've murdered him, Taniu, just like his father. It's worse. After all that treachery he came to help us—and we betrayed him! I'll kill myself for shame!'

She took the bridle reins. It would do King Owain no good if her brother broke their necks. In spite of her shock and disgust, her mind was busy.

'Brude and the others—did they get away?'

'The Cumbrians cut down Talorg and Nechtan. Brude—he put himself on my spear. I cursed him; he threw his dirk away and let me kill him.' Gwalchmai sounded dazed. 'They must have gone mad. They fought bravely all through the battle—they were near me all the time.'

'Do the Cumbrians know they were your men?'

'No, we were all busy about the king, then I came to fetch you. I haven't had a chance to explain.'

'Say nothing.'

'Shame on you, Taniu! Do you think I'm Morcant? I don't cheat my allies. I'll stand before them and tell them the truth. They can take his blood-price out of my body!'

'You don't owe them a blood-price! Those three were Picts. They went back to their own people to share their defeat—God help them, that's warriors' honour. But if you claim the guilt, you're the cheat. And what's worse, you'll give a cruel wound to our allies, as if they haven't suffered enough already. You'd turn their generosity into a mockery, make it meaningless.'

He didn't answer. She turned her head and stared full into his face, her eyes blazing.

'Gwalchmai, I order you, by the Holy Name of God, say nothing!'

They had been so locked in their own battle that they took little heed of the journey. They owed it to the sense and goodwill of the horse that they arrived at the gate of the Castle of Maidens, now occupied by the Cumbrians.

They had taken their king to Monenna's cell and laid him on her bed. Most warriors and hunters who outlived boyhood had a working knowledge of wound care. They had already stripped him, cleaned his wounds, lit the brazier and collected some linen from the nuns' stores.

The still-room had not been emptied; she thanked God for that as she made a hasty selection. She'd need to examine him before deciding on his treatment but she was glad to find enough of the healer's chief allies, muttering their names as she filled her basket: 'Saint John's Wort for wounds; yarrow for bleeding inside—please God he isn't!—comfrey, boneset—all-heal for sleep—they'll do for now.'

When she came to the bedside, the Cumbrian nobles stared at her with the same look she had seen so often on the faces of the poorest peasants, making her heart sink——humble, pleading, yet hopeful that she would begin her wonder-working at once. As she wasn't a witch or an elf-woman, she settled to a slow, careful examination of every inch of the king's body, her mind intent on what her eyes and hands were telling her. Taniu was a true healer; she would have given the same care to a serf or a war-captive. Even so, she could hardly forget that this was the great king of Cumbria, who had saved Lothian and Eidyn—and who might have been her husband.

She had no call to remember her own youthful disaster; there was nothing about the stately, black-bearded man lying like a corpse under her hands to bring it back to her. She felt his limbs, noting their long fine bones and slender well-muscled lines. Nothing broken there, but various cuts and slashes with the blood beginning to clot. These would be wounds he'd got in the earlier fighting; the sort that men call 'scratches' and laugh about, then get angry if you offer to tend them. Nothing serious in itself; but he'd bled too much before the last attack; he was thirsty and tired too, no doubt.

His loins and belly, flat and firm, the skin that clear gold that sun and air put on fairness. His flesh was as spare as a hunting wolf or falcon—at least, his body would fight for him; it hadn't been wrecked, like her poor father's, with drink and gluttony. There seemed no damage to the guts, none that she could feel, anyway.

The chest, broad under wide shoulders. One side was very badly bruised, and over the bruisings, dozens of brandings and scratches from the rings of the lorica. Some dreadful weight must have crashed into him to drive chain mail through his leather tunic. Yes, three ribs had cracked on that side. If his lungs or liver had been torn, his case was desperate. There was no sign of bleeding from mouth or bowels—yet; when that came there was nothing she could do but make death easier.

If I could really do magic, as they say, there are just two spells I'd like to make: to see inside the body and to put spilled blood back into the veins.

There was a deep gash on the right side of the neck; Brude had been going for the throat but he must have turned aside before the blow. His men had cleaned and padded the wound but it must have bled profusely. She remembered that Picts sometimes poisoned their dirks, and shivered. But there was no use in terrifying herself; if that had happened she had nightshade to finish him quickly.

Gently, she slid her hands under him to feel the shoulder blades. Her left hand moved across his upper arm, her fingers spelling out a faint scar from some old injury, shaped like a forked twig . . .

'*The boar swung me against the rock. It's only a scratch, I'll bind it when I've unsaddled.*'

Her healer's training held firm. The Cumbrians, who had not taken their eyes off her, saw no more than a moment's check; then the seeking hands went on.

He had been lying with his face away from her. She lifted and turned his head, staring at the face while her fingers combed through the heavy blue-black hair, questing across his skull for any injury. There were the fine features, the long black lashes lying so quietly now across his high cheek bones. She had the hollow of his cheek cupped in her palm, feeling the strong lines of his jaw and chin. His mouth spoke to her memories, though it was as still and silent now as a Roman carving. It had been tightened by years of command but she could see it smiling at her in mockery or tenderness when they were both young, before the world's evil had infected them.

She let his head rest back on the pillow; made herself breathe deeply to steady her voice; then looked up at his anxious warriors, forcing herself to speak more boldly than she felt.

'He's got broken ribs but I hope there's no worse injury inside. It's a pity he lost so much blood, but he's a strong man. Help me to raise him—so—and prop his side with the bolster. Some of you go to the sisters' cells and bring some more pillows. Make sure you keep the brazier going—he mustn't take cold. Now, I'm going to salve his hurts and give him an infusion against wound fever.'

The Cumbrians followed her orders with well-trained promptness; but in this fight they could be no more than her shield-bearers. She was in single combat with death.

As the long evening wore into night and the night crawled towards morning, Taniu began to taste the bitterness of defeat. The wound fever had come upon Owain and nothing she could do would check it. The fever distressed his breathing; it was difficult to keep him still; she feared he would drive his broken ribs in upon his lung. More than all, as he burned and shivered into the second night, she dreaded his heart would give out.

He had lost too much blood; death was attacking with too many weapons and he had no strength to oppose them. She had been wrong to think his body would fight for him; it was destroying itself before her eyes. If she couldn't find anything to ease him, he wouldn't last many more days like this.

There were things she could give him; she had them in her stores. Foxglove, nightshade, cowbane: all strong and all deadly. Any one of them was powerful enough to ease Owain's heart—and to stop it for ever. No healer was happy to use them; they were not healing herbs but poisons, used in killing-magic. To give them to a patient was knowingly to give a death-bringer. Ancarat had given nightshade once or twice; Sister Agatha kept all three herbs reluctantly, to complete her collection but had always refused to use them. How would she guess the dose? Anything strong enough to help his condition would be strong enough to kill him in his weakened state. She decided she could not take the risk.

Another hour of listening to his rasping breath and

watching his face burning away to a skull changed her mind. If she made a mistake she was only giving a quicker, easier death than the one that was coming anyway.

She rose, lit a taper and signed to one of the Cumbrians to take her place, saying she was going to mix a different draught. Owain's men had seen enough of death after battle to know their king was in grave danger; their faces were set and strained.

She decided she would use foxglove. Sister Agatha's books recommended it for the heart, it did not have such an evil name in sorcery as the other two. As she counted out the drops, the thought came to her that this was the last and bitterest of the jokes that life had played on her. If she was mixing Owain's death-brew—and likely she was—then at last she was doing her duty as Loth's daughter. She was going to kill the man who had dishonoured her, in the time-honoured way of her sex, who were not allowed to take up arms for themselves.

She came back to Owain's bedside and raised his head.

I can mix some more for myself; I'll see that's strong enough.

She put the cup to his lips.

Owain was crossing a moor. It stretched all around him, mile after mile. He had forgotten how many days he had been lost; he was so tired now, he couldn't stand. He had to crawl; the tough heather stems tore at his limbs and chest; the sun blazed pitilessly on his head and neck. His throat was parched; his heart was beating like a smith's hammer. His body screamed to be still, to stop struggling; but if he gave up now, he would never find what he was looking for. He had forgotten what it was but he had to keep searching or he would never have peace. He crawled painfully on, gasping for breath.

At last, his groping hands touched something that was not heather, that did not give way when he pressed against it. He forced his agonized head to look up and saw he had reached a sheer wall of grey rock. His heart nearly stopped with despair; he could never climb that height; he had reached the end and found nothing.

As he swept his hands down the rock face, it melted under his touch and turned into a shimmering curtain of water drops. A figure stepped through it, a girl made out of grey moorland, sunlight and clear water. It was the Goddess herself, the Lady of the enchanted springs. She filled her silver goblet at the waterfall and gave it to him. He drank greedily.

The Goddess smiled and he saw that she was Taniu. She lifted her arm and brushed aside the waterfall like a curtain, stretching her other hand to him as she turned to go. He took it gratefully and followed her into the dark.

CHAPTER
30

Monenna came quietly into her cell. The Cumbrians, crouched with their arms round their knees, looked up to watch her. Taniu was sitting by the bed, her eyes open but unseeing, her face grey in the cold morning light. The bloodstains on her robe had darkened and stiffened.

The abbess bent over the still figure on the bed, checked, stooped lower, drew back the blankets and touched him. Then she replaced the coverings.

'You can go now, my daughter. Your work is done.'

Taniu neither moved nor spoke.

'It's over. The fever's broken; he's sleeping.' She took Taniu's arm. 'Go and get some sleep yourself, child. Sister Agatha's coming.'

She half-lifted Taniu to her feet, steered her to the door and beckoned to one of the nuns to lead her away. She went without a backward glance.

Owain swam up reluctantly from the deep pool of sleep. Surfacing into wakefulness brought pain, which was bearable. It also brought the frustrations of being helpless, imprisoned and tended like a baby, which nearly drove him mad. He could have raged himself back into his fever; but that would be stupid as well as insulting to his devoted followers and to the abbess and her nuns, who were giving him such unfailing care.

Sometimes, as he watched Sister Agatha, stout and breathing like a bellows, the contrast between her and the shimmering goddess of his dream made him start to laugh and hurt his ribs. He would have liked to go back into his dream; at first, he tried to make it happen by fixing his mind on it as he drifted off to sleep. He never succeeded. He settled grimly to the task of getting back his health and fighting skills.

His body was very strong, hardened by years of hunting and war. He began making it answer to his will again, with the same deadly patience he used in training a falcon or a war-horse. Though Sister Agatha often cried out in horror at what she called his recklessness, he worked with a slowness agonizing to himself, well knowing that too much haste could set him back for weeks.

As summer died into autumn, while strength and movement crept back into his limbs, he got more impatient to be in Cumbria. He'd been too long away; he had full trust in Rhun but he wanted to take the reins into his own hands.

Above all, he wanted to get his warriors away from their grateful allies. It was all very well for Cumbria and Lothian to fall on each other's necks in time of danger. Peace gave time for thought: time for easterners to remember that Cumbrians were greedy, ambitious land-grabbers; time for Cumbrians to remember that easterners were shifty traitors who stabbed their trusting allies in the back.

He knew Gorthyn wanted to get back to Din Pelidr. The Angles had got that far; they'd burned the houses of the township. But Brychan had held the citadel and given the invaders such a mauling that they'd gone back south. Gorthyn told Owain he wanted to see what damage they'd done; quite true, and spoken in a friendly way but Owain sensed that the Lothian war-leader would be glad to see the back of him. Gwalchmai too; Owain knew from Madog that the boy had kept a sleepless vigil at his door while his life was in danger; he kept repeating how glad he was that Owain had recovered. But he didn't always meet Owain's eyes; there was always some strange constraint.

The exalted joy Owain had felt in fighting for Taniu's land and people had vanished; so had the haunting sense of her presence. Perhaps that strange dream had been her farewell to him: he had offered to pay her blood-price, now he was free of her. Freedom was such dull emptiness that he would have preferred her bloody spectre weeping by his bed every night.

Suddenly he was sick of the whole business. It would soon be October; days were shortening; he didn't want to spend the next months winter-bound in Eidyn. He gave orders to prepare to ride next day; he'd get to Cumbria if he had to be carried in a litter like a breeding woman.

Monenna met him trying how well he could walk, supported by his spear-shaft.

'You're eager to leave us, I see, my son.'

'I could never be eager to leave a true friend like you, Mother. But you're a ruler yourself; you wouldn't want to linger far away from your realm and your duties.'

She nodded, her bright eyes fixed on his. He was glad to tell some part of the truth because he respected her.

'Besides, I want to get my men away while there's still goodwill between West and East. Warriors can do more damage in peace, when they're idle, than they ever do to the enemy in war. It only needs one quarrel over dice or a whore—I beg your pardon, Reverend Mother, but you don't know what fighting men can be like.'

'Do I not?' asked the Irishwoman drily.

'I'm truly grateful to you, Mother, and your nuns, especially Sister Agatha. I'd like to thank her—with your permission, of course. She saved my life, I wouldn't want her to think I was ungrateful.'

'As you've thanked her every time she's given you a draught or felt your pulse, she's not likely to think that. Though as it happens, the one who tended you when you were at the worst was our herbalist. Sister Agatha says that, under God, she was the one who really saved you. You may speak to her, if she isn't away on some errand of healing. She's a lay sister, a noblewoman of Lothian who took refuge with us some time ago. She'll be leaving us when King Gwalchmai goes home, so you won't have the chance to thank her much longer.'

She smiled; her quick dark eyes more than ever like an alert robin's.

'Try if you can get as far as our herb garden, it's the most likely place to find her. Up there—it's a nice little climb for you.'

Taniu needed no excuses to keep away from Owain's sick-bed. There was more than enough work for her during her last days in Eidyn, among the wounded in the city and with the old and new-born among the country folk, struggling to rebuild their burned hovels and get some harvest in before the winter. Nefyn often rode out with her on these missions; she spent the rest of her time with Monenna or Agatha. The company of women she could respect, the use of her mind and energies, brought her peace and a hope of happiness after the loss of her brother. Taniu was training her to take her place in the still-room; she sensed that one day Nefyn would succeed Monenna.

If excuses had been needed to avoid Owain, she would have lied her soul away rather than be in the same room with him when he was conscious and could watch her.

That bold plan of offering a marriage alliance to hold the peace between their two peoples, so easy when she thought he was a stranger, was laughable now—a child's tale at bedtime.

Whatever could I say to him when we met? she was thinking all that afternoon, while she pointed out the herbs that were ready for picking and got Nefyn to say their names and properties over to her.

'You loved me once; I've borne you a son.' And then, if it was a story told by a bard, he'd take me in his arms and that would be the end of the story and all the hearers would applaud.

As it is, I'd have to watch him trying to remember who I was—which one I was. Watch him trying to think of something courteous and kind to say to me. Watch the knowledge in his face that whatever else he said, he couldn't afford to say 'No' to the King of Lothian's sister. And all the while, his captains would be shuffling their feet outside the door, coughing and cursing, wondering how long I'd be before they could get back in to talk about horses and supplies!

'We've got enough today, dear,' she said aloud. 'Would you take them back to the still-room and sort them, please. I'll join you in a little while.'

She watched Nefyn go down the path with her basket; then turned back to stroll between the beds, glad of a moment's rest and silence, she'd been driving herself hard for weeks. The convent's herb garden was in a pocket of earth just below the crest of the rocks. It opened to the southwest, holding all the warmth and sweetness of the October day like a chalice.

Life's not a story made up by bards. She had taken up her former train of thought. *How much simpler for us if it were, with a tidy ending. But the only ending to our real life-stories is death, and we're not here to enjoy the effect! And up till then, life's all endings—or all beginnings. Which is which, I wonder?*

A little spring trickled through the rocks, falling into a pool below, set round with water-plants. It made a drowsy sound; she remembered how tired she was and sat down beside it. The air was sultry; she unwound her wimple from her head and neck, loosed her hair and rested her cheek against the cool stone.

So Owain found her: grey rock, sunlight and clear water, taken up into the form of a girl. His shadow lay across the pool; she looked up and saw him watching her, leaning on his spear.

After all, there was no need to wonder what she would say. They just went into each other's arms, like childhood friends meeting after a long exile, stammering and talking in broken snatches because they have so much to say they can hardly speak.

'I came back for you—I found out the truth and I came back for you next spring—as soon as the snows had melted. But the place was in ashes. They told me you were dead—yet I've never stopped wanting you—can you believe me?'

She believed him. Belief was so bitter, for a moment she felt she had drunk poison. What a waste of life and happiness! But then her mind and her deeper feelings rebelled.

Waste?

That I've kept house for a swineherd and a fisherman? That I was sent out to my death alone in the sea? That I bore a child on the beach? Is that waste? And Owain—if he hadn't known sin and betrayal, how could he have found true honour and courage? He's a great king now—and I'm a great healer. Let's be grateful for what life gave us, not waste time whimpering about what we lost.

'I found out the truth too—the truth about myself. If you'd come back then, I'd have gone with you.'

'I never meant to hurt you. I never planned treachery against you. I thought I'd teach you how to love—the proud fool I was!—I wanted to do better for you than you could for yourself, and I did so much worse!'

Taniu hardly knew if she were laughing or sobbing —hadn't she said just that to Monenna? She wanted to explain what Monenna had told her, to comfort him, but she could feel he was shaking. She brushed the tears out of her eyes and briskly hitched her skirt up into her belt.

'You're not half cured yet. Give me your arm, I'll help you back to your bed.'

He smiled with some of his old mockery. 'It seems I'm getting some of my Purgatory in advance. To have you in arms' reach at last and not enough strength to hold you with them.'

'Perhaps it's as well.'

'Oh God—and we ride for Cumbria tomorrow!'

'All the more need, then, to rest today.'

She turned to go and reached her hand to him, smiling, as she had in his dream. He took it, but held her there, deadly serious.

'Taniu, you're free of me. I'll never try to force your will again; not by love, or pleading, or getting your brother to urge you. If you answer *No*, I'll be silent.'

She became very still.

'I've got to go back to Cumbria, and winter's coming soon. If I send my messengers to Din Pelidr in the spring and ask your brother, will you come to me then?'

'No.'

Her face was quite calm; she had come to her decision before he spoke.

'I fought death for you, Owain, it was the hardest struggle I ever had. I'm not going to have my good work wasted if you decide to try how well your new war-horse goes over the Cheviots at the gallop. I'm coming with you now.'

His eyes were gleaming with laughter but he kept a straight face.

'Dressed in your wimple and habit, of course, and perched up in front of me on the war-horse. You eastern folk have put every hard name on Cumbrians that their tongues could find, but nobody's ever accused me of seducing a nun—yet.'

'I'm not a nun! And you're not seducing me.' She laughed back at him. 'Oh, my dear love, you don't need to!'

They were still laughing when they came down the path to the abbess's cell.

Elcu the pedlar had lent his cart to Arthgal to bring up the fish for the Friday fast; they were unloading the creels by the gate and stopped dumbstruck at the sight. The King of Cumbria with his arm round the Healer of Eidyn and she with her hair tumbled down her back and her skirt hitched over her knees! She looked for all the world like a farmer's daughter being taken off in a cattle-raid—and not at all unwilling to be taken, by the look of things.

Arthgal just stared but Elcu spat.

'Cumbrians! What did I tell you? It's time they went home.'

GHOST IN THE SUNLIGHT
BY KATHLEEN HERBERT

It was the heroic age, and the misty hills of Old Britain were to witness the last great battle between the ageing kings – South of the Humber was Penda, the blazing heathen leader of Mercia – North was Oswy, Christian, subtle, and determined to weld the land into one mighty kingdom.

And between the two stood Alchflaed, the beautiful impetuous princess of Bernicia, who casts herself into a marriage to save the peace of the land – and thus stirs up the evil ghosts of the past – ghosts of murder and treachery, of her dead mother's first love, and the ghost of a terrible secret that should have stayed buried forever.

0552 12896 1

LEGACY
BY SUSAN KAY

MAY 1536: A turbulent love affair ends in murder, and a headless queen is laid to rest in a common arrow chest in the Tower of London. Behind her is left a small silent girl who should have been a boy – legacy of the unholy union that shook the world.

Accusations of 'possession' were levelled at Elizabeth Tudor all her life, based on her incredible luck and her uncanny hold over the men who served her. LEGACY is the story of a Queen who sometimes thought herself possessed, who spent a lifetime in search of a master, and whose unparalleled love affair was with England, her country, for which she was prepared to lie, cheat, flatter and scheme.

'Remarkably accomplished, detailed and arresting'
GOOD BOOK GUIDE

'The story is vigorously told . . . a stirring read'
JANE AIKEN HODGE

'The story of Elizabeth and the men who devoted their lives to her has been told and retold but rarely as well as by Susan Kay . . . long may Miss Kay, newly crowned queen of the historical novel reign!'
DAILY MAIL

'Quite simply, the most exciting, most moving, most passionate novel of Elizabeth I have ever read'
DIANE PEARSON

0552 127205

I AM ENGLAND

BY PATRICIA WRIGHT

'I AM ENGLAND NOW, LET THAT BE MY LIFE. THE FIRST QUEEN ELIZABETH SAID THAT, AND WAS LOVED BY HER PEOPLE FOR HER PRIDE IN ENGLISHNESS. THE REST OF US, WHO MADE THE LOOK AND FEEL OF ENGLAND, SHOULD ALSO BE REMEMBERED. WE ARE ENGLAND TOO.'

In this remarkable epic, which spans fifteen centuries from AD 70 to 1589, Furnace Green in the Weald of Sussex is England. Set about with great trees, abundant with deer and boar and wolves, the first people to come to the Ridge were the shy forest people, then Brac the ironsmith, who used a deer sign as his mark to express his love for his wild strange wife.

Then came Edred, the Saxon, who left the Ridge to kill the hated Danes, and returned with a Danish slave girl with whom he could found a dynasty.

Their descendants, over many years, many calamitous events, continued to love and fight and build and pray on the Ridge. Robert the Falconer, doomed to die if he did not carve out a Fief by the Ridge, and Benedict, the priestly knight, fighting his last fight, and the Elizabethan yeoman who forged the cannon to defeat the Armada – these were the people of the Ridge – the people of England.

Winner of the Georgette Heyer Historical Novel Award.

0552 13290X

COMING OF THE KING
BY NIKOLAI TOLSTOY

A world of magic, mysticism and enchantment.

The first volume in Nikolai Tolstoy's epic *The Book of Merlin* trilogy is as rich and vivid an evocation of the world of Celtic Britain as one might expect from the pen of a direct descendant of the author of *War & Peace*.

The narrator and chief character, the poet and magician Merlin, takes us into an unfamiliar but utterly convincing world of warrior aristocrats, bards and druids, a world of cruelty and of exquisite beauty, mingling high adventure and mysticism, tragedy and laughter.

A *tour de force* of literary recreation, it will be recognised for years to come as the most convincing Arthurian saga written in modern times.

'I was entranced . . . the book has so many strands, so many layers of meaning that it defies summary . . . here is a novel in which imagination and scholarship make a perfect marriage with craftsmanship and narrative drive, buy it, I beseech you.'

Ted Willis, Sunday Telegraph

'Grips the reader . . . I felt I could read this story for evermore'

Roy Kerridge, Spectator

'I much preferred it to *The Lord of The Rings*'.
John Bayley, Professor of English, Oxford University

0552 13221 7

THE BELGARIAD

BY DAVID EDDINGS

David Eddings has created a wholly imaginary world whose fate hangs on the outcome of a prophesy made seven thousand years earlier. The fulfilment of this prophesy is entrusted to a young farm boy named Garion, aided by his aunt Pol and the mysterious Mr Wolf. Together they embark on their quest to retrieve the stolen Orb of Aldur and confront the ageless malice of the god Torak.

The story of their quest unfolds with a magical blend of excitement and enchantment. *The Belgariad* is an outstanding piece of imaginative storytelling, destined to achieve the classic status and following of Tolkein's *The Hobbit* or Stephen Donaldson's *Chronicles of Thomas Covenant*.

Pawn of Prophesy   0 552 12284 X
Queen of Sorcery   0 552 12348 X
Magician's Gambit   0 552 12382 X
Castle of Wizardry   0 552 12435 4
Enchanter's Endgame   0 552 12447 8

THE AWAKENERS

BY SHERI S. TEPPER

'Tepper creates a true refuge, one of those rare worlds into which the reader can escape completely'

Locus

In the savage and magical world of the River, the pace of life is dictated by the ebb and flow of the great tides – and by the power of a fearsome religion. Yet dangerous currents gather force beneath the placid surface.

Together, Pamra Don and Thrasne the Boatman seek to uncover the terrible truth about the river and its awesome strength. But in the world of the Awakeners, the truth can kill you . . .

'Sheri S. Tepper has a remarkable talent, and with each new book she outdoes herself. I don't know which I like more, the worlds she creates or the way she writes about them'

Stephen R. Donaldson

'The plot is rich . . . the characters come alive. The whole is imbued with a marvellous sense of dream . . . Don't miss'

Analog

'Tepper is something special'

Orson Scott Card

0552 13295 0

A SELECTED LIST OF FINE NOVELS
AVAILABLE FROM CORGI BOOKS

THE PRICES SHOWN BELOW WERE CORRECT AT THE TIME OF GOING TO PRESS. HOWEVER TRANSWORLD PUBLISHERS RESERVE THE RIGHT TO SHOW NEW RETAIL PRICES ON COVERS WHICH MAY DIFFER FROM THOSE PREVIOUSLY ADVERTISED IN THE TEXT OR ELSEWHERE.

All Corgi/Bantam books are available at your bookshops or newsagents, or can be ordered from the following address:

Corgi/Bantam Books,
Cash Sales Department,
P.O. Box 11, Falmouth, Cornwall TR10 9EN

Please send a cheque or postal order, (no currency) and allow 60p for postage and packing for the first book plus 25p for the second book and 15p for each additional book ordered up to a maximum charge of £1.90 in UK.

B.F.P.O. customers please allow 60p for the first book, 25p for the second book plus 15p per copy for the next 7 books, thereafter 9p per book.

Overseas customers, including Eire, please allow £1.25 for postage and packing for the first book, 75p for the second, and 28p for each subsequent title ordered.